Praise for *Over the Moon at the Big Lizard Diner*

"Lisa Wingate delivers an insightful, heartfelt, and sometimes crazy novel of romance, redemption, and personal change. A journey you simply must not miss."

> —Julie Cannon, author of the Homegrown Series and *Those Pearly Gates*

"A feisty, flirtatious, home-grown Texas tale."

> —Dixie Cash, author of *My Heart May Be Broken, But My Hair Still Looks Great*

Praise for *Texas Cooking* **and** *Lone Star Café*, **companion novels to** *Over the Moon at the Big Lizard Diner*

Lone Star Café

"A charmingly nostalgic treat. . . . Wingate handles the book's strong spiritual element deftly, creating a novel that is sweetly inspirational but not saccharine."   —*Publishers Weekly*

"A beautifully written, heartwarming tale about finding love where you least expect it."   —Barbara Freethy

"Leaves you feeling like you've danced the two-step across Texas."
> —Jodi Thomas

"A remarkably talented and innovative writer, with a real feel for human emotion."   —Linda Lael Miller

continued . . .

Texas Cooking

"A delightful love story, as heartwarming and vivid as its setting in the beautiful Texas hill country."　　　　　—Janice Woods Windle

"*Texas Cooking* . . . will have readers drooling for the next installment . . . [a] beautifully written mix of comedy, drama, cooking, and journalism."　　　　　—*Dallas Morning News*

"Sure to touch the heart and reach down deep into the well of hope within each of us."

　　　　　—Debbie Macomber

"Takes the reader on a delightful journey into the most secret places of every woman's heart."　　　　　—Catherine Anderson

"The story is a treasure. You will be swept along, refreshed and amused. . . . Give yourself a treat and read this tender, unusual story."
　　　　　—Dorothy Garlock

Praise for Lisa Wingate's NAL Accent novels, the Tending Roses Series

The Language of Sycamores

"Heartfelt, honest, and entirely entertaining . . . this poignant story will touch your heart from the first page to the last."
　　　　　—Kristin Hannah

"Wingate's smoothly flowing prose fills the pages with emotional drama."　　　　　—*Romantic Times,* 4½ Stars, Top Pick

Good Hope Road

"A novel bursting with joy amidst crisis: small-town life is painted with scope and detail in the capable hands of a writer who understands longing, grief, and the landscape of a woman's heart."
—Adriana Trigiani

"Wingate has written a genuinely heartwarming story about how a sense of possibility can be awakened in the aftermath of a tragedy to bring a community together and demonstrate the true American spirit."
—*Booklist*

Tending Roses

"A story at once gentle and powerful about the very old and the very young, about the young woman who loves them all. Richly emotional and spiritual, *Tending Roses* affected me from the first page."
—Luanne Rice

"You can't put it down without . . . taking a good look at your own life and how misplaced priorities might have led to missed opportunities. *Tending Roses* is an excellent read for any season, a celebration of the power of love."
—*El Paso Times*

LISA WINGATE

Over the Moon at the Big Lizard Diner

New American Library

New American Library
Published by New American Library, a division of
Penguin Group (USA) Inc., 375 Hudson Street,
New York, New York 10014, USA
Penguin Group (Canada), 90 Eglinton Avenue East, Suite 700, Toronto,
Ontario M4P 2Y3, Canada (a division of Pearson Penguin Canada Inc.)
Penguin Books Ltd., 80 Strand, London WC2R 0RL, England
Penguin Ireland, 25 St. Stephen's Green, Dublin 2,
Ireland (a division of Penguin Books Ltd.)
Penguin Group (Australia), 250 Camberwell Road, Camberwell, Victoria 3124,
Australia (a division of Pearson Australia Group Pty. Ltd.)
Penguin Books India Pvt. Ltd., 11 Community Centre, Panchsheel Park,
New Delhi – 110 017, India
Penguin Group (NZ), cnr Airborne and Rosedale Roads, Albany,
Auckland 1310, New Zealand (a division of Pearson New Zealand Ltd.)
Penguin Books (South Africa) (Pty.) Ltd., 24 Sturdee Avenue,
Rosebank, Johannesburg 2196, South Africa

Penguin Books Ltd., Registered Offices:
80 Strand, London WC2R 0RL, England

First published by New American Library,
a division of Penguin Group (USA) Inc.

First Printing, November 2005
10 9 8 7 6 5 4 3 2 1

NEW AMERICAN LIBRARY and logo are trademarks of Penguin Group (USA) Inc.

LIBRARY OF CONGRESS CATALOGING-IN-PUBLICATION DATA:

Wingate, Lisa.
Over the moon at the Big Lizard Diner/Lisa Wingate.
p. cm.
ISBN 0-451-21664-4
1. Women paleontologists—Fiction. 2. Horses—Therapeutic use—Fiction.
3. Dinosaur tracks—Fiction. 4. Ranchers—Fiction.   I. Title.
PS3573.I53165095 2005
813'.6—dc22   2005009007

Set in Bembo
Designed by Ginger Legato

Printed in the United States of America

To Uncle Pug
Otherwise known as Wonderful Winfred,
Who said,
"Some of the best adventures of my life never really happened."

Here's another adventure.
I hope they have a good library
Up there in heaven....

Acknowledgments

The story of Lindsey Draper's trip to Big Lizard Bottoms would not have been possible without the help of some very special people. As always, my undying gratitude goes out to all the booksellers and media personnel who have shown such devotion to the previous books in the Texas Hill Country series, *Texas Cooking* and *Lone Star Café,* as well as the books in the Tending Roses series. My thanks also to the many readers who have shared the books with friends, taken time to send letters of encouragement, and asked for sequels. I hope you enjoy the trip to Big Lizard Bottoms as much as I did.

My gratitude also goes out to those who helped me in the writing and research of Big Lizard. Thank you to Fred and Gwen Owens for sharing information about and articles about the theropod tracks stolen from your ranch. May your big lizard someday find its way home. Thank you to Kent Munden for providing information on the workings of the USDA. Thank you to friends in San Saba for offering stories and memories of the real Wedding Oak. Thank you to my father-in-law, Lawrence, for information on windmills and other ranch machinery. Last, but certainly not least, thank you to our neighbors, the Webbs, for letting us borrow Wally, the wandering Great Pyrenees, for the back cover photo shoot, and for providing the numerous dog biscuits required as Wally's modeling fee.

As always, my heartfelt gratitude goes to the staff at New American Library, my editor, Ellen Edwards, and my agent at Sterling Lord Literistic, Claudia Cross. Special thanks also goes to my family, including my wonderful mother-in-law, Janice, for helping with address lists, newsletters, soccer games, baseball practices, and always having the door open at the Nanny in Pajamas bed and breakfast. Thanks also to my mother for being a willing reader, a traveling companion, writer's helper, and super grandma to my boys.

Last, thanks to all the friends far and near, who have encouraged me along the way. We all need the help of a few special angels in this world, and I've received more than my share.

ONE

<hr/>

GRITS AND HORSE PSYCHOLOGY. NOT EXACTLY THINGS YOU THINK of as life altering. When I tell people it was grits and horse psychology that brought me to an epiphany, they look at me like I'm crazy—just one more single mother who finally cracked under the demands of career and parenthood. One more lost, lonely thirty-something woman who read too many romance novels, developed a Bridget Jones obsession, and decided to do something impetuous for love.

But love was the farthest thing from my mind that summer. Romantic love was an idea completely beyond the realm of my existence, another planet I'd landed on just long enough to conceive a child with a husband who didn't want to be a father. The blastoff from that world was so painful that I lay for eight years in suspended animation, drifting through space, isolated in my protective bubble while Sydney grew up dreaming that one day her father would come back.

When she learned to write in first grade, she started sending him letters, which, of course, went unanswered, except for an occasional child-support check. She read about him in *National Geographic, Paleontology Magazine*, and on the archaeology Web sites. She reasoned that he was too far away to hear her, and kept sending letters.

The year Sydney turned seven, a check arrived for all the back child support. I should have been suspicious. Geoff never did anything without a motive. The payments came on time for a couple of months, and then a courier showed up with a letter from a lawyer. Goeff had remarried and settled down, and he wanted Sydney for the summer. In Mexico.

I've never ached the way I did hugging her good-bye at the airport, as she stood with her pink backpack, her long sandy-brown hair—his color hair—curling over the straps. I hugged her so hard I thought she might break. Then there he was, looking like the *National Geographic* portrait Sydney kept taped to her mirror. She slipped her hand into his like it was the most natural thing in the world. For an instant in the gateway, she lifted her hand and waved before he led her away. She was beaming. I wanted to die. In eight years, Sydney and I had never been separated for more than the length of a school day.

The first weeks of summer were a blur. I was nonfunctional. Catatonic. I drifted back and forth between my apartment in downtown Denver and my job as a paleontology lab supervisor in the basement of the museum six blocks away. Somehow I ended up on sabbatical, in Texas.

"Grits, baby?" I should have known I was a long way from home when the waitress called me *baby*.

"Pardon?" I muttered, staring at the menu, reading the same words over and over.

The waitress, a portly lady in her forties, gave me a sympathetic look. I imagined what she was seeing—a desperate woman in old jeans, a wrinkled T-shirt, and worn-out sandals. Stringy, uncombed dark brown hair pulled into a sloppy ponytail, eyes red and puffy around the brown centers, a body that used to be tan and in shape from hiking and mountain-bike riding with Sydney, but now hung pale and sallow, bent over the menu in some middle-of-nowhere Texas café. Lost as lost could be, even though I knew exactly where I was on the map.

"You need a cup of our crossroads coffee," she said to my pathetic self as she filled the cup on the table.

"It shows, huh?" I rubbed my forehead because my eyes were starting to sting. Driving all night from Colorado was catching up with me.

"Well, you know, working here, you learn to spot when somebody needs a little pick-me-up." She patted my shoulder, and suddenly I wanted to tell her everything. Which would have been completely unlike me. "Our coffee cures a multitude of ills," she offered. "Cream and sugar?"

"No, thanks. Just coffee," I said miserably.

"Grits?"

"Huh?"

"With your breakfast platter, baby," she said tenderly. "Mernalene's got some grits cooked up. Wouldja like some on the side? They'll stick to your ribs. Comfort food."

"Sure," I answered, thinking that Sydney would have jumped at the chance to see a real live grit. Grits played a cameo role in her new favorite movie, *My Cousin Vinny*. She loved the part where Vinny used grits to disprove the court case against his client. Sydney adored lawyer shows these days—probably because, thanks to Geoff and Whitney's phone visits, Syd was way too privy to the ongoing custody litigations.

My eyes teared up completely without warning. "No," I said quickly. "You know what? I'll just wait to order. I'm meeting my sister here for breakfast."

The waitress drew back, giving me a sudden look of recognition. "Oh, my goodness, are you *Laura's* sister?"

I blinked, surprised. "She told you I was coming?" It seemed unlikely, since I'd called Laura only a few hours ago to tell her I'd driven straight through last night. She'd suggested we meet for breakfast at this crossroads café, which was on her way to work in Austin.

It was hard to picture my sophisticated sister eating in cafés where the waitress served grits and called everyone *baby*. Perhaps that was because I hadn't actually seen Laura in her new environment yet. In the eleven months since she had fallen in love, eloped to Cancún, and moved permanently to Texas, I'd been tied up with Sydney's custody case, fighting it right up until the moment I slipped her hand into Geoff's and sent her off to Mexico for the summer. Laura had been to Colorado twice to visit me, but I hadn't come down to

Texas. Maybe it was jealousy that kept me away. Laura seemed blissfully happy in her new life.

"Oh, we just love Laura around here," the waitress gushed. "She called while ago, said to tell you she'd be a few minutes late."

"Thanks." I nodded, looking glumly at my coffee, hoping the too-cheerful waitress would leave so I could brood about Sydney's latest e-mail from Mexico. Without knowing it, my daughter had explained a lot of things about her father's sudden interest. In the back of my mind, alarm bells were whispering like foghorns, still far out at sea.

The waitress rested the coffeepot on the table. "I'm so glad to finally meet ye-ew. Your sister brags on you all the time, and your daddy can't stop talkin' about that granddaughter of his."

My father? I wanted to say. I couldn't imagine my father's name and the words *can't stop talking* in the same sentence.

Smacking her lips, the waitress pointed a finger at me. "I thought y'all were twins."

"What?"

"You and Laura. I thought y'all were twins. Y'all don't look anything alike."

"We're the fraternal kind. Laura takes after Mom's side, and I got the height and dark hair from Dad's side," I answered absently, my mind whizzing like a computer on overload. My CPU wanted to lock up, post a system-failure message, and hang there in limbo, as it had the past three weeks since Sydney's departure.

The waitress rubbed my shoulder, propping me up like a rag doll. "You look wiped out. I'm sorry. I'm just standin' here talkin' your leg off. I should get you some biscuits. By the smell of things, Mernalene and Hasselene just now took 'em out of the oven." She checked her watch. "Good thing. The breakfast rush'll be startin' in about fifteen minutes."

"Oh," I muttered. It was hard to imagine a rush of any kind here.

"You bet," she said as she crossed the room and slipped behind the counter. "The old Lone Star Café's real popular with commuters since your sister put those articles in her magazine last year. After folks read about it, they all wanted to come try some of our special coffee. Of course, they had to wait until we were back open after the asbestos removal on the café building, but that's another story. Don't you worry, though. There's no asbestos in the food or nothin'. We had crews in white spaceman outfits workin' here for weeks. Cleaned the place top to bottom, and did an extra-special job, because Mernalene and Hasselene stayed in a camp trailer outside and kept the workers full of biscuits and coffee. Our coffee's special—did I mention that?" Picking up the pot, she headed for the kitchen. "Cures a multitude of ills. Try some. It'll perk you right up."

I wish it were that simple. Drink some magic coffee. Relax. Accept the fact that my daughter's life was changing in ways I couldn't control. Ignore the warning signs in her e-mails. Believe that everything would be all right.

Taking a sip of coffee, I sat hoping for denial to set in. Halfway through the cup, I started to feel better. My pulse slowed and the whirring in my temples quieted as the place filled up and the breakfast rush began. The waitress whizzed by my table, leaving behind butter, jam, and a basket of biscuits wrapped in a blue gingham napkin.

My stomach rolled with sudden hunger. For the first time in three weeks, it felt like I might actually taste the food.

I took out a biscuit. It was warm and soft in my hands, the scent comforting in a way I couldn't explain. It tasted impossibly good, and I realized I was starving. Taking another bite, I chewed slowly, savoring, relaxing, falling into the rhythm of clinking pans, the low hum of voices, and the rich, golden warmth of sunlight streaming in the window. The sounds conjured images of my mother, working in the kitchen years ago. . . .

I sat staring at the inside-out letters on the glass, entranced, comfortably numb. The café door opened, and I heard it, but couldn't focus.

"Lindsey?" My sister's voice barely penetrated the fog. She stood at the end of the booth, seeming uncertain. I wondered if I looked so bad that even my twin didn't recognize me.

"Hi, Laura." I swallowed a sudden rush of emotion, hoping she hadn't noticed the tremor in the words.

Her brows knotted in the center, a sure sign that she had. "Are you all right? You look terrible."

"Thanks," I said, self-consciously tucking unkempt strings of hair behind my ears. Fifteen hours of driving and crying had, no doubt, left me looking like the basket case I was.

Forcing a tired smile, I made an excuse. "Long trip."

"Well, why didn't you stop for the night?" She slid into the seat across from me. "You shouldn't have tried to drive straight through alone."

"I caught a couple hours' sleep at a rest stop." All I could remember about last night was the vague thought that Sydney loved hotels, and staying at one without her would be unbearable. "I wasn't tired."

Laura knew better, of course. "Yes, you were," she said softly, slipping her hand over mine. "Come on, Lindsey. What's wrong?"

"Everything." My voice was a thin, choked whisper. "Everything about Sydney being gone this summer is wrong."

"I know," Laura commiserated, squeezing my hand. "But it's just for the summer, Lindsey. It's what Sydney wanted. It's what she needs right now."

"Is it?" A litany of my darkest fears ran through my mind. Anger followed quickly like a noonday shadow, and words spilled out of me in rapid succession. "Because I'm starting to wonder. Oh, Sydney's trying to put the best light on it in her e-mails, but I'm starting to get a pretty clear picture. Her father is hardly ever there. He's gone to some dig site two hours into the interior, while she sits home patiently waiting up late, hoping he'll spend a few minutes with her. Most of the time, she's not with him; she's with his new trophy wife, Whitney. They're doing hair and makeup and touring the open-air market—in between Whitney's Zen infertility treatments, which, by the way, she feels completely free to tell my eight-year-old daughter all about. Whitney felt so sorry for Sydney, sitting around waiting for her father all the time, that she ordered voice-recognition software so Syd can write me e-mails without having to type everything. She must be spending hours each day on the computer, but what she really wants is to be with her father. She's been dreaming of this for eight years, and he can't even take a few weeks off to spend time with her." Tears spilled over as I thought of my little girl in a strange house, waiting for something she might never get. "I'm afraid she'll end up with her heart broken. I want to fly down there and bring her home."

Laura squeezed my hand and I felt the connection we'd always had. The twin thing. "Lindsey, you have to calm down about this." She offered me a napkin, and I wiped the raw, puffy skin around my eyes. "You *cannot* fly down there and get Sydney. Geoff has custody for the summer. It's always been joint custody, Lindsey, even if he never chose to exercise his right to visitation before. That was what you wanted when she was a baby—for her to have some kind of relationship with her father."

I knew Laura was right. I knew it, but for the past three weeks I'd been sliding down a hole so deep that rational thought had disappeared. I needed Laura to tell me what was logical. Letting my head fall into my hand, I admitted how far gone I was. "I was on the Internet the other day, buying a ticket to Mexico, when you called."

Laura gasped, slapped back against her seat by the statement. "My God, Lindsey . . ."

"I know."

"It's a good thing I called."

"Is it?" Part of me still wondered. "I could be with my daughter right now."

Laura leaned close, her blue eyes stern. "You could be in jail right now, Lindsey. In Mexico, for God's sake. How would that be for Sydney?"

I squeezed my eyes shut, nodding. *She's right. She's right. You know she's right.*

Laura continued on the attack. "You are *not* buying any airline tickets."

I nodded again.

"You have got to get a grip. Sydney is not in imminent danger.

She's staying the summer in a nice little hacienda with a maid and a swimming pool, and a stepmom who comes from money and likes to spend it. Hopefully, she's having a little time with Geoff and things will grow from there. If you try to take Sydney away from her father now, she'll never forgive you."

"But what if it's not good for her to be there? What if she ends up getting hurt?" Laura didn't have children. She couldn't possibly understand the depth of a mother's protective instincts.

My sister sighed, stroking a hand along the side of my face. "Have a little faith, Lindsey. Sydney's a smart kid. She's spent a lot more time in the adult world than most eight-year-olds. Give this a chance to work itself out. Just because you don't have control of the situation every minute of every day doesn't mean there's an impending disaster."

I laughed miserably at Laura's famous last line. I was the notorious control freak in the family. "Yes, it does." I groaned.

"No, it does not." She sounded and looked like our mother, who always knew how to bandage the wounds and soothe the hurts.

"I wish Mom were here," I whispered.

Laura smiled tenderly. "I know. But you've got me and you've got Collie. One way or another, we're going to girlfriend our way through this thing without your buying a ticket to Mexico."

"OK." I took a fortifying breath, strengthened by the image of Laura, Collie, and me together. Ever since college, we'd been the unstoppable gal trio. Strong. Determined. At least two-thirds sane at all times. Now that I was the one bungee jumping over the edge, I knew they would anchor the rope.

"So . . . speaking of Collie . . ." Laura's tone told me she had concocted some sort of plan to save me from myself. "She's working on a story down there in San Saline and she needs your help."

I drew back, smelling a setup. Laura was busy today, so Collie had been assigned to babysit me. "What help could I possibly be on something for Collie's newspaper?"

"The story isn't for the *San Saba County Review*. It's for my magazine. I've contracted her to expand a little piece she wrote last week, so that we can run it as a feature in the next issue of *Texcetera*."

"I don't think I'd be much help writing a magazine story," I hedged.

Laura raised a hand impatiently. "Give me a minute. Let me explain. It's a story about dinosaur bones."

"Really?" Now she had my interest. Writing wasn't my area of expertise, but fossils were. I hadn't heard of any big new finds in Texas lately. . . .

Laura leaned close, as if she were about to share a mysterious secret and the walls had ears. "There's a ranch near Collie's place—Jubilee Ranch. Anyway, one of her husband's cousins owns it, and it's been in the family for a hundred and fifty years. These days, they run some kind of New Age therapy camp where screwed-up suburbanites come to get a dose of pioneer life and horse psychology."

I lowered an eyebrow at my sister, and she raised her hands palms-up. "I know, it sounds strange, but here's the thing. One of the big attractions on the ranch has always been the dinosaur tracks in the riverbed. In fact, that area has always been called Big Lizard Bottoms because of all the fossils. People come from miles around to see the dino footprints. Schoolkids take field trips to it. Lots of old folks around here had their pictures taken as babies, sitting in the dinosaur tracks like a bathtub. So, two weeks ago, guess what happened? In the middle of the night, someone came in with heavy equipment and stole the dinosaur tracks. No kidding. They chiseled a huge section of limestone right out of the riverbed, and somehow managed to load it onto a truck and make off with it."

"They came prepared. . . ." Mentally, I calculated the tools required for such an operation—diamond-blade saw, generator, portable air compressor, pneumatic driver and tools, steel wedges and splitting feathers, hoist, and hydraulic lift. Not a small endeavor. "What kind of tracks were they?"

Laura tapped a finger on the table contemplatively, watching her wedding ring glitter in the angular sunlight. "I can't think of the name. Collie knows it. Some kind of meat-eating dinosaur with three toes. Thera-something."

"Theropod?"

"I guess." Laura had never shared my interest in long-extinct animals and other antiquities. "They were some of the smaller tracks, but they were the most perfect ones—the ones that were stolen, I mean. There are still some others from some kind of bigger dinosaur. I guess they were too large to steal."

"Or else the thieves are coming back for them after they get the first ones sold." Which was what often happened. Black marketers who sold fossils and other antiquities often pillaged sites a bit at a time.

Laura grimaced. "I hope not. The old man who owns the ranch was so upset, he ended up in the hospital with heart trouble. The trackway was always a part of his family's place, and now it's gone."

"Poor man." After these past few weeks, I understood how it felt to have something precious and irreplaceable taken from you.

"I know." Laura was pleased at having me hooked and largely distracted from the Sydney situation. "So Collie was hoping that you'd go down there, help her with the story, and maybe assist the local sheriff in getting the word out to places where the fossil might turn up for sale."

"I'd love to." A surprising buzz of excitement zinged through me. Other than flying to Mexico, I couldn't think of anything I'd rather do than help track down thieves who sold fossils on the black market. I had long suspected that, in addition to his legitimate work, Geoff dabbled in illegally selling antiquities to the highest bidder. "Call Collie and tell her I'm on my way to San Saline."

Laura laughed. "Well, it's good to see you so charged up. Don't you think you ought to eat first?" She waved at the waitress, who quickly brought over two breakfast platters, complete with grits.

"Did y'all get everything all worked out?" the waitress asked. Obviously, she had been poised for Laura's all-clear signal. I wasn't sure, but I thought she winked at my sister.

Laura gave her a *keep quiet* look, then blinked innocently at me and started in on her breakfast.

"Well, y'all just enjoy." The waitress backpedaled. "Eat them grits;

they're good for ya. Those'll stick to your ribs all the way to San Saline." Eyes flying wide, she popped a hand over her mouth and gave Laura a look that said, *Whoops.*

I smelled a setup larger than just my going to San Saline to help Collie with a story. Lowering my fork, I dead-eyed my sister, who was turning red, but trying to look nonchalant. "All right, Laura. Out with it. What's going on?"

TWO

<hr style="width:30%">

L AURA WOULDN'T ADMIT THERE WAS ANYTHING GOING ON, OF course. Or that her sudden phone call the day before, and her insistence that I come for a visit, had anything to do with a plot to save me from myself.

"Oh, Lindsey, don't be so paranoid," she said, as we ate our breakfast platters, and for the first time, I saw a real, live grit up close. Lots of grits, actually. They looked like lumpy Malt-O-Meal and tasted like wet potato chips. I ate the whole bowl and asked the waitress for more. My throat was raw from crying all night, and the grits felt warm and soothing.

Laura laughed as I started on seconds. "I didn't know you were such a fan of grits."

"I'm not," I said, pushing the bowl aside after a few bites. The grits were expanding in my stomach and I felt like a pop bottle that had been dropped down the stairs. "I was starving." Which was true in more ways than one. There had been a ravenous emptiness inside me since the day Sydney left. My sister's presence and the warmth of the grits filled it in some way. It felt good to be here, eating, talking, watching the world pass by outside the window instead of hiding out in the basement lab of the museum.

"So, tell me about this horse psychology place," I said. "Sounds interesting."

Laura shrugged casually, but I suspected she was hiding something. "Don't know too much about it," she said, glancing at her watch.

"Collie can tell you more. It's a cousin that runs the place—True's cousin, I mean, that would be Collie's cousin-in-law. It'll take you around two hours to get there. Collie said just to meet her at the newspaper office in San Saline, and you can drive out to the ranch together. She has an appointment to do an interview there at ten."

I glanced at my watch as the waitress cleared our plates from the table. Seven thirty-seven. "Guess I'd better get going."

The waitress paused. "Aren't you going to wait around and see your dad? He comes in every day about this time. He and Hasselene are so cute together. Just shows you that romance can happen at any age."

Laura gave her the *be quiet* look, and the woman winced, then mouthed, *Ohhh,* and quickly changed the subject. "I'll put your leftovers in a to-go container. It'd be a shame to waste all that food." Hurrying to the counter, she plopped my grits into a container, then brought it back.

Sliding to the end of the booth, Laura stood up, suddenly in a hurry to be gone. "Well, that was good. Don't worry about the check. Graham and I pay our tab at the end of the month."

I waited while Laura crossed the room, said hi to the people in the kitchen, then met me at the door. "What's Dad doing driving way out here every day?" I asked as we stepped onto the porch. A new-old worry needled my mind, pushing aside the Sydney obsession. "And what's this about a romance?"

Laura stiffened, tucking her short blond hair behind her ear, her chin jutting out defensively. "He's fine, Lindsey. Don't worry about it."

"He isn't supposed to be driving, and do you really think it's a good idea for him to be having some senior romance when he's still trying to get over losing Mom?"

Huffing, Laura crossed her arms, and I could tell we were about to get into one of our bossy-sister versus nice-sister arguments. "He's fine. He passed his driver's test. *You're* the only one who thinks he shouldn't have his keys. Mark, Daniel, and I agreed that there's no reason Dad can't drive, and we're all OK with his dating Hasselene. Mom's been gone over a year, and he's lonely. Mark thinks Dad and Hasselene ought to get married and Dad should move out here."

I stood blinking at Laura, openmouthed. Apparently, there had been a family conference involving my brothers and my sister, and no one bothered to include me. "Well, it would have been nice if someone had told me."

"Leave it be, Lindsey." Laura sounded so much like my mother that my heart lurched. "I know you wanted him to hang around the senior center and take up woodcarving, but he isn't interested. He's been afraid to tell you that. He doesn't go to any of those senior activities you send him e-mails about. He likes spending his days here at the café, doing little repairs and odd jobs, and, as it turns out, he likes Hasselene. He's happy. End of story."

I coughed in disbelief. Everyone in my family had been lying to me. Normally such a realization would have caused a temper flare, but I just stood there feeling hurt and unwanted.

Running a hand down my arm sympathetically, Laura tilted forward to catch my gaze. "Lindsey, it's OK. It really is. You had so much on your mind this last year with Sydney, we didn't want to burden you, and . . . well . . . we didn't want to deal with your reaction to Dad dating Hasselene. It's like you go into a panic about anything you can't micromanage. Life happens, Lindsey. It just . . . does. The fact that you didn't plan something doesn't mean it's going to end in disaster. Let loose a little bit before you kill yourself. Have a little faith."

"Faith isn't my forte," I whispered, scrubbing my eyebrows with my fingertips, feeling my lips tremble into a wan smile. "Control works much better for me."

Laura laughed, pulling my hands away from my face and holding them in hers. "Control is an illusion."

"I can't lose Sydney." My darkest fear bubbled up like stagnant water trapped below the surface.

"You're not going to lose Sydney." She squeezed my hands and I felt the bond between us, her strength flowing into me. "Go do the story with Collie. Have fun. Relax. Distract yourself for a while and you'll be that much closer to Sydney coming home, right?"

Taking a deep breath of the fresh air, I gave her hands a resigned jiggle. "You're right. You're right. I have to get myself together."

"Good." Seeming satisfied, she reached into her briefcase and pulled out a couple of newspapers. "Here are some articles about the ranch. Collie wrote the one about the stolen dinosaur footprint. The other one is a *USA Today* article about the horse therapy program. Apparently horse psychology is all the rage, ever since Oprah, or somebody, featured it on a talk show."

"Really?" I said, glancing at Collie's article and then at the one printed in full color in *USA Today*. "Where in the world have I been?"

Laura chuckled. "Apparently not in Texas."

"Apparently not. I didn't . . ." I paused, losing my train of thought as I studied the picture of a solemn-faced cowboy next to the article. In the photo, he was standing with his elbows braced on an old wooden fence as he looked thoughtfully into the distance. His black cowboy hat was pulled low, so that it framed his silvery green eyes and straight, dark brows. "Who's this?"

Laura craned her neck to see the picture. "That's one of Collie's cousins-in-law from the horse psychology camp."

When I looked up, my sister was studying me, seeming contemplative, slightly expectant. Pasting on an artificial smile, she gave me a quick hug and said, "Guess you'd better get going. Tell Collie hi for me," then practically shoved me down the stairs toward my vehicle. "Collie's newspaper office is right in downtown San Saline. You can't miss it. You've got a map in your car, right?"

"Of course," I replied. "And a new GPS system, actually."

Laura rolled her eyes. "Good Lord, Lindsey. You don't leave anything to chance."

"Not if I can help it." I gave her a quick sneer, playfully snide, like I would have done when we were kids competing against each other on the same softball field. Laura was always petite, puny, and afraid of the ball. I knew that the key was to learn to control it. Once you had control of the ball, there was nothing to be afraid of.

"You're such a brat," she shot back over her shoulder, as she headed to her car. "Call me later." Opening the door, she put one foot in, like a bank robber about to make a getaway. "You'd better head out. You'll miss Collie." She added a little head bob, her short blond hair swinging like a Clairol commercial. "Love ya. 'Bye." Then she disappeared into her car.

As I climbed into my Jeep, I caught her watching me again as she answered her cell phone. I had the strangest feeling she was talking about me.

She smiled and waved, then put her car into gear and drove away like she was afraid I'd change my mind. My original plan had been to hang out at Dad's place and spend the day rearranging his pills, cleaning up the farmhouse, or finally sorting through Mom's things and sending them off to Goodwill. Something, anything, to put life in order. Someone's life.

Only now, Laura was telling me that Dad had better things to do. He had a life of his own. Laura had a life of her own—new husband, in-laws, a comfortable little ranch house that I'd seen only in pictures. Worst of all, Sydney had a life of her own. New father, new stepmother, new bedroom that she said was bright-pink stucco decorated with lively Mexican-tile mosaics.

Everyone was moving on, and no one had bothered to consult me.

"Do you think I have control issues?" I said to the horse psychologist in the newspaper. I propped him up against the door handle so that we could see each other better. "Because I don't think I have control issues."

The horse psychologist studied me with his faraway look. If he had the answers, he wasn't sharing. The big brown doe eyes of the horse in the picture next to him regarded me tenderly from beneath a mop of frosty white hair. He didn't think I had control issues. To him, I was just a normal, well-adjusted, thirty-something single mother having a bad day . . . bad week . . . bad month . . . bad year. . . .

Anyway, the point was that I didn't have control issues. Once I got Dad's life and Sydney's situation back in order, I'd prove that to Laura. Admittedly, I needed for things to be on an even keel, reasonably predictable. That wasn't the same as being a control freak.

Was it?

The horse psychologist answered me with the slightest hint of a sardonic, know-it-all smile. He thought I had control issues.

I laid the paper facedown, because I really didn't need his opinion anyway.

Picking up the road atlas, I glanced at the route to San Saline. I was heading from nowhere to nowhere. Nothing between me and San Saline but two-lane roads and towns in small print. Easy drive. I punched the starting point and destination into the GPS console, and an electronic map displayed the route. Estimated travel time, 108.5 minutes. Adequate fuel. Outside temperature, seventy-two degrees, weather fair, wind speed eight mph.

The GPS pinpointed my current location on the digital map. "Proceed east point-one miles. Turn left onto FM 47-B," the electronic voice instructed pleasantly as I put the car in gear. Sydney and I laughingly called the woman in the dashboard "Gertie."

Circling the parking lot, gazing at the wild Indian blankets blooming around the edges, I sifted out a childhood memory of my mother picking a bouquet of the bright yellow flowers with velvety crimson pinwheel centers. I couldn't even remember where we were living then. My childhood was a series of army towns that all ran together.

"Make a legal U-turn. Proceed east point-one miles. Turn left onto FM 47-B," Gertie repeated, her electronic frustration obvious, despite the singsong voice.

Gertie had control issues. She liked to stay right on course, no side trips. Normally, we got along very well.

She quieted as we pulled onto the two-lane. I pictured her inside the dashboard like *I Dream of Jeannie* in a prim gray business suit, hair in a tight French twist. Right now she was mopping her forehead, saying, *Whew, that was a close one. For a minute there, I thought she was going to stop and pick flowers. . . .*

Gertie went into snooze mode as we wound along the old two-lane highway, slipping through the gnarled fingers of overhanging live oaks, past roadside pastures vibrant with wildflowers and crystal-clear streams still swollen from spring rains. The rhythm of the road and the melody of sunlight and shadow soothed my mind, and I found myself letting out a long breath, taking in another, breathing out again, feeling drowsy as the miles passed.

Gertie must have sensed it, because she spoke up eventually, guiding me through a bypass of Killeen, near a few vague signs of civilization, a metal fabrications shop, a giant red barn with a cross on the top that said COWBOY CHURCH, a sports complex where golfers were whacking balls on the driving range and Little Leaguers were perfecting their swings in the batting cages. After that, civilization faded away again, and Gertie ran out of things to say.

I fell into the rhythm of the road, not thinking for a change, just driving and breathing in air, scented with growing things and damp spring earth, as another fifty miles drifted by. It was good to be far from home, beyond the boundaries of the museum and our apartment in downtown Denver. Here, the countryside was foreign, empty, distinctly Southwestern. Lacy mesquite trees waved lazily as I drove by, and spiny yucca plants stood at attention, their white plumes thrust into the air like the banners of the Spanish explorers who once traveled these rambling hills.

I passed a ranch where a herd of horses grazed peacefully, now and then raising their heads and flicking their ears, instinctively alert for danger. I slowed to look at them, black, blond, brunette, gray. Sydney would have known the technical terms for those colors. I would be sure to tell her about them tonight in my e-mail. She loved horses, even though I was terrified of them. If she could have found a way to smuggle one into our apartment, she would have. As it was, she had to settle for a guinea pig and a goldfish, which were staying over with one of her school friends for the summer, because she didn't trust me to feed them. "I'm not trying to be mean, Mom," she had said. "But you're not an animal person. I think they can tell you put together bones and stuff for a living."

Slowing a little more, I studied the horse herd, memorizing the details so that I could impress my animal-crazy daughter. She would never believe—

The horses raised their heads and started suddenly, and a blur of movement flashed past the corner of my eye. I turned back to the road just in time to see something large and white bolt into my path and stop directly in front of me. My heart rocketed into my throat, exploding like a bomb. Grabbing the steering wheel with both hands, I slammed on the brakes. The Jeep squealed and fishtailed as I spun the wheel left, then right, struggling to keep the car on the road, trying to make out the hairy white object ahead. Sheep? Pony?

The car wasn't going to stop in time. Closing my eyes, I braced for the impact as the SUV slid sideways, then started to spin. The steering wheel vibrated wildly in my hands, and I hung on as the force threw me against my seat belt, then back into the seat.

Please don't let it roll. . . .

Thank God Sydney's not in the car. . . .

I imagined her being raised by her father and Whitney.

No!

It's going to hit now. . . .

The SUV came to a stop and everything was silent. The spin was over as quickly as it began. I opened my eyes, shaking, my pulse booming like a bass drum. The Jeep had done a complete three-sixty, so that it was facing forward again. In the correct lane. Idling just like nothing had happened. In the road, not more than two feet from my bumper, just now turning its head and noticing me, was a huge, hairy, white . . . dog?

Parting his massive jaws, he hung his tongue out, wagging his tail casually, completely unaware of what had almost happened.

"What in the . . . ?"

In the dash, Gertie came to life. "Proceed seven miles on Highway 190," she said, apparently neither confused nor affected by the wild spin, just frustrated with the unauthorized stop. "Proceed seven miles on Highway 190," she said again. *Ding, ding, ding.* Apparently, she couldn't see the enormous dog in the road, though, at his size, he should have been clearly visible from any orbiting satellite.

Sticking my head out the window, I looked up and down the road. No cars. No one. No ranch house visible anywhere. The dog had apparently escaped from somewhere, because he was dragging a length of chewed-off rope.

"Shoo!" I hollered.

He promptly sat down in the road and scrubbed his long, furry tail back and forth against the pavement.

"Shoo!" I hollered again. "Shoo! Scat! Get off the road, you idiot."

Inching the car forward, I honked the horn, backed up, and pretended to make a run at him. No reaction. I pulled alongside, waving my hands madly out the window to chase him off the road before he got killed or caused another accident.

He only lolled out his tongue, long and pink, dripping slobber between enormous canines perfect for making a quick snack of tourists foolish enough to exit their cars.

"Get out of the road, you big, stupid dog!" I screamed, honking the horn.

The mat of weeds and loose hair on his head shifted upward, then back down like a giant, overgrown eyebrow. There were probably eyes in there somewhere, and behind that a brain that was saying, *Just a little longer . . . here she comes . . . she'll get out of the car, and then . . . lunch.*

"I don't believe this!" I muttered, clamping my hands over my eyes, then bolting them to the sides of my head, looking around the car for a weapon, something to scare him with, maybe one of those long poles they used to catch wild crocodiles on TV.

I ended up with a fold-up umbrella and a stadium seat. Hitting the hazard lights, I opened the car door a crack.

Gertie went crazy. *Ding, ding, ding.* "Door ajar. Proceed on highway. . . ." I left her there, talking to herself.

Inching forward, one step, two, three, I moved around the side of the car, holding the stadium seat and the umbrella like a toreador advancing on a wild bull. The bull only cocked his woolly white head to one side and looked at me, unconcerned, yawning with a bite radius the size of my thigh.

That was definitely the biggest dog I'd ever seen. He stared at me from almost chest level. Covered with pounds and pounds of thick, dirty white hair, he looked like something from *Star Wars*. The wookiee.

"Shoo! Ha! Scat!" I screeched, sounding, I thought, fairly fierce.

The dog stuck his head forward and let out a huge, baritone noise . . . something between a bark and a growl . . . a sound completely unlike anything I'd ever heard a dog make. It echoed against the rim of rocky hills that surrounded the highway.

"Geez!" I jumped back, and the wookiee stood up, barking at me three more times.

"Ooooh, gosh." I started backing toward the car, muttering, "Good job, Lindsey. Really smart. You're going to get eaten by a gigantic white dog in the middle of nowhere. . . ."

In the car, Gertie piped up again, "Door ajar. Proceed . . ."

The dog turned his attention to the car, bounding back and forth in front of the headlights, sending out a deafening series of raspy barks. When he finally stopped, I heard a sudden clatter on the road. I turned around just in time to see a cowboy on horseback come running through a break in the barbed-wire fence and gallop toward me.

Thank God! The beast had an owner, and there he was.

The cowboy skidded to a stop on the roadside, sending up a shower of flying gravel and waving his hand urgently with a lasso in it. "Lady, is that your dog?"

"What . . . ? My . . ." I glanced toward the dog, which had left the road and disappeared around the side of my car. The rope slid past the tire like a snake. "I was just trying to get him off the—"

Jumping sideways, the horse spun around in the ditch, flinging specks of foamy white lather in all directions. "Whoa, idjut!" the cowboy hollered, bringing the nervous animal under control, so that it stood stomping and trembling. Ears flicking back and forth, it snorted at the rope slithering past my car. "Listen, if that's your dog, you better git him outa here, because he's fixin' to git shot."

"He's not my . . ." I felt a wet nose on the small of my back, hot breath seeping through my T-shirt. *Oh, God . . .*

I stood very still, the umbrella and the stadium chair dangling at my sides, my arms like overcooked noodles. The dog rubbed his head against me, knocking me sideways into the open door of the Jeep. Bracing his feet on the door frame, the dog climbed halfway in and tried to kiss me. I smelled old sneakers and tuna fish.

"Get down!" I pushed him away with more command than I thought I could muster. Rejected, he cowered in the doorway, pinning my leg against the seat as the cowboy forced his horse a few steps closer. "He isn't mine," I insisted, as the odor of swamp water crowded my nose, flipping the wad of half-digested grits in my stomach.

"Well, then he's fixin' to git kilt." Pushing his hat back, the cowboy wiped his forehead with his sleeve. I realized he was younger than I'd originally thought. Twenty-one, twenty-two, maybe, baby-faced despite a pathetic attempt at a mustache. He didn't look like the type to do something so heinous as shoot a helpless animal.

I felt the need to defend the dog. "Listen, you can't—"

Pointing a finger, the cowboy cut me off impatiently. "That dog just run two hundred head a' cattle through the fence. He's been causin' trouble around here for a solid month. The boss is gonna shoot him this time and take care of it for good."

THREE

———◆———

I GAPED AT THE COWBOY. AGAINST MY KNEE, THE DOG WHIMPERED. The mother in me, the soft, tender part that yearned to protect little people and big stray dogs, rose up and leaned menacingly out the door. "You are *not* going to shoot this dog."

The cowboy glanced over his shoulder in a guilty way that told me he didn't want to shoot the dog. "Lady, as soon as the boss lays eyes on that dog, it's dead. We got tore-up cattle and a half mile of downed fence over there." He winced, his eyes beseeching me. "You sure he ain't yours?"

"Well, he's somebody's." I motioned to the animal, now pressed so tightly against my leg that my foot was going numb on the door frame. "You can't shoot him. He's obviously somebody's pet. I'm sure they want him back."

"Doubt it." Dismounting, he tied his horse to a fence post, then came back, gesturing with the lasso still coiled in his hand. "That thing's part Great Pyrenees. Them kind ain't supposed to be pets. They're supposed to live out with the sheep to keep predators away. They're raised with the herd and mostly they don't like people, but every once in a while, you git a dud that won't stay in the sheep pasture. This one's a dud, I reckon. Either wandered off or somebody dumped him. He's been hangin' around the area awhile raidin' trash cans and causing trouble. Then today he took up chasin' cows." Glancing over his shoulder at the ruined fence, he gave the dog a disgusted look. "If you don't want him to git shot, you better load him up and git him outa here."

"I can't . . ." I stammered. "I don't . . . don't live here. I don't have anywhere to take a giant . . . *dog*."

"Listen." He raised his hands, pleading, looking at the dog and then me. "You're only a few miles from San Saline. My mama runs the Hawthorne House Bed-and-Breakfast there. If you don't want him, drop him off there. Tell her Jimmy sent you. She's always takin' in stray animals and finding homes for 'em."

The dog laid his woolly head on my thigh, gazing hopefully upward. "Oh, for heaven's sake. All right," I heard myself say. What was I thinking? "Back up, OK. He's afraid of you and he won't get off my leg."

The cowboy, Jimmy, walked up the road a few steps, his spurs jingling against the asphalt. "You better hurry up and git him loaded. Boss is gonna be comin' any second."

"Just give me a minute. You're scaring him." Pushing the button to open the back hatch, I grabbed a huge handful of matted neck hair, pushed the dog off my leg, and slid to my feet. This had to be one of the stupidest things I'd ever done. "Come on, boy," I urged as the stadium seat toppled from the floorboard and clattered against the pavement. The dog responded by compacting me against the side of the Jeep, while eyeing the folding chair warily, so that all I could do was inch sideways along the car, my rear end wiping a clean streak in the dust of three states.

When we got to the back, I patted the empty space next to my suitcase, saying, "Come on, boy. Come on."

Cocking his head to one side, the dog perked his ears and wagged his long tail at my singsong, friend-to-animals voice. "Get in the car. Come on." Still no progress. "The mean cowboy men are going to shoot you. Get in the car."

Gertie started talking in the dash, and the dog let out a deafening series of barks. The cowboy hollered, "Lady! Here comes the boss!" His spurs jingled as he ran through the ditch to his horse. Peeking around the side of the Jeep, I saw three riders galloping up the fence line, coming straight toward us, no doubt following the barking.

I developed sudden superhuman strength. Wrapping my arms

around the massive animal, I lifted. "You're"—front end in, stiff-legged, claws digging furrows in the carpet—"going"—arms around the back end, and lift—"in"—*ooof!*—"here"—brace shoulder, shove—"darn it!" *Grab hatch, shut quick.*

"There," I breathed, wiping my forehead, then striding forward to meet the boss before he could see inside my vehicle.

". . . took off," Jimmy Hawthorne was doing a very poor job of lying to his employer, while waving vaguely toward the hills. "Over there someplace, I think. This lady durned near run him over. Scared him away. Don't think he'll stop runnin' for a while."

The boss swiveled slowly in his saddle, so that instead of looking at the hills, he was looking at Jimmy, then at me, our bodies reflecting off his sunglasses like figures in a funhouse mirror. His lips, made stern by the glasses and the square line of his chin, straightened into a thoughtful frown beneath the shadow of his cowboy hat. There was something familiar about the expression, but I couldn't decide what.

"He's probably all the way to Lampasas County by now," Jimmy added, his voice a little too quick, too high-pitched. He sounded like a teenager who'd just been caught ditching class.

"That so," the boss replied. It was neither a statement nor a question.

I nodded, motioning vaguely over my shoulder. "I was looking at the horses, and the next thing I knew there was this huge dog in the road. I hit the brakes, and somehow I missed him." All true. Just not all of the truth.

The boss scratched beside his ear, then pulled off his sunglasses. His eyes were surprisingly bright against his dark skin. Surveying the round-robin skid marks on the road, he rested an elbow on his saddle and leaned closer to me. "You're lucky that Jeep didn't roll."

"Boy, is that the truth. I thought it was going to for a minute. It all happened so fast," I babbled, suddenly nervous. The intensity of his regard was unsettling. If he hadn't been a dog hater, he would have been . . . well . . . good-looking, in a rugged sort of way.

"Bet that shook you up a little bit," he commented with apparent concern. His gaze shifted past me to something else.

"You have no idea."

Lips parting slightly, he clicked his tongue against even white teeth. "Guess that's how you left your door open, and the dog got in your car."

Jerking back, I glanced over my shoulder. The dog was . . . climbing into the passenger seat, a huge mass of white hair squeezing past the console, filling the front of the Jeep, turning around and around in the cramped space before finally stopping. He was looking at us, I thought, but at this distance, it was hard to tell one end from the other.

The boss gave his cowpoke a scathing glance, as did the two men behind him. "Jimmy, you want to tell me what the heck's going on?"

Jimmy's gaze darted back and forth, like those of a rat in a trap. "I didn't . . . It was . . . She . . ." He raised a hand, lowered it, then raised it again and pointed at me. "It's her dog."

"It's *not* my dog." I had a fleeting vision of having to pay for two hundred cows and miles of fencing. Bracing my hands on my hips, I straightened my shoulders, suddenly feeling like my old self. The self who could handle pushy museum patrons, dishonest customs officials, and smart-mouthed high school kids on field trips. The self who wouldn't let anything happen to a helpless dog, even if he was chewing on my dashboard. "Listen, mister, you are not going to do anything to that poor dog."

The boss drew back, craning his neck. "That *poor dog* just chased two hundred cows through a half mile of barbed wire fence."

"I don't care." I was suddenly on fire with the righteous indignation that had been simmering inside me ever since the family court judge chose to sympathize with Geoff's sudden desire to be a father. This cowboy man would be taking that stupid, smelly dog out of my Jeep over my dead body. "That doesn't justify what you were going to do."

"Really?" The hard line of his jaw jutted from beneath the shadow of his hat, catching the sunlight. He needed a shave.

"Yes, really." Riding his horse forward, he dismounted, and my heart started thudding against my chest. He was tall and intimidat-

ing, and he obviously knew it. In one swift move, I grabbed the dis-
carded stadium seat, brandishing it without even thinking about
what it was. In my mind, I saw Geoff standing there, smirking at me
in the airport, letting me know he'd won.

Stopping midstride, the boss pushed his hat brim back so that I
could see his eyes again. He squinted at the stadium seat, then me.
"Lady, are you all right?"

"I'm fine!" I snapped, still holding the fold-up seat like a weapon.
"I'm just sick of people who . . ." *Who take advantage of a child's desperate need for love.* ". . . who go around . . ." *Living by their own rules,
taking things just because they feel like it, no matter who it hurts.*
". . . shooting dogs."

"What?" His head snapped back like an oversize yo-yo. "Lady, I
wasn't going to shoot the dog."

"Yes, you were," I shrieked, waving a finger toward Jimmy, feeling
nearly out of my mind with exhaustion and pent-up anger. "Don't
even try to deny it. Jimmy the Kid over there told me. I know what
you were doing. What do I look like—an idiot?"

His expression said, *Well, actually, yes. You look like a crazy lady in the
middle of a deserted highway threatening a perfect stranger with a stadium
seat.* Swallowing whatever he was going to say, he braced his hands
on his hips and turned halfway around, silencing the cowboys, who
had started to chortle and snort. "Jimmy, did you tell this lady I was
going to shoot the dog?"

Red-faced, Jimmy shrugged. "Well . . . I . . . It was . . . Dan . . . Dan
said you said to shoot the dog."

The boss stiffened, some unreadable emotion crossing his features.
Anger? Guilt? Embarrassment at all of this being brought out in
front of a third party? He seemed to think carefully about what to
say, then finally bit out a tight-lipped, "I didn't tell anyone to shoot
the dog."

Jimmy looked down at his hands uncertainly.

"I'll bet," I heard myself mutter.

The boss put on an impassive mask and turned back to me.
"Ma'am—"

"No . . . just . . ." Backing away, I hatcheted a hand between us, my emotions being sucked down a backwash now that the immediate crisis was over. I felt ridiculous, exhausted, confused, suddenly unsure of myself. It was hard to tell what was real anymore. "You know what . . . ? Never mind. No blood. No foul. The dog is fine. Whatever." I didn't care what his explanation was. I just wanted to get out of there. My emotions were sliding out of control again. I had a feeling I'd just made a complete fool of myself.

Opening the car door, I tossed the stadium seat into the back and glanced at the clock. Ten fifteen. Great. I couldn't do anything right anymore. "I'm late. Good-bye. I'll take the dog with me."

A glint of sunlight from the car windshield slid beneath his hat as he stepped closer, squinting doubtfully at me. "You might want to—"

"I think I can handle it," I interrupted, in a hurry to be out of there before the situation degenerated any further. A dark-colored pickup was barreling across the pasture toward us, and Jimmy the Kid looked worried. "It's just a dog," I added.

The boss raised his straight, dark brows, looking at me like I was nuts. "That's a Great Pyranees sheepdog mix. They aren't pets. That one—"

"Good, because I'm not looking for a pet." I cut him off before he could tell me again that the dog had run his cattle through the fence. Next thing he'd be asking me to pay for the damage. Not that I could have. With the legal bills and taking this unexpected time off work, I was pretty well tapped out.

Bracing his hands on his hips, he drew back to his full height, smiling slightly . . . appreciatively, I thought, though I couldn't imagine why. I could picture what I looked like, standing there after twenty-four hours with little sleep and no shower, wild tendrils of brown hair flying all around my face. I felt like something off *O Pioneers!*—Ma all haggard and exhausted after a battle with the wilderness, forced to confront unfriendly natives.

Another hostile had just arrived in a pickup, jumped out, slammed the door, and was headed our way. With wrinkled, leathery skin, beady, dark eyes, and thin lips pressed into a severe frown, he looked like the type to shoot a helpless dog. He paused to talk to Jimmy, who, judging from the body language and hand motions, was telling him the whole story, complete with the bit about the umbrella and the stadium seat.

I turned back to the boss. "Well, like I said, I think I can handle it." My fingers closed on empty air as I reached for the door handle.

"Door's open," he said.

"No kidding." I felt like an awkward teenager at a middle school dance.

"Your partner's eating something in there." His gaze cut toward the vehicle, then back to me. He delivered a broad, white smile that might have been charming in any other circumstances, but right now the old guy with the bad attitude was finishing up with Jimmy and heading toward us. "Hope it's not your checkbook."

"My checkbook wouldn't make much of a meal." Glancing into the vehicle, I could see that the dog was, indeed, consuming a half-eaten honey bun, wrapper and all, and sniffing the container of leftover grits on the dashboard.

The boss shook his head, clearly ready to abandon me to my fate. "Good luck." He tipped his hat before turning to meet the surly-faced cowboy. "Well, Dan, you missed all the excitement," he said, as if he couldn't see the stiff-armed posture and the man's murderous glare aimed at my car.

"There's gonna be some excitement when I git my hands on that dog." The older man's voice was rough, his tone gravely serious. I slid closer to my vehicle.

"Leave it be, Dan." The boss walked back to his horse, picked up the reins, and prepared to mount.

Bristling, Dan pulled off his hat and slapped it against his leg. "Like heck I will. We been trying to git that mutt took care of for a week. I ain't letting him drive off with some half-cocked do-goodin' out-of-town city woman who'll probably turn him loose a mile down the road. That dog's got to be took care of before he can do any more damage around here. Old Neville down the road's missin' three baby goats. Mrs. Bradshaw's got a tore-up vegetable garden. I hear he broke into some lady's house in town, scared her and her kids half to death; then he raided the potluck at the Baptist church. Yesterday, that mutt jumped Mrs. Horn's fence and got after her best border collie female, not to mention all that ruckus in town when he stole the beef from the locker plant, and now we're gonna be fixin' fence and sewin' up cattle from now till next Tuesday."

"Then we'd better get to it." The boss climbed onto his horse with the authority of a man who assumed his orders would be followed. Leaving Dan standing in the road, he pointed at Jimmy and the other cowboys, who, so far, hadn't said a word. "Go ahead and get the cattle penned and sorted. I'm late for an appointment with the windmill salesman at headquarters. I'll bring some penicillin and sutures when I come back." He glanced at Dan, who was still eyeing my vehicle with his nostrils flaring. "See what you can do about the fence. Looks like you've got wire in your truck. I'll bring some T posts and a driver after a while."

Yanking a pair of gloves from his back pocket, Dan turned to the other cowboys, his shoulders clenched. "You heard the man. Git to work." He walked away, muttering under his breath, "Stupid son of a . . ." It was hard to tell whether he was talking about his boss or the dog.

Watching him go, I reached for the car door and realized again that it was already open. Climbing in, I slammed the door, trying not to look as stupid as I felt. In the passenger seat, the dog thumped his tail and investigated me with a slobbery sniff.

"No! Now stop," I scolded, pushing him back to his side of the car. "Just . . . just stay over there. You smell . . . disgusting." My stomach rolled over. No wonder the cattle had stampeded.

Sensing that he wasn't welcome here, either, the dog turned to face the front window and emitted a huge sigh. The hopelessness of the sound resonated within me, touching that part that could identify with wandering lost in a world unfamiliar and unfriendly.

"Don't worry," I whispered, pulling back the mat of weeds and hair and looking into the sad, bewildered eyes underneath. Brown eyes, like Sydney's, heavy with a need I couldn't fulfill. I couldn't be this dog's owner, any more than I could be Sydney's dad. Nor could I make the need go away. The desires of the heart are what they are, no matter how long you try to deny them.

"Don't worry." Giving the dog a last pat, I shifted the car into gear. "We'll figure it out."

Outside, the cowboys backed their horses off the road, and Dan stalked to his pickup, then disappeared in a hail of uprooted grass and roadside gravel. The men on horseback stood looking at me like I was an alien presence about to blast off for my home planet.

I rolled down the window as I passed them. "How do I get to the Hawthorne House?"

Jimmy delivered a grin that was genuinely grateful. "Through town, on your right, just across from the Sale Barn Café. Can't miss it, ma'am."

"All right . . . well . . ." Thanks? Thanks for what? My car smelled like the inside of a sewer. " 'Bye."

"Good luck, ma'am." Something in his tone worried me. As I rolled up the window, he leaned over and whispered something to the cowboy next to him and both of them laughed.

The drive to San Saline seemed longer than seven miles, but in the dash, Gertie was once again pleased with our progress. She rang in, "Destination four miles."

My copilot jumped in his seat, then stuck his head forward and sniffed the dash.

"Estimated time to destination, six minutes," Gertie went on.

Jerking back, the dog stuck its head out and let out a baritone bark that rumbled through the car like thunder.

Gertie went on, completely unfazed. "Estimated arrival time, ten thirty-five."

"Ten thirty," I muttered, checking the clock on the dash. The dog rescue had made me terribly late. Not only that, but I still had a dog to get rid of. Collie would never believe my reason for not being on time. I pictured arriving at the newspaper office, saying, "Sorry I'm late, Col. I had to stop out on some deserted highway and rescue this huge, hairy stray dog. No kidding. The thing was the size of a small pony and had jaws like something off *Wild Kingdom.* . . ."

Collie would never buy it. Neither would Sydney, when I put it in tonight's e-mail. They would all think I was making it up, covering for some lapse in time, during which I pulled over to the side of the road and sat staring into space, unable to function. . . .

Rolling down the windows, I let the fresh breeze chase away stale air and unhappy thoughts. My passenger barked approval and stuck his head out. The unibrow sailed upward in the breeze, giving him a surprised look as his jowls flapped, fanning into a gigantic smile.

I felt a tickle in my stomach, heard a puff of air press past my lips, and suddenly I was laughing for the first time in weeks. Shaking his head in the wind, the dog sent a shower of slobber fanning back against the Jeep, his face distorted as if he were a pilot undergoing major g-force. I laughed harder, and he barked happily, his tail thumping against the seat.

Gertie must have sensed the unplanned moment of wild abandon, because she piped up on the dash, "One mile to destination."

I came back to earth as we topped a hill. Below in the valley, the town of San Saline was nestled among the mesquite and wild sage along the San Saba River. Slowing the car, I gazed absently at the outlying pecan farms, their fields neatly groomed beneath towering trees, bright with the fresh growth of a new summer. Near the river, a beekeeper dressed in a protective white suit was harvesting honey, and along the banks three young fishermen, happy to be out of school for the summer, had set up camp on a rock ledge. Lulled into momentary complacency, I smiled at the peacefulness of the scene.

Fortunately, Gertie was still on track. "Proceed point-six miles to B Street," she commanded, growing more active now that we were entering civilization.

The dog sniffed the dashboard, growling and whining, then lifting a paw and batting the instrument panel.

"Not a fan of GPS, huh?" I said, pushing him away, then hitting the button to turn it off as we passed a park and a small grocery store. "Not much need for Gertie around here, anyway," I muttered, scanning the tiny town square ahead. It was just as Collie had described in her letters. Ancient, quiet, almost a still life of a town, with a towering German-style limestone courthouse in the center of the square, surrounded by buildings constructed of brick and heavy limestone blocks. Wide porches overhung the sidewalks, offering shade and a resting place on park benches that seemed content to sit idly in front of stores with names from a bygone era—Harbison's Farm and Home, Dandy Dime, Harvey's Boots and More, San Saline Dry Goods, Harvey's Ladies' Store (sale on new summer dresses, and girls' sandals two for one). The flowered dresses in the window looked like they'd jumped off the fashion train about 1960 and remained there ever since.

Watching them pass, I had a sense of nostalgia for the quiet days of my childhood. I remembered my mother at the post exchange with other army wives, passing the days trying on dresses like those, waiting for my father to return home from one tour of duty or another. Most of her life was about waiting for my father to come around. She did it with the grace of an angel and the style of a Palmolive ad—the ones in which the mom did dishes in a new dress and pearls. She held everything together through a dozen moves, four children, the ups and downs of an army career, my father's stubbornness, his battle fatigue and depression, and more homes than I could count. The silverware was polished, the plates were clean, the clothes were ironed, and Mom was smiling, gentle, serene. She never once had a meltdown like I was having now.

If she could have seen me these past weeks, she would have been ashamed. She would have said, *Lindsey, what is, is. Sometimes you just have to be patient and trust that the answers will come. In the meantime, wash those dirty dishes.*

Mom was a firm believer in doing something useful as therapy for life's ills.

Beside me, the dog whined low in his throat, resting against the seat. I'd done something useful today. Rescuing a lost dog—that was useful. A random act of kindness. My mother would have approved.

"All right, big boy," I said, smoothing the hair out of his eyes, watching him blink at the sunlight. "Let's go by and catch Collie, tell her what's going on, then find this Hawthorne House and drop you off."

He batted brown eyes at me just before I dropped the matted brow back into place and made a left turn, circling the square and pulling up in front of the *San Saline Record* and *San Saba County Review* office in an old frontier-style building. Beyond the plate-glass windows, the place looked dark, and there was a note taped to the door with my name on it. I retrieved the note and came back to the Jeep to read it.

> Lindsey,
> Had to go on without you—10:15.
> Meet me at Jubilee Ranch. Here's a map.
> —Collie

Below the note was a quickly scrawled map, starting at the *Record* office, routing west of town through a network of county roads delineated with landmarks like *cemetery*, *big tree*, and *old church*. It looked easy enough to follow, but first I had to get rid of the dog. He was on the driver's side now, hanging his head out the window, watching me. "Get out of my seat," I hollered, shooing him as I trotted back to the Jeep. I had a vision of him hitting the gearshift, jumping the curb, and driving through Collie's front window. "Go on, get out of there." The last line came in the this-time-I-really-mean-it voice I sometimes used when Sydney didn't want to do her homework. The mommy voice.

Ducking his head in the window, the dog squeezed back to his own seat, panting happily, ready for our next adventure.

"Oh, no, big guy," I said. "It's the end of the line for you. As soon as we find this Hawthorne House, you're out of here."

He only stretched out his neck, his big black nose almost touching the ceiling as he yawned and smiled, filling the car with dog breath.

My stomach, now empty of grits, rolled over. "Gross," I wheezed. "If this lady at the Hawthorne House has a sense of smell, we're in trouble."

As it turned out, the Hawthorne House was easy to find, but it wouldn't have mattered if the proprietor, Jimmy's mother, had a sense of smell, because the front gates were chained shut with a sign that said, CLOSED FOR WEDDING PREPARATIONS. BACK FRIDAY.

Friday, which was four days away.

I sat idling in the driveway, wondering how Jimmy Hawthorne could possibly not have known his mother was out of town. Or . . . maybe he did know, and he was trying to trick me into removing the dog before Dan shot it. Now what? The doggy drop-off spot was closed until Friday. *Think. Think. Think. Think of something.*

Nothing came to mind. This was absolutely a problem I'd never confronted before. How to get rid of a large, smelly, unwanted dog, the kind of dog that didn't make a good pet, in a town where you didn't know anybody and didn't know your way around. In a hurry.

Not possible, a voice inside me concluded.

Another voice, one closer to my churning stomach, said, *Just tie it to the front gate and drive off. Someone will find it. It smells really bad. . . .*

The mommy in me insisted that I couldn't abandon the poor animal. I let out another long sigh, and the dog sighed with me.

"Any suggestions?" I asked, but of course the dog didn't answer. "You know, I can't talk to you with your hair in your face." It was something I used to say to Sydney when she was younger. As a toddler, her favorite trick was to pull her knees into a ball, tuck her head, let her long sandy brown hair fall down like a curtain, and pretend she was invisible. Eventually, she figured out that, even though she couldn't see me, I could see her.

"How about this?" Impulsively, I grabbed one of Sydney's hair bands off the dash, pulled the thick mat of weeds and loose hair away from the dog's eyes, and gave him a new 'do. He sat blinking at the bright light, the hairball newly secured in a glittery pink Barbie hair band. He looked like a Pomeranian on steroids. "How about we run by the Dairy Queen, and grab a couple of burgers and drinks—I don't think my stomach can take this much longer—then we go out and meet Collie, so I can get a look at the missing dinosaur tracks. You sit in the truck and promise not to eat anything of mine, and when we're done, we'll get Collie to help figure out what to do with you. How does that sound?"

The dog seemed happy with the plan. Sticking his big head out the window, he lapped up air, his jowls flapping like the wings of a stingray underwater as we drove to the Dairy Queen, pulled up to the sign to order, then proceeded to the pick-up window.

"We're in kind of a hurry," I said as the waitress, a twenty-something blonde with a pert nose and too much makeup, slid open the window. Working the register, she held the tail of the receipt while the machine slowly punched out numbers, making an old-fashioned *ca-ching, ca-ching, ca-ching* rather than the sterile *beep-beep* of modern models. The sound was rhythmic and relaxing in a way that promised the food would be cooked by hand and the waitress would take time to chat about the weather.

Tearing off the receipt, she turned slowly toward the window to hand it to me. "That'll be seven ninety—" Her eyes as big as Dilly Bars, she jumped back. "Holy crap, what is *that*?" Motioning to the dog, she craned away from the window as if he might jump through and eat her right along with the burgers.

I laughed. "I'm not sure. I found it on the road." Pulling money out of my wallet, I held it out to her. "I think it's a really big dog."

She made a quick grab for the money and handed the food out the window, followed by the drinks. "Your change is three cents."

"Keep it," I said, busy finding a place to put the food, realizing that this might not have been such a good idea. The bag smelled like hamburgers, and the dog was getting excited. "Thanks," I said, elbowing my copilot back into the passenger seat.

He collided with the dash, awakening Gertie. "Destination error. Make a legal U-turn, proceed east six-tenths of a mile on Highway 190."

The dog barked, and the waitress cried, "Lord have mercy!" The hamburger sack fell onto the floor, and limeade spilled on my knee, dripping, cold and sticky, into my shoe. Scenting the aroma of fresh meat, the dog tried to scramble over me onto the floorboard.

"Stop it!" I hollered in my mean–mommy voice, and the dog, surprisingly enough, froze. "Get back in your seat."

Ducking his head, he backed across the console, slunk into the passenger seat, and turned his face, pink hair band and all, away from me, sulking.

"Geez," I muttered, wiping my jeans with a napkin, then putting the limeade in the drink holder next to the dog's water glass. The hamburgers, fortunately, were still wrapped in the white Dairy Queen papers with a toothpick stabbed through the middle. Rescuing them from the floor, I tucked the sack between me and the driver's-side door. Everything under control, finally.

Leaning out the window, the waitress flashed a customer-friendly smile, and said what was probably the most enthusiastic thing she could think of at the moment. "He sure minds good. . . ."

FOUR

FOLLOWING COLLIE'S MAP TURNED OUT TO BE MORE DIFFICULT than I had anticipated, not because the map was unclear—Collie had noted all of the landmarks—but because trying to drive while sharing lunch with a ravenous hundred-pound canine presented a challenge.

We traveled east, back out of town the way we had come. By the time we passed Mill Creek Park, and then the river, the dog had finished his hamburger and wanted mine. Grabbing the leftover container of grits from the dash, I opened it and set it on the floorboard on his side, as we turned onto a smaller county road. "There you go. See how you feel about Lone Star grits."

He felt fine about them, of course. It was hard to dislike a dog who appreciated the value of a good grit.

"Careful. They expand in your stomach," I said, and he looked up, his snout covered with grits and a smear of mustard. He tried to sniff my hamburger. "Stop that," I said, and he backed off, but sat watching me, his face soulful beneath the pink Barbie fliggie. I took a bite, and he licked his lips, sweeping a long slobber string and a few leftover grits into his mouth.

"Mr. Grits—" I muttered, vaguely aware that I'd fed the dog, and now I'd named it, which was not a good thing.

Mr. Grits continued watching the hamburger like a marksman homing in on a target. Up to the mouth, down to the lap, up to the mouth, down to the lap, salivate, lick lips . . .

"Oh, for heaven's sake. Here you go," I said finally, surrendering the remaining burger bit as we came to an enormous live oak tree that Collie had listed on the map. Next to the tree was a historical marker. I coasted slowly past, reading a few lines of text before the sign drifted out of sight.

THE LOVER'S OAK

Mentioned in the diaries of the earliest set-
tlers, The Lover's Oak is said to have been
considered a sacred matrimonial site by Native Americans. According to legend, young
couples passing beneath these branches
would be destined for true love and . . .

Giving a rueful snort, I turned back to the road. Considering that my date today was a smelly stray dog, this was not good news, but it was par for my luck lately.

Just past the Lover's Oak, a small settlement crouched nearly for-gotten in a riverside thicket of lacy mesquite. A faded sign marked the entrance to town with the proud proclamation: WELCOME TO LOVELAND, TEXAS. HOME OF THE LOVER'S OAK. POPULATION 77.

I checked my map. Collie had, indeed, noted the location of the town with a quickly scrawled abbreviation, *LL, Tex.* Somewhere near here, I was to turn onto a dirt road, then drive six more miles to my destination.

Slowing the car, I watched for the turn, absently surveying the de-caying town. "Population 77" was hard to believe. Unpainted and overgrown with mustang grapes and wild mustard weed, the build-ings on the left were abandoned except for a tiny one-room post of-fice and a hardware store that might or might not have been operational.

On the left side of the road was the Lover's Oak Chapel, where you could get married or book a float trip down the river, or both. Across the street stood an old clapboard-sided building, aptly named Over the Moon General Store, which advertised everything from bait and souvenirs to decorative river rocks and plumbing supplies. Next to the store, separated by a grass-and-gravel parking lot, was the Big Lizard Diner—an odd conglomeration of two antique railroad cars set parallel to the road, with an ancient silver Airstream trailer crammed sideways in between. Collie had abbreviated it on my map, *BL Diner. Cross bridge, turn right.* She'd drawn the river and three odd-shaped boxes that hardly did justice to the café. Permanently marooned in a sea of white gravel, it looked like something that might have floated down the river during a flood and landed there by accident, a cross between a giant catamaran and Noah's Ark.

"Now that's something you don't see every day," I commented, craning to look out the window as I passed. There were vehicles in the parking lot—four pickup trucks, two cars, and a propane tanker of some kind. People sat in the railroad cars, happily settled in for a train trip to nowhere. Down the hill on the riverbank, a crowd was throwing what looked like flower petals into the water, while on the river, a canoe drifted toward the bend. In the boat a woman pulled something from her long blond hair and tossed it into the air, where it floated, light and diaphanous, seemingly weightless in the breeze. A wedding veil.

"That's something you don't see every day, either," I muttered, feeling like Alice falling down the rabbit hole. This adventure was getting stranger by the minute, and I hadn't even made it to the ranch with the missing dinosaur tracks yet. I couldn't wait to see what surprises were awaiting me there.

In the seat beside me, the white rabbit blinked his long lashes and yawned like he'd seen it all before. Reaching over, I stroked his fur absently, speeding toward our destination, the last landmark on the map, an arched rock gateway that marked the entrance to the Jubilee Ranch, at least on Collie's map.

The ranch melted out of the heat waves in the distance ten minutes and six miles of gravel road later—a lone sign of civilization. Past the Jubilee Ranch, the road faded through an open gate into a pasture, where it wound across the flatlands and disappeared into a canyon. I wondered where it went. . . .

The brakes gave an impatient squeal, and a cloud of white dust enveloped the car as I turned into the driveway. From where I was, I couldn't see a house, barns, or any other signs of civilization. A hawk sat perched atop a gnarled wooden fence post perhaps ten feet away, so close that I could see sunlight glinting on golden eyes as it clicked its head sideways with robotic precision, and regarded me.

In the passenger seat, Mr. Grits barked, and the hawk took wing.

"Good boy," I said, touching the dog's fur like a toddler grabbing a security blanket. This place felt more like the end of the world than some guest ranch where beleaguered urbanites came to have a rugged vacation.

I glanced at my map again. I was definitely where Collie's directions had specified. The stone nameplate on the gateway read JUBILEE RANCH, EST. 1855 BY JEREMIAH MICHAEL TRUITT AND CAROLINE ANNE TRUITT. I recognized the names from somewhere—probably the newspaper article, which I had only glanced over. The article was now somewhere under the dog. Slipping my hand beneath the mass of dog and hair, I found the paper wadded against the seat back and stuffed partway down the crack. It tore as I pulled it out, the bottom half remaining wedged. Fortunately, the article about the dinosaur tracks was on the top section . . . mostly. I had the horse psychologist's hat, but the rest of him was still somewhere under the dog.

"I hope this isn't Collie's only copy," I muttered, turning it right side up, so that I could look at the pictures of the dinosaur tracks and read the commentary from the local sheriff. Mr. Grits leaned closer, tipping his head to see what had emerged from his seat, probably thinking, *Is it edible?*

"Not for dogs," I said, guiding the car across the bumpy metal gateway. A tingle of excitement ran through me, an electric sensation I couldn't quite explain, a sense that something was about to happen. Beside me, the dog tried to catch a noon nap as the Jeep bounced over potholes and loose gravel, traveling an expanse of flatland, then winding uphill.

When we crested the rise, I could see that the road split ahead, one branch descending toward the west, disappearing into a thick stand of trees, where I could barely make out buildings, and the other path heading south and east into the valley. According to the newspaper article, the east branch was the one that led to the dinosaur tracks in the riverbed.

I sat at the fork in the road, trying to decide which way to go. Collie's map directed me to the house, but by now she might be down at the track site. The old me, Archaeologist Lindsey, tingled at the idea of driving down the rough, washed-out road to the riverbed, observing the site, cataloging the strata and composition of the rock layers, estimating age, looking for more possible track locations, other fossils that might help index and date the missing tracks—a treasure hunt, of sorts, with a long-hidden treasure. I hadn't been to a field site in years. The only digging I did these days was through prepackaged display materials in the basement of the museum, things other people discovered, which I only measured, cleaned, molded, and mounted for display.

Now, looking out over miles of country, I remembered when the idea of finding undiscovered treasures was a passion that took precedence over anything else. A first love. A quest that had once prompted me to write stacks of applications for fellowships and grants so that Geoff and I could travel all over the world trying to make that one big discovery that would put our names in all the magazines. All of that stopped after I had Sydney. Geoff knew it would. When I told him about the pregnancy, he'd wanted to terminate it, terminate her.

"Think about it, Lindsey," he'd said, standing in the doorway of a hotel in Cairo. "It'll be the end of everything. What are you going to do, drag a baby all over the world? Put it in a little backpack and haul it around the dig? Let it play in the dirt with the sand fleas, and the scorpions, and the snakes? What?"

"Yes," I said, "I guess we are." I should have known that there was no *we* at that point. The look in his eyes, two dark, cool mirrors, should have told me. But I still didn't think he'd leave. Two days before that, we'd been blissfully happy. A team, a partnership, desperately in love, living a dream life. Still wild for each other after four years of marriage.

Then he looked at me with a gaze as cool as brown glass and said in that slight California accent, "Well, you know what, Lindsey? You can have it your way—you always do. But I won't have any part of it. I'll do the decent thing, but I won't have any part of it."

He walked out the door and never came back, even when Sydney was born, all tiny and pink, with his eyes, his straight dark brows, his sandy-brown hair. His idea of the decent thing was to give her his name, to remain separated but married until she was two years old and I was able to get a job with health insurance. To sign joint custody papers, never arrange visits, send off-and-on child support, then take Sydney off to Mexico at age eight because his new wife wanted children and couldn't get pregnant.

A fork in the road. Then, now, over and over, it seemed. Six years ago I'd taken the museum job in Denver, relegated myself to cleaning samples in the basement lab, setting up displays, and talking about paleontology to schoolkids on field trips, so that Sydney could have a normal life. Now here she was traveling without me, and I was in Texas at the mercy of Laura and Collie's plan to break me out of my funk, watching the road divide again.

Once again, I took the safe fork, the one that wound through the trees toward the ranch headquarters. The play-it-safe-mommy me was saying, *Better not take any chances. What if somebody thinks you're trespassing down there and you get shot? What if there's a gang of dangerous fossil thieves lurking and you run into them out here, alone? Something could happen, and who would take care of Sydney?*

I hated that voice—the careful, paranoid one that prattled on in my head, warning me of all the things that could go wrong, inventing scenarios that hadn't happened and might never happen. Sighing, I thought of the bride on the river. Oh, to be young and carefree, just starting out in life again. As loose and light as the wedding veil floating on air.

Who are you kidding, Lindsey? the mommy voice said. *You're a grown woman with a child to raise and a deadbeat ex-husband.*

The only similarity between me and the wedding veil was that, after years of working in the basement of the museum, I was about as pale and filmy as it was.

In the passenger seat, Mr. Grits started snoring. As we bumped down the hill, he slid forward, fell onto the floorboard, and never woke up.

"Now that is serenity," I said, smiling at the shapeless mound of hair. Mr. Grits looked completely content. There was a lesson in that. Settle down, stop worrying so much, appreciate the little things—like a full stomach and a warm place to curl up. It was a beautiful day. Around me the watercolor landscape stretched to the horizon in tranquil shades of sage and gold. I was on an adventure rather than sitting in the basement of the museum fretting about Sydney. My sister and my best girlfriend loved me enough to drag me out of my pity party, bring me all the way to Texas, and come up with something interesting for me to do. My boss at the museum cared enough to let me take off at a moment's notice on a sabbatical of unspecified length.

All things to appreciate. My situation could have been much, much worse.

Ahead, I could see the ranch headquarters. I was on the right road, and I'd almost reached my destination.

Drifting slowly through the grove of trees and into the headquarters area, I studied the buildings—a huge hip-roofed stone barn, a long stable with horses hanging heads over stall doors, dozing in the sun, a small cottage house near the barn, a couple of outbuildings, a well house next to a tall windmill, an empty kennel, a chicken house with chickens pecking in the sand, a long stone building with a sign that said BUNKHOUSE, and at the end of the lane where the gravel drive circled around, a tall white limestone home with an old picket fence around it. An enormous pair of pecan trees stood like sentries in the front yard. Their lofty shade and downward-fanning leaves gave the place a slightly Southern feel, though the house itself, with its wraparound porch and steep dormers on the third story, could have been plucked from a valley in Norway. Over each window on the lower story, the rockwork formed an arch, which was inset with plaster. Small colored stones pressed into the plaster created a mosaic of sunflowers, crafted piece by piece in an age when people took the time to do things by hand.

I watched the reflection of my SUV in the wavy plate glass as I drove up to the front gate, stopping in the shade next to a red pickup truck, which I could tell was Collie's. On the door it said, SAN SALINE RECORD AND SAN SABA COUNTY REVIEW. I tried to picture my formerly glamorous Washington, D.C., reporter friend, Collie, cruising the backroads of Texas in a pickup truck. She'd left D.C. and opted for the slow life, and from the looks of things around here, it couldn't get much slower than this. No sign of anyone, no movement, no human sounds. The place looked deserted.

I waited in the car a few minutes, watching lace curtains sway inside the open windows, hoping someone would see me and come out of the house. When no one did, I finally rolled down the car windows and stepped out, leaving Mr. Grits sleeping on the floor. "Stay right there," I whispered. The place seemed too quiet for anything more than a whisper.

Tiptoeing around the Jeep and through the yard gate, I curled my toes to stop the *slap-slap* of my Birkenstocks against my feet. Even that seemed like too much noise. An eerie quiet stilled the pecan trees and let the curtains close against the screens, as if the place were holding its breath, waiting to see what I wanted. Gooseflesh rose on my arms as I walked closer. The house seemed to grow in stature, stretching toward the sky and blocking out the sun. Tilting my head back, I surveyed the second-story windows, the old glass reflecting sky and trees in misshapen rainbows of color and form. It felt like someone was up there, watching.

I shuddered, climbing the steps. There was a piece of paper taped to the front door with something written on it. My name? I couldn't quite tell.

A horse whinnied in the stable, and I jumped. Tripping on the last step, I sprawled forward, landing with one shoe on, spraddle-kneed on the porch, like a baseball catcher trying to block a dirt ball.

"Graceful," I grumbled, climbing to my feet, relieved to have broken the imposing quiet.

As if in response, a breeze swept across the porch, and the weathered rocking chairs started rocking. The note on the door twittered in the wind, flipping upside down. I pulled it off and unfolded it, hoping it wasn't another map.

Laura, Collie had scrawled, obviously in a hurry.

Jocelyn and I went to look at something. We'll be back in a minute. Go on inside and wait. Don't tell anyone why you're here. If anyone asks, just say you have an appointment with Jocelyn. Long story. Will explain later.
—Collie

Frowning, I surveyed the porch, not sure what to do next. I didn't want to go inside some stranger's house, no matter what the note said. Especially not this house, with its shadowy windows and eerie silence.

I turned to look at my car. In the driveway, a sudden breeze coaxed a dust devil to life, whipping it until it collided with the yard fence and shook the lower tree branches, rattling a wind chime made of horseshoes and old silverware. Every horse in the stable neighed in reply, sending up a deafening cacophony of equine chatter.

A heebie-jeebie ran through me, and I reached for my shoe. "I'll just be waiting in the car now."

"Pardon?" A man's voice jolted me upright. Stumbling down three steps, I caught my balance at the bottom and spun around with my heart pounding in my throat, and my mind conjuring Hollywood images of ghostly apparitions.

Instead I saw cowboy boots, real enough, and I worked my way upward, past dusty blue jeans to a gray chambray shirt. Catching my breath, I muttered, "Sheesh, you scared me to . . ."

Oh, my God. It was the guy who wanted to shoot Mr. Grits. And now, in this light and up close, I realized something else. He was also the horse psychologist—minus the mustache—from the newspaper article. That was why he'd looked familiar to me on the road. "You!" I heard myself gasp.

He blinked in disbelief, his mouth hanging slack and his eyes bugging out as if he'd just come face-to-face with his worst nightmare. For a moment, neither of us said anything. I stumbled sideways on the uneven stone path, catching my balance on one shoe and one bare foot.

He rushed down the steps with an arm outstretched, like he thought I might faint, and he'd need to catch me.

"I'm all right." Collie's note still in my hand, I waved him away. "You just took a couple years off my life, that's all."

"Guess that makes twice today." He started to smile, but instead opted for a hard look, as if he'd just remembered who he was talking to. "Listen, if you're here about the dog—"

"I'm not here about the dog."

Crossing his arms over his chest, he drew up to his full height, a good six inches taller than me, which most guys weren't, since I was five-eight. "I wasn't going shoot the dog." Thick dark hair fell over his forehead, covering the hat line where his suntan ended. He combed the hair back impatiently, then threaded his arms again.

"Really," I scoffed, unsure why I felt the need to argue with him. Justifying my position was a compulsion that my mother claimed I'd developed as soon as I could talk. "Because Jimmy the Kid sure seemed to think you were. According to him, the dog was in mortal danger, and if I didn't want it to get shot, I'd better get it out of there." I imitated Jimmy's words on the last part, twang and all.

The horse psychologist's gray-green eyes twinkled as if he were picturing the scene. "Jimmy needs to learn not to listen to Dan. Dan's a crotchety old fart. He probably said that because he was irked. I just wanted the dog caught. That animal's been causing trouble from here to San Saline for a solid month."

I shifted uncomfortably, beginning to feel like the butt of a really bad joke. If no one was going to harm the dog, then there was no reason for me to have crammed the big, smelly beast in my car and driven around with it for hours. I felt . . . gullible. Or just flat out stupid. "Well . . . Jimmy Hawthorne made it sound like an emergency. All I know is what I was told."

"I'm sure that's true, ma'am." He had just enough Texas accent to make the line sound like something from an old cowboy movie.

"It was a very strange situation."

"I don't doubt that." His lips twitched, though he was kind enough not to laugh. Looking down at his feet, he absently rolled a dried-up pecan under the toe of his boot. "So how'd you finally get rid of the dog?"

I winced, crinkling the note in my hand and glancing sheepishly at the Jeep. "I didn't."

Head jerking upward, he squinted toward my vehicle.

"I mean, I tried to drop him off," I rushed. "But the friend I was meeting was already gone from her office, and the Hawthorne House was closed for wedding preparations until Friday." Now he looked like he wanted to kill both me and the dog. He probably didn't appreciate my bringing it back on the property, but how was I supposed to know this was his place? The Jubilee gateway and the headquarters had to be several miles from the road where the dog had run out in front of my car. "Don't worry; he's not going to get out. He's sound asleep on the floorboard." The cowboy gave me an exasperated look, and I added, "It's not so easy to get rid of a gigantic smelly dog, you know. I didn't have any choice but to bring him along."

He slanted a mischievous glance at me. "Guess your luck's under a bucket today, isn't it?"

I felt myself laugh, then heard it. I realized I was smiling at him, a strange giddiness in my stomach. "Under a bucket and down the well, just lately."

"Well, guess there's nowhere to go but up, then." His lips parted into a wide, slow grin.

"Guess so." I smiled back, an unexpected jolt of electricity zinging through my body and revving up my senses.

With a quick backward step, he scooped my shoe from the porch step and held it out. "Lose your glass slipper?"

I flushed at the dingy sandal, one half of my dirtiest, oldest pair. Comfort footwear. The footwear of a mommy who never even bothered trying to look sexy anymore. Reaching out to reclaim it, I lamely said, "Thanks," and slipped it back on the foot with the half-peeled toenail polish.

We stood there in awkward silence for a moment, until finally he asked, "If you're not here about the dog, ma'am, what can I do for you?"

"Well, for starters, stop calling me ma'am." Self-consciously, I tucked loose strands of hair behind my ear. I could just imagine what I looked like. "It's Lindsey. Lindsey Attwood."

Shaking my hand, he reached up to tip an invisible cowboy hat, then seemed to realize there wasn't one there, and said, "Glad to meet you, Lindsey. Zach Truitt. You're not here about the windmills, are you?"

I'm sure he could tell by my blank look that I had no idea what he was talking about. "No, I'm here to meet my friend, Collie, and . . . " *Don't tell anyone why you're here.* The words from Collie's note ran through my mind. "I had an appointment with . . . uhhh . . . Jocelyn."

His demeanor changed completely, the smile fading to an *aha* look, and then a worried frown.

I had a feeling I'd said exactly the wrong thing.

FIVE

⸻◆⸻

An uncomfortable silence descended again, and Zach Truitt eyed me like I was an alien presence on his front steps. All traces of flirtation were gone. The playful twinkle in his eyes, the loose, forward angle of his slim hips, the self-assured smile disappeared, and he looked stiff, uncomfortable, businesslike.

The strange thing was that I felt . . . disappointed? I was enjoying the chance to flirt. Or enjoying flirting with him. Either way, it wasn't like me at all. Another completely out-of-character moment in a completely out-of-character day.

Zach squinted toward the driveway, clearly wishing that someone would take me off his hands. "Well . . . uhhh . . . the entrance to the horse therapy camp is past the Jubilee Ranch entrance. You keep going straight through the cattle guard. Usually Jocelyn sends you people . . . uhhh . . . her clients a map. I told her she needs to put a big sign up there at the gate, so people won't"—he flushed, cleared his throat, and finished with—"get lost."

Great, now he thinks I'm a therapy patient.

I debated telling him my real reason for coming, but Collie's note said not to tell anyone. "She said to meet her here." Folding the note, I stuck it in my pocket. "She's supposed to be back in a minute."

Zach nodded and silence descended again. I followed his gaze down the driveway, struck by the beauty of the view. It was the kind of scene that belonged in some pastoral painting of the idyllic West—the pale ribbon of gravel road winding through the trees and disappearing up the hill, the feathery grass, the dusty green of wild sage, spiny yucca holding plumes of white flowers high in the air, crimson and vermilion patches of Indian blankets, prickly pear cactus with pink fruit and lacy yellow blooms. . . .

The moment fell out of focus, taking on a dreamlike quality, as if any second I would awaken, and the events of the day would be nothing but a figment of my imagination. I'd be back in the museum basement, having laid my head down on the lab table and fallen asleep to the hum of the furnace.

A noise caught my attention, a rattling and clawing from the vicinity of my car. "What in the world . . ." I turned to see Mr. Grits with his head and one front leg hanging out the partially opened window, trying his level best to squeeze through the ten-inch crack without being noticed.

Awakened by the gyrations, Gertie came to life and alerted the antitheft system, sending the car into a spasm of horn honking and light flashing, while an electronic voice commanded over the din, "Step away from the car. Step away from the car. Step away . . ."

Mr. Grits descended into full-scale panic, let out a sound like the off-pitch *baa-roo-ooo* of my trombone in seventh-grade band, and began frantically trying to claw his way through the glass.

"Stop! No! Wait!" I squealed, running for the car.

Behind me, Zach called out, "Whoa, there, easy now, fella!"

Terrified by the racket, Mr. Grits let out another, "Bar-roo-ooo!" braced his feet against the glass and pulled back, then attempted to push out, then in, then out, rocking the entire Jeep.

Gertie continued over the blaring horn, "Step away from the car."

"Bar-roo-ooo!"

"Step away from the car!" *Honk, honk, honk, honk.*

"Bar-roo-ooo!"

"Step away . . ."

Zach reached the passenger door first. The dog growled, and Zach held his hands out, saying, "Easy there, fella. Hold still. You're in a fix, aren't ya?"

Hurrying to the driver's side, I yanked open the door and leaned sideways across the seat, hitting the window button and the antitheft alarm at the same time. Gertie went silent, and the window lowered with an electronic groan, freeing the dog bit by bit, until he lurched forward, hooked his feet on the frame, and launched himself into Zach's arms. Climbing out of the car, I dashed around the hood to find Zach flat on his backside against the fence, struggling with a tangle of rope and frantic dog. Scrambling backward, the dog pulled free, and lumbered off at a high rate of speed.

Diving for the rope, I landed on my knees in the grass beside Zach. "Shoot!"

"Don't tempt me," Zach grumbled, sitting up. Resting his elbows loosely on his knees, he hung his hands and watched the dog disappear around the barn. "Some days it just doesn't pay to get out of bed."

I guess I could have been offended by that, but I looked at him, covered in white hair, slobber, and dusty dog footprints, and a giggle bubbled up in my throat.

Zach went on muttering, "Lord, I started the day out chasing the dog, and I'm still chasing the dog. You sent the crazy lady to take away the dog, and then the dog was gone; then the crazy lady came back with the dog. . . ."

"Hey!" Laughter burst from my lips. I couldn't help it. Some days you can either laugh or cry, and my mother always said it takes fewer muscles to smile than to frown.

Zach smoothed his thumb and forefinger over his straight, dark eyebrows, trying to hide a grin. "It's not funny."

"No, it's not," I agreed, attempting to sober, then bursting into laughter again. "It's . . . really . . . not," I coughed out.

Quirking a brow, he frowned at my hysterics, or my Northern accent, or both. "Where in the world are you from, anyway?"

"Not here." Sitting back on my heels, I pulled in a long breath, wiping my eyes and trying to straighten up. "I'm just visiting."

"That's the first good news I've had all day," he said, giving me a wry, one-sided smile and a flirtatious wink.

Something inside me tightened in response, and my mind went

blank. A hot flush ran through my body and the laughter burned away. I found myself gazing wistfully into his eyes.

What in the world are you doing? a voice reprimanded in my head. *Hel-lo-oh . . . anybody home in there? Flirtation alert. Make a legal U-turn; return to the straight and narrow.*

"I guess we'd better go catch the dog." The words sounded breathy and soft—not the right tone for, *Let's go catch the dog.* More the tone for, *Kiss me, you fool. . . .*

"Guess that'd be a good idea." His slightly lowered eyelids answered, *Kiss me, you fool,* with a silent, *Come closer and see what happens. . . .*

For just a moment, I thought about it. I pictured how it would be, dusting off the rusty Romance Lindsey, long hidden in some box in the back closet of my mind, under piles of more important boxes filled with Work Lindsey, and Mommy Lindsey, Divorce Court Lindsey, and now Shared Custody Lindsey, and Depressed Insane Lindsey.

Was Romance Lindsey even there anymore? Probably not. She had sat forgotten for so long that, like the Skin Horse and the Velveteen Rabbit, she had ceased to be real. I never even thought about her anymore. Until now. Which was a bad sign that the boxes were getting jumbled up and Control Freak Lindsey needed to get to work.

I pushed to my feet, wiping my eyes and slapping my hands lightly on my cheeks, though I suspected that what I needed was the kind of slap that brought hysterical women to their senses in old movies. "I'm sorry," I said, looking off toward the barn instead of watching him stand up. I imagined the way he would do that—in one smooth, graceful movement. *Stop. Now,* Control Freak Lindsey scolded. "I wonder how far the dog went." That was better. A serious voice. A normal voice.

"No telling." His tone was still light, flirtatious. "If someone put that pink girlie thing in my hair, I'd run, too."

I glanced sideways—a mistake, because he was smiling just slightly—and I felt glitter sprinkle through me like magic dust. "Well, you know, I don't go for the Mick Jagger look. Hard to talk to a guy with hair in his eyes." That was not Control Freak Lindsey or Depressed Insane Lindsey. That was Romance Lindsey, sounding not so dusty at all. Mommy Lindsey was about to have a heart attack.

As we walked toward the barn, the cowboy leading the way and the Lindseys following beside and slightly behind, I noticed a few stray strands of dark hair falling over his forehead. He combed them back with his fingers, a wicked twinkle in his eye that told me Romance Zach was pretty well up to speed. "What look do you go for?"

I blinked, surprised. There were a million ways to answer a question like that. Inside me, Mommy Lindsey and Control Freak Lindsey were going into panic mode, and Divorce Court Lindsey was setting off the alarm system. *Beep, beep, beep. Step away from the cowboy. . . .*

"The white, furry kind with sort of a . . . fishy smell," I said finally, a cute but fairly innocuous answer.

Zach stopped, motioning as we rounded the corner of the barn. "Well, then, yonder stands your prince, Cinderella."

Mr. Grits was sitting at the end of the barn aisle next to a tall stone watering trough, ears perked beneath the pink fliggie, as if to say, *What took you so long?*

Standing up, he wagged his tail, looking at the water trough, then back toward us.

"I'll bet he's thirsty," I said as we cautiously moved closer, though Mr. Grits didn't seem as if he intended to run away. "I bought him a glass of water at the Dairy Queen, but he drank it all with his burger. Have you got a bowl or something that I could . . .?" Zach was looking at me with one eyebrow raised and one lowered. "What?" I said, grabbing the end of Mr. Grits's rope. One rogue dog, successfully captured.

"You bought him lunch at the Dairy Queen?" Zach coughed. "Bet that gave Becky a surprise at the window."

I shrugged. "We were hungry. It seemed like a good solution." Reeling in the rope, I patted Mr. Grits on the head. "We did have a little incident at the drive-through window, but it worked out all right. He likes hamburgers—a lot, actually."

Zach chuckled. "Next time, try dog food. Too much people food isn't good for these big fellas. Large breeds tend to have joint problems, hip dysplasia, things like that. Eating people food doesn't help." Slipping a hand under the dog's chin, he checked teeth and ears with one expertly efficient motion. "People food for people. Dog food for dogs, all right?" I couldn't tell whether he was talking to me or the dog. Mr. Grits wagged his tail, as if he understood the F-word—food.

"I don't know anything about dogs," I admitted. "I was an army brat growing up, and we moved quite a bit. Pets weren't a very good option." Why I was telling him this, I didn't know. The moment seemed inexplicably comfortable. A soft breeze wafted along the barn aisle, and the afternoon sun cast soft amber streamers through the gaps in the old wooden stall doors. The scene was serene, the kind in which, if this were an old Western movie, the hero would kiss the heroine. . . .

Romance Lindsey poked her head out of the box, intrigued by that thought. Mommy Lindsey shoved her back in, slapped the lid on, and said, "My daughter's been begging me for a dog, but we live in an apartment in downtown Denver, so it's not really a good idea." Romance Lindsey popped up unexpectedly, like a jack-in-the-box, and added, "With just the *two* of us, it would be pretty hard to take care of a dog." I noticed Zach watching my hand on the rope, checking for a ring.

Leaning against a stall door, his long legs crossed, Zach rubbed the dog's ear, and Mr. Grits relaxed into his hand. "Well, this guy wouldn't make much of an apartment dweller. He's meant to be a sheepdog. This kind needs room to roam."

"Oh, I wasn't thinking about keeping him." I punctuated the sentence with a quick shake of my head. "I hope I can find a place for him before I have to leave, though."

Zach was watching me through soft, dusty green eyes with boyishly long lashes. Interested eyes. Interesting eyes. "How long have we got?" I watched his lips move, but barely heard the words.

"What?"

"How long"—he seemed to forget what he was saying, and for just an instant, we stood gazing at each other before he finished with—"are you in town?"

"Oh." The word was a breathy whisper. I looked away, trying to clear the heady fog from my mind. "I'm not sure."

Pushing off the stall door, he cleared his throat. "Well, we'll see what we can do . . . for the dog, I mean. For now, why don't we get him a drink and put him in the dog kennel so he doesn't cause any more trouble?" He patted the top of the watering trough, saying, "Here ya go, fella. Jump up."

Mr. Grits responded by cocking his head, one ear flipping upward as if he were trying to hear better.

Zach's eyebrows drew together. "Well, I can see how, with that fancy hairdo, you'd be expecting Perrier, but this'll have to do." Bending over, he lifted the dog's front end, hooking the paws over the edge of the trough. "There you go, hotshot." He frowned at me. "Poor thing doesn't even know how to drink out of a horse trough. Wonder where in the world he's been."

"Don't know." I stepped closer to look into the stone tank, which was about two feet deep and filled with clusters of slimy-looking green stuff. "Yuck. I wouldn't drink that, either." I was teasing, of course. The water did smell bad, but not as bad as the dog. "There's something swimming down there."

Zach turned his attention to the water. "Those are goldfish. They eat the algae and keep the water tanks clean."

"I think you need more goldfish," I observed, watching a small orange fish swoop to the top of the water, give Mr. Grits the once-over, then dart beneath a clump of algae. Intrigued by the movement, the dog leaned closer, his head tracking the herky-jerky movements of the fish.

Shrugging, Zach sat on the edge of the trough, seeming in no hurry to go anywhere. I stared into the water, feeling his gaze on me. I could imagine what he saw. A ragged-out, tired woman in washed-out jeans, a nondescript white T-shirt with a fading Abercrombie logo, no makeup, hair in a degenerating ponytail with a pink hair band that, now that I thought about it, matched the dog's, and old Birkenstock sandals, worn so many years that my feet had made shiny black imprints in the suede insoles.

Why, I wondered, would he even look twice? Why was he looking now?

I glanced up and he turned his attention to the water trough. "The ranch hands used to put algaecide in them every so often, but Josie went to some farm seminar in Austin, and now she's got them trying to be more *organic*." He bracketed *organic*, making little quotes with his fingers, then rolling his eyes. "The goldfish were her idea."

"Oh." My mind cataloged the information. Who was Josie? Daughter? Girlfriend? Wife? I caught myself checking for a ring. Nothing. But, then, men didn't always wear rings. Geoff never would, even though I bought him one when we married. A few weeks after the wedding, he put it in a box on the dresser, and it stayed there. He said it got in the way. Got in the way of what? I wondered.

I blushed, embarrassed by the pointless train of thought. "Well, the fish are pretty, anyway, although, to tell you the truth, I think they're eating bugs down there, not algae." I'd been absently watching the goldfish dart to the surface, grab little squirmy things, and race for cover while Mr. Grits tracked their maneuvers. "I think you have meat-eating goldfish."

Zach leaned closer to study the activity in the tank. "Well, Josie won't like that. Meat-eating goldfish probably aren't politically correct."

"I don't think goldfish follow politics."

Zach chuckled low in his throat, a warm, appreciative sound that sent a tingle down my spine. "No. Probably not."

I looked up, and he looked up, and we hovered there above the water, just . . . looking. My heart lurched and my stomach fluttered into my throat, and Romance Lindsey jumped all the way out of her dusty box, saying, *Wow! Let's flirt a little and see what happens. . . .*

A blur of movement flashed past the corner of my vision, and I came to my senses just in time to see Mr. Grits slip headfirst into the trough. Jumping back, I hollered, "Watch out!" But it was too late. The leading edge of the tidal wave hit the side of the trough and drenched us both.

Holding my arms out to my sides, I looked down at the wet, slimy mess as Zach fished the dog from the water like a hundred-pound mackerel and set him on the ground, grinding out the words, "If I never see this dog again, it'll be too soon. How in the hel—pardon me—world can one animal cause so much trouble?" Throwing up his hands, he turned to Mr. Grits, who looked chagrined by the incident. He was only half as much dog with his hair wet. "Answer that for me, will you?"

Mr. Grits sighed and turned his face away, seeming that much more pathetic.

"I think you hurt his feelings." I started to giggle, peeling the front of my soggy Abercrombie T-shirt off my skin and fanning it in the air. "After all day with the dog, I didn't think I could possibly look or smell any worse, but this is worse."

Zach's expression could have melted ice. "I think you look great. Smell . . . well, that's another matter."

"Look who's talking." I motioned to his shirt and jeans, now molded to his body with water, slime, and dog hair.

"Yeah, but I'm used to smelling bad. You . . . well, you're an uptown girl."

I braced my hands on my hips. "Who says?"

"You said."

"Well, I'll have you know that you are looking at a former hardcore tomboy, thank you very much." I hadn't thought of myself that way in years, but suddenly I felt as bold as that ten-year-old girl who loved sports and firmly refused to wear dresses. "I am *not* afraid of a little slime."

"That so?" Pulling a little piece of slime off his jeans, he pitched it at me.

"So," I confirmed, dodging the throw, then dipping a little slime from the water trough and tossing it at him.

He caught it, winged it back, and hit me on the leg. "Oh, that's it!" I warned, pointing a finger. For my next throw, I made a slimeball, used a windup, and hit him square in the chest. My high school softball coach would have been proud. "Take that, buddy."

"Oh, a ballplayer, huh?" he observed.

"You bet."

He moved around me toward the tank, and suddenly I had a sense of things degenerating completely out of control.

"All right, that's enough," I said, but ten-year-old Tomboy Lindsey raised a hand above the water and added, "Don't come any closer."

"Oh-ho." Zach coughed. "Is that a threat?"

"Absolutely."

The next thing I knew, we were having a water fight, Mr. Grits was running around the tank barking, and the goldfish were swimming for their lives.

"What in the world is happening here?" I heard someone say. "Zach, what's—"

"Lindsey?"

I recognized that voice. It was Collie's. She and some woman I didn't know were gaping at us from the end of the barn. The expressions on their faces said it all, and suddenly I got the total picture of what this must look like.

No . . . actually, I couldn't imagine how it looked. *Lindsey has lost her mind*—that was what Collie's expression said. Her blue eyes were bugging out beneath a shock of curly red hair.

The other woman, who was probably about our age, slightly shorter than Collie, with dark hair and green eyes, twisted her head to one side, her face saying, *Who is this strange woman?*

Zach cleared his throat, motioning to Mr. Grits. "The dog fell in the water trough," he said lamely.

"And then I thought I lost my earring in there," I added, trying to make things more convincing. "But we found it. See?" I smiled and pointed to my ears, then hurried forward, putting distance between myself and Zach. "Hi, Coll. I'd hug you but"—I motioned to my clothes, now even wetter than before—"well, I'm a little bit of a mess right now. It's been a really crazy day."

Collie grinned, the light dusting of freckles over her nose crinkling up. "I can't wait to hear about it."

SIX

I DIDN'T TELL COLLIE ABOUT MY DAY, OF COURSE—AT LEAST NOT the part about my flirting with the cowboy and acting like a crazy woman. I stuck with the story about having lost my earring in the water trough while rescuing the dog. I even made a show of thanking Zach for his help.

He gave me a lopsided grin and said, "My pleasure. Glad you got your . . . uhhh . . . earring back." He wasn't much of an actor.

"Me too," I said, shifting uncomfortably, nervously fanning my shirt. "That was a close one."

"Yes, ma'am." Cutting a sideways glance at me, he winked. Fortunately, his back was turned to the other women, who were eyeing us and making a snap analysis of the situation. Zach seemed to suddenly remember that we weren't alone. Picking up the dog rope, he said, "Guess I'd better get this fella in the kennel before anything else happens. Hi, Collie, how's the newspaper business?"

"Great," Collie said, seeming overly cheerful, even for Collie. "I was just down at the camp with Jocelyn, watching one of her group therapy sessions. It's amazing how she uses the horses to work with the people. I'm going to do a piece on it for *Family Circle.*"

Zach nodded with a thinly veiled lack of enthusiasm. "Yeah, Josie's amazing." He gave Collie's companion a hooded look, filled with some hidden meaning. "As many things as she's got going on around here lately, pretty soon none of us will recognize the place."

Josie, Jocelyn—whatever her name was—crossed her arms and

jutted her hips to one side with a patient but slightly irritated smile. Clearly, this was a conversation they'd had before, but she didn't want to have it in front of us. "Well, you know we always love to have your input, Zach. If you'd come home more often, you'd probably recognize the place a little more easily."

Zach lowered his lashes, his eyes flinty. "I'm home now, Jocelyn. Not that it does much good. Pop's down at the Mundy Canyon Trap, straw-bossing the fence crew."

Jocelyn gasped. "He's not supposed to be doing that. He said he was going by the Big Lizard to play dominoes."

"Well, what can I tell you?" Zach massaged the back of his neck like an actor on a tension headache commercial. "The man's down at the fence line. He's going to do what he's going to do. It doesn't matter what you, or I—"

"But the doctor said—"

"—or the doctor tells him." Zach finished over Jocelyn's objections.

Pursing her lips, she exhaled what yoga professionals call a cleansing breath. "He's going to work his way right into another heart attack."

Zach frowned, his forehead a worried knot. "I tried to get him to come up here and wait for the windmill salesman, but he wouldn't. He wanted to be out there with the crew." He glanced at his watch, then at Mr. Grits, who was leaning on Zach's leg, gazing upward adoringly. "Apparently your windmill guy isn't coming. I've been here for an hour, and I haven't seen any sign of him. Who did you say you called?"

Jocelyn studied the doorway contemplatively. "I called B and B Windmills. Pop said he's had the maintenance contract with them for years. Bo Bales was here a few weeks ago, and we toured the entire place. He was supposed to come back today with a bid for replacing some of the old units that aren't working anymore and refitting the ones that can be salvaged."

"Pop's confused," Zach replied. "If he's been using B and B, it's no wonder the windmills are in such bad shape. Ever since Bo and Benny took over the business from their dad, they've let the old mills go downhill on purpose. They're just taking advantage of Pop, trying to sell him new ones. And you know Pop. If someone says hi to him at the café, he thinks they're friends." Zach's jaw hardened, and then he shrugged it off. "I've got some supplies coming by UPS. I can probably get the old ones greased and going while I'm here."

Jocelyn didn't seem pleased, and I had a feeling we'd stepped into an ongoing family confrontation. "The new ones are more efficient, and we won't be repairing them every time we turn around. The old ones have just seen their better days, that's all."

"The old ones have charm." There was a stubborn tilt to Zach's chin that said he didn't want shiny new windmills any more than he wanted goldfish in the water troughs. "Some things ought to stay the same."

Jocelyn delivered a peeved glare. "You know, you could at least talk to Bo Bales, maybe look over the literature before you make up your mind. It seemed to me like he knew what he was talking about, and I didn't get the impression he was trying to take advantage of anybody, or that he didn't intend to come back. I probably wrote the appointment time down wrong, or maybe he called to reschedule and you were outside"—pausing, she surveyed Zach, the dog, and me, then finished with—"getting the dog out of the water trough." Mr. Grits perked his ears at the word *dog,* and Jocelyn turned her attention from the windmill argument to him. "Is that the mutt who's been causing all the trouble around town?"

Zach nodded with a rueful shrug. "This is the one." He waved the rope loosely toward me. "Lindsey caught him."

Giving me a speculative look, Jocelyn reached out to shake my hand with a wide, friendly smile, saying, "I'm sorry. I'm Jocelyn Truitt—Zach's cousin. I feel like I already know you through Laura and Collie."

"Nice to meet you," I said. Laura hadn't mentioned that she knew the horse psychologist. Why would she leave out a detail like that?

Jocelyn turned back to the dog. "He looks harmless enough."

Zach scoffed. "You know what they say about looks being deceiving. This is not your ordinary, white-bread city dog." He glanced privately at me, and I blushed, trying not to laugh as he made a production of pulling a strand of slime off his clothes and dropping it. "This dog's got attitude."

"Just a little," I admitted, noticing that Collie was watching me, intently. The last thing I needed was her telling Laura that, on top of obsessing about Sydney, I was now running around the countryside picking up cowboys and stray dogs.

Straightening my posture, I cleared my throat, saying, "Well, he can't cause any more trouble now."

"Let's hope," Zach agreed. "Guess I'd better haul the prisoner off to jail and get back to the fence line to see if I can keep Pop out of trouble. If Bo Bales does decide to show up, he'll just have to track me down." He waved good-bye with the rope in his hand. "Nice meeting you, Lindsey. Collie, tell your husband I'll be by to talk to him about that three-point cedar grubber sometime while I'm here. Tell him, at that price, I expect the kissin'-cousin discount on the thing."

Collie chuckled. "Good luck. True's so attached to the cedar grubber, I don't think he'll be able to sell it. He's on a mission to eradicate cedar from this part of the country. He's already cleared our whole place and half of the neighbors'. He has this gigantic spreadsheet on the computer, breaking it down into time per tree, size of tree, cost per acre, you name it. The man goes around measuring how much root came up and calculating potential regrowth. He has a spreadsheet for that, too. He's possessed. Yesterday he stood Bailey out there and took her picture with a pile of cedar and the grubber. He's going to put it on his desk at the tractor dealership."

Zach flashed her a charming grin—one that, I now noted, he used fairly often. "Tell him I'll trade him a three-legged bull, two blind cows, and a slightly used sheepdog." Turning around, he started down the aisle with Mr. Grits trailing at his side. "I've got a dog Bailey will just love. Comes with a pink hair bow and everything."

"No *way*," Collie called after him. "And don't you dare show that dog to Bailey. That mutt has a reputation, and if Bailey falls in love with him, True will knuckle under and say yes."

"That's what I'm counting on." Zach raised a hand and waved. "See you later, Collie."

"Zach . . ." Collie threatened. "Don't you . . . Zach . . ."

He didn't look back, just waved again and continued on. I watched him and Mr. Grits leave the barn aisle, a tall man and a tall dog, strolling out of view. The dog definitely wasn't the one with attitude.

Bracing her hands on her hips, Collie turned to Jocelyn. "Do I need to go after him? He wouldn't really bring that dog to my house, would he?"

Jocelyn pulled her lip between her teeth thoughtfully. "You know Zach—he likes a good joke, and he pretty much owes you one after what you did to him at the Christmas gift exchange."

"That was *last winter*," Collie protested.

Jocelyn's green eyes twinkled at the memory. "Yes, but you took Mrs. Hawthorne's pecan pie gift basket away from him and stuck him with the used set of Dr. Phil *Relationship Rescue* books."

Pressing a hand over her lips, Collie muttered, "He needed the Dr. Phil books more than he needed the pecan pie."

Jocelyn shrugged her agreement. "Now, whenever he does come home, everyone in town asks him if he's read Dr. Phil yet." She squinted speculatively toward the spot where Zach and Mr. Grits had disappeared. "I'd say he's going to bring you the dog."

Collie huffed a sigh. "Well, you're his cousin. Tell him no."

Jocelyn rolled her eyes. "He doesn't listen to me, in case you haven't noticed. How many times have I asked him not to call me Josie anymore? What does he call me? Josie—in front of clients and everyone else. He does it just to irritate me. He'll definitely bring you the dog. He—"

"It's a nice dog, Collie," I interjected, and both of them blinked like they had completely forgotten I was there. "It . . . uuuh . . . it is," I added uncertainly, feeling like the dorky girl in the cool girls' section of the locker room. "Sweet, I mean . . ." Why were they looking at me that way? "It's very sweet . . . the dog. It's very sweet."

Collie's brows went so high they practially touched the wispy red ringlets at her hairline. "That's public enemy number one around here." Waving a finger toward the doorway, she indicated the dog. *My* dog. Mr. Grits, my friend. "You can't even imagine. He's becoming a legend—the biggest thing to hit this area since Billy the Kid. He's been raiding chicken coops and breaking into houses everywhere. He stole an entire leg of beef from the locker plant in San Saline and crashed the potluck supper at the Baptist church. One lady found him in her bathtub trying to pry the lid off a container of cottage cheese. It almost gave her a heart attack. The newspaper has been tracking his movements all over the county—like UFO sightings, or something."

"Really?" I said, trying to picture the poor, lazy creature who was afraid of my GPS system terrorizing an entire county.

"The sheriff's been trying to catch him for a month." Collie made it sound like serious business. "Nobody has even been able to get close to the thing."

"He walked right up to me," I said, picturing the scene with the umbrella and the stadium seat, and trying not to laugh. "I loaded him in the car, no problem."

Jocelyn seemed impressed. "Amazing. You must be an animal person." Beside her, Collie gave a mystified frown. She knew I wasn't an animal person.

"Actually, no," I admitted. "I don't do well with animals, at least not ones that aren't fossilized. My daughter's guinea pig hides in his shoe box every time I walk into the room."

"Hmmm." Jocelyn shrugged. "You should have an interesting time in the horse psychology class then."

I gaped at her with what was undoubtedly a completely confused look. Apparently, Collie had failed to explain my presence here. Jocelyn thought I had come for some offbeat therapy session. "Oh, didn't Collie tell you? I'm here to help her with the story on the dinosaur tracks. I'm the paleontology lab supervisor at the Colorado Museum of Natural History."

Jocelyn didn't seem surprised by any of that information, but at the word *paleontology* her bottom lip pulled to one side, and she checked the barn aisle like she was afraid someone might be listening. "Collie told me." She lowered her voice. "But there's a little bit of an issue with it, so we're keeping it quiet. Basically, I think someone who works here must have been in on stealing the dinosaur tracks, and I want to find out who before anything else disappears. Zach and Pop don't agree, and they want me to drop it. They're more trusting than I am, I guess. They think that just because everyone has either been here a long time, or is local from town, they couldn't be involved. Anyway, it's a bone of contention—sorry, bad pun—among us, and then right after all the fuss about the tracks being stolen, Pop had a minor heart attack, and Zach wanted to drop the issue about the theft completely, so as not to upset Pop any further. Pop's memory is fuzzy, and some days he doesn't even remember the tracks are gone. Zach thinks it's better that way. Denial works well in Zach's usual scheme of coping mechanisms." Snapping her lips shut, she glanced at Collie, indicating that she hadn't meant to add the last line. "Anyway, while we were driving back from the therapy camp, Collie came up with a good idea."

"I did," Collie piped up a little too quickly, as if she'd rehearsed the next lines. "When we were down at the camp, I thought, Wouldn't it be great for the horse psychology article to have the perspective of someone actually going through the sessions? Someone who didn't know anything about it and didn't have any preconceived notions? I thought, since you're on vacation anyway, maybe you could stay a few days, attend some of the sessions, check out the dinosaur track site, discreetly look around and see what you can find out."

I turned to Collie with my arms and jaw hanging slack. "You want me to go undercover as a therapy patient so I can investigate a fossil theft, which was possibly an inside job?" I summarized. "What is this—an episode of *Scooby-Doo?*"

Collie shoulder-butted me good naturedly. "Come to think of it, it does kind of sound that way, but it really is more serious than that. There's a man at the general store in Loveland who has spent the last several years photographing fossils and petroglyphs all over Texas and New Mexico. They're disappearing like crazy. He said that nearly half of what he's photographed in the past five years has disappeared, either stolen or vandalized. It's a much bigger story than people think."

"Hmmm," I mused, sensing a sudden awakening in the part of me that lived to solve old mysteries. "OK, now you've got my attention."

"You wouldn't really have to spend much time at the horse therapy camp. Just enough to make it look good, and maybe help Collie with her article a bit," Jocelyn chimed in. "And you wouldn't have to stay at the camp with the other campers. Actually, this week I have a group of psychology students from UT, and they're very sweet. You'll like them. Last week I had businessmen from Taiwan, which was kind of crazy, so it's a good thing you weren't here then. Anyway, there's a separate cabin about two miles from the camp. It's just up the hill from the dinosaur tracks, so it would be perfect. It was the original homestead house on the place, completely restored for guests, of course, but it's kind of neat and historic, a little rustic. It's in a beautiful setting overlooking the river."

"Sounds nice," I said, picturing the scene—a pioneer cabin on a hillside beneath the sheltering limbs of overhanging trees. An old rock fence around the yard, crumbling slightly, built from white limestone that the homesteaders would have harvested by hand from the riverbed. "But I really have to . . . I should . . ." Should what? Hang around the honeymoon house with Laura and her new husband? Go to the farm and rearrange my dad's life when Laura claimed he was doing just fine? Spend my vacation days sitting in the Lone Star Café, waiting for Laura to come by on her way home from work, watching Dad do odd jobs and talking to the waitress about my troubles, eating grits and obsessing about Sydney?

Or studying dinosaur tracks, staying in a quaint, historic, rustic cabin by the river, tracking down fossil thieves and attending horse psychology camp. *Hmmm* . . . Not much of a decision, really.

Go for it, ten-year-old Tomboy Lindsey said.

Think about what you might be getting into, Mommy Lindsey warned.

It's a completely unpredictable situation, Control Freak Lindsey complained. *Ask more questions.*

Live a little. I didn't know which Lindsey that was.

It's close to Zach, Romance Lindsey chimed in, sending Mommy Lindsey into a spasm of what-if scenarios.

"I don't know . . ." I muttered.

Collie's hopeful expression turned to a worried scowl. She knew I was on the fence, so she pushed me to her side with a little verbal nudge. "Come on, Linds, a vacation is just what you need. I promise I won't work you too hard on the horse therapy thing."

It occurred to me that, since I was hearing voices in my head, maybe I needed some kind of therapy, horse or whatever. "All right. I'll do it."

"Great!" Collie and Jocelyn both exhaled the word at once, as if they had been holding their collective breath, hoping I would agree. They gave each other quick, triumphant smiles. I couldn't help wondering why this was all such a big deal. It seemed like more than just an idea Collie and Jocelyn had dreamed up that morning. "With any luck, you can help break open the fossil theft case," Collie added. "The deputy sheriff is waiting down at the fossil site and can fill you in on the evidence so far. There's very little—just some tire tracks and a cigarette butt left at the site."

"That's not much to go on," I agreed, as we left the barn and climbed into a pickup truck. I took the backseat and let Jocelyn and Collie sit in front. They chatted about the sheriff's inability to solve the case, which led to a discussion about lack of funding for the sheriff's department, the latest city council election, and how the price of gasoline was affecting sales of farm equipment at the Friendly's Tractors dealerships.

"The big farm equipment sales are down right now—the economy and all that," Collie said. "But then, we're selling tons of smaller tractors and hydrostatic mowers over at the Llano dealership, and quite a few in Lampasas, too. Seems like we can hardly keep up over there. Lots of people moving out from Dallas and Austin—gentleman farmers, buying ranchettes and weekend places, recreational lots on Inks Lake, things like that." She gazed out the window, the breeze combing the amber ringlets of her hair. "Guess people are starting to discover our secret out here."

Jocelyn ducked her head between her shoulders like a turtle. "For heaven's sake, don't mention that to Pop or Zach. You'll get them started on their half-hour tirade about people moving in and dividing up the old ranches and selling the property to out-of-towners. The other day a real estate agent came by, and Pop chased him off with a shotgun. Can you believe that? I had to catch the man at the gate and tell him Pop just got home from the hospital, and he wasn't himself. The poor salesman wasn't even trying to get a listing. He was lost, for heaven's sake."

Collie chuckled. "Guess your horse psychology customers had better watch out, huh?"

Jocelyn made an irritated sound in her throat. "Don't even get me started. Pop's not so bad about it, but Zach . . . Gee whiz, you'd think I'd destroyed the ranch by moving back here and starting the therapy camp. It's ridiculous. In the first place, the camp has always been there. Years ago, when it was a kids' summer camp, Pop used to supply the riding horses. The camp land wasn't even part of the ranch until Pop bought it when the camp went belly-up. It's perfect for me because it has its own entrance, and it's self-contained, but to hear Zach talk, I've moved home and taken over the ranch. This from Zach, who hasn't stayed here for more than two days at a time in the last six years. And then there's Dan. He thinks I'm trying to take over his foreman's job and kick him off the ranch, which isn't true. He's an ornery old turd, but he's been here a long time. Both he and Zach think the whole horse therapy thing is a bunch of malarkey."

"I thought Zach was a horse psychologist," I interjected, and instantly I wished I had kept silent. Collie and Jocelyn both jerked in the front seat, looking over their shoulders.

Jocelyn winced guiltily. "I'm sorry. I shouldn't have brought all that up. It's a family thing. Sibling rivalry, territorial boundary issues, and all that. Zach and I grew up competing with each other in just about everything—sort of a brother-sister thing, even though we're cousins. Collie understands, because she's close in age to her brother. It's all perfectly normal, but sometimes . . . well, even therapists need to vent. Moving back home and starting up my practice here has been a transition."

Collie swiveled in her seat and quirked a brow. "Did you say you thought Zach was the horse psychologist?"

"That's what Laura told me. When she gave me the newspaper article with his picture in it, she said she thought he was a horse psychologist."

Collie coughed like she had a bone stuck in her throat. "Well, she must have been in another world. Zach's a horse doctor, not a horse psychologist. He's a veterinarian. Laura knows that."

"I probably misunderstood her." I was so frazzled this morning, there was no telling what Laura had said. "After driving all night, I think I'm running on fumes."

Jocelyn frowned sympathetically. "You must be really tired." She gunned the truck through a mud hole and the three of us bounced around like pinballs. "Tell you what, after we go by the track site, we can show you the cabin. It's fully furnished, so you should have everything you need. You can catch a little nap this afternoon, eat or whatever, and enjoy the evening. I have a session with this week's campers later today, but there's no need for you to be there. We'll just tell everyone you arrived late, and you can join us for the first horse therapy session tomorrow morning."

"That sounds good." No, it didn't. I was just starting to realize the ramifications of what I had agreed to. If I hadn't been on a natural high after rescuing lost dogs and having splash fights, I would have thought about it earlier. I didn't like horses. In fact, I was terrified of horses. Me masquerading as some kind of a horsewoman was going to be about as convincing as trying to pretend I was a brain surgeon. "I don't know anything about horses," I hedged. "I don't even like them. They scare me. It might be better if—"

"Oh, no, that's the point." Jocelyn clipped off my objections with one quick snip. "Horse therapy is all about learning to react constructively to unfamiliar and sometimes unpredictable situations. You'll be a perfect subject for Collie's article."

"I just don't think—" *horse therapy is for me.*

Jocelyn went on like she hadn't heard me. "I promise not to take up too much of your time. You can come to the morning sessions, and we'll tell the group you're spending the rest of the day on individual contemplation, journaling, and completing the personality patterning workbook. That will give you plenty of time to investigate the tracks. From the cabin, you'll be able to go back and forth to the track site as much as you need to. Collie mentioned you'll probably be wanting to get on the Internet and things like that, which might be a little complicated, since . . . well, we don't have phones in any of the cabins. It's part of the therapy. We take up all the cell phones and PDAs at the start of the week, so clients can focus on actual face-to-face relationships for a change."

Glancing in the rearview, she must have noticed I looked concerned, because she added, "But don't worry. I have a computer in my office at the house, and there's never anyone there during the day, so you can have access to that. Also, if you have a PDA or laptop and cell phone, you can walk up the path to the scenic overlook behind the cabin and connect to the cell tower across the valley. That's top-secret, of course. If the clients knew, they'd be sneaking off to the hilltops to do business and check voice mail while they're here."

I chuckled, trying to imagine some of the people I knew in Denver, who were accustomed to speed-of-light access to everything, trying to cope with life deprived of e-mail, and voice mail, and satellite news. "So this is like detox for tech-toy junkies."

Jocelyn winked into the rearview mirror. "You'd be surprised how much clarity can be achieved when all the distractions are stripped away. Modern life has people on stimulation overload. We don't function as well as we could at home or at work. We've lost the ability to communicate, to sense other people's needs and respond in appropriate and productive ways. Horses are a useful tool, because they react instinctively to what we do, rather than to what we say or how we look. The way you form a relationship with an animal says a lot about how you form relationships with people."

Collie pulled out her notepad and jotted that down. "That'll be perfect for the article," she remarked, then craned to see out the window, and pointed as we topped a hill, winding toward a clear-running river in the valley below. A sheriff's car was parked beneath the trees. "There's the track site. You can see the white spot where they chiseled the tracks out of the limestone."

Scooting forward, I took in the riverbank. The displaced square was clearly visible, a man-made shape in an otherwise natural landscape. "They took that out with a diamond saw." That much was clear, even at a distance. The lines were too clean to have been made by a chisel. "These were definitely not amateurs. They knew what they were doing."

SEVEN

I SPENT A HALF HOUR EXPLORING THE CRIME SCENE WITH THE sheriff's deputy. Gracie Benton was not at all what I'd expected in a small-town law enforcement officer. I'd pictured a big man in a cowboy hat and Western boots, with an overhanging stomach, a large belt buckle, and a Texas drawl that made it seem like nothing could possibly be urgent. Gracie Benton was tall and willowy, with thick blond hair rubber-banded into a bun like she didn't have time for it. She moved like a basketball player on her way down the court with the ball and talked like a Harvard lawyer. Every time I looked up, she had changed locations—ahead of me, behind me, across the river, back, climbing a pile of boulders near the track site, checking for evidence. Like a hyperactive bloodhound, she followed me up and down the riverbank even after Collie and Jocelyn gave up and went to sit in the shade.

"I keep thinking I've missed something," she said, pulling off her hat and mopping her brow as we walked back to the track site. "There's something more here, and it's right under my nose, but I'm not seeing it."

"They knew what they were doing and which tracks to take," I said, squatting beside the white scar in the rock. In the golden afternoon light, the remaining tracks were as clear in the mottled Edwards limestone as if they had been made yesterday by some ancient creature stalking through soft, wet earth. "There's a fairly long track-way here, but most of it is ambulatory—the animal was walking, so the tracks are spread apart and not as deep. But in this spot"—I pointed to the cutout—"the animal stopped momentarily, so there was a right and left track close together, more deeply imprinted. These were made by a theropod. Judging by the size of the remaining tracks and the spread of the digits, probably an Acrocanthosaurus, a meat eater with three long, thin toes. These are Triassic or Cretaceous period, most likely, though without an index fossil to date the rock formation, it's hard to say for sure." At the edge of the rock shelf, there was a compressed formation of coquina, filled with the fossilized shells of tiny sea creatures, Texigryphaea marccoui, Lima wacoensis, and Anchura mudgeana, which would undoubtedly date to the Lower Cretaceous. The tracks were several feet above that level, probably somewhat more recent.

Gracie wrote furiously on her notepad while I examined the white scar in the trackway. The prints had been carefully lifted out in a section approximately six to eight inches deep and three feet by three and a half feet across. The cut was a neat rectangle, a perfect ornament for the patio or fireplace of some wealthy collector, or a showpiece for a museum overseas, where no one would know or care that the fossil had been indiscriminately removed from context and stolen away in the dark of night.

Gracie was muttering to herself, guessing at how to spell Acrocanthosaurus.

"I can e-mail all the technical information to you later, if that would be helpful," I offered, and she seemed relieved. "Without having seen it, I'd estimate the value of this piece at between forty and sixty thousand dollars. If I can look at some pictures of the actual fossil, I can give you a better estimate."

Gracie pursed her lips and whistled, clearly surprised by the valuation, then wagged her pencil toward the road. "We have a pretty clear idea of how they did it. There was some kind of dual-wheel truck—it left pretty deep tracks up there in the grass. They turned around and backed down the hill, as close to the site as they could get. We figure they used a portable generator to run some kind of rock-cutting machinery."

"It looks like a pneumatic chisel and a diamond saw, maybe a few other tools. It would have taken some kind of heavy-equipment truck with a hoist to transport a slab this large," I said, dipping my finger in the powdered limestone. "They probably insulated the equipment as much as they could to cut the noise. Even so, the saw blade would have made a squeal you could hear for a mile. Was there anyone staying in the cabin when it happened?" From the riverbank, I could see the road to the cabin, but not the structure itself. The dense foliage would have cut the sound, but anyone staying there would have heard.

"Not that week," Gracie answered. "Unfortunately." The radio on her belt beeped, and she turned up the volume, listening as a dispatcher relayed a report of an escaped Brahman bull on the highway. "Guess I better get over there," she said, slipping her notepad into her pocket, then pulling out a business card and handing it to me. "My number's on there, and so is the office e-mail. As soon as you send me the description of the tracks, I'll put it on the wire. We've got one out already, but yours will be more accurate. So far, we haven't heard a thing. It's like this gigantic slab of rock just disappeared." Another report came over her radio, and she turned down the volume. "I'll talk to you soon."

"All right," I said, shaking her hand and slipping the card into my pocket. "I'll be in touch." As she walked away, I squatted by the tracks, making a mental sketch of the area. Later I could do a grid and catalog the site, but it was good to note first impressions with a fresh eye. The second or third time through, it was easy to miss things you would have noticed on your first time, like . . .

. . . like the barely visible evidence of smaller prints beside the large ones. Blowing away the white dust, I traced the smaller tracks with my finger. Three little toe prints here, three little toe prints there, the tiny pinprick imprint of claws. Juveniles, traveling with an adult.

A rush of excitement went through me, followed by a leaden sensation. No wonder someone was willing to risk coming this far onto private property to steal the tracks. They showed the movement of adults with young, lending credence to the most recent theories that the ancient reptiles did not nest, lay eggs, and abandon their off-spring, but raised and schooled the young, perhaps for several years until maturity. No doubt, the stolen fossil not only had adult tracks, but some of the juvenile ones, as well. This was the kind of fossil find that would definitely turn up on the black market at a big price. The kind that should have been studied and cataloged in context.

"Do you have any pictures of the site before the tracks were stolen?" I called up to Collie and Jocelyn.

"We have some at the house," Jocelyn answered. "Everyone used to come down here and take pictures of their kids by the tracks. I can look tonight."

"Good." Standing up, I dusted the powdered lime from my hands. "I have a feeling these tracks were more valuable than you thought. Right here, there's . . ." Over Jocelyn's shoulder, a truck was coming up the road.

Snapping to her feet, Jocelyn peered around the base of the tree as a truck rolled to a stop with a lazy squeal of brakes. "Oh, God, it's Pop." She headed toward the clearing where we'd parked.

Collie stood up and followed, and I started out of the riverbed. Fortunately, Pop was slow, and Jocelyn intercepted him before he could manage to get the door open and come to investigate what we were doing.

The old man paused with one foot in the grass and his walking cane caught in the seat belt, which was still fastened around his waist. "Well, hang!" he grumbled, trying to pull the cane loose, but suc-ceeding only in hooking it around the steering wheel. "This blamed seat belt's all herky-jerked, Josie. I got myself trussed up like a chicken."

Sighing patiently, Jocelyn worked to unwind the cane. "Well, Pop, what are you doing down here? Zach was supposed to send you home to rest."

Pop shrugged, waiting for Jocelyn to free the cane, then smiling when Collie reached in to unhook the seat belt. "Hi, uhh, Collie." Craning his neck, he looked over Collie's shoulder as she steadied his elbow while Jocelyn helped him get his other foot out of the truck. "Where'za baby? Did ya bring her down for a swim?"

Collie smiled at him fondly. "I didn't bring her today, Pop. She goes to Mother's Day Out on Mondays."

Pop's silvery-green eyes—Zach's color, I noted—twinkled and his thick gray mustache twitched upward. "Well, ye're in a pretty sad state if comin' here's your idear of a day out. Unless, a'course, you come to take me out dancin'." Laughing at his own joke, he gave Collie a flirty wink that reminded me of Zach.

Collie seemed properly charmed. "Well, I hear your dancing feet are supposed to be in temporary retirement. True says to tell you to behave yourself."

Pop shook a finger at her. "You tell True to keep his nose to hisself." The petulant look showed that Pop wasn't all fun and flirtation. "I got enough people fussin' over me already. Between Josie and Zach, they're all over me like hens on a grasshopper."

Collie patted his arm sympathetically. "Now, Pop, you know they're just trying to make sure you follow the doctor's orders."

Pop *foof*ed a puff of air past his mustache, then noticed me, and asked, "Who'zis?"

Collie made introductions. "Pop, this is my friend, Lindsey Attwood. She's here for Jocelyn's therapy camp, but we thought we'd do a little touring around the place first. Lindsey, this is Jocelyn's grandfather, True's great-uncle Jeeve, but everyone calls him Pop."

Elbowing past Jocelyn, Pop shook my hand, saying, "You're a darned sight prettier than them Japan businessmen Josie had down to the camp yesterday. They's nice enough, but I couldn't understand a word they was sayin'." Still holding my hand, he grinned over his shoulder at Jocelyn. "Yer taste in customers is lookin' up, Josie."

Jocelyn tapped his arm lightly with the cane. "Stop flirting with Lindsey, Pop. And it was last week when you surprised the Incani group while they were out on their nature quest, not yesterday. They left two days ago. And they were from Taiwan, not Japan."

Pop seemed momentarily befuddled, then shrugged off the statement and muttered, "Well, that explains why I didn't understand 'em. I knew some Japanese from when I was in the army, but I never learnt to speak any Taiwan." Gesturing toward the river with his cane, he changed the subject, "So, did y'all come down here to take the baby swimmin'?"

A sad look crossed Collie's face; then she smiled patiently at Pop. "She's at Mother's Day Out in town today, Pop."

"Oh, that's right. That's right." He snapped his fingers beside his head, his knobby hand trembling. "Y'all down here lookin' at the dinosaur tracks?"

Collie and I glanced at each other, unsure of what to say. Jocelyn put on an easy smile and covered like a professional. "Lindsey wanted to see them. She's into historical things. It's kind of a hobby of hers. She's making some notes that Collie might use in her newspaper articles about the ranch."

Pop puffed up like a balloon. "Well, we're sure 'nough proud of our dinosaur tracks. This set here was discovered around 1855, when Jeremiah and Caroline Truitt homesteaded the place."

"That's amazing. That long ago?" I said, gathering that, as Jocelyn said, he didn't remember that the tracks had been vandalized.

Jocelyn pressed her lips into a regretful frown as Pop went on.

"A' course, the Indians knew about 'em long before then. They had a whole slew of legends about how giant dragons and such had left them tracks here in the ancient days." Pop gestured down the river like a museum docent handing out the tourist spiel. "The big round tracks downriver was cataloged around 1851 by Caroline. She was a bit of an early-day bone hunter, I guess you'd say. She made a hobby of it, even kept journals and wrote some serials about the tracks. She drew pictures for the newspapers back east about what the dinosaurs might of looked like, and people took to callin' this part of the river the Big Lizard Bottoms." Chewing the tail of his mustache thoughtfully, he pointed at me. "I got a Big Lizard box up in the attic to the house. I can get it down if you want." He chuckled, his cheeks flushing red. "Course, maybe I ought to go through it myself first. As I recall, there's a picture in there of me as a baby, sittin' naked as a newborn piglet in one of them big round dinosaur tracks. We liked to play in them things as youngsters. So did the kids and grandkids. Come to think of it, somewhere there's pictures of Zach and Josie sittin' there in their birthday suits, too."

"Really?" Collie stretched out the word, raising a brow. "I have dibs on the one of Zach. That might come in handy if he gets any ideas about bringing that dog to my house."

Jocelyn nodded and Pop frowned, putting a hand up to his ear. "What about the log house?"

"No, Pop, she was talking about a dog," Jocelyn said a little louder, turning to face him as she spoke. "They caught that dog today. The one that's been causing all the trouble around town."

"Oh, all right, all right." Pop's expression was as blank as the summer sky. Clearly he didn't remember about the dog. He turned back to me. "If ye're interested in the Big Lizard, I got some stuff up at the house you ought to look at. There's a whole box of writings and things was done by Caroline Truitt. A'course, what I got here at the house are just copies. The originals are in the county museum in San Saline, but lots of them writings was done when the ranch was homesteaded back in . . ." He continued through the story of the journals and old photos of the tracks, not seeming to realize he was repeating himself. Behind him, Jocelyn shrugged apologetically.

"That sounds fascinating," I said when he'd finished for the second time. I felt the irresistible tingle of an emerging mystery. "I would love to look at Caroline Truitt's notes and the old photographs—whatever you have, really. I enjoy studying that kind of thing."

Pop seemed pleased. Clearly I was his new favorite person. "Well, all righty, then. You just come on up to the big house when you git a chance, and I'll have some things for ya about the Big Lizard. I'll git busy and hunt that stuff up."

"Sounds good," I replied.

"All righty," he said again, then peered past me toward the drop-off, as if he were thinking about going to the riverbank. "Guess the tracks are above water, bein' as the river's low right now."

Jocelyn chewed her bottom lip nervously. "Pop, you'd better get back to the house. You've had way too much activity today already."

"Oh, for hang's sake, Josie. I'm fine."

Jocelyn nodded, trying to usher him back into the truck. "Yes, and let's try to keep it that way. You go on back to the house and get some rest, and this evening Zach or I can help you find that box of Caroline's things."

Pop grumbled in his throat, "Oh, all right," then climbed laboriously into the truck, letting out a long groan as he pulled his legs in. He patted Jocelyn on the head as she handed him his cane. "See ya this evenin', Josie."

"Have a good rest, Pop. I love you." Kissing him tenderly on the cheek, she stood back and closed the door.

Pop smiled, leaning out the window. "Collie, you bring that baby by swimmin' next time."

"I will, Pop," Collie said. "She's taking toddler swim lessons down at the pool, so maybe she won't be so afraid of the water this year."

"Toddler swim lessons?" Pop repeated, rolling his head back and squinting at us. "Heck, back in my day, we just threw 'em in the river and let 'em figure it out."

Collie chuckled. "These days you'd get arrested for that, Pop."

Shaking his head, Pop started the truck. "There's a lot of 'em need to be throwed in the river these days. It'd do them some good." He punctuated that with a nod, then started the engine, waved good-bye, and coasted off toward home.

Letting out a long breath, Jocelyn massaged the base of her neck as we climbed into her truck and followed Pop's dust trail. "That was close. Sometimes he forgets about the tracks being stolen, and then when he does remember, he's upset all over again. He hasn't come down here and actually seen the damage since his heart attack, and I think it's better that he doesn't, for now." Glancing at her watch, she started. "My gosh, look at the time. I've got an introductory session with this week's group in thirty minutes. If it's all right with you, Lindsey, I'll just point out the cabin as we pass, and you can drive back out here in your car, unpack, settle in, rest and relax for the evening."

"That sounds good." I envisioned taking my things to the cabin, falling down on the bed, and passing out for a while. Later, I could send an e-mail to Sydney, as I did every evening—my way of electronically being with her when bedtime came and she was lonely. She would read it when she wandered off to her room for the night, then stay up late answering, hoping her father would come home before she fell asleep.

"So where is this top-secret place I can go to use the cell phone? I try to e-mail my daughter every morning and evening, at least. She's visiting her father for the first time this summer. In Mexico." My stomach twisted into the usual knot as I painted the picture of Sydney so far away in a strange house, strange country, strange life.

"The cabin is right up there." Jocelyn pointed through the trees. "Just keep going on this road instead of turning off at the river. You can barely see the roof from here. Out back, there's a trail that leads up the hill. There's an observation spot at the top, with a little picnic bench under a tree. From there you'll be able to pick up a cell tower. Your cell phone won't work down in the cabin."

Leaning close to the window, I peered toward the cabin roof, considering the steep slope behind it. "This will be an adventure," I commented. "E-mail with a view. I should also call Laura and tell her I'll be staying here a few days."

"I told her you might be," Collie said as we turned the corner and the river disappeared from sight. "Staying, I mean. I called her when I had the idea of your staying here and helping me on the horse therapy story. She said that was fine, that she'd see you in a few days. It sounded like she and your dad had kind of a busy week coming up, anyway. They were getting ready for some barbecue cook-off there in Keatonville. Laura's husband is the event chairman. Your dad was going to be helping them get the grounds ready this week."

I squinted at the back of her head, again getting the feeling that people were having long conversations about me behind my back. "Hmm . . . Laura didn't mention that." Obviously I was the patsy in some kind of grand plot to . . . to what, exactly? Maybe they thought that the remote location and difficulty with e-mail would keep me from sneaking online and buying tickets to Mexico. Maybe this was some grand save-Lindsey-from-herself plan they had cooked up. Then again, maybe I needed a friendly intervention.

Collie put on a falsely casual air. "Well, you know, it came up suddenly. The whole idea of having you help on the articles, I mean. Laura thinks it's great, though."

"Laura thinks I'm neurotic," I muttered, and Collie glanced over her shoulder.

"You *are* neurotic," Collie said in a way that only a really good friend could get away with. "But we love you."

Clasping a hand over my eyes, I rested my head against the seat, bouncing up and down with the bumps in the road. "I'm sorry. I feel like such a loser, interfering with everyone's summer. You're all down here in never-never land, falling in love, and getting married, and having babies, and then along comes Lindsey raining on the parade. I don't want to dump on you this way. I should have waited to visit until after Sydney was back and I had my head together again." I was suddenly aware that I was speaking in front of Jocelyn. No telling what the psychologist in her was thinking. *Here is a woman who needs therapy....*

"Are you kidding?" Reaching over the seat, Collie laid her hand over my knee, her fingers a warm circle of comfort. "Laura and I have been waiting forever for you to fall apart. You're the Miss Together who's made the rest of us look bad all these years. We couldn't be more thrilled that you're having a breakdown."

"Thanks," I said miserably, swallowing a lump of emotion and smiling wanly at her. My best girlfriend, who'd stood by me through everything.

Jocelyn gave me a sympathetic look in the rearview. "You know, the feelings you're experiencing are perfectly normal. Of course you'd have separation anxiety and concern in a situation like that. How old is Sydney?"

"Eight." The word trembled from my mouth with a sudden rush of emotion. "She's only eight. Her father has never shown any interest, but all of a sudden this summer he's interested. Coincidentally, he has recently remarried and has a new young wife who's bored, wants children, but has infertility problems. Mind you, they talk about all of this where Sydney can hear them, so she tells me about it on e-mail or during our weekly phone calls. That's bad enough, but the real truth is that Geoff never wanted any children, and I doubt he wants any now. He's just using my daughter to distract Whitney from pursuing it. Faced with the idea of going through in-vitro, or exercising his joint custody of Sydney, it's much easier for him to take Sydney. I'm afraid that my little girl will end up hurt and disappointed."

Jocelyn nodded with the empathic-but-detached mask of an accomplished therapist. "Well, that is a hard thing to predict, isn't it? Do you feel that Sydney is in any danger—physically, I mean? At risk of abuse, anything like that?"

My eyes widened, and I jerked back against the seat. "Well, no. Of course not. I wouldn't have sent her if I did. I would have found some way not to."

Jocelyn nodded thoughtfully. "In the past, did Sydney ever display any evidence that she had issues with her father not being an active participant in her life?"

"Yes. Definitely," I answered, the vessels in my heart twisting, shrinking, wringing out blood and leaving behind an old, hollow ache. "She's been sending notes to him ever since she learned to write. Last year she started keeping a picture of him taped to her dresser mirror. She's been obsessed with the idea of meeting her father."

Jocelyn nodded again. "Would you say that is a natural longing on her part?"

I slouched in my seat, feeling strangely exposed. "Well . . . yes, of course."

"But you're afraid that she will come out of it disappointed—that her father won't be everything she had hoped for?"

"Exactly," I replied. That was it exactly.

In the mirror, her eyes cast a thoughtful reflection, a deep green like a pool of water in a grassy field. "Would you say that most people are disappointed in their parents in some way? That often a parent is not all we could have hoped for, in some capacity or another?"

"Well, of course. I think most people have some of those feelings toward their parents." I thought of my own father, an old-school military man, obsessed with his career, often gone on duty for months at a time, suffering from battle scars we couldn't see, wounded in a way that prevented him from reaching out to us. He was a face behind a newspaper. I never knew him well, but of all four kids, I knew I was his favorite, and that was enough for me. I thought of my mother, who waited patiently but never pushed, who held the family together and tended the home, who forbade us to complain about Dad. Who swept the issues of our youth under the rug, neat and tidy. Of course most people had issues with their parents. Parents, I'd learned since becoming one, were imperfect people, feeling their way through the uncharted wilderness of their children's lives.

"In my experience, some parental resentment is a common life theme," Jocelyn summed up. "Even given whatever issues you had with your own parents, would you have chosen for them not to be there?"

"What?" I stammered, trying to picture growing up without Mom or Dad. As a child, I wasn't aware of their flaws. I cared only that they were there, that our home was stable and reliable day after day, year after year, a safe place to be, even if we didn't get mushy-gushy over each other or have big family meetings. We had our routines, our spaces to fill, family dinner out on Friday night, chores on Saturday, and church on Sunday, work and school. A normal life.

"Would you have chosen not to have either of your parents in your life because they could not be perfect for you?" Jocelyn restated as we wound through the grove of trees to the ranch headquarters.

"Of course not," I replied, shocked by the suggestion that I would ever voluntarily give up one of my parents. My mother's stroke the year before, losing her, was one of my most painful experiences. "As a kid, I didn't care if my parents were perfect. I just cared that they were there."

"Exactly. That is what children care about, for the most part. Most of the time—now I'm not speaking into the realm of situations that include abuse and neglect here—but most of the time, children are better served by a relationship, even an imperfect relationship, with both parents. Give yourself credit for loving your daughter enough to put your own resentments aside and allow her to discover this relationship with her father, whatever it is going to be. Only time and God know the answer to that, so in the meantime, there isn't much point in second-guessing and worrying, is there?" Parking the truck in front of the ranch house, Jocelyn glanced at me with a wise, empathic expression. "Sorry. I didn't mean to analyze. Habit."

I sat there stunned, muttering, "Oh, no . . . that's . . . It's fine, really. . . . I . . ." Suddenly I saw Sydney's situation in an entirely new way, through the eyes of my daughter, who could accept Geoff for what he was, because he was her father. "Thanks," I said, but Jocelyn was already getting out of the truck with Collie, the two of them exchanging a private look. I had the feeling, again, that Collie had told her about me ahead of time, perhaps set me up for a little of Dr. Jocelyn's impromptu analysis.

Maybe that was why she and Laura had concocted this scheme to send me to horse psychology camp. Maybe it had nothing to do with Collie's writing a magazine article at all. I considered the idea as we said good-bye and departed in separate vehicles, Jocelyn heading toward the therapy camp, Collie toward town, and me to my cabin.

A long, mournful howl broke the afternoon quiet as I passed the barn and the chicken coop. Stopping the car, I glanced at the dog kennel, where Mr. Grits was dividing his time between howling and trying to dig his way to China. He had created a hole large enough that the front half of his body disappeared when he dug, leaving only a woolly white rear with dirt flying out.

"Oh, you bad boy," I muttered, backing up. I'd have to tie him up or something. In another hour or so he'd have completed his escape tunnel, and would be on the loose again.

As I pulled up to the fence, Mr. Grits came out of the hole, mustache and jowls painted brown. "You are going to dig your way right back into trouble," I warned, shaking a finger at him, and he turned his face away. "But on the other hand, then you won't be here if Zach really does decide to take you to Collie's house. . . ." *Hmmm.* Some wicked part of me had an idea. *Wouldn't it be funny to kidnap the dog? Then if Zach decides to go through with playing the adopt-a-dog joke on Collie, he won't be able to find Mr. Grits. He'll think the dog escaped.*

It was too tempting to resist. I was out of the SUV in a flash, opening the chain on the dog kennel, and ushering Mr. Grits into my car, before even considering the fact that he smelled like a combination of damp garden and goldfish tank. Still, the plan seemed worth it as I chained the gate, slipped into my SUV, and left the headquarters with my hairy, smelly partner in the passenger seat. Mutt and Jeff, together again, on the road to adventure.

A giggle pressed from my throat as I rolled down the window, enjoying the late-afternoon breeze. I found myself checking the rearview mirror, watching the ranch house disappear from sight, thinking, *Maybe he'll come looking for the dog . . .*

Shaking off the idea, I relaxed against the headrest as I drove slowly out of the trees, through the grassland sea beyond, then up the rocky hillside to the place where the roads forked. Following the fork to the river, I took in a deep breath, feeling . . . good for the first time in weeks. It was hard to imagine now, winding along the hillside with the soft wildflower-scented breeze swirling through the windows, that this morning I had been falling off the edge of a cliff.

I had a newfound faith that things would turn out all right. I had a peace for which there was no explanation, except perhaps the quiet magic of this place with its wispy sage-green grass swaying hypnotically in the dappled shade of the live oaks. There was an incredible silence here. No voices, no car horns, no cell phones ringing or television sets droning. Just the low hum of the engine and the relaxing rumble of tires traveling over the stone and earth.

This was a beautiful place, serene like a scene from an artist's painting, old and unchanged. It was no wonder that people came here for therapy. The yawning trees and the boulder-strewn hillsides made human problems seem temporary, insignificant, all part of some larger plan as vast as the sun-drenched landscape itself.

We rounded a bend and our destination came into view on the hillside ahead. The cabin was just as I had pictured it, a sturdy one-story limestone structure with a loft window upstairs and a stone fence around the yard. It looked like a lithograph from a turn-of-the-century storybook, nestled beneath the shade of a gigantic oak—the kind of scene in which Goldilocks might show up to steal the three bears' porridge or Little Red Riding Hood might skip by with her basket of apples. I'd brought the wolf with me. He turned his dirty snout my way, licked his lips, and yawned a smile, as if to show that he liked the cabin.

Parking near the yard gate, I killed the engine. A sigh wound through my body, and I sat there with my fingers dangling on the keys, filled with the strange sense that I was finally someplace where I could close my eyes and rest.

EIGHT

◆◆◆

Dear Sydney,

Sorry Mommy didn't answer your e-mail last night. Do you know what happened? I lay down to rest for a minute after supper, and I slept until morning. I woke up a little while ago when the clock on the mantel (long story) chimed six. Outside, the light is just beginning to turn gray, and I'm writing this e-mail to you so that when it's bright enough, I can climb to the top of the hill (another long story) and send it. You won't believe where I've ended up and what I've been doing.

I'll play our little game first, so you'll know what it's like this moment where I am, and it will be just like you're here.

Right now, I'm in a little stone house on a ranch not far from where Aunt Laura lives. The ceiling is low and cozy, with heavy tree-trunk timbers to hold it up, and the walls are a thick white plaster like the ones in Mexico. I'm sitting at the table in the tiny kitchen, next to a living room with a stone fireplace. There's also a bedroom (where I slept last night) downstairs. Upstairs is a loft with two bedrooms and a low, sloping ceiling. One room has pink quilts and one has blue, all sewn by hand sometime long, long ago. I imagine that the pioneer mom who lived here pieced them together from

FLOUR SACKS (FLOUR USED TO COME IN CLOTH SACKS) AND OLD WORK CLOTHES AND BABY THINGS HER CHILDREN OUTGREW. SHE PROBABLY PULLED THOSE QUILTS UP SNUG UNDER THEIR CHINS, SMOOTHING THEIR HAIR AND KISSING THEIR FOREHEADS. IF ALL THE BUNKS WERE FULL, THERE WOULD HAVE BEEN SEVEN KIDS. IMAGINE THAT! YOU'VE ALWAYS WANTED A BROTHER OR A SISTER, BUT CAN YOU PICTURE HAVING SEVEN!

THE FURNITURE HERE HAS CARVINGS OF FLOWERS AND LEAVES. ON THE BEAM ABOVE THE FRONT DOOR, THE WORDS "ENDE GUT, ALLES GUT" ARE CARVED INTO THE WOOD. I DON'T KNOW WHAT THAT MEANS, BUT I THINK IT'S GERMAN. THE CHAIRS AT THE DINING TABLE HAVE OLD MAN WINTER'S FACE ON THEM. FROM THE LOOKS OF HIM, HE'S BLOWING UP A MEAN SNOWSTORM, BUT I DON'T THINK THERE WILL BE ANY SNOW HERE TODAY. THE BREEZE FEELS COOL NOW, BUT IT'LL BE HOT LATER.

WELL, LOVE, THERE'S ALMOST ENOUGH LIGHT OUTSIDE TO SEE, SO I'M GOING TO GET DRESSED AND CLIMB THE HILL TO SEND THIS. OH, I FORGOT TO TELL YOU WHY I'M HERE. AUNT COLLIE IS DOING A STORY ABOUT SOME DINOSAUR TRACKS THAT WERE STOLEN OUT OF THE RIVERBED, AND I'M HELPING HER. WITH ANY LUCK, WE'LL CATCH THE THIEVES. THEY THINK IT MAY HAVE BEEN AN INSIDE JOB—LIKE ON SCOOBY-DOO, WHEN THE CULPRIT IS ALWAYS SOMEBODY YOU KNOW. I HAVEN'T MET TOO MANY SUSPECTS YET, BUT I DO HAVE A SCOOBY. HE'S GIGANTIC, WITH THICK WHITE HAIR. I RESCUED HIM FROM SOME ORNERY COWBOYS WHO SAID HE WAS CHASING THEIR CATTLE. (BY THE WAY, DON'T GET ANY IDEAS ABOUT KEEPING HIM—HE'S AN OUTSIDE DOG, NOT AN APARTMENT DOG.)

RIGHT NOW HE'S SLEEPING BY THE DOOR, WEARING YOUR PINK BARBIE FLIGGIE IN HIS HAIR. IT LOOKS VERY CUTE ON HIM, AND HE SAYS HE HOPES YOU DON'T MIND. HE ASKED IF I WOULD GRAB THE DIGITAL CAM AND SEND YOU A PICTURE, BECAUSE IT WOULD MAKE YOU LAUGH. IF YOU COULD HAVE SEEN ME CRAMMING HIM IN THE BACK OF THE JEEP YESTERDAY, YOU WOULD HAVE REALLY LAUGHED.

HE SMELLS BAD, BUT HE'S ACTUALLY PRETTY GOOD COMPANY,
SO DON'T WORRY ABOUT ME. I MISS YOU, BUT I'M DOING JUST
FINE. I HAD REAL LIVE GRITS YESTERDAY MORNING FOR BREAK-
FAST. THEY WEREN'T BAD. I'LL TELL YOU MORE ABOUT THAT
IN THE NEXT E-MAIL.

ENJOY YOUR DAY. I LOVE YOU TO THE MOON AND STARS, AND
BACK.

MOM

The light outside was finally becoming bright enough to see by as I dressed in khaki shorts, a white tank top, and hiking boots, and tucked the laptop into my backpack. Standing by the door, I glanced at myself in the little antique mirror, noticing that I looked surprisingly rested. My hair had dried in dark waves while I slept, and the dark circles under my eyes had faded. There was a blush in my cheeks and a touch of color in my skin from being out in the sun the day before. I looked like I'd returned to the realm of the living. The hollow-faced woman who'd stared back at me from the rearview the day before was gone.

"Must be the fresh air," I muttered. On the entry rug, the dog rolled one eye open and thumped his tail against the floor.

"You ready to take a little walk?" I asked, grabbing the rope from the coat hook and slipping it on him.

As I opened the door, and we stepped out side by side, I was glad to have Mr. Grits along. The predawn light was still dim, and the twisted live oaks cast odd shadows in the low-hanging mist. Somewhere nearby, a dove called clear and mournful, and its mate answered from the fog. Mr. Grits squatted on his haunches and howled out a reply as I closed the cabin door. The sound sent goose bumps down my spine, but I pictured Sydney wondering why I hadn't answered her e-mail last night, and knew I couldn't wait for the rising sun to burn away the fog.

As we left the porch, the dog bounded playfully ahead, pulling me across the yard. "Whoa there, wait a minute." Laughing, I braced both feet as he started toward the river. "This way, big guy. Up the hill." He switched paths with a playful yip, and we were headed up the hill at a trot.

We climbed the narrow trail in record time, Mr. Grits plunging ahead, scrambling over loose rock and tree roots, and me stumbling at the end of the rope like a reluctant mountain climber. The hurried ascent was probably beneficial, because I didn't have time to think about snakes or other crawly things, or wonder about the rustles in the underbrush. Before I knew it, we'd wound through the trees and emerged from the fog on top of the mountain. Mr. Grits skidded to a halt so fast we collided, and I ended up astraddle him like a kid playing leapfrog. The dog swiped his tongue across my face, and I smelled fish.

"Eeew!" I coughed, pushing him away.

Batting his eyes beneath the pink fliggie, he looked at me soulfully, as if to say that I looked like I needed a kiss. For just an instant, I had the feeling he could see things in me that I didn't let anyone see. The loneliness. The sense of being lost, drifting with only Sydney as my anchor, and now she was far away.

It's not much of a life, I heard him say.

"It's all I've got," I whispered, then realized I was having a moment of insanity in which I thought the dog was talking to me. Worse yet, I was answering.

"All right, Lindsey, I don't know what that was, but you need to shake it off," I muttered, following the path into a maze of towering boulders. In my father's old John Wayne movies, the bad guys would have ambushed the hero there. Ahead, Mr. Grits sniffed the air suspiciously, slowing down.

"Let's go," I whispered, anxious to be out in the open, and Mr. Grits picked up the pace.

Beyond the boulders, the path crested the hill, where an old stone bench cast a long morning shadow over a carpet of Indian blanket blossoms beneath a lone live oak.

To the east the sky was afire, and below in the valley, the shadow of the jagged hills slowly receded, allowing diaphanous streams of sunlight to breathe life into the silent earth. Nestled among the trees like part of the landscape, the buildings of the ranch headquarters caught the sunlight, the metal roofs reflecting amber tones like embers in a fire. Far off in the pasture, a herd of horses grazed, their sleek coats golden and copper and silver-gray.

In my mind, I pictured them as a herd of wild mustangs, the descendants of noble Spanish horses, roaming free on the dusty green prairie. I imagined the pioneers who'd come to this place when it was wild and new. Strong men and bold women like Caroline, who posed staunchly beside her husband in the portrait on the cabin wall. Had she once stood in this very spot, gazing into the valley? What thoughts did she find here? What did she dream?

Someday we'll build a fine house there in the valley, she whispered in my mind. The voice was so real, I glanced over my shoulder. There was no one there, except the Caroline from my imagination. Caroline and Jeremiah. Jeremiah, with dark hair and eyes like tarnished silver. In my imagination he smiled at me, and I was Caroline.

Letting my eyelids drift closed, I sat on the bench and allowed the fantasy to sweep me away. The wind touched my cheek, featherlight, and I felt his hand, a strong, sturdy hand, his fingers combing into my hair, gentle, familiar, loving. I leaned into him and whispered, *In that big grove of live oaks below. That's where we'll build our home.*

A hawk shrieked overhead, and I jerked upright, the vision evaporating like a wisp of morning fog. Loneliness stung like a slap, sudden and sharp. For just an instant I'd let myself remember how it felt to be with somebody, to be one half of a whole, rather than a single self-subsisting entity. When was the last time I'd opened myself to that yearning, even for a moment in the unguarded hush of morning? Most days the morning hour was filled with rushing to get dishes into the dishwasher, or clothes folded, trash taken out, lunches packed, homework folder signed, myself off to work, Sydney off to school. . . .

Sydney . . .

Anxiety crept over me, blocking out the sunrise and the cool, sweet breeze. *You're not up here to loll around in a teenage fantasy,* I reminded myself. *You're up here to e-mail Sydney.*

A new sound cut through the stillness, a human sound, someone whistling long and loud. Mr. Grits perked his ears, and I leaned forward on the bench. Below, the horses lifted their heads, whinnied and cavorted in a whirling waltz of motion. The whistle came again, and as if by some silent agreement, the herd bolted, racing across the valley like the shadow of some giant beast gliding between earth and sky.

Sydney should be here to see this, I thought, grabbing the digital camera from my backpack just as the herd topped a hill. The picture captured the moment perfectly—the valley, the shadows, the crimson-lined clouds, the ranch buildings squatting among the trees, the cowboy sitting atop a silvery-blue horse near the pasture gate. . . .

The cowboy? Lowering the camera, I noticed him for the first time. He'd emerged from the trees while I was taking pictures. He whistled once more as the horses streamed past, bolting through the gateway into the barnyard. I knew him even from this far away. There was something unmistakable about his movements as he steadied his nervous mount, then swung the gate closed behind the horses.

I moved to the edge of the bluff, watching as he latched the gate, then stood gazing at the far hills for what seemed like forever. All of a sudden, I realized it wasn't Jeremiah Truitt I had fantasized about a few minutes before; it was Zach.

He turned, looked up the hill, as if he knew I was there, and I blushed from head to toe, as if we were face-to-face. Surely he didn't know I was watching him. Surely he couldn't see me all the way up here. . . .

Beside me, Mr. Grits threw his head back and let out a long "Ba-roo-roo-oooo!" that echoed through the canyon like a foghorn.

So much for remaining undetected.

Shading his eyes, Zach zeroed in on me and waved. Sheepishly, I lifted my hand in return, then proceeded back to the bench, my heart pounding and an odd tingle of excitement ping-ponging through my body.

I tried not to think about what that meant, as I set up my communications equipment like a secret agent in a low-budget spy thriller. It felt fairly ridiculous, but Jocelyn was right; the cell phone picked up a signal, and within moments I was on the Internet. Snapping a quick picture of Mr. Grits in his pink fliggie, I downloaded the photo of him and the one of the horse herd, attached them to my e-mail, and sent them whizzing through the Internet to my daughter. When the message was safely away, I punched up Sydney's message to me, which she would have probably written before bed, and normally I would have read late the night before.

Her e-mail didn't say much, just the normal things. Her dad was busy working. He left before she woke up, and she wasn't sure when he'd be home for the night. Whitney had taken her shopping. She was learning some more Spanish. She played dolls in the courtyard with the housekeeper's little girl, but Sydney's dolls didn't speak Spanish, so it was hard for them to talk to Rosa's dolls. All the TV programs were in Spanish, so she couldn't understand them, but it was funny to see Barney the Dinosaur singing "I Love You, You Love Me" in Spanish. She missed me a lot, especially when she went to bed at night, but I shouldn't worry about her, because she was eight, after all. Tomorrow night wouldn't be so bad, because her dad was having a party for his crew from the dig. They'd found several partial hadrosaurid skeletons, one of which had an actual tooth of a predator, possibly a Gorgosaurus, in it. Everyone was excited. Her dad said that could be a big enough find to make some of the magazines, which would bring in "big bucks" to fund a longer dig. He was sure they were close to unearthing a nearly complete skeleton. If he could dig long enough, he would find it, and then there would be really "big bucks," and he'd get in *National Geographic* again. Sydney thought that would be "cool."

Cool, in spite of the fact that this was his first summer with his daughter, and all he could think about was the dig.

Really cool. I wondered if he spared her a single thought in the course of his day, until he drifted in, exhausted, mellow, and probably halfway looped from stopping off for *cerveza* with his crew. If he was going to bring them home with him tonight, I hoped he made sure that they were reasonably sober and decent around Sydney. I didn't want her hanging around the fringes of some grown-up party, exposed to . . . well, who knew what? Geoff wouldn't think to look out for her, and he hired all kinds of riffraff on his crews.

Panic tightened my throat, and I let my head fall into my hand, muttering, "God," trying not to imagine the worst. Surely Whitney would watch her. She seemed to be trying to make a go of things with Sydney, even if Geoff wasn't. Surely, if things got out of hand with the drinking and the partying, Whitney would send Sydney to bed.

Then again, she didn't send Sydney to bed on any other night. Whitney didn't have any idea that eight-year-old girls needed bed-times. To Whitney, Sydney was just like another college friend, visiting for the summer. Bedtime didn't mean *bedtime*; it was just the time when Whitney went to her room to take a bath and lounge in front of the bedroom TV. Sydney went to the computer and used her talk-and-type software to compose her nightly e-mail to me, then wandered around until midnight, one, two a.m. until her father came home or she fell asleep somewhere, exhausted.

I blew out a long breath, took in another, and blew out again, remembering Jocelyn's advice from the day before. Sydney wasn't in any imminent danger, and I had to allow her time to find out who her father and new stepmother were, and what kind of a relationship she could have with them. If I didn't, she would never forgive me, and she would always wonder. I had to be patient, give it some time, *have faith*, Laura would have said. It was exactly the kind of thing my mother would have told me. Laura was becoming more like Mom every day.

Who was I becoming more like? Dad? More off in my own world, more solitary and self-contained? Disconnected like he was, shell-shocked, not from tours of duty, but from a bad divorce and a husband who couldn't love my perfect little girl? Did I really want to be like that, a sleepwalker insulated from everything, including the yearnings of my own heart?

Shaking off the thoughts, I composed one last message to Sydney, with a delayed delivery time so it would arrive in the evening.

MOMMY LOVES YOU, BABY GIRL. HAVE A GOOD SLEEP. DON'T
WORRY ABOUT ME. I'M FINE. IF I DON'T GET TO E-MAIL YOU
AGAIN TODAY, HERE'S YOUR GOOD-NIGHT KISS, OK? IT'S A
GREAT BIG SMOOCHEROO ON YOUR FOREHEAD. SWEET DREAMS,
ANGEL. MOM.

Hopefully, she would get the second e-mail before she went to bed and be reminded that someone out there loved her desperately and missed her every moment.

It would be just like tucking her in. From a thousand miles away.

Sitting there looking at the blank screen, I considered something else—another possibility, an idea that was both tempting and repulsive. I could e-mail Geoff about the stolen tracks. If anyone knew where something like that might turn up for sale, it would be him, since he teetered on the edge of shady paleontology himself. If we talked about the tracks, it might open the door to dialogue about Sydney. Right now, we weren't speaking at all.

Swallowing hard, I punched up a new mail window. My pride burned going down. *Dear Geoff.* I wanted strike his name from the page, erase it from my life and my memory. *I wonder if I could ask you about something totally unrelated to family issues. . . .* Family issues. Such an innocuous-sounding euphemism. *I am in Texas right now, working on a project.* See? Not sitting home, curled in the fetal position crying my eyes out . . .

I paused with the cursor on the delete button, again considering erasing the message. Beside me, Mr. Grits laid his head on the bench, lending moral support. Stroking his soft fur, I thought through the facts of the fossil theft—just the facts—then typed them into the computer. I added Gracie's name and the sheriff's department e-mail address so Geoff couldn't accuse me of inventing the story as an excuse to pump him for information about Sydney's visit. Gritting my teeth, I pushed send before I could change my mind.

"I hope that was a good idea," I muttered, then opened a new window to type a message to Gracie at the sheriff's department. I copied the fossil description I'd sent to Geoff, then listed tools that

had probably been used in the removal, including parts and supplies that might have been purchased recently, such as blades for the
diamond saw, compressed air, and rock-splitting feathers. If those
things were bought locally, perhaps Gracie could track down the
buyers. It wasn't much of a lead, but at least it was something. I forwarded a copy of the e-mail to Collie, in case some of it might be
useful for her article about the fossil theft. At the bottom I added
a note.

EVERYTHING'S GOOD SO FAR THIS MORNING. THE CABIN IS
ADORABLE. YOU WERE RIGHT: I NEEDED A VACATION. TODAY
SHOULD BE AN ADVENTURE. I'LL SEND MORE INFO FOR THE AR-
TICLE LATER, AFTER I'VE HAD A CHANCE TO LOOK THROUGH
POP'S MEMENTOS ABOUT THE TRACKS.
                    LOVE FROM THE BIG LIZARD BOTTOM—
                                            LINDSEY

Clicking the send button, I closed the laptop and took one last
look at the valley. Both the horse herd and the cowboy had disappeared into the tree-covered barnyard. Below, only the occasional
sound of a horse whinnying, or the clang of metal on metal, or the
far-off rumble of an engine testified to the fact that the ranch
headquarters was waking up. Which meant that I needed to get
moving, as well. I had a full day ahead of me. There were the dinosaur tracks to investigate, and the very intriguing possibility of
more tracks or other fossil evidence in the vicinity. The notes and
journals of Caroline Truitt might provide more clues, but to get
them, I'd have to go see Pop at the ranch house. That would probably take a while. Pop obviously liked to tell stories. If I hung
around the ranch headquarters part of the day, I might get to talk
with some of the cowboys who worked there. Given time, I could
probably get Jimmy Hawthorne to spill just about anything he
knew. My cover as amateur historian and curious-tourist-slash-
psychotherapy-patient would allow me to ask all sorts of dumb
questions.

My cover . . . I groaned under my breath. Before I could do anything else, I had to attend horse psychology class with the college students from UT.

I tried to picture what it might be like, as I picked up Mr. Grits's makeshift leash and followed him across the meadow of Indian blankets, through the maze of boulders, and down the hill. No potential images of horse therapy class crystallized in my mind, because I had absolutely no idea what I'd gotten myself into. I hadn't really read the article Laura had given me, or asked any questions of Collie or Jocelyn. Nor had I told anyone about my bad experience years ago at Girl Scout camp, which was the beginning of my lifelong fear of horses. In Cairo, I'd once walked six miles through the desert, alone, in 120-degree heat, because I'd refused to get on a horse.

Why hadn't all of that occurred to me yesterday, when I was letting myself be talked into acting as an amateur sleuth? Everything had seemed perfectly logical, or at least reasonably close to logical, when I was road-weary and sleep deprived. Now, in the growing light of morning, it seemed idiotic.

Surely Jocelyn didn't intend for me to actually participate in the horse therapy class, whatever that entailed. Hadn't she said something like, *Just come by enough to make it look good?* Undoubtedly that was why I hadn't panicked when she and Collie suggested that I work "undercover."

Stop worrying, a voice said in my head. The confident voice of ten-year-old Tomboy Lindsey. *You can handle it. It'll be different. Fun. An adventure. You need something different. Your life is boring. Capital B.*

Which was true, for the most part. Cleaning fossils in the basement of a museum wasn't the most thrilling day-to-day existence, but it was safe. There was no horseback riding involved, and never once had I been required to save a marauding dog from a band of gun-wielding cowboys. . . .

I dropped the thought as we rounded the last bend in the path. Sighting the cabin, Mr. Grits lunged ahead, yanking me off my feet so that I stumbled forward, slid on a patch of wet dirt, hit the dewy lawn slightly off-balance and splay-footed, and proceeded to ski down the hill, clinging to the rope with the dog blazing ahead like a high-powered speedboat.

Rounding the corner of the house, he skidded to a sudden halt, and I tripped forward, ending up in leapfrog position again. When I caught my balance, I realized we had an audience. He was leaning against the gate with his long legs crossed and his dark brows knotted like he'd seen one of those can't-be-real acrobatic maneuvers on the Cirque du Soliel.

His lips twisted into a wry one-sided smile, and I watched them with a strange fascination. "Guess now I know how my dog got out of the kennel."

NINE

I QUIRKED A BROW AND SLANTED A GLANCE AT HIM THROUGH SLIGHTLY lowered lashes—a decidedly flirty maneuver. *Stop that!* Mommy Lindsey scolded. *What in the world do you think you're doing? You are somebody's mother. Act like a grown-up.*

I barely heard her. *Come on, live a little,* Romance Lindsey countered. *You're a mother, not an android. You're entitled to have a life.* Lately even Sydney had been asking why I never dated. The divorced mothers of her friends dated. . . .

Jutting a hip out jauntily, I twirled the dog rope around my finger, looking from the man to the beast, and back again. "*Your* dog?" I said sweetly, batting my lashes in false bemusement. "There must be some mistake. I believe this is *my* dog."

He drew back, making a *tsk-tsk* sound against his teeth. "I had plans for that dog. I know where I can find a great home for it. Nice house up on a hill. Little girl with curly red hair to play with. Just the place for him." He grinned wickedly, and my stomach fluttered like a firecracker the instant the chain reaction starts inside the casing. Romance Lindsey and Tomboy Lindsey grabbed Mommy Lindsey, shoved her into a box, and sat down on the lid. Control Freak Lindsey ran away screaming.

"Collie doesn't want this dog," I said, but I might as well have been saying, *Hey, handsome, what's your sign?* I felt my lips slipping into a slow smile, tongue sliding along the edge of my teeth in a silent challenge. "Besides, he's busy protecting me."

Zach's dark brows lifted beneath his cowboy hat. "From what?" The words were so suggestive that a hot flush went through my body, pheromones or something racing in all directions.

I swallowed hard. "Any number of things."

"Like . . . ?"

"Like . . ." *Like cowboys with crooked smiles and copious attitude.* "Like . . . snakes, and"—*and the things I'm thinking right now*—"and wild"—*urges . . . uhh*—"animals, and other things."

"Other things?" His lips twisted into a question mark, waiting for me to further clarify.

Which, of course, I did not. I pointed at him, saying, "You're repeating me. That isn't nice."

"I didn't realize you thought I was."

"Was what?" Tipping my chin down, I watched him from the corners of my eyes, my mind tingling at the verbal repartee.

"Nice."

A puff of air burst past my lips, and I raised my hands into the air, palms-out. "I'm not even going to go there. Actually, Collie said you were . . ."

He cocked a dark brow, waiting for the rest.

". . . well, kind of a pain," I finished. He took on a slightly wounded look, and I couldn't tell if he was serious or just pandering for sympathy, so I added, "But she meant it in an affectionate way, I could tell."

Shaking his head, he looked down at his boots, his face hidden except for the slightly crooked, definitely overconfident smile. He knew Collie liked him. He knew I liked him, too.

Normally that would have sent me running the other way. Men with easy smiles and flamboyant charm were not at all my type. Not since, at twenty-something, I fell for Geoff. After that ended so badly, I'd stuck to being friends with safe, studious guys, which was predictably uninteresting, which was just as well, because I had a daughter to raise, and that took up my free time. I didn't want her involved in a parade of would-be stepdads and short-term suitors. She was better off, much better off, being raised in a solid, predictable single-

parent home without all the unnecessary drama of dating and relationships.

Which made me wonder why I was lingering in the gateway with
the cowboy. Perhaps it was the change in location and the fact that
Sydney was so far away that made this seem . . . well . . . harmless.
Not harmless, exactly, but manageable. Anything that might happen
between Zach and me was acceptably doomed, like falling for one
of the crew members on a cruise ship. Next week I'd be off the boat,
headed for distant shores. No risk, just the chance to unearth an ancient part of myself that hadn't seen daylight in years. The ruins of
Romance Lindsey had been buried under a mountain of divorce
rubble, resentment, and unrealized hopes, but now that I'd excavated
her, she was in surprisingly good shape.

Glancing at his watch, Zach pushed his hands casually into his
pockets. "So I guess you're off to your first horse therapy session this
morning." He studied me in a narrow-eyed way that told me he was
wondering why I needed psychotherapy—what I was *in for*, so to
speak.

I blushed, and not because I felt the least bit flirty. There was
nothing romantic about masquerading as a head case, especially
since, lately, I'd been one. "I'm here working on an article," came out
of my mouth. "About the ranch and the therapy program. But don't
tell everyone. I want to observe things in their natural state." Odd
how easily that big fat fib rolled off my tongue.

"A writer, huh?" he said with interest.

"Mmm-hmmm," I chirped. *I write signs for museum exhibits, notes to
Sydney's teacher, occasional copy for museum brochures.* "But, like I said,
we're trying to keep it quiet. I don't want to disturb anybody."

"You don't look like a writer." He scratched the dog's ears absently, and Mr. Grits laid his head against Zach's leg, suddenly
smitten.

I gave the rope a little jiggle, feeling mildly betrayed. "Great, then
I'm doing a good job of blending in."

Arching a brow, Zach scanned me from head to toe in a way that
said that I wasn't blending in at all, and that had him interested.

"So . . . then I guess I shouldn't hold you up. Don't want to make you late for class." He watched my reaction very closely. I got the feeling that Zach was astute about people, and he didn't exactly buy my story about being a writer.

"Wouldn't miss it," I assured him with a load of false enthusiasm, which quickly evaporated when I thought about horse therapy class. "Actually, I don't quite know what to expect," I admitted. "We aren't actually going to be *riding* the horses, are we?"

He had the nerve to laugh at my question, which worried me, until he shrugged and said, "Not today."

"Oh, good. I don't get along very well with horses. I never have."

He gazed toward the river with the faraway, pensive look from the picture in the newspaper. "Getting along with horses is just like getting along with people."

"I don't always get along with people very well, either." It was a surprisingly honest admission for me.

"Why not?"

"Oh, you know, lack of patience, I guess," I said evasively, trying to make the comment sound light.

He chuckled. "Don't tell that to Jocelyn. She'll have a field day. She loves to get her hands on the impatient ones who have to be in control."

"I'll act very patient." Recalling my impromptu counseling session with Jocelyn yesterday, I wondered if I'd already revealed myself as one of the impatient ones with control issues. "Thanks for the tip."

He winked conspiratorially. "No problem." Giving Mr. Grits one last pat, he pushed off the gate. "Don't let Jocelyn get you rattled. No riding on the first day. All you'll have to do today is catch your horse and groom it. Tomorrow you'll learn to pick up its feet and clean them out."

"Eeew, really?"

Waving a hand over his shoulder, he headed for his truck.

"Really?" I said again. How did one clean a horse's feet anyway? And why bother? Horses walked around in dirt and horse poop. What would be the point in cleaning their feet?

Zach climbed into the truck and closed the door. Bracing an elbow on the window frame, he leaned out. "Want me to watch your dog while you're at class?"

"Absolutely not. Do I look stupid to you?"

He pulled his hat off and set it on the seat, so that damp strands of dark hair fell over his forehead as he grinned. "Not a bit," he said, then started the truck and drove away, leaving me standing there wondering what I was going to do with the dog while I went to horse psychology class.

I didn't have a good answer, so I decided to tend to breakfast first. Class started in twenty-five minutes, and, judging from the hand-drawn map that Jocelyn had left in the cabin, I would have to go back to the main road, turn into the other entrance, and drive two miles down a gravel driveway to reach the camp. After doing all that, I would be only a short distance, perhaps less than a mile, down the river from where I was, but there was apparently no direct road from here to there.

The cabin was well stocked with food, and in the bread drawer I found just the right thing for breakfast. "Instant grits." *Huh. Who'd have thought?* My mouth actually started watering as I rummaged for a bowl and turned the porcelain handles on the sink. Overhead the pipes groaned and belched, then coughed out a puff of brown water, which slowly turned clear and smelled of minerals. The hot faucet yielded cold water, and the cold produced hot. It reminded me of the hotel room in Cairo, which I had shared with Geoff while we were working there, and where I stayed after he left, rambling around the dusty stucco rooms, empty except for the realization of a husband gone and a child on the way.

I stood staring at the water running down the drain, lost in those lonely months before Sydney became a reality, and I wrapped her life around mine like an insulating cushion. I hadn't thought about that time in years. I hadn't felt this deep ache, this mournful longing that caused me to look toward the door and sense the lack of someone there. Someone who would walk in and smile with love and desire in his eyes.

Why now? Why was I feeling it now?

Perhaps it was this place, this tiny cottage home where the beams, and the stones, and the mortar spoke of a husband and wife building a life together. Here, it was hard to escape the sense that this was how things should be. It was hard to pretend that I didn't want it, that part of me didn't yearn for a cottage and someone to share it. . . .

Something warm touched my leg, and I started, then realized it was only the dog. Eyes rolling upward, he whined and nuzzled my leg sympathetically.

"Hey, big guy," I said, then went on with hurriedly fixing a breakfast of toast and grits, which we shared in the dining area. The grits soothed my stomach and my mood. By the time I was finished, I felt ready to conquer horse psychology class, lonely-heart longings, fossil thieves, flirty cowboys, and anything else that might come my way.

My confidence lasted all the way to out the Jubilee driveway, and down the two-mile gravel road to the camp. But all the bluster started to fade as I parked among the 1950s-vintage stone buildings, labeled with cute wooden signs that said things like CHUCKWAGON, DRY FORK BUNKHOUSE, GUNSMOKE HALL, and so forth. Zeroing in on the sounds of human activity behind an enormous red barn, I drove around to the back and parked. I got out with Mr. Grits on his leash and walked to the horse corral, where Jocelyn was holding some kind of horse gear in her hand and talking to about two dozen people.

An equal number of horses milled around loose in the opposite corner of the enclosure. Big, unfriendly-looking horses, like the ones who took advantage of little girls at scout camp, carrying them docilely to the farthest point in the pasture, only to suddenly jump, snort wildly, and bolt into an out-of-control gallop toward the barn, crashing over boulders, through creeks, and under low-hanging branches—jumping small bushes while said Girl Scout clung to the saddle, seeing her life pass before her eyes, and promising God that if she survived, she would never come near a horse again. Ever, ever, ever. Amen.

It was a promise I'd kept for many years, quite happily, and something I should have thought about before letting Collie and Jocelyn talk me into this ridiculous plan. I was not meant to be a horsewoman. I'd proven that at a very young age. Even if today's lesson didn't include riding, I didn't want to get in the corral with the horses, or brush them, or clean their feet, or do anything else horse-related.

My stomach rolled and I felt sick. I considered turning around, ducking behind the corner of the barn, leaving, and later coming up with some excuse as to why I didn't make it to class this morning. Then I thought of Zach's know-it-all smirk when he mentioned horse psychology class. He didn't think I could do it, which meant, of course, that I had to prove I could.

Tying Mr. Grits in the shade, I stepped from the shadows of the barn. Jocelyn saw me and waved. "Good morning, Lindsey. Come on in."

The crowd turned, and I realized that most of them were under-legal-drinking-age young. There were about a dozen man-boys looking less than their ages in their baggy T-shirts and grunge-style droopy pants, and an equal number of girls, desperate to affect an appearance of maturity through tight midriff T-shirts and hip-hugger pants. Most were wearing shirts or clothes with orange-and-black UT logos, or sorority and fraternity letters—all-important symbols of group identity.

They watched me like I was a creature from another planet, an unwelcome invader from grown-up land. On the fringes of the group, two middle-aged women and a balding forty-something man gave me kindred looks, clearly hoping I was joining the group.

Jocelyn came forward, and the crowd parted like the Red Sea. "Everyone, this is Lindsey. She'll be participating in our lessons this week." She motioned to me, and the kids worked hard to contain their enthusiasm. "Lindsey, this is Dr. Vaneyken's Psychology 101, and on the fence over there is Dr. Vaneyken."

A frumpy-looking elderly man, perched atop the fence, nodded at me and wrote something in his notebook. I wondered what.

Jocelyn turned back to the group and finished the introductions. "Class, this is Lindsey. Lindsey, this is the class."

"Hi," I said, holding a hand up uncertainly.

"Hi, Lindsey," the crowd replied in singsong unison.

Shifting uncomfortably, I tried to move the focus away from myself. "Well, listen, don't let me disturb you. Go right ahead with what you were doing. I'm just here to watch."

Jocelyn frowned, slightly parental, mildly reproachful. "Of course not. There are no observers here, only active participants in the group. We're here to do a basic study of relationships, outcome-based motivational learning, and our own people skills. We're happy to have you with us." She motioned for me to open the gate and come on in, and the crowd swiveled toward me like spectators at a tennis match, waiting for the return volley.

I stood with a white-knuckled grip on the latch, thinking that—hoping that—maybe I'd accidentally pass out, extricating myself from horse psychology class without having to look like a total wimp. Suddenly it seemed very hot, and my skin felt clammy.

"Sure." *Whose voice was that? Was that me? Did I say that?* "Do you want me to come on in now? Because I can wait, if you're in the middle of something."

"She's worse than I was," muttered one of the middle-aged ladies, the heavyset one with the spiky red hair. Several of the college kids chuckled.

I suddenly understood how the klutzy kids felt in grade school, when no one picked them for dodgeball.

"Nothing but positive energy here," Jocelyn reminded. "We must remember that horses are instinctive animals. They mirror what they see. If they sense hostility, aggression, and fear, they will react with hostility, aggression, and fear. Because they do not have the power of speech, horses form their opinions of others based on nonverbal communication—body language, if you will. They will react to you based on your body language, on the nonverbal signals you give off. They will deliver nonverbal signals in order to communicate their thoughts, feelings, and needs to you. If you perceive the horse's needs and respond in appropriate ways, the relationship will progress. If not, the animal will grow frustrated and fearful. Neither horses nor people do well with relationship partners they do not understand. In order to form a bond of understanding with other people, you have to first understand yourself."

Jocelyn took several rapid strides toward the horse herd, and the horses eyed her warily, lifting their heads and swiveling their ears, the closest ones shrinking back into the pack. "You see, right now these horses are communicating uncertainty through flicking their ears, drawing their faces away, watching me from the corners of their eyes with the lids slightly narrowed. They're reacting both to my aggressive approach and to the presence of strangers in the corral. They're worried about the unfamiliar situation, and their body language is telling me that. If I'm perceptive, if I'm focused outward, rather than inward, on what *they* need rather than what *I* want, I'll stop now, slow down, and give them time to assess the situation, to relax, begin to lower their heads, fully open their eyes, and incline their posture toward me."

Pausing a moment, Jocelyn pointed toward a large beige horse that had stepped from the group and started to approach. "From here, I can begin to build a relationship, if I'm careful. If not . . ." She took another quick step forward, and the horse ducked away, disappearing into the herd. "If not, I'm going to find my efforts unsuccessful. Building a relationship—between a horse and a person, between two people, between a husband and a wife, between estranged family members, between a salesman and a customer, between a therapist and a client, and so forth—is all about the giving and observing of signals. It's all about action and reaction, and mostly about silent cues. Once you learn to read the silent language of a horse, you'll be better able to read the silent language of a person. We tend to think of human relationships, of relationship building, as verbal, but that is a mistake. In any contact between animals of any kind, including humans, studies tell us that up to eighty percent of the meaningful communication is nonverbal. As humans, we want to fall back on the verbal, but in a relationship with a horse, you don't have that option. Your relationship with the horse is strictly nonverbal, and as you improve your relationship with horses, you'll find that you improve your ability to build a bond of trust between yourself and another person."

Jocelyn left the horses and faced us. "For the next two hours, you're going to learn about how you relate to human beings by working with a horse. Your failures and successes in relating to the horse will tell you how you succeed and fail in forming relationships with people."

As if on cue, a cowboy—Jimmy Hawthorne, I recognized when he came closer—entered the corral with a bunch of horse headgear and leashes. Smiling and flirting with the girls in their hip-huggers, he passed them out to students, then gave one to me, grinning and saying, "And one for the dog lady."

My lip twitched feebly. I felt like dropping the nylon-and-rope contraption and running for the hills. Right here in front of all of these strangers, I was about to reveal two long-hidden facts about myself: I wasn't good at relationships, and I was terrified of horses.

Glancing toward the barn, I considered my options as Jimmy finished handing out the horse gear and positioned himself on the fence. From the shadows of the barn aisle, Dan, the cranky ranch manager, was scowling—at me, I thought. Eyes narrow, he glared at Mr. Grits, now rolled over in the shade and licking himself in a less-than-polite way. I walked to the fence and stood near him, just to let Dan know that if he planned to do anything to the dog, he was going to have to go through me.

"Thank you for bringing the extra horses and halters, Jimmy. This group turned out to be a little larger than usual," I heard Jocelyn say. She smiled at Jimmy, then acknowledged Dan with a detached but businesslike nod. "I know you and Dan have work to do, so I won't hold you up any longer."

Disappointed to be missing the show, Jimmy jumped down from the fence, tipped his hat to the fresh-faced college girls, and slouched off toward the barn. Dan delivered one last narrow-eyed glare before heading for his truck. Obviously, Jocelyn's I'm-OK-you're-OK relationship-building techniques were not working on him at all.

TEN

WITHIN A HALF HOUR, IT WAS CLEAR THAT I WAS GOING TO BE A horse psychology washout. Nearly half of the students had managed to catch a horse and tie it in the adjacent corral, where they were to brush the fur while waiting for the rest of us to capture our animals.

I could see immediately that there were problems with the plan. Number one, all of the more docile horses had already been caught. Number two, all of the people who were good with horses had already progressed to the second corral. Which left the horses who didn't like people and the people who didn't like horses together, quite unhappily, in one place.

Even I, who knew nothing about psychology or horses, could see that there was a hole the size of Montana in Jocelyn's lesson curriculum. We could keep at it all day, and the picture would still be the same—three blond sorority sisters, who sounded like part of the cheerleading squad, two nerdy-looking college guys, one middle-aged woman, one middle-aged man, and me, endlessly pursuing horses who walked just fast enough to elude us, and stopped just often enough to tease us into attempting again and again. I suspected that the horses knew what they were doing and saw this as a game.

As Jocelyn had predicted, communication between me and my horse, a whitish-gray animal with long neck hair and a decidedly bad attitude, was mostly nonverbal; however, at one point, I heard him say to another horse, *Hey, look here, I'll let her get just close enough to touch my back; then I'll swing around, put my butt in her face and let out a huge fart.*

He-he-hey, laughed the cappuccino-colored horse the middle-aged woman was trying to catch, *that's a good one. Watch mine. I'm going to let the red-haired lady touch my nose this time, and then . . . Hey, wait, she's holding out a big handful of grass. . . . That's . . . mmm . . . not bad. . . .*

I ground my teeth as the woman slipped the head harness on her horse while he munched the handful of grass. I wanted to raise my hand, point a finger, and say, *She's cheating. Teacher, the lady in the blue sweat suit is cheating. She bribed her horse with grass.*

I didn't, of course, but it was unfair that neither Jocelyn nor the professor noticed the bribe. Nor did they react when the two remaining college boys teamed up to capture their horses, then led them triumphantly from the enclosure, leaving only me, the middle-aged man, and the three sorority sisters, two of whom were in conference on the other side of the corral. The third, a blonde in hip-huggers and a sexy halter top, had slumped down on the fence and dropped her horse harness in the dirt. Resting her chin petulantly on her hand, she rolled her eyes and huffed, "I quit. Like, my horse hates me and he isn't going to just, like, stand there and let me put this thing on his head. This is so majorly lame. If I flunk this class because of this horse deal, my dad's going to be at the dean's office, like, the next day."

Professor Vaneyken glanced up from his notepad, studied her impassively, then wrote some more. I had a feeling he was writing about her. Which also meant he was probably making notes about me. He paused again, watching as two of the sorority sisters teamed up, captured their horses, and led them away, leaving only me, the middle-aged man, and the whiny cheerleader on the fence.

Jocelyn returned to our corral and stopped near the gate. No doubt she was ready to move the class along, and we were holding things up. She observed us with the impassive but hopeful expression of a mother watching toddlers trying to fit the pieces into a puzzle box.

The cheerleader smacked her lips, squinting at her companions in the next corral. "This is impossible, and my horse is a jerk."

That seemed to be Jocelyn's cue to intervene. "Is it impossible, or are you just making it impossible?"

"Uhhk, no-o." The cheerleader coughed, throwing up her hands. "All the good horses are already gone, and, like, this one is a butthead."

Jocelyn's dark brows straightened thoughtfully. "So, because the horse is not reacting as you would like, he has a problem. Is that correct?"

"Uhhh, yeah. Ex-*act*-ly." Standing up, she brushed off her hip-huggers, peeled a piece of horse hair from her shirt, and let it float to the ground. "It's, like, impossible. I got a bad horse, you know?"

"Would it change your opinion to know that, last week, that very same horse—who is called Boggy, by the way—completed all five tasks of the horse therapy class in record time, in partnership with an elderly Chinese gentleman who grew up in Taiwan and had never been within twenty feet of a horse before?" Jocelyn asked. "In fact, on day one last week, Boggy was the very first horse haltered and taken to the other corral."

The cheerleader flushed, properly chagrined for a moment before she lifted her chin with a defiant jive. "Well, it must be in a bad mood today. Maybe it's PMS-ing." Chuckles came from the other corral, and she snorted irritably.

Jocelyn answered with a patient smile. "Well, in the first place, the horse is a male, so PMS is unlikely, and in the second place, horses are who they are. They aren't emotional; they are reactionary. They react to their environments. Boggy isn't trying to prove anything, or make you mad, or hurt your feelings. His behavior is not aimed at you; it is a reaction to your behavior, which, of course, means that you have complete control over this situation."

Jocelyn raised her voice for the benefit of the students in the other corral. "Remember that, in any encounter, the only thing you can control is your own actions and reactions. You cannot dictate the actions of the other person, or in this case, the horse, but you can send the right signals to get what you want. If you are often baffled by the reactions others have to you, it is probably because you are unaware of the silent signals you send through your posture, your facial gestures, your tone of voice, the amount of personal space you maintain, and so forth. Ever wondered why people don't listen when you try to assert yourself, or why people back away when you're trying to be friendly, or why you're never the one people seek out in a crowded room? Body language. Silent signals. Mixed signals. The trick is to focus outward, not inward."

Jocelyn retrieved the harness from the dirt and the cheerleader smiled, obviously assuming that Jocelyn was going to catch her horse for her.

Jocelyn only laid the harness over the fence, and said, "It's not good to leave these lying around. The horse could step in it and go into panic mode, and then we would have a crisis." Clasping her hands behind her back, she silently indicated that she would not be bailing us out. The last thing I wanted to be was an object lesson for a bunch of college kids. I made up my mind that, one way or another, if I had to jump on like John Wayne and tackle it, I was going to get the head harness on my horse.

Determined, I strode toward the animal and firmly said, "Hold still," which seemed to work. He waited while I untangled the harness and inched forward, hoping, silently praying that he would put his muzzle in the noseband, so I could buckle the remaining part behind his ears.

I moved closer, one baby step, two, three, as Jocelyn worked with the cheerleader on the other side of the corral.

"Madison, do you often find that building new relationships doesn't come as easily as you would like it to?"

Madison, close to her breaking point, sighed. "Yes."

"And why do you think that is?"

"I don't know. Some people are just jerks. They don't like me because I'm . . . well . . . pretty."

Jocelyn paused. I realized I'd stopped the advance toward my horse and was frozen with a cold sweat dripping down my back. I glanced over my shoulder at Jocelyn, and my horse swiveled and stuck his rear end in my face. He proceeded to pass gas and stroll off, looking self-satisfied.

The rumble of a vehicle passing the corral caught my attention, and I glanced up just in time to see Zach slowing down to watch me as I fanned away the cloud of methane. Glancing over her shoulder, the cheerleader noticed the truck, flipped her blond hair, and gave the cowboy a sexy smile and a little wave.

Zach waved in response, then turned his attention back to me. Stopping the truck by the fence, he had the nerve to point at me and my horse and make a hand motion that indicated we were supposed to be in the other corral by now.

Giving him a disgusted look, I held out the head harness and mouthed, *Help.*

He grinned and shook his head, then pointed at the harness and pretended to buckle an invisible version on his own head. *Simple, see?* his pantomime said.

Shrugging I let the harness fall to my side and sagged pathetically. For just an instant I thought he was actually going help me, but then Jocelyn delivered a territorial glare that clearly meant, *Buzz off.*

Winking, Zach gave me the thumbs-up, then let off the brakes and drove away.

I groaned, feeling like a failure as Jocelyn resumed her one-on-one therapy with the too-sexy-for-her-horse cheerleader.

"So, then, your focus is mainly on you in a given encounter. On how you look, and your perceptions of what the other party is thinking about you?"

Crossing her arms, the cheerleader jutted her slim hips to one side. "I dunno. I guess so."

"Did you ask the name of the horse?" Jocelyn queried. "Did you consider that knowing his name might be useful in building trust?"

The cheerleader slouched. "Yeah, I guess it might have."

"Do you often forget people's names when you're introduced, or fail to retain information about them after the conversation is over?"

The coed's eyes widened in surprise. "Yeah, I do."

Jocelyn nodded with the keen look of a spider luring a fly deep into the web. "When you enter a conversation, are you listening to what the other person has to say, or are you mostly focused on what you're going to say and how you think the other party will react to it?"

"The second one."

Jocelyn nodded. "You see, self-focus is death to personal encounters and to relationships. If, when you approach people, they perceive genuine interest, if they see that your focus is on them, they will respond positively, and I can promise that ninety-five percent of the time, it won't matter how you look. The horse, obviously, is not reacting to your looks. He is reacting to your lack of empathic behavior, to your silent signals. Try approaching him this time with your focus on him. Say his name with interest and warmth. Think about what he is feeling and what you're asking from him. The horse's natural instinct is to flee from entrapment. You are asking him to submit control of his head, the most vulnerable part of his body, to someone he doesn't know. He has to feel that he can trust you not to hurt him, to keep his feelings and needs and fears in consideration if he enters into this partnership with you."

The cheerleader was clearly having what Oprah would have called a lightbulb moment. "OK," she breathed, suddenly becoming animated. "I get it." Lips parting into a broad, perfect smile, she blinked in astonishment. "I really get it."

Jocelyn nodded with approval. "Good, then try it again."

Shaking the dust off her head harness, the cheerleader moved toward her horse, talking and cooing, saying his name, looking him in the eye and promising that they were going to be very good friends. The treatment worked. After only a small misstep or two, she had successfully haltered Boggy and led him to the other paddock. Passing from the failure corral to the success corral, she stopped and jiggled up and down, giggling and saying, "Yes! Yes! Yes!"

Her boisterous exit left only me and the middle-aged man in the loser's bracket. The man had somehow managed to lock his arms around his horse's neck and was trying to get the harness on without letting go. Meanwhile, the horse was dragging him through the corral, occasionally stepping on the toes of his Nikes, while the man cussed a blue streak.

Jocelyn redirected her attention to him. "How are things going between you and Snowflake, Robert?"

"Fine," Robert grunted, his voice strained with the effort. "I'm just . . . trying . . . to get this—owww, my foot—thing on his—owww . . . head." The horse yanked away, pulling the harness from Robert's hand and dragging him across the enclosure.

"How are things going now, Robert?" Jocelyn asked patiently.

"Great," Robert ground out. When the horse finally stopped, he fished for the harness with his foot, trying to snag it without letting go of the horse. Sensing the ploy, Snowflake dragged Robert a few feet farther away, so that the harness was out of reach.

Robert roared, then let his forehead drop against his arm and wiped the sweat from his eyes. "This is impossible. This horse is uncooperative. He knows what I want. He's just trying to irritate me."

Pursing her lips thoughtfully, Jocelyn commented, "Actually, Snowflake is a female."

"No wonder she's such a pain in the butt."

Jocelyn smiled at the joke, then turned serious again. "Do you often find that people are uncooperative with you? Unwilling to consider your ideas or acquiesce to your wishes?"

Robert regained his footing. "Well . . . yeah," he barked gruffly, as if Jocelyn were wasting his time and everyone else's. "Some people get off on being a pain in the butt. I've been with the sheriff's department for fifteen years. I ought to know."

"So in your years as a police officer, did you find that some people were uncooperative, or most people were uncooperative?"

"Most people," Robert answered. "Most people don't want to do what you want 'em to do. That's life. I don't care what some candy-pants psychology book says; sometimes you gotta get tough." He swiveled toward Jocelyn. "Listen, lady, I'm not one of your little college kids. I know how the real world works. I'm only here to get through this class so I can move up on the pay scale at the department, *sabe*?"

"Well, I can see how you would feel that way," Jocelyn's tone was sympathetic. "It's never pleasant when you're forced to do something you don't want to do."

"No, it ain't."

For the first time Robert and Jocelyn were simpatico. Scooping the horse harness out of the dirt, she handed it to him. "People generally don't respond well to being bullied."

"Darned straight," Robert agreed, trying to sort out the harness while keeping his arms around Snowflake.

"In fact, the more someone feels leaned on, the more they resist. It's kind of like Newton's Law—for every action, there's an equal and opposite reaction, right?"

"Exactly. Tell that to the county commissioners. They're always trying to cram this New Age, liberal, politically correct stuff on us. First they're hiring a girl deputy because she's got some ignorant college degree, and now they want us all to do this continuing-education crap. Like we've got time for that."

Jocelyn watched Robert renew his struggle with the horse, the corners of her lips turning up. "People need to feel like they have . . . well, some control over things. Like with you, for instance. It probably isn't taking the courses you resent, as much as the fact that you were forced into it."

"Darned straight. And on my own time, too. You know, I got a life."

Jocelyn sighed sympathetically. "Everyone does. Being bullied into taking coursework just to keep your job is bound to cause resentment, especially when you weren't consulted first. It's always more productive to try working with someone first, instead of descending into a confrontation. Given the situation, of course you're going to be less than cooperative. I mean, it's kind of like having someone walk into your corral, grab you around the neck, holler threats in your ear, and try to force a halter onto your head." Without waiting for an answer, she turned around and started across the paddock.

Everyone in the far corral suddenly fell silent, and Robert choked like he'd swallowed an ice cube. Muttering niceties through gritted teeth, he released his hold on the horse, and Snowflake stood calmly as Robert untangled the halter and buckled it into place. No problem.

He led Snowflake away, which left only me in the corral. Lindsey Attwood, the biggest failure in horse psychology class. Outdone by a bunch of wet-behind-the-ears college students, two empty-nesters returning to college, and a disgruntled sheriff's deputy. What was wrong with me? Had these last six exceedingly tame years of working at the museum completely asphyxiated the intrepid, independent woman who traveled the world seeking magnificent treasures? Where was the woman who ignored her fear of heights to scale a hundred-foot cliff, worked hanging from a belaying harness to unearth the remains of a woolly mammoth in Siberia, or dug up fossilized sauropod eggs on a riverbank in Argentina, with hungry alligators practically in her hip pocket?

Who was this sniveling weenie who let herself be intimidated by a horse?

"How are things going, Lindsey?" Jocelyn asked. "How are you getting along with Sleepy?"

"Just fine." The horse even had a docile name. Sleepy, like one of the Seven Dwarfs. "I'm trying not to be too aggressive. I wouldn't want Sleepy to feel forced into anything."

Jocelyn chuckled at the joke, and on the fence the professor glanced up with a mildly surprised look, then went back to furiously writing on his pad. About me, I was sure. *Thirty-something female, unable to capture horse. Obviously suffers from horse phobia. Displaying mildly uncooperative behavior and extreme signs of stress, possible symptoms of recent nervous breakdown. Note perspiration on forehead and damp, clingy nature of T-shirt, flush in facial region. May be suffering from acute embarrassment and—*

"Well, that's good thinking," Jocelyn remarked. "But you've pretty much maintained a distance of several feet throughout this entire exercise. Have you any idea why that might be?"

I hate horses, and in particular, I hate this one. No doubt he senses hostility. "None," I said. "When I get near him, he moves away. I don't think he . . ." Remembering her conversations with the cheerleader and the cop, I astutely glanced under my horse's belly. Boy parts. I didn't know much about horses, but I knew enough to tell boys from girls. ". . . he feels very good today. He seems to be a little flatulent."

A puff of laughter burst past Jocelyn's lips, cracking her therapist's mask for a moment before she wiped away the grin. "That's normal for horses," she informed me. "So have you any other ideas as to why you and Sleepy are maintaining a distance?"

"Not a one," I replied. "I'm trying to be as open, honest, nonthreatening, unself-centered as I can, but it isn't working. When I approach, he walks away."

Tapping a finger to her lips, Jocelyn did her pretend psychologist-think. "And have you noticed that when he stops walking, you stop advancing?"

"I do?" Squinting upward, into my brain, I tried to remember. I had the uncomfortable feeling that Jocelyn was right. The best thing, I decided, was just to admit the truth, and in a backhanded way, let Jocelyn know not to expect much from me in horse class. "Well, to be honest, I don't like horses very much. I had a bad summer-camp experience when I was young. I'm afraid of horses."

Jocelyn didn't look surprised. "Do you follow this pattern with people, as well—pursuing contact only at a nonthreatening distance, backing off when it looks like the other person might be interested in closing that space, forming a relationship, so to speak?"

I turned to her with the strange sense of having my mind read. "Well, I wouldn't say . . . I don't . . . I mean, I have close friendships. There's my sister, and Collie, my daughter, of course. I'm not afraid to be close to people, if that's what you mean."

"New people?"

A lump rose in my throat, and I swallowed hard, surprised by the sudden rush of emotion, or indignance, or whatever it was. "Well, not . . . I work in the basement of a museum, and when I'm not working, I'm shuttling Sydney to her activities. I don't meet new people."

"Don't meet them, or aren't willing to try to meet them? Do you think it's possible that you're letting past pain dictate present behavior? That you've decided to forgo relationships altogether, rather than suffer through another loss of someone you care about?"

Suddenly I felt like a drug addict at an intervention, or a defendant on trial for my life. A thirty-something divorced mom charged with willful injury to potential relationships. In the innermost part of my soul, I knew she was right. The breakdown of my marriage, and then Geoff's betrayal when I needed him most, had left me emotionally raw. For eight years now I'd done everything I could to insulate myself from further damage. "I don't know. Maybe."

Laying a hand on Sleepy's shoulder, Jocelyn stroked his hair as she spoke privately to me. "It's absolutely up to you where you want to go from here, Lindsey—with the horse, I mean. It isn't like you've any need to pass the course. You and Sleepy can continue circling the corral all week. No one's going to force you to go any further."

I nodded, feeling relieved. Even if Jocelyn's diagnosis was right, she still remembered that I wasn't really here for horse psychology class.

Winking, she patted my arm and started off, adding, "Of course, you could do that forever, and all you would have done is walk around the corral."

She was gone before I could answer. I stood in her wake, feeling as if I were stepping outside my body, hovering overhead, watching the terrified dark-haired woman standing in dust with a useless bit of rope in her hands. For eight years she'd been wandering around the corral, dancing with various partners at a distance.

I slipped back into my body as Jocelyn rang the cowbell on the gate. "OK, people, that's class. If you managed to complete the first task of the week—haltering your horse and beginning the bonds of a relationship—please take your horse through the corral to the pasture gate, give him a big hug, and turn him loose in the grass. Enjoy your time today journaling about your experience and completing the treasure hunt on today's handout. I'll look forward to seeing your answers. We'll meet in the picnic grounds down by the river at three o'clock for our afternoon discovery and sharing session."

Jocelyn returned to the failure corral as the students took their happy horses to a lush, green pasture that looked like heaven compared to the dry, dusty paddocks.

"What about Sleepy?" I asked. "Should I open the gate so he can go with the others?"

Jocelyn's forehead straightened into a bewildered line. "Oh, no. Of course not. Horses are allowed to move to the pasture only after they and their therapy partners have completed step one. Sleepy will have to stay in here." Seeing the shocked look on my face, she added, "Don't worry. There's plenty of food and water in here for him. Of course, he'd rather be in the pasture, but we've got to stick with the rules."

"Oh . . ." I muttered, glancing reluctantly at poor Sleepy, now standing in the corner of the corral sorrowfully watching his friends stride off into the knee-deep grass.

Jocelyn motioned toward my car. "You know what? You might run on into town to the Big Lizard. It's lunchtime, and Melvin Blue will be there. He's the one I told you about, who's made a project of photographing the fossil sites and petroglyphs around here. I think it would be worth your time to talk to him, but after the lunch hour he's harder to catch. Anyway, just go by the diner and ask anyone for Melvin Blue, and they'll introduce you."

"All right," I said, checking the time. Noon. Not much time to waste, if I was going to catch this Blue fellow. "See you later, then." Giving Sleepy one last guilty look, I headed for my car, trailing an invisible cloud of horse psychology failure behind me.

ELEVEN

I LEFT FOR TOWN WITH SOME BOTTLED WATER AND A TUPPERWARE dish from the cabin, supposing that I could tie Mr. Grits in the shade with water to drink and buy him some dog food at the general store. As we cruised along the Jubilee driveway, he seemed happy to be riding shotgun on another adventure. Sticking his head out the window, he let out a giant "Baa-roo!" as the breeze lifted his ears and fanned his jowls into a huge smiley face.

A giggle tickled my stomach, breaking through my lingering horse psychology worries, until they fell away in tiny pieces, and I just laughed and laughed and laughed. I hadn't felt that light in months, maybe years. As we topped the hill, I stretched my hand out the window, touching the breeze, sensing that if I let go, I could soar away from all the debris of my life, and land in a completely new place.

The surreal feeling followed me out the gateway of Jubilee Ranch and all the way to town. The tiny village of Loveland seemed to take on an otherworldly glow in the golden midday light. Crossing the river, I watched the sun glitter like diamond dust on the water. I pictured the young bride floating away into adventure and love, like something from a movie or a storybook, the kind of thing that didn't happen in real life. Women with jobs and bills and custody problems didn't just drift off on the whims of a river. Did they?

Lost in thought, I almost missed the turnoff to the Over the Moon General Store and the Big Lizard Diner. The brakes squealed a complaint as I whipped into the parking lot, which was crowded with cars, pickup trucks, and livestock trailers. Apparently most of the local population gathered at the Big Lizard at noon. Which made me wonder if Zach did. I caught myself looking around for the Jubilee Ranch truck as I pulled up near the general store. Disappointment pinpricked inside me when his truck wasn't there. Shaking off the thought, I hopped out and trotted up the stairs onto the wide front porch. The old wooden door with its oval-shaped glass was unlocked, so I turned the handle and went inside, even though the place seemed to be empty.

The Over the Moon looked like a combination general store, rock shop, tourist trap, and museum; the wall shelves lined with various rocks and fossils, intermixed with boxes of bolts, nuts, lightbulbs, food, camping items, shotgun shells, fishing bait, and plumbing supplies. The high rock wall behind the counter was covered with framed pictures of fossils and petroglyphs. On the counter was a display of postcards and photo albums with a handwritten sign that read, *Disappearing treasures of Texas. Original petroglyph and fossil photography by Melvin Blue.*

"Hello?" I said, crossing the room. The old-fashioned Coke machine rattled and belched in answer, but other than that, the place was silent. Taped to the cash register was a note saying that Melvin was at the diner having lunch, and if I needed something, I should come over there and find him. If it was an emergency, I could take what I needed now and pay for it later. Signed, *Melvin. Have a good day, y'all.*

"Imagine that," I muttered, surveying the store, considering a world where doors were left unlocked and people paid for things on the honor system. A little utopia, an island of blind trust in a suspicious world.

Melvin's pictures told another story. Flipping through the dusty photo album, I gaped at his collection of before and after pictures— sites that once contained petroglyphs and fossils, plundered and destroyed by vandals and thieves. Huge pieces of rock had been removed, sometimes with surgical precision, sometimes through the clumsy work of a hammer and chisel, but always leaving behind a jagged white scar like the one at Jubilee Ranch. Occasionally the items had not been removed, but merely defaced with cans of spray paint, destroyed in one careless, thoughtless instant, after having survived the wind and the weather for hundreds of years.

Each set of photographs had been carefully labeled as to the location, the time the photographs were taken, and whether the stolen items had been recovered. Notations in the recovery column were few. The final set of photographs, also bearing an empty recovery/prosecution column, were from Jubilee Ranch.

Letting out a long sigh, I closed Melvin's book, his proof of dozens of horrible offenses. Less than a foot away hung his hastily scrawled greeting, extending blind trust to all who passed through the Over the Moon. How did he find the strength to do that in a world where people were not always trustworthy?

Sometimes you have to trust anyway. . . . The voice in my head surprised me. I didn't recognize it. It was unusually serene and confident, comforting in a way I couldn't describe. A sort of Zen Lindsey. She seemed wise, and very together. She was like my laughter as I topped the hill at Jubilee Ranch and felt like I could fly. She was like the bridal veil floating lighter than air, destination unknown.

She was something completely new.

I thought about her as I left the store, hopped into the Jeep, and idled across the parking lot to the café. I liked the way Zen Lindsey felt. No fear, only a blind faith that things would turn out as they were supposed to, a trust like that in Melvin's note, a willingness to embrace life's possibilities and the existence of a larger plan directed by a higher authority.

I tried to hold on to the feeling as I parked under a mesquite tree close to the Big Lizard, and tied Mr. Grits to the bumper with his water bowl nearby. "Now you stay right here," I said. The voice sounded like Zen Lindsey's, and Mr. Grits cocked an ear, his head turning to one side, so that both he and Barbie regarded me from a bemused angle. "It's OK," I said, scratching his ears. "I'm having a moment of . . ." What exactly? "Something."

Walking toward the diner, I looked up at the railroad car windows, trying to decide where to go in. There was only one visible entrance—a storm door hanging partway askew on the silver Airstream trailer between the cars, but from the sound of things, that was the kitchen. I could hear the *clink-clink* of dishes rattling and the sizzle of someone flipping meat on a grill. The windows on the dining cars were open, the weathered screens catching the sun at an angle that made them practically opaque, so that I couldn't see anything inside. I stood squinting upward, taking in the lay of the place, listening to conversations drifting through the screens.

"Door's on the end," someone said from up above. "Either car. South car's got a domino game goin' on."

"Thanks," I replied, feeling like I should have said, *Much obliged*, or something more down-home. Opting for the north car, the one closest to the general store, I walked around to the wooden steps on the end.

The door opened before I got there, and a tall man stepped onto the platform, tipping the brim of his cowboy hat. "Welcome to the Big Lizard, young lady. I'm Dandy Roads. I'm the part-time cook, game ranger, head fly swatter, pastor at the weddin' chapel, and occasional constable around here. You need a mess a' barbecue, got a skunk under your house, legal problems, or want to get married, I'm your man. You must be Lindsey Attwood." When I didn't answer right away, he added, "Jocelyn called and said you were comin'. Melvin's down at the last table on the right, waitin' on ya."

"Oh . . . good," I replied, a little surprised that he knew why I was there, since Jocelyn had said to keep the Jubilee investigation a secret.

Poking his head in the door, Dandy Roads called out, "Hey, Melvin, here's your gal from Denver." Patting me on the shoulder, he explained, "We get a lot of writers around here. What with them dinosaur tracks that got stolen out at Jubilee Ranch, and the Lover's Oak, and then all them couples that got hitched here last month. Set a record. Got our bid in for the *Guinness Book* to certify it. Most simultaneous nuptials on an inland waterway. The ABC station come all the way out of Austin and got it on videotape." Lowering his brows, he turned momentarily serious, wagging a finger at me. "Wasn't no publicity stunt, neither. We did 'em once under the Lover's Oak, then again on the river, just to be safe. No one knew if it would be good enough just to be near the oak, or if you'd have to be under it."

"Good enough for what?" I wasn't sure I wanted to know.

Skewing one eye, he peered at me as if it were a silly question. "Why, for the marriages to stick, of course. A couple gets together under the Lover's Oak, it sticks. Guaranteed."

"Oh," I muttered, thinking cynical divorce thoughts I knew I'd better not share. Dandy Roads clearly took this oak-tree thing seriously. If only keeping a marriage together were really that simple.

"Well, guess I'd better get goin'. Got a weddin' to perform, let's see . . . in about two hours." Checking his pocket watch, the constable, game warden, and barbecue cook excused himself.

"Nice meeting you."

"You too, ma'am." Stepping back, he held the door open wider so that I could go in. Remembering the bride and groom in the canoe the day before, I contemplated hanging around town for a while after lunch, so I could see today's wedding for myself. "Do they all go canoeing down the river after they get married?"

"Well, most of 'em." Dandy's eyes narrowed thoughtfully as he gazed toward the water. "Ya see, it's a good way to start off, a good reminder to these young folks . . . well, they ain't all young. Last week I performed nuptials for a man eighty-two and a woman seventy-nine—but anyway, setting out together in a marriage is a lot like setting out on the river. Some parts will be rough; some will be smooth. You can't see from the start where it's gonna travel and where it's gonna end up. Sometimes it'll turn a sharp corner; sometimes it'll drift along awhile. Thing is, no matter what the river does, both parties gotta paddle equally, see? Piloting a canoe down the river is all about working together to keep things afloat. One party doesn't paddle, the canoe gets all whompy and turns over in the water. Paddle against each other, the canoe doesn't go anywhere, and eventually the current runs the boat into the rocks, see?"

He nodded expectantly, and I commented that I could see how it would be similar. Not that I was any authority on the subject of marriage and relationships.

"Dandy!" Melvin Blue called from inside the diner. "Quit talkin' her ear off and send her in. We ain't got all day. I gotta get the nuptial canoe ready before the weddin'."

"All right, all right." Dandy ushered me through the door, then leaned through after me and called out in a booming voice, "Weddin' at two o'clock, everybody."

Murmurs of interest went up from various customers in the booths, and a gray-haired woman about halfway down the car asked, "How many?"

"Just one," Dandy answered. "That ain't bad for a Tuesday. So far we got two nuptials on Thursday, a double-double with two sets of twins on Friday night, and then, don't nobody forget, this Saturday's the big Hawthorne shebang. Dinner on the grounds by the river, then the nuptials under the Lover's Oak. Only thing better than a weddin' is a re-weddin'."

Everyone else murmured in agreement, and as I passed down the aisle, I could see that matrimony was popular entertainment in this town. People were checking their watches and hurrying to finish eating. The lady in the middle booth called out, "Could you hurry up my chicken-fried steak, Vanita? I have some tea cakes I made last night, waiting in the Frigidaire. I just knew there would be a wedding today. I'll use these up this week, and bake fresh ones on Saturday for the Hawthorne renewing."

The waitress, a woman in her sixties with graying hair pulled into a leather ponytail holder, rolled her eyes and leaned close to me as she passed by. "Belvanne's been bringing those darned tea cakes to the weddings for fifty years. They're as dry as paste and the icing tastes like lard, but she's sure they're good luck. Maybe after eating those, the new husband appreciates his wife's cooking. I bet poor old Jasper Hawthorne still remembers Belvanne's tea cakes from his first wedding, all those years ago. Heck, he probably still has some. They last forever. Like rocks." Shuffling the tray onto one arm, she shook my hand. "I'm Vanita Blue. Jocelyn called to say you'd be coming by."

Vanita escorted me to the last booth on the left, the one right by the doorway to the Airstream trailer, which was, indeed, the kitchen, a strange conglomeration of blackened fry grills, three old refrigerators ranging from harvest orange to olive green, and a pink stove that looked like it was from the fifties. Overhead, the ceiling tiles were caked thick with grease. The floor was a combination of peeling Formica, plywood, and press-and-stick faux brick that seemed not to have been applied in any particular pattern.

Looking at the kitchen made me wonder if I should eat there or not. If anyone else in the room was bothered, they didn't show it. Throughout the dining car, people were happily shoveling down gravy-covered meals, and in the dining car across the kitchen, customers were eating while playing dominoes.

The cook stepped into the Airstream from the outside door, carrying a huge bag of potatoes, and I could see why no one was complaining. He was at least six-foot-four, with broad shoulders, strong arms, an ample stomach, and legs that bowed slightly under the load. He was wearing an undersized Chiquita bananas T-shirt that made him look like Baby Huey. Smiling, he lifted a greasy spatula, greeting me in a friendly manner that belied his crusty appearance. I waved back as I slid into the booth across from Melvin Blue. Vanita introduced us, then hurried off to fill someone's coffee cup.

His gaze darting around suspiciously, Melvin leaned across the table, as if we were secret operatives having a clandestine rendezvous. He looked like Santa Claus on a Western vacation, with wavy white hair, partially covered by a straw cowboy hat, a thick beard that curled around his turquoise and silver bolo neck tie, and twinkling eyes that matched the stones in his necklace. His skin was leathery from hours in the sun, and thick wrinkles fanned from his eyes. The sleeves of his plaid shirt were rolled up, showing a tattoo that said, IWAKUNI USMC 62. A marine. My father would have loved him. His gaze swept one side of the room, then the other, as if he were checking for bugs or hidden cameras.

I waited, not at all sure what to say, and wondering if Melvin Blue might be a little touched in the head—an aging soldier who'd spent too many years in the wilds of Texas, cataloging rocks.

The elderly ladies at the table across the aisle appeared to be wondering, too. Pausing in the middle of sharing a slice of pie, they eyed us with wary curiosity.

"So you're the one," Melvin said, loud enough that they could hear.

The ladies leaned closer, their forks dangling in midair.

"The one?" I repeated.

"Sure. The *one.*" Wheeling a hand in the air, Melvin leaned over the table, whispering, "Just play along for a minute, all right? This'll give the old Blum sisters something to talk about all day."

"Ohhh-kay." I nodded slowly, though I had no idea what kind of game we were playing. "I'm the one."

Across the aisle, the vinyl seat made a flatulent sound as one of the Blum sisters scooted closer. Melvin glanced over, and she batted her lashes, delicately scooping her napkin off the floor.

Melvin winked at me and said, "Everything go as expected?"

"Huh?" I felt like an actor who'd forgotten to read the script. "Oh . . . sure. Definitely."

"Any surprises?"

For some reason, I thought about my splash fight with Zach Truitt, and a little smile tugged my lips. "A few. Nothing I couldn't handle."

The Blum sisters were about to tumble out of their seats. The taller one pretended to scratch her ear, but instead held her hand cupped around it.

Melvin grinned. "Looks like they were good surprises."

I sighed thoughtfully. "Well, I don't know. It was definitely . . . something . . . unexpected." I realized I was blushing, reliving the Zach Truitt fantasy I'd entertained atop the mountain that morning. I wondered again what it might be like to kiss him.

Melvin leaned close, and my daydream popped like a soap bubble. "I've got the goods over at the store."

I wasn't sure how to respond to that. *Goods? What goods?* Across the aisle, the Blum sisters widened their eyes beneath tall hairdos, and whispered to each other.

Melvin grinned like the Cheshire cat. Seeming satisfied that we'd stirred the ladies up enough, he gave a little shrug toward the door. "C'mon," he said, sliding to the edge of the booth and sticking his head into the kitchen. "Hey, Cookie, send her order over to the store, will ya?"

"She didn't order," the cook hollered from somewhere within the Airstream.

Melvin glanced back at me. "Did you want something?"

"Cheeseburgers," I replied, thinking that, since Zach wasn't here to see it, I'd treat Mr. Grits to one last hamburger meal before we switched over to dog food. "Three."

"Comin' up," the cook replied. The kitchen door opened with a rusty groan, and I heard him say, "Afternoon, Gracie. What can I getcha today?"

"Coffee. But don't stop what you're doing there. I'll get it. I just came by to fill my thermos. It's been a long night. We had a stakeout at the locker plant in San Saline. Finally caught the hamburger thief around midnight. Had him red-handed, so to speak." Crossing the kitchen, Gracie noticed Melvin and me in the first booth and poked her head through the door.

The Blum sisters sat motionless with anticipation.

Gracie exchanged greetings with Melvin, then turned to me. "I got your e-mail. Didn't have time to answer back right then, but I put out some feelers to see who around here might be buying diamond blades and so forth. Things go all right last night at the Jubilee?" she asked, and I nodded in response.

The Blum sisters jerked closer together, whispering something about *Jubilee* and *diamonds*.

"Maybe something will come of it," I replied, having the uncomfortable feeling that more than just the Blum sisters were listening. In the surrounding booths, people were regarding Gracie, me, and our conversation with mild curiosity.

Opening the top on her thermos, Gracie tipped her hat back and peered inside. "I hope so. Anything else I can do to help?"

"Nothing so far," I replied. "I want to look around some more this afternoon. And I sent an e-mail out to"—*my ex-husband*—"a business associate to see if he could add any helpful information. I don't know if it will lead to anything, but I thought it was worth a try. You may hear from him. Geoff Attwood."

The Blum sisters whispered, *business associate* and *lead to something*.

Frowning over her shoulder, Gracie exchanged a private glance with Melvin. "All right, then, let me know what you come up with." Pushing off the door frame, she said good-bye to Melvin and me, suddenly turning on the Texas charm. "Y'all have a good day now, y'hear?"

"See you later, Gracie," Melvin replied, then glanced covertly toward the Blum sisters and smiled at me. "So, like I said, I got something at the store you need to see."

We stood up and Melvin tipped his hat to the Blum sisters. "Afternoon, ladies."

"Why, Melvin," the taller one said, fanning her lashes innocently. "I didn't even notice you over there."

TWELVE

——◆◆◆——

MELVIN STARTED APOLOGIZING AS SOON AS WE WERE OUT THE door. "Sorry about all the dramatics in there. It's part of my God-given mission to give the old Blum sisters something to talk about. This ought to keep them going awhile. They'll be all over town trying to figure out who you are and whether you're here to get married or buy some of my pictures."

"More likely the latter," I said, as we crossed the parking lot. The words had a wistful sound that surprised me—a sad, lonely, looking-for-love quality that was both obvious and embarrassing.

Melvin delivered an acute glance, his round red cheeks lifting into a smile. "Well, never say never. Strange things happen in this town. We're famous for a reason, you know. Folks pass under the Lover's Oak, and bang, next thing you know we're hitching 'em up and sending 'em down the river. That's how it was with Vanita and me." Stopping in the parking lot, he gazed down the road toward the massive tree, and I sensed a story coming on. I had a feeling he'd told it many times before. "She was sitting on the fender of a broke-down 'forty-two Ford in a pretty blue dress, waiting on her brother to hitch a ride into San Saline and come back with a replacement for the radiator hose. I came along on my way to meet some chums for the big USO dance, and I patched that radiator hose with some rawhide and a piece of tire tube." He illustrated with his hands, and in my mind I saw the young woman in the starched blue dress, peeking carefully over her rescuer's shoulder, trying not to muss her clothes.

His face clouded with memory, Melvin went on, "When I got the thing running, she wanted to drive to town and find her brother, only she didn't drive, so I got in the car and gave her a driving lesson. We went off down the road all catywhompus. I never laughed so hard in my life, and by the time we'd got a mile or so, I was sure she was the prettiest thing I'd ever seen. She had the biggest brown eyes, and a smile that looked like a movie star's. I knew if we got as far as the USO dance, some better-looking fella was gonna snap her up, so I wasn't even sorry when that car broke down again. I could have put the patch back on the radiator hose, but by then neither of us cared if we made it to the dance. We just walked back to the Lover's Oak and danced right there under the branches. Two weeks later we were married right on that spot." Eyelids lowering, he drew a long breath, then exhaled a slow, contented sigh. "I tell that story to the young folks who come through here, so they'll know it doesn't matter what you read in the magazines, or what those TV talk shows say. It's possible for two people to be in love all their lives. That's why Vanita and I named the store Over the Moon, because that's the way it is when you're in love—you're over the moon."

"That's really nice," I said, but in my experience love was a fickle and sometimes painful thing, better left alone. "The story, I mean. It's a nice story." I knew, of course, that the Lover's Oak was just a tree, and it couldn't really bring people everlasting bliss. Melvin and Vanita were just lucky.

Still, there was an ache, a yearning in me as I gazed toward the oak and thought of the young soldier and the brown-eyed girl in the blue dress. I wanted to believe it was possible to stumble upon true love completely by accident.

Shaking my head, I banished the fanciful idea. "Well, I passed under the tree with a big, smelly white dog. So I suppose there isn't much hope for me."

Melvin raised a finger astutely as we started toward the store again. "Yeah, but did you like the dog better after you passed under the tree than before?"

I chuckled. "Well, I'm not an animal person, and he's still with me"—I pretended to consider the question—"but that's really just because I'm trying to keep Zach Truitt from making off with him."

"Ahhh," Melvin replied thoughtfully, steepling his fingers in a wise way that made me uncomfortable.

"Long story." I changed the subject. "Anyway, I was in the store a few minutes ago, looking at your pictures. I hope you don't mind. I guess Jocelyn told you why I'm really here?"

"Sure." Suddenly Melvin was all business. The jolly backwoods philosopher was gone. "I hope you catch whoever stole the tracks from the Jubilee. There's been an awful run of that kind of thing lately, and I think some of it's got to be connected. A few of the jobs are real professional, like the one at the Jubilee, and then some it's obvious are done by amateurs. I think the shoddy jobs might be folks who saw newspaper articles about the thefts and got ideas that they could make themselves a little money."

I nodded gravely. "I'm putting some feelers out to see if the fossils have surfaced anywhere for sale. It might be possible to trace them back that way. If they do turn up, we can use the rock strata and composition to match them to the site and prove they came from the Jubilee, even if the rock has been recut by now, or the edges polished. The amazing thing to me is that the fossils were deep onto private property, yet the thieves were able to get in there, remove the fossils, load them, and disappear without anyone hearing or seeing anything. Jocelyn thinks someone on the crew might have been involved in setting it up and making sure there was no one in the cabin at the time."

Melvin drew back, surprised. Glancing nervously around the parking lot, he opened the door and ushered me into the store. "You better watch who you say that to around here. The reporter from *USA Today* made that suggestion to the ranch foreman, Dan Daily, and got himself run out of town. Dan's a tough old bird, and he didn't appreciate his cowboys being maligned that way. Most of those boys have been at the Jubilee for years. They got their housing, their work, their families, their whole lives out there, and they're devoted to the place and to Pop. Jimmy Hawthorne's new there, but he's from a good family in San Saline, and besides, he's just an aimless little pup. He's not enterprising enough to think of stealing dinosaur tracks."

We stepped inside the store, and Melvin closed the door behind us, then crossed to the counter where his pictures were. "Dan thinks it's likely the theft had to do with that horse psychology camp of Jocelyn's—maybe one of her customers was involved. Lots of folks have been on the ranch since she started that camp. Maybe word got around until finally someone saw dollar signs. Fossils and petroglyphs sell for some serious money these days, especially ones that are small enough for some rich fella to put out by a fireplace or a swimming pool. Heck, people make coffee tables out of them and everything else."

Thumbing through his book, Melvin made a disgusted sound in his throat. "I can't tell you how many sites I've photographed, only to find out sometime later that the site's been vandalized or robbed. And with the petroglyphs, those that haven't been destroyed are just fading away." He flipped to a page in his book, and I leaned closer to see the photos. "I call this one my spaceman. The picture on the left is thirty years ago. The one on the right is last year. See how he's fading right off the rock? Something in the atmosphere is eating the pigments away. Another ten years, he'll have disappeared for good." He pointed to the succession of photos, and it was easy to see that the petroglyph was rapidly disappearing. I was struck by the sense of ancient history being lost.

For a moment Melvin and I stood staring at the pictures, neither of us able to think of anything to say.

"I hope you catch the people who destroyed the Jubilee site," Melvin said finally. "Maybe that'll put a stop to some of the thefts around here. Sometimes, when the war's too big, you have to be satisfied with the little battles, you know?"

"True enough." I thought of my life lately. The situation with Sydney felt like a war I couldn't win. Sometimes, when I went to bed at night, and I couldn't kiss her on the forehead as she slept, or when I woke in the morning without her sounds in the house, I felt as if my life were like that giant petroglyph, slowly fading into oblivion, being dissolved by some invisible force of nature. I felt as if I couldn't breathe another minute, as if the atmosphere were too thin, too polluted with old resentments and lingering pain.

But today I'd won a little battle. I'd gone through an entire morning without breaking down in tears, or suddenly feeling sick to my stomach, or picking up the phone, tempted to call Sydney, even though it wasn't my day to call, and I knew the sadness in my voice would upset her. Today I'd had a pretty good morning. I'd e-mailed from a mountaintop, I'd learned a little bit about myself in horse psychology class, I'd laughed and flirted with a total stranger. Not bad accomplishments. I felt like I was a far cry from the exhausted, emotionally bereft woman who had arrived in Texas just a little over a day ago.

Shaking off the thought, I returned to the conversation with Melvin. "Anyway . . . if you hear anything, will you let me know?" I said. "In the meantime, I'm going to ask around the ranch, do some exploring up and down the riverbed and see what other sites are nearby—if there's anything the thieves might come back for."

Melvin snapped his fingers like I'd reminded him of something. "There's one more thing I ought to show you." Stepping from behind the counter, he opened the door to what looked like a storage room. "Come look at this thing." Inviting me in with a shrug and a hooded look that added mystery, he pulled a string, turning on the overhead light before he lifted a flowered sheet off something in the corner. The something turned out to be a gigantic fossilized leg bone, a femur, to be exact. It was an absolutely perfect specimen.

"Oh, my gaa . . ." I whispered, stepping closer so that I could get a better look. Definitely a biped, possibly even a tyrannosaurus. If it was a tyrannosaurus, it would be the first confirmed T. rex discovered in Texas. There had been a suspected rex in the Big Bend area, but nothing could be proven. If this femur could be authenticated as belonging to a tyrannosaurus, it would be a major find. I touched the smooth surface, amazed by how clean and well preserved it was. "Where did you get this?"

Melvin hatcheted a hand back and forth in front of himself. "Now, I didn't take it out of context, if that's what you're worried about. I wouldn't ever do that. I'm not a scavenger, and I understand the need to keep a site undisturbed. All the rocks and fossils I keep here in the store washed up on the river at one time or another. This one turned up a few weeks ago in a flood. Vanita and I found it just layin' there on the bank one day when we were out walking."

Melvin paused to glance out the door, then came back. "Anyway, it was just sitting on the path where we walk, not a mile out of town, I'd say. That was right after we heard about the tracks being stolen at the Jubilee Ranch, so we brought this home and didn't tell anyone. All the land upstream belongs to the Jubilee Ranch, and Vanita and I figured that if word got out about it, on top of all the news articles about the stolen tracks, well, then, the place would be crawling with treasure hunters. Pop doesn't need that kind of worry right now, and with the way Dan feels about outsiders coming on the ranch, and all the trouble between him and Jocelyn about her starting that horse camp . . ." He stopped, like he was telling me too much, then finished with, "Well, Vanita and I just thought it'd be better if we kept this find under wraps."

"I see." I was still focused on the dinosaur bone, but my thoughts had wandered to the nest of family intrigue Melvin was describing. Paleontology was all about solving mysteries, and I was beginning to piece together the archaeology of Zach's family. I couldn't help digging for a little more. "I can understand why you wouldn't want to cause any more problems in the family. I gathered that it's kind of a tough time, with Pop having had a heart attack and then the problems on the ranch. . . ." The statement was purposely open-ended, like a fill-in-the-blank question on a test.

Melvin answered it with an essay. Relaxing against the wall shelves, he laced his thick arms across his barrel chest, looking at his feet and shaking his head. "It's been a rough few years for that family, you know. Pop kind of fell apart when Nan died a couple years ago. Then Jocelyn got hit by that drunk driver, and they darned near lost her, too. After that, she moved back home from Austin to start the camp and care for Pop. Dan had pretty much been running that place in the years that Pop was wrapped up with nursing Nan, and so when Jocelyn came back, there were some hard feelings. It probably would of all gone smoother if Zach had moved home again, but he never did."

"Why didn't he?" I traced a finger along a fissure in the dinosaur bone, a long, thin crack that showed the animal had a broken leg that had healed slightly crooked. It would have walked with a limp, one leg slightly shorter than the other.

"Why didn't he what?" Melvin seemed to have lost track of the conversation. I wondered if he was aware that we were unearthing the Truitt family skeletons along with this one.

"Take over the ranch," I answered, my thoughts alternating between theorizing about the fossil and postulating about why Zach never came back home. Apparently Zach had lived there at one time. What happened?

Stroking his beard, Melvin studied the cluttered shelves over my head. "Well, you know, Zach didn't grow up there like Jocelyn did. Jocelyn's daddy ran the place, but Zach's dad went into coaching and moved off, and it was always a sore spot between him and Pop. Zach's folks live up in Oklahoma now, and his daddy coaches at one of the colleges there. I think the absolute last thing he wanted Zach to do was come back here and run the ranch, but Zach came back to the Jubilee right after he graduated vet school, and—" Melvin snapped shut like a clam, and abruptly finished the sentence with, "Well, that's a long story. How'd I get started on all that, anyway?"

The doorbell jingled in the main room, and Melvin and I jumped like bank robbers caught safecracking. Tossing the sheet over the dinosaur bone, Melvin walked out ahead of me.

"Well, speak of the devil," I heard him say as I finished covering the fossil and followed him from the storeroom.

Zach Truitt was standing at the counter, holding a paper plate with three gigantic hamburgers. I had a momentary note of panic that he might have heard me quizzing Melvin about him.

Turning from Melvin to me, he quirked a dark brow, and my

heart fluttered upward, then slapped back into place like a hippo in toe shoes. There were a slight narrowing of his thick lashes and crinkles at the corners of his eyes that testified to his suspicion of my presence there.

"Hungry?" He held the plate up. "Vanita asked me to bring these over to 'that cute little city girl with the pretty brown eyes.' "

Quite obviously, the last part was a quote from Vanita, but all I could think was, *He called me cute.* He smiled slightly, and I felt myself going all moony again. "Thanks," I said, with a smile.

Zach leaned a little closer. "She also said you didn't look like such a big eater. I told her you'd had a tough morning in horse therapy class."

I flushed red. I'd almost forgotten about my humiliating performance. "Very funny. Two of the burgers are for the dog." Before he could lecture me on proper dog feeding, I added, "It's just one last treat, and right after that I'm switching him over to dog food. In fact, I came in here for dog food. Didn't I, Melvin?"

"Sure enough," Melvin chimed in, and went to the shelf for a bag.

Zach squinted toward the front door. "Where is the dog, anyway?"

"Wouldn't you like to know?" I teased.

Zach coughed in playful indignance. "I was just wondering, because—"

"You are *not* stealing my dog, Zach Truitt." I wagged a finger at him playfully. "So you can just forget about playing your little joke on Collie."

"I wasn't going to. . . ." He could tell I wasn't buying, so he changed tactics and tried begging. "C'mon. I owe Collie one."

Shaking my head, I made a *tsk-tsk-tsk* through my teeth. "What would Dr. Phil say about that?"

At the counter, Melvin coughed out a chuckle. I'd forgotten we had an audience.

Zach rubbed his forehead. "See? Now I've been putting up with the Dr. Phil jokes since last Christmas. Every time I come home, someone's got to bring that up. Collie deserves this dog, and little

Bailey's going to love him. Heck, he's big enough that she can use him for a pony."

I vacillated, picturing Mr. Grits and my adorable red-haired goddaughter, Bailey, frolicking in the fields together. "You can't take the dog to Bailey . . . unless Collie says yes."

"It wouldn't be any fun if Collie said yes." Zach shifted his posture, bracing one long leg in front of himself so that his slim hips angled to the side. "How about a loan? I'll just"—he leaned closer, and for a moment I thought he was going to kiss me right there in front of Melvin—"borrow him for a while."

"I don't think so," I said, but my voice was thick and welcoming like warm honey. Taking a step back, I tried to shake off the heady feeling before things got out of hand. "The dog is safely tied to the car. Where he is going to stay, thank you very much."

Glancing out the window, Zach drew back slightly. "No, he's not."

"Very funny. Yes, he is. I tied him in the shade."

A muscle twitched in Zach's cheek as he scratched his ear with the tip of one finger. "I just walked by your car. There's no dog."

I thought about the big double knot I'd tied in the rope. "There has to be. There's no way he could have gotten loose."

"He's not there." Zach was starting to smile, as if the joke were on me.

"He has to be."

"He's not."

"Did you?"

"I didn't."

"But then, where—"

Melvin interrupted, wagging a finger toward the door. "That the dog?"

Zach and I turned in unison. Mr. Grits was standing in the doorway with a piece of the chewed-up water dish hanging from his mouth like bubble gum.

"Oh, no." I gasped.

"He's loose again." Zach's head fell back in disbelief. "I think we've played this game before."

Turning carefully, I walked toward the door, patting my leg and saying, "C'mere, boy, c'mere. Good boy. You just stay there. You're a very bad boy, untying yourself." Through the screen I saw that the rope, or some of it, was trailing behind the dog. He'd chewed completely through it. "And look, you ate the water dish. That wasn't nice. You bad dog. Shame on you."

"Better talk sweet to him until you catch him," Zach interjected.

"This is sweet," I replied, reaching gingerly for the screen door. "Hey, there, big boy. You need your hair fixed. Sta-ay there, staaa-ay there."

As I lifted the latch, Mr. Grits smiled at me, dropped his bubble gum, let out a baritone yip, and took off. He was across the parking lot and headed up the road before I made it onto the porch.

"Oh, no!" Squealing, I started after him in the fastest sprint I'd managed since high school track.

Zach followed, hollering, "I'll get the truck!"

Crossing the parking lot, I dashed up the side of the road after Mr. Grits, who was loping along just fast enough to stay out of reach. Occasionally he glanced back over his shoulder with his tongue lolling out, ignoring me when I breathlessly called, "C'mere, boy, c'mere."

He had the nerve to yip and wag his tail as he continued down the tiny main street, past the little post office, the closed-up brownstone stores, the Lover's Oak Chapel, and into open territory, where he really started to run.

I skidded to a halt in the gravel next to a sign that read:

**LOVELAND, TEXAS
HOME OF THE LOVER'S OAK
A GREAT PLACE TO FIND
YOURSELF**

Only right now it didn't seem like a great place. My legs felt like wet spaghetti, and the dog had just disappeared into the brush beside the road. I didn't know how we'd ever catch him now. A rush of panic went through me. I felt like a mom who'd just lost my child in the mall.

Zach's truck rattled up, and I crossed the ditch, jumping into the passenger seat without waiting to be invited.

"Hurry!" The tremor in my voice surprised even me. "He's gone. If he gets away, someone might shoot at him for real this time."

Zach gave my rush of emotion a double take. "We'll find him," he said with calm assurance. "Which way did he go?"

I pointed. "He went under that fence and disappeared into the brush. Then he was just . . . gone."

Zach surveyed the escape route with the expert eye of a man who knew the terrain. "I bet he followed the deer trail through the fence." He indicated a tangle of spiny brush that looked impenetrable to me.

"I don't see a trail." Stretching across the seat, I tried to see out his window.

Zach winked. "That's because you're a city girl."

My stomach did a strange little hula. "Am not." For just a second I forgot all about the dog. "I'll have you know I'm a p—" I was about to say *paleontologist,* and my mind snapped into gear just in time to yank the word back into my mouth. *Stupid, stupid, stupid. Didn't Jocelyn tell you not to tell him that?* "Hiker," I finished lamely.

"That's not what you were about to say."

Think. Think fast. "P . . . retty serious nature lover," popped out of my mouth. *How idiotic.*

He swung the truck through an open gateway so fast that I had to grab something to keep from falling over. I ended up clutching his arm.

"Sorry," I said, righting myself in my seat. "Warn me next time."

He gunned the truck through a rut, and we jounced through the gateway into the pasture where Mr. Grits had disappeared. "I thought you p . . . retty serious tomboy nature-lover types were ready for anything."

"Very funny," I retorted as we plowed over a three-foot cedar bush, bouncing together, then apart again. My hair fell across my face like a dark curtain, and I reached for the grab handle above my door. "Gee whiz. Do you always drive like this?"

"Not always." The flush in his cheeks told me he was enjoying the chase. "But there's your dog." He hit the gas, and the truck shot across the pasture like a cowboy hovercraft, whizzing over a layer of cactus, assorted wildflowers, and cedar brush. Ahead of us Mr. Grits loped along, fanning his tail like a propeller and occasionally glancing at us as if this were a fantastic game.

A jackrabbit darted from its hiding place, and Mr. Grits kicked into overdrive after the rabbit.

"Shoot!" I hollered, leaning out the window to see if calling the dog would help. "Mr. Griii–its, Mr. Griii–its . . ."

"Don't worry. We'll catch him." Zach shifted gears, and we burst forward at what felt like an insane speed, given the lack of pavement. Grabbing the back of my T-shirt, Zach yanked me in, calmly saying, "Look out," just before a branch slapped my side of the truck, whipping in the open window, then back out.

"Whoa! My gosh!" I squealed, falling against him, then scrambling back up.

"Duck," he said again, and another branch snapped in the window, depositing a few addled grasshoppers, who were quickly sucked out again by the g-force. "There he is."

I swung around in time to see Mr. Grits follow the rabbit down a small canyon and up the other side. "We're not going to . . ." Before I could finish the sentence, the truck plowed down the slope, bumped across some rocks in a dry creek bed, and scrambled up the other side like a mountain goat. Just as we topped the arroyo, I saw the rabbit dart off under the overhanging branches of a huge live oak near a barbed-wire fence. Mr. Grits followed, and we closed in just as the rabbit jumped into a hole beneath the tree. Skidding to a halt, Mr. Grits stuck his head in the burrow, then withdrew it, sneezed violently, and proceeded to calmly lie down in the shade beside the rabbit hole.

Zach hit the brakes, the truck slid to a stop, and we reverberated back and forth in the seat from pure inertia. Raising his head, Mr. Grits thumped his tail against the ground.

Untangling my Jell-O legs, I turned to Zach, openmouthed. His hair was sticking up in all directions, the wind having slicked it into sharp points. He looked good that way. Really good. "You are insane." My voice quavered, either with terror or laughter, I wasn't sure which.

Zach must have thought it was laughter, because he grinned and said, "That was fun, huh? There's your dog. Looks like he had almost as much fun as we did." I blinked at Zach, and he lifted his hands, palms up. "What? You've never chased jackrabbits with a pickup truck before?" He smiled in a boyish way that really was adorable.

I chose to be playfully coy. "Not until now," I said, opening the door and stepping out.

He met me at the front of the truck, and we stood there for a moment, waiting to see if our quarry would bolt again.

"Well, then, it's about time." Zach's voice was warm and low, and it occurred to me that we were standing shoulder to shoulder in the wildflowers. A breeze whispered by, lifting strands of hair and blowing them across my cheek. I felt him watching me. Overhead the branches of the ancient tree rustled, stirring the dappled shade and lifting the scent of wildflowers. I looked up into the branches, then down again into his eyes, the clear, pale green of desert sage.

The breeze lifted my hair again, and his fingers combed it away softly, as light as the touch of the breeze itself. Turning toward him, I leaned close, felt his body warm against mine. My heart stopped, and the breath caught in my throat. Lifting my chin, I gazed into his eyes, waiting, falling into an age-old dance to which I hadn't forgotten the steps, after all. My eyes fell closed, my mind a heady swirl of his touch, his scent, his nearness. His lips touched mine, and everything else seemed a million miles away.

I abandoned myself to the kiss, my mind swirling until I felt dizzy, lighter than air, as if I were floating, or flying. The warm, strong circle of his arms caught me, and I lost all sense of who and where I was.

The only thing I knew for sure was that I'd never, ever felt like that before. Every thought in my head exploded into a burst of color and light.

Skyrockets.

Then the dog barked, and the rumble of a car engine wound into the mist of my thoughts. I heard voices. The sound of tires on asphalt told me that, in our wild drive through the pasture, we had come full circle, back to the road.

Zach's lips parted from mine, and I stepped away unsteadily. Opening my eyes, I turned around in time to see a cream-colored Cadillac passing very slowly on the opposite side of the barbed-wire fence, the driver and passenger leaning to gape through the open window. Between us and the car, there was a wooden sign supported by old stone pillars. I knew what it said, even though I couldn't see the letters.

My mind snapped to reality, and all at once I realized that the tree Mr. Grits had led us to wasn't just any tree.

I had just kissed Zach Truitt beneath the Lover's Oak.

And the Blum sisters had seen it all.

THIRTEEN

————◆·◆·◆————

SOMEHOW I ENDED UP GOING WITH ZACH TRUITT TO FIX A windmill. I wasn't sure how it happened, except that when we came back from the Lover's Oak with Mr. Grits safely tied in the back of his truck, I was feeling light-headed. When Melvin met us in the parking lot and pointed out that I had a flat tire on my vehicle, I didn't even care. That was odd, because right before the dog chase and the Lover's Oak incident, I'd been gung ho about getting in my Jeep, racing back to the ranch, getting Caroline Truitt's journals, and searching for the rest of whatever had yielded the femur that Melvin had found. Archaeologist Lindsey knew it was a scintillating mystery, and she might be on the verge of something big. And, of course, there was still the issue of tracking down the fossil thieves. Archaeologist Lindsey was very interested in that.

But she was nowhere to be found when we returned to the Over the Moon. Romance Lindsey was turning handsprings in my head, and there was no room for anyone else in there at the moment.

She couldn't have cared less about the Jeep's flat tire, especially when Melvin handed Zach a UPS box, which he must have come there to pick up before being sidetracked by the dog incident.

"Here's your order for the windmill supplies." Melvin studied Zach and me with a practiced eye. "You know, you ought to take Lindsey, here, with you. It's a pretty drive through the canyon. Bet she doesn't have any idea how a windmill works. Might be a couple hours before I can pull that tire off her Jeep and get it plugged for her." On top of being the store owner, UPS agent, and fossil expert in town, Melvin was also the head mechanic and tire fixer. He had a shop out behind the store, it turned out.

I looked up from where I was sitting at the corner counter, eating my now-cold hamburger with a Dr Pepper in a real glass bottle. Melvin was also the dealer for what the locals called Dublin Dr Pepper—the real old-fashioned syrupy stuff bottled at the original Dr Pepper factory in nearby Dublin, Texas. It shouldn't, Melvin told me, be confused with the other kind that came in mass-produced plastic bottles at Wal-Mart. Dublin Dr Pepper was the real thing—not to mix soda-pop metaphors—but you haven't been to Texas until you've had one.

It was pretty good, I had to admit, but at that moment everything seemed good. I was in a state of floaty, fluttery goodness. I eyed the UPS box with interest. *Windmill maintenance . . . interesting . . . hmmm . . .*

Zach seemed to read the thought, and glanced at me with a twinkle in his eye. There was a ruddy flush in his cheeks that hadn't been there before. Maybe it was just my own wishful thinking or some Cinderella fantasy, but he seemed in favor of my going along. "What about it, Lindsey? Want to play hooky from the afternoon session of horse headshrinking and go play windmill doctor?"

Melvin backhanded Zach in the shoulder, and a chuckle burst from my lips. "Sure," I heard myself say. "Sounds . . . interesting."

Melvin appeared to be pleased, and hustled us toward the door, even though I hadn't finished my burger and Zach was occupied with opening the UPS box. "Guess you two'd better go, so you don't have to rush. Zach, you ought to take this little lady 'round the long way and show her some of the countryside. Now, don't worry about the car. I'll get the tire fixed and drive the car out to the ranch later."

"Oh, you don't have—" I began, but Melvin cut me off.

"No. Now, that's all right. I don't mind a bit. I was going to drop by and look in on Pop anyway. I'll just leave a bill for the dog food and the tire repair in the car, and you can settle up when you're in town again." He turned to Zach. "Speaking of animals, I was hoping maybe you'd take a look at Vanita's old cat before you go. That broken leg you set last week is healing up, but he doesn't seem very spry. He's just lazing around behind the café. I could take him to the vet in Lampasas, but I figured maybe I could trouble you for a little more free veterinary advice."

"I already looked at him," Zach answered. "Melvin, that's the fattest tomcat I've ever seen. He can hardly waddle. I told Vanita she's got to cut back on the food, especially now, while he's largely sedentary. I bet he's gained two pounds since I saw him last week."

Melvin grimaced. "That's what I was afraid you'd say. It'd be easier if he had some rare disease and needed a vaccination or something. I could get Vanita to give him medicine, but it'll be tough to stop her from handing out table scraps. Vanita likes to feed people ... and animals." He patted his ample stomach. "Well, you two get on with your windmill fixing. I'll run the Jeep out there to you later."

I hesitated—a brief return to sanity, perhaps. I could almost, but not quite, hear the voice of reason in my head. But since I didn't want to listen to reason, I downed the last of my Dr Pepper, left my keys on the counter for Melvin, grabbed the two extra hamburgers, and headed toward the door, saying, "Well, let's go. This will be a first. I didn't even know windmills had heads."

Zach tipped the box so that I could see the nuts and bolts inside before he hefted it onto his shoulder, then grabbed my bag of dog food from the counter. "The head is up top by the fan blades," he explained as Melvin said good-bye and we stepped onto the porch. "You're not afraid of heights, are you?"

"No." *Lie, lie, lie.* That was such a lie. I was afraid of heights almost as much as I was afraid of horses. Both phobias were born at the same Girl Scout camp. After the runaway horse incident, there was an event that involved a poorly executed trapeze maneuver on tree branches over the swimming hole, and me doing a painful belly flop into the water. Sometime after that, I discovered I didn't like heights or tree climbing anymore. Funny how life is a process of developing fears, one by one. Eventually, or at least in my case, that became a fear of failure, which compounded into a near-phobia of anything that wasn't firmly under my control, making me, of course, a control freak of legendary proportion.

Fear. The enemy of faith, my mother used to say in Sunday school.

Out the window with the fears! Today. I laughed in fear's face as I left the Over the Moon with Zach to climb windmills. *Ha, ha, ha, ha*. Not afraid. Not me. I was one out-of-control oversize tomboy headed for adventure . . .

. . . or else a delusional thirty-something single mom trying to pretend she was something she wasn't.

I tried not to analyze it as we crossed the parking lot, and Zach put the package and the dog food in his truck. My SUV was, indeed, parked nearby with one back tire flat.

Vanita Blue poked her head out of the Big Lizard, waved, and said, "Hey, there! You two need drinks for the road or anything? I heard you were headed out to fix windmills." I glanced from the diner to the store and back, wondering how word had traveled from there to here in the time it took Zach and me to walk across the parking lot.

"I need to pay my tab," I answered, but Vanita shook her head.

"Don't worry about it, hon. Zach already took care of it." Waving again, she added, "Have fun!" and disappeared back inside.

"Guess I need to settle up with you, then," I said to Zach.

He shook his head. "My treat." He frowned as I unwrapped one of the burgers for Mr. Grits. "But if I'd known they were for the dog, I would have let him get his own tab." Patting Mr. Grits, he checked the dog's eyes and teeth.

"I know, I know." I sighed playfully. "Dog food for dogs. People food for people. Do you work for a pet food company or something?" It occurred to me to wonder what, exactly, he did in the real world. Collie had said he was a vet and traveled a lot, but that was all I knew, except that he didn't come home much.

"I'm a section vet for the USDA," he said. "It's been a few years since I've been into casting broken doggy legs and prescribing diet food for overweight house cats."

Something told me there was more to the story, but it was obvious that he didn't want to talk about it. Leaving off the subject, I handed Mr. Grits a cheeseburger. Engulfing it in one bite, he thumped his tail, and smiled at the remaining burger. "Here you go." I unwrapped the prize, and he inhaled it, then licked his chops, resting his chin on the truck like a hairy Kilroy. "Sorry, that's all there is, big fella." Reaching up, I fixed his Barbie hair band and patted him fondly, even though he had been a very, very bad dog that day.

Shaking his head, Zach opened the truck door for me, waiting like a valet while I climbed in. "You're going to have that dog completely ruined before I ever get him to Collie's house," he joked, but I could tell he'd given up on his plan to shanghai the dog and surprise Collie's little girl with it.

"You can't ruin something by loving it." An unusually soft and New Age comment for me.

"You sound like Jocelyn," Zach quipped, and I chuckled. Pausing with his hand on the door, he watched as a rusted B & B Windmills truck pulled into the parking lot and stopped on the other side of my Jeep. Hooking an arm over the door, Zach waited while two men in dusty coveralls and ball caps disembarked the truck and started toward the café.

"In a rush today, Bo?" Zach asked, and one of the men started, surprised by our presence there.

Before he could answer, the shorter man stepped forward and stuck his hand out, smiling at Zach through a set of teeth that needed dental attention. "Hey, Zach," he said enthusiastically. "I didn't know you was back in town. How you been doin'?"

"OK, Benny." Zach shook the man's hand with a brevity that said he wasn't looking for friendly conversation. "Don't suppose you boys are headed out to fix Pop's windmills today?"

Benny turned questioningly to the taller man, who shook his head and rubbed the back of his neck, looking at the ground. "Well, dang, I wish I could get out there today, Zach. Sorry I missed you yesterday. I got tied up with a job down toward Austin and couldn't make it back. Anyway, I'll give ya a call and we'll get out there real soon about putting in some new windmills. I hope I didn't put a hitch in your day yesterday."

Zach glanced at me, losing his ire for a moment; then he turned back to the two men. Pushing off the truck, he stood at his full height, towering over both of them. "Why don't we just skip that altogether, Bo." His tone was flat, leaving no room for argument. "Because I've checked the windmills, and they don't need to be replaced. All they need is some oiling and some maintenance, which, come to think of it, is what Pop pays you boys for."

Bo, disappointed at the prospect of losing a sale, quickly began backpedaling. "Oh, well, since we'd decided to replace the old ones anyhow, I just figured, why not save Pop some money on the maintenance? That's all it was. Not a lot of need to fix windmills we're gonna replace, right? We're a little behind schedule in putting in the new units, but we'll be there."

"What say we skip it?" Zach's gaze was cool and unwavering. He leaned comfortably against the door again as the other man shoved his hands into his pockets and jingled coins.

"Well, Zach, it's really Pop's decis—"

Zach cut him off. "If you bring this up with Pop, you and I are going to have a problem. We don't have a problem, do we, Bo?"

Shaking his head, Bo backed away, his pale blue eyes shifting back and forth. "No . . . sure, of course not, Zach. Listen, we'll get out there and get those old units running."

"Don't bother." Zach pushed off the truck again. "I'll take care of getting the units going again. I'm not going to cancel the maintenance contract, because that would upset Pop, but once I get them running, I expect every one of those windmills to be as slick as a Sunday-morning skillet. You're going to give Pop what he's paying for. We clear?" He stuck his hand out, and Bo took it with an audible sigh of relief.

"Sure thing, Zach." Pulling his cap off and mopping his balding brow, Bo backstepped toward the café. "Thanks for being understanding. It's been tough keeping up with the business since Dad passed away."

Zach didn't answer, just shook his head as Bo and Benny Bales turned around and scooted off toward the café. Sighing, Zach glanced at me with a sardonic smirk. "Sorry I didn't introduce you."

"It's all right," I said, suspecting that the Bales brothers weren't anybody I wanted to meet. From the café window, I heard someone hollering out a jovial greeting as they went in.

Zach stiffened, listening a moment, then shook it off and closed my door before he walked around the truck and got in. We drove in silence for a while as we left the Big Lizard and turned onto the gravel country road that wound like a lazy brown snake toward the gateway of the Jubilee. Zach, I noted, was not the wild speed racer I had anticipated from our earlier trip through the pasture. He drove at a leisurely pace, his body slowly relaxing in the seat, elbow resting on the open window frame, so that the breeze blew under his shirt and puffed the chambray fabric out like a parachute.

Since Zach wasn't in the mood to talk, I watched the miles pass in an airy rhythm, considering the rich golden glint of the sun on the dry native grasses, and the faraway hills, stacked row upon row, like torn strips of colored paper on the horizon. A study in shades of green—sage, dusty green, forest green, and a rim so far away it was some hue between green and pale sky blue. Somewhere in that mix was the color of Zach Truitt's eyes. . . .

Slowing the truck, he drove past the Jubilee gateway and contin- ued on the road to the camp. I was glad when we stopped to put cow food in several feeders and perform minor repairs on a barbed- wire fence. It was a welcome distraction from watching Zach brood about Pop and the Bales brothers. By the time we'd finished feeding cows and fixing fences, Zach was his usual jovial self. Unfortunately, I could feel my mood deteriorating as we drew nearer to the ther- apy camp. I knew we were going to pass by the horse corral and I was going to feel guilty because the other horses were out in the grassy pasture while Sleepy stood locked in the dusty paddock. At least I wouldn't have to face the other campers as we drove through. By now they would be entrenched in the afternoon sharing session down by the river, where they would cheer their horse psychology successes and emote about all the things they had learned. Why was it that every one of them could make friends with a horse, and I couldn't? What was wrong with me?

When we came within sight of the camp headquarters, Zach gave me a contemplative look that made me wonder if he was reading my thoughts. "So how did horse therapy turn out?"

Failure slipped over me like a dark cloud. "I flunked. Jocelyn made Sleepy stay in the corral because I couldn't catch him. All of the other horses got to go to the pasture and eat grass." Slouching in the seat, I tried to decide whether to laugh it off or succumb to a bout of general insecurity and latent feelings of inadequacy. Somehow Zach's presence made the latter seem like a nonpossibility. I'd just had my first real kiss in . . . well . . . counting the years was humiliating, so I didn't bother. Actually, I didn't think I'd ever felt that way during or after a kiss. There was a giddiness buzzing around like a bee in my brain, stirring up my thoughts and keeping things slightly out of focus.

I had the misty thought that there were things I should be doing, rather than trekking out to perform first aid on a windmill. I should be retrieving Caroline Truitt's notes from Pop, or searching for Melvin's mystery dinosaur. With a femur so perfectly preserved, there were bound to be other components of the fossil, perhaps even enough to positively identify it as a tyrannosaurus.

A species heretofore unconfirmed in Texas . . .

An exciting possibility that didn't seem to matter in the least right now.

Hard to explain, even to myself.

"You couldn't catch *Sleepy?*" Zach asked the question with the kind of disbelief that might have accompanied words like, *The sky turned polka-dotted and a UFO landed in the horse corral? Really?*

"Sleepy and I did not get along," I said defensively. "He didn't like me and he wouldn't let me get close." I left out the part where Jocelyn said that I was keeping my distance from the horse as much as the horse was keeping his distance from me. "It just didn't go very well. I'm terrified of horses." *And relationships, actually.*

Funny, I didn't feel terrified right now. Just disappointed in myself for having flunked horse psychology.

"But you couldn't catch *Sleepy?*" Zach repeated. "I grew up on that horse. He loves people."

"He didn't love me." I craned to see around the barn as we came within view of the corral. "I'm not very good with animals."

Zach eyed me with disbelief. "Oh, come on, any girl who can rescue an outlaw dog with a stadium seat and a folding umbrella can't be too bad with animals."

The image made me laugh. Who'd have thought, as I was fending off Zach with my stadium seat and my umbrella, that a day later I'd be kissing him under the Lover's Oak? How was that possible? "The dog was a fluke. He was desperate. There was a big, bad cowboy out to do him harm."

Zach grinned and said, "Well, the cowboy was having a big, bad day until that point." The earnest admission stirred my emotions like a mixer on high.

"Did it get better after that?" I couldn't believe I'd said it. My heart did a strange tattoo, waiting for the answer.

Letting the truck roll to a stop beside the horse corral, he looked sideways at me like he was bemused by the strange chemistry between us. "Yeah, it did. There haven't been"—he clipped off the sentence, turned away, and finished with—"a lot of laughs around here lately."

I wondered what he'd intended to say before he stopped himself. I wanted to peer into his mind and see what the words were. As he gazed at Sleepy in the corral, I saw a mirror of the loneliness I felt. But maybe I was only projecting my own needs onto him. It was impossible to tell. Even the horse, standing forlornly in the long afternoon shadows beside the barn, seemed like a portrait of my feelings.

"Poor thing," I said. As if on cue, Sleepy lifted his head and nickered at us. Far away in the pasture another horse answered, and Sleepy whinnied so hard his entire body shook. "Can we let him out?"

"Sure." Zach stepped from the truck, and I followed him through the gate into the corral. Nickering, Sleepy crossed the enclosure and stuck his head against Zach's chest like a big lapdog. Scratching the tuft of long hair between the horse's ears, Zach commented, "See? He's friendly."

Even as he said it, I could see Sleepy watching me with one eye, plotting strategy. "To you, maybe, but he doesn't like me." Equine-o-phobia crept up inside me like the mercury rising on a thermometer, until my stomach knotted and my body went stiff. Swishing his tail, Sleepy kicked a back foot against his stomach, and I jumped. "See? He's trying to kick me."

"He's chasing flies." Zach had the nerve to loop an arm over Sleepy's neck and use him as a leaning post. Eyes drifting closed, Sleepy rubbed lovingly against Zach's shirt. "The first thing you have to know about horses is they don't like or dislike anybody. They just react to trust, or the lack of it. Sleepy's an old grouch, but he understands people. He spent years in the summer camp string." Scuffing the ground with his boot, he watched a filmy puff of dust rise and settle, then smiled and shook his head. "Sleepy's mother, Belle, was one of the original camp horses, and I think she taught Sleepy everything she knew. Belle understood kids, and the kids loved her. Every year, when we'd come here to help get the horses ready for the camp, Dad would put Belle in the camp string. Belle was really supposed to be my horse, so I'd cry and fuss and carry on."

Resting against the fence, I pictured Zach as a little dark-haired boy with a big pouty lip. I chuckled, and he smiled sideways at me.

"Hey, now, this was serious business. Belle was the only thing around here that was the right color for playing Lone Ranger. Pop gave her to me for that very reason."

I imagined Zach as a pint-sized Lone Ranger. Adorable in little Western boots and a big white cowboy hat, like the pictures of my older brothers the Christmas that Santa brought cowboy suits and Red Ryder BB guns. For the strangest instant I yearned to be the mother of sons and buy them tiny Western boots and little cowboy outfits. I realized I probably never would. There was just Sydney and me, and probably that was all there would ever be.

I laughed, a slightly wistful laugh. Half at him, half at my own misguided train of thought, off on a track that came from some uncharted part of myself and led to somewhere I couldn't imagine.

"It's no laughing matter." He drew me back from the train trip to divorced-mother despair. "You can't say 'Hi-ho, Silver' on a brown horse. It just doesn't have the same effect."

"I can see where it wouldn't."

"Pop had some sympathy for me." There was a hint of the little boy as he went on. "Pop would put Belle back in the barn, and Dad would put her back in the camp string, and they'd go back and forth about it for a while, until finally Dad won out. I'd stomp off, thinking my father was the meanest man in the world. I'd sit down by the river and plan to make a raft and run away. Dad would let me stew for a while, and eventually he'd come around and tell me how Belle was the only horse he could count on to babysit any kid who came through the camp—even the ones who were scared to death of horses, or the ones who wanted to pick a switch off a tree and make the horse go faster, or the ones who yanked the reins too much. By the time Dad was done with the team-player talk, I felt like Belle could cure world hunger, end the Cold War, and make the Cubs win the World Series all on her own."

Giving Sleepy an adoring look, he smoothed the long white hair tenderly away from the horse's cloudy eyes. For an instant I was jealous of the horse. "You know, the day Sleepy was born was the day I knew I'd go into vet med. Belle was old by then, and she had a hard time foaling because one of Sleepy's legs was folded back. Old Doc Ham from Lampasas pushed him back in, pulled the leg around, and out Sleepy came. I thought, 'Man, I want to know how to do that.' " A flutter of amusement formed crinkles at the corners of his eyes. "Which was a pretty profound thought for me at the time. I was sixteen and didn't think about much except baseball and girls. Watching Belle have Sleepy gave me the guts to tell Dad I didn't care about getting a college baseball scholarship, that what I really wanted to be was a vet. Dad wasn't thrilled, but Pop thought it was a fantastic idea."

"That's a great story." I had new respect for Sleepy—babysitter, patient teacher, friend to would-be Lone Rangers and frightened summer campers far away from home. Dividing line and bridge between father and son. A lesson in life. "He must be quite a horse."

"Yes. He is," Zach agreed, walking to the gate. "Of course, he's old and arthritic now. It's hard on him standing in the pen all day."

A mammoth slab of guilt fell on my shoulders. "I know. Let's bust him out of here, OK?"

"Good idea." Grabbing a head harness, Zach tried to hand it to me.

I held my hands up like a traffic cop signaling *halt*. "Oh, I didn't mean . . . you just go ahead. I don't know how to put the harness on him or anything."

"Halter," he corrected, holding up the tangled mess of nylon webbing and rope. I vaguely remembered throwing it in the dirt and stomping on it in a fit of frustration earlier that day. Straightening out the apparatus, Zach shook off the dust and held it up, demonstrating the proper working of the buckle. "This way. That part goes over his nose, and this buckles behind his ears. It's pretty simple."

"For you, maybe." I knew I was being a baby. Zach was offering to help me redeem myself, and I was wimping out. "I can't do it," I admitted, rubbing my forehead, feeling like the lost, ragged woman who had arrived in Texas yesterday morning. "I'm scared to death of horses, all right? It's like a phobia. I can't do it."

"Come on, anyone can catch a horse," he said, his eyes acute in a way that made me suddenly aware of his nearness. He stepped closer, and I forgot all about the horse. My body crackled with latent electricity. "There's nothing to worry about."

That couldn't have been farther from the truth. "I'm not worried," I lied. "I'm terrified." The truth.

"Don't be." His voice was low and thick, and for a moment I thought he was going to kiss me again. It seemed like a good idea. I arched onto my tiptoes and started to tilt my face upward, gazing at the suntanned contours of his face. . . .

And then I felt him slipping the halter into Horse Psychology Lindsey's arms, turning her around slowly, his hands on hers, moving her like a limp puppet toward the horse, guiding her fingers upward to stroke the soft gray velvet muzzle. His fingers curled over her fingers, intertwined with them in a way that was both natural and frightening. She drew back just enough to feel the barrier of Zach's body curved against hers, the caress of his breath on her skin.

"Like this," he whispered just inches from her ear, his breath making her draw her own as she watched his hands and hers slide the halter over Sleepy's head, his fingers dark from the sun, hers pale from hours inside. She watched them work together to slide the buckle into place. A triumph for Horse Psychology Lindsey.

But something more than that, as well.

A bridge over the troubled waters of fear.

All the Lindseys felt it being built, piece by piece, inch by inch, as dark hands and pale hands slid into Sleepy's thick white mane, over the bridge of his back, down the tightly corded muscles of the shoulder, the bow of the stomach, and then the soft curve of the hip.

The muscles twitched beneath the skin, and neither hand drew back.

No fear.

For the moment, only faith.

FOURTEEN

I squealed like a giddy adolescent as I watched Sleepy trot off into the pasture to join the horse herd. Standing there with the halter in my hand, I experienced a burst of triumph that was ridiculously out of proportion to the event. I felt like I'd just climbed Mount Everest, or rowed across the ocean on a homemade raft, or trekked to the North Pole with nothing but snowshoes and a sack lunch. It seemed as if the moment should have a headline: *Woman Leads Imprisoned Horse to Freedom.*

Trotting off to his companions, Sleepy jumped into the air and bucked like a rodeo horse, kicking his hind legs and farting all the way.

"Hi-ho, Silver!" I called after him, which was a completely dorky thing to say. If Sydney had been there, she would have rolled her eyes to let me know I was being terribly uncool.

Zach chuckled. He had one arm looped over the gate and his legs crossed comfortably, as if he had nothing more important to do than watch my moment.

It felt good. I had a sense of friendship that had nothing to do with the way his eyes twinkled in the light, soft against his tanned skin like circles of frosty green glass cast ashore by some invisible tide. Quiet waves of thought moved in and out as his gaze flicked from me to the galloping horse and back.

He was trying to figure me out. Right then he looked very much like Jocelyn, mapping those wounded parts of me, penciling in a landscape of despair and broken promises, self-defense mechanisms and control issues, where Trust was a tiny place with no access roads.

But Sleepy had found the way in, blazed a trail where there hadn't been one since Geoff left.

Sleepy and I had traveled across the barren space together—a simple, dusty corral, but metaphorically something larger. He had stood patiently with his head resting on my shoulder as I loosened the halter to set him free. Then he lingered a moment longer, unbridled as I stroked his nose, his ears, his long white forelock. His whiskers tickled my skin as he sniffed my arm, my shoulder, and blew softly in my ear.

I didn't pull away, just rested my cheek against his muzzle and closed my eyes for the barest of moments.

Trust.

It was possible to trust that which you could not predict, or plan, or control.

In fact, it was essential. It was the only way to really live.

I realized it all in an instant, and Zach's expression said that he'd seen every naked bit of it. I should have felt overexposed, vulnerable, but instead I felt grateful not to have experienced the moment alone. There was an inexplicable level of comfort in being there with him. As Sleepy trotted off to the pasture, Zach and I stood smiling at each other, the experience so perfect that no words were needed.

The squeal of brakes and the grinding of tires shattered the moment, and I turned to catch the approach of my SUV, followed by a pickup truck with a dealer tag in the window. Zach glanced over his shoulder. "Guess Jimmy brought your car back from town. Must be that Melvin got it fixed quicker than he thought," he said as we started across the corral together.

But it wasn't Jimmy Hawthorne who exited my car and stalked toward the fence—it was the petite blond waitress from the Dairy Queen in San Saline. "That thing won't shut up." She waved a hand toward the Jeep. "Every other minute it pipes up and says something. I think it's trying to get me to drive to Dallas. Melvin didn't tell me it was gonna do that." Jimmy climbed out of the pickup, and she turned to him, pointing at the car again. "That talking dealie didn't shut off like you said it would. It gave me orders all the way out here."

Jimmy grinned impishly beneath his stringy blond mustache. "Bet that didn't go over well," he drawled, stretching the words like rubber bands, each one playing a slightly different twang.

"Very funny." The waitress dangled my keys over the fence like she couldn't wait to get rid of them. "Here," she said to Zach. "I was by the Big Lizard to meet Jimmy, and Melvin asked if I'd drive this out here. He said one of Jocelyn's *campers* left it to get a flat tire fixed, but he couldn't find any hole in the tire, so he wanted to get the Jeep back out here in case the *camper* needed it." She scrunched up her pert nose like the word *camper* had a bad taste, and gesticulated toward my car with my keys swinging from her hand. "Man, have you been in that thing? It stinks like rotten fish and there's hair *everywhere* and containers of dried-up food and clothes and junk. It looks like something Jimmy would drive." She gave Jimmy a dirty look, but he only shrugged, unconcerned. "Of course, now it doesn't, because he went out yesterday and signed on a new truck without even asking me." Clearly she was talking to Jimmy now and not us. I stepped back, embarrassed for myself and my car, and for Jimmy, who was having a fight with his . . . wife, I assumed, right in front of his boss. "Like we can afford that with my classes to pay for and everything," she added, bracing her hands on her waist and jutting her hips toward Jimmy in a way that demanded, *So what have you got to say for yourself? Huh? Huh? Huh?*

Jimmy ducked like an ostrich trying to bury his head in the sand. "Becky, I told you it was a good deal, and—"

She didn't wait for him to finish. "You don't just go on out and buy a car because it's a good deal, Jimmy." With a huff, she turned to Zach and threw a hand in the air. "You tell him, Zach. You're my ex-brother-in-law. Tell him how stupid it is to go out and sign up for a truck loan when we're tryin' to pay for college, and rent on the trailer, and . . ."

I lost track of Becky's tirade. My mind lit on one part of that sentence: *ex-brother-in-law. You're my ex-brother-in-law.* My stomach flipped over, dumping out all the warm fuzzies and the butterflies. The stuff that was left felt like three-alarm chili. How long had Zach been her brother-in-law, and then her ex-brother-in-law? Why did I care? Why was I surprised? Did I really think Zach had existed in a vacuum for . . . what . . . maybe thirty-eight, thirty-nine years—just waiting for me to stumble onto his ranch looking for . . .

. . . for horse psychology lessons and temporary romance?

Or . . .

Or what? Those two words came with a big blank at the end. A blank line. Blank slate. Blank page. An essay question not easily answered. With no logical answer.

". . . won't even tell me where he got the money for the down payment," Becky was saying. Jimmy went on to defend the fact that he *had some money*, and besides the dealership gave him a real bargain, because . . .

Somewhere in the back of my mind I pondered a new question. Where did Jimmy get the money for the down payment on the truck, and why didn't he want to reveal the source to his wife? Fossil-theft suspect number one: impish cowboy with seemingly too-expensive new truck. No explanation for down-payment money. Suspicious wife. Zach's ex-sister-in-law.

Zach's ex-sister-in-law . . .

Who was Zach's ex-wife? Did she look like Becky, only older? Becky couldn't have been more than twenty-five. Cute and petite with a smattering of freckles that made her seem more like a spoiled girl than a married woman on a tirade.

She let her hands slap to her sides, the jingling keys raising a puff of dust from her Dairy Queen uniform. "I swear, Jimmy. You can't just call me at the end of my shift, when I have a big early childhood development test to study for, and tell me you bought a new truck."

"I told you we can afford it." Jimmy stiffened his arms like he was working up the guts to confront a schoolyard bully. "You could just trust me for once, Beck. I ain't stupid. I'm not no big junior in the college of education like you, but I'm not stupid, either. Am I, Mr. Truitt?"

Wincing as if that point were debatable, Zach gave Jimmy a sympathetic look. "I think you'd better work this out between the two of you," he advised, quite wisely, I thought. "Beck, you know, ever since you were a little girl in pigtails you've tended to get mad first and ask questions later. You might give Jimmy, here, a chance to explain."

"Yeah, you might," Jimmy echoed, then he realized that all three of us were focused on him, waiting. He blushed fiercely. Clearly the conversational floor was not what he'd wanted.

"You're a fine one to be giving out marriage advice," Becky grumbled, turning on Zach. "After all, you—"

"Ssshhh." Zach held up a hand, then turned it over with a flourish, serving Jimmy up like fine hors d'oeuvres. "Jimmy?"

Studying the ground, Jimmy let out a long breath. "Oh, hel"— glancing at Becky, he winced and corrected—"heck. I sold my gun. All right? The one I got at the estate sale last Christmas."

Becky's mouth fell open and the color drained from her face. Her arms hung slack at her sides. "The old one with the octagon barrel? The one you had in pieces on the dining room table all winter? That gun?"

Jimmy's mustache twitched like someone had just pinched him. "Yeah. That gun. Old man Carver has been after it ever since I used it at the turkey shoot last spring. Yesterday I called him and said what I'd take for it."

"Jim-mee." Becky breathed his name in two distinct syllables, her plump bottom lip dangling open. She looked like she might cry. "That rich old fart. He gets everything he wants. You shouldn't of let him have your gun. No pickup truck is worth that. You call him and tell him you want your gun back."

Shaking his head, Jimmy regarded her from beneath his hat, his face surprisingly determined, steadfast. "Beck, you've got to have a good vehicle to go back and forth to them night classes. You can't be breakin' down on the highway at twelve o'clock midnight anymore. It's not safe."

Tears filled Becky's eyes and spilled over the flush in her cheeks. "But, Jimmy, your gun . . ."

"It's just a gun, Beck. It's just a *thing*," he said softly, then leaned over and kissed her on the top of her head, both of them disappearing behind his cowboy hat for a moment. "It don't matter, OK?"

"OK," she choked out, but all of us knew it mattered. I wondered if old man Carver, whoever he was, would ever realize the true value of his purchase.

Slipping under Jimmy's arm, Becky stood on her toes and kissed him on the cheek. "I love you, Jimmy."

"I love you too, Beck," he drawled as they turned to leave.

Becky remembered the keys and paused to offer them to Zach. "Whose are these, anyway?"

"Mine," I said sheepishly, and Becky slipped them into my hand.

"I think that thing in the dashboard is still talking." She sniffed, wiping her eyes and blinking at me like she'd just realized she'd had a marital disagreement in front of a perfect stranger. She studied me for an instant; then her gaze flipped speculatively back and forth between Zach and me. "I didn't know how to shut it off."

"That's OK. It'll stop on its own now that the car is off," I assured her, wishing she would leave. Given that she was Zach's ex-sister-in-law, there was no telling what she might be thinking right now.

The look in her eye was becoming territorial and mildly predatory. "Sorry. I forgot to, like, introduce myself. I'm Becky Hawthorne."

"Lindsey Attwood," I replied, shaking her hand and hoping I would come out with all five fingers.

Beside me, Zach shifted away from the conversation, a silent but polite signal that it was time to break things up. Becky chose to ignore the hint, and pointed at me with a look of discovery. "You're Collie's friend, right? Laura's sister—the one from Colorado."

"Yes," I answered, but I was more focused on Becky's tone than her words. She said my name with a disturbing level of recognition, considering we'd just met.

In the space of an instant, she turned all girlfriendly, smiling and nudging my shoulder. "It's so good to finally meet ye-ew. How's your visit going? Are you, like, getting back on your feet again? How's your little girl doing down in Mexico?"

I blinked, stunned then mortified. "Good . . . umm . . . fine."

Becky giggled at my confusion. "Oh, I'm sorry. You're probably wondering how I knew all that. I work at the newspaper part-time, too. Collie's my boss."

An explanation, but not a comforting one. I imagined the little blonde listening in on Collie's end of all the conversations about Sydney leaving for Mexico and my plunge into depression. There was no telling what bratty Becky knew about me, and she was ready to spill all of my secrets, like cats out of a bag.

Clearing my throat, I attempted to take charge of the situation. "Thank you for asking. It was very nice meeting you, Becky. And thanks for driving my car out. I don't want to hold you up."

Becky didn't budge, but widened her eyes like I had all the glitter of a new toy. "Oh, that's all right. I'm not in a rush."

Darn. Please be in a rush. Rush off to somewhere. Else.

Glancing at the sky, I wished a sudden storm would blow up. A plague of locusts, a tornado, an earthquake. UFO attack. Something to break up this uncomfortable scene.

"Yeah, we are, Beck," Jimmy interjected, pulling out a pocket watch and glancing at the time. "We gotta go sign the papers on the truck before the car dealer closes. We're just barely gonna make it."

I had a sudden flood of tender feelings for Jimmy Hawthorne. Suspect number one had just turned into a lifesaver.

Becky emitted an irritated huff, then remembered that he'd sacrificed the treasured rifle with the octagon barrel for her. Slipping her arm into his, she hugged herself against him and said, "Guess we better go. It was nice meeting you, Lindsey."

"You, too." Couldn't have been farther from the truth. I waved a little toodle-oo as they hurried off to the new pickup and disappeared in a cloud of silty white dust.

Zach and I stood in her wake like survivors assessing storm damage. Hurricane Becky had just blown through and dumped a whole lot of completely unwanted information. A layer of muck over the glittering surface of the day.

"Guess we'd better get on with doctoring the windmill," Zach said finally. His attention flickered to my vehicle, like he thought I might prefer to return to my cabin, since I had wheels now. I didn't want to. I wished the tire would go flat again.

"I guess we should," I said, answering the unspoken question before he could put larger parameters on it. "Get on with doctoring the windmill, I mean." And then, before I knew it, I added, "I've never played doctor on a windmill before."

Zach raised a brow and my cheeks flamed so hot I could have fried an egg. Grinning, he shook his head and ushered me toward the truck, saying, "I'm not touching that one."

"Thanks," I muttered.

We passed the drive to the windmill making pleasant chitchat, like I was a tourist and Zach the tour director. He told me about Jubilee Ranch: comprised of nearly fifteen-thousand acres, homesteaded in 1855 by Jeremiah and Caroline Truitt. Home to Pop Truitt, who was born there in 1921, was married beneath the Lover's Oak, served in World War II, and lived the rest of his life with Nanny Pearl Truitt, whom he dearly loved, and lost two years ago. They raised two sons—Zach's father, who moved away, and Jocelyn's father, who lived on the ranch and ran things until a few years ago, when he and his wife surprised everyone by buying a motor home, in which they were now touring Canada, footloose and fancy-free, and, at Jocelyn's insistence, completely unaware of Pop's minor heart attack. The younger son was Zach's father, who was a high school sports star, played minor league baseball after college, and was so much like Pop that they tended to butt heads, which was why he wasn't here overseeing Pop's health. Zach's mother and younger sister also now taught at the university, where his dad was currently coaching a play-off-bound baseball team, and Zach's mom was directing the university's summer theater. Zach laughed when he talked about having been a high school baseball star like his father.

"Fathers aren't always realistic about the abilities of their sons," he said in a way that seemed both wise and gentle. "Vet school was a better idea than bucking for an athletic scholarship and professional ball. Deep down, I think Dad knew that, but he was afraid anything having to do with animals would eventually lead me back here to Pop and the ranch."

I pictured the invisible tug-of-war between father and son, a timeless struggle of diverging dreams, disappointed hopes, and learning to accept ourselves for who we are.

"I know what you mean," I said. "My father always envisioned that my brothers would have careers in the military, like he did." Laughing softly, I pictured Dad with his curmudgeon face, complaining about my brothers' high-tech civilian careers. "He still hasn't gotten over the fact that they didn't. If you ask him what they do for a living, he acts like he doesn't know. By the time Laura and I came along, he wasn't so opinionated, or maybe it was because we were girls. I think he was just glad to survive raising twin daughters after the age of forty."

Zach peered curiously through the window into my past. "I'll bet that was an adventure."

"We gave him a few gray hairs," I admitted. "Laura more than me, of course." Which was exactly the opposite of the truth. Laura was the sweet one. I was the stubborn, strong-willed pain in the butt who took after my father. Which meant that we both understood and clashed with each other. My father could not imagine digging up dinosaur bones for a living; nor was he in favor of my marrying a man who wanted to spend his life bumming around the world on grant money and a moderate inheritance, looking for the big discovery that would make him famous.

But I was determined to do it, and I did. I married Geoff and took off seeking buried treasure. Now here I was fixing windmills. Strange, the twists and turns that life takes . . .

I had the feeling that Zach was looking way too intensely through the portal into my past, and was about to send in a probe, so I changed the subject back to him. "Jocelyn said you travel often. How is it that you travel so much?" Actually, *He never comes home*, was what she'd said. Why would he avoid this place when he seemed to love it? He seemed as much a part of the landscape as the towering sky and the brooding live oaks.

"The USDA job comes with a fair amount of travel. I'm a section VMO, so that means I cover anything that comes up in my area, and then assist in other areas across the country when something big happens." We crossed a dry creek bed, and he gunned the engine to make it up the other side. The view out the back glass went straight down as we scratched and clawed our way up the narrow trail. I wondered if this was a good idea, if maybe we needed a mountain goat rather than a pickup truck to make it to the top.

Zach approached the climb with perfect confidence, hitting the gas, then letting the truck roll and bump over washes of loose gravel. He kept right on talking, his attention focused partly on the road and partly on the conversation. "If there's an outbreak—Exotic Newcastle Disease, West Nile, possible mad cow, things like that—it falls under USDA jurisdiction." He shrugged, making the job seem routine. "We chase a lot of phantoms, especially the last few years with the whole bioterrorism issue going on, but then we get involved in a lot of the real stuff, too. We were on the Navajo reservation during the outbreak of HPV."

"Oh, I read about that," I said, thinking back several years to an issue of *National Geographic* I'd read in the pediatrician's office during one of Sydney's appointments. "Something like twenty-six people died before they tracked down the cause." I remembered staring long at the image of a young Navajo woman in blue jeans, sitting forlornly by the grave of her daughter. I'd imagined how it would feel to lose my little girl, and tears had fallen on the page.

Zach confirmed my recollection of the story with a solemn frown. "It was a tough bug to chase. Turned out to be bacteria in dust contaminated with rodent urine—a strain of hantavirus. It can lie harmless for years, but when it's stirred up and goes airborne, it's a killer bug."

"Sounds bizarre," I agreed, imagining him traveling the reservation with a vet bag and a biohazard suit, placing himself in harm's way to save lives.

"Not as much as you might think," he replied. "It's something fairly common in Asia, but not in the U.S. until recently."

I imagined Zach, the hero, holding up a microscope slide, hollering across a makeshift field lab, *I've got it. Here it is!* "Seems like interesting work."

"Sometimes," he allowed as we topped the hill and drove along a mesa. Below, the valley floor spread for miles, and ahead, a windmill stood like a sentinel tower. "I needed a change. I'd already been doing some work for the USDA, and the section VMO job came up. It's been . . . hmmm . . . five years now."

A change, after the divorce? I wondered, but of course I didn't ask. Five years since he was Becky's brother-in-law?

The questions went unanswered as we pulled up to the windmill. I stood at the edge of the butte while Zach unloaded the parts and a toolbox and arranged them at the bottom of the metal tower. Overhead, the windmill squeaked softly like a suffering animal, its arms motionless in the wind.

"What a view," I said, admiring the rolling pastures, crisscrossed with streams and strewn with limestone boulders and groves of trees. Here and there the naked cones of prehistoric volcanoes jutted above the landscape, surveying what had once been the floor of a primordial sea. I breathed the moment in like heady incense, filling my lungs and body and mind with this quiet place, unchanged and unchanging.

"You ought to see it from up here." Zach climbed the metal skeleton that held the windmill fan high overhead. "The view goes all the way to Loveland."

"Really?" Standing on my toes, I shaded my eyes from the late-afternoon sun, trying to make out the town in the heat mist on the horizon. "I can't see it from here."

"Come on up." He settled himself on the wooden platform beneath the windmill head, his long legs straddling the tip of the tower as he wound a rope around the disabled rudder and bound it securely.

Squinting upward, I considered the prospect of teetering twenty-some feet in the air on top of a cliff. "I . . . don't think so."

Shaking his head, he grinned down at me, then proceeded to take the case off the windmill head and balance it on the platform. A bolt came loose and clattered down the tower like a pinball, *ping, ping, ping*, then landed in the grass near my foot.

"Hand me that bolt, will you?" He waved his wrench in the general direction of the ground.

The next thing I knew, I was climbing up the windmill tower, playing Jane to his Tarzan. He leaned down to receive the bolt, and our fingers met for a moment, so that I didn't notice I was twenty feet in the air atop a cliff. I just felt the warmth of his hand and the urge to go wherever he was.

It was a powerful sensation, and strange. A compulsion that was almost irresistible. Climbing back down the tower, I stood at the bottom, trying to decide if I'd ever felt anything like that before. There were few enticements on the face of the earth that could have convinced me to climb that high. I'd lived in Colorado for six years, but I didn't ski because I was terrified of the lifts. I'd never been across the Royal Gorge, even though Sydney begged me every time we were in Canyon City. I was petrified of both the suspension bridge and the gondola. It was all I could do to stand at the edge and look through the chain-link fence.

It occurred to me that I'd been looking at life through the chain-link fence ever since Sydney was born. For eight years I'd been afraid that something would happen to me and Sydney would be left alone. I'd been playing it safe.

Afraid of life.

And the thing was, that wasn't me. Before I became an abandoned single mother, I'd been a risk taker who loved hiking and rock crawling and sports of all kinds. A world traveler who didn't worry that I couldn't speak the language.

Now I had the lily-white complexion of a woman who hung around in basements being careful.

Squinting against the late-day sun, I watched Zach perch atop the tall, pyramid-shaped tower, his long legs spraddled, boots hanging off the platform. He wasn't the least bit worried about the height. He drove like a crazy person and climbed towers like Spiderman. He had a mysterious past and lived a thousand miles from where I lived. He definitely wasn't safe.

Yet when I was with him I felt grounded, even on top of a tower dangling on the edge of a cliff. Even handling a thousand-pound horse or driving breakneck across a pasture. I felt like I'd found the one place in the whole world that was right.

It made absolutely no sense, but it was impossible to deny.

I studied him, trying to figure out what it was—the *it* that made me feel like a giddy teenager. I tried to piece together the mystery as I would re-create an artifact, making suppositions and educated guesses where there were no facts, filling in the absent parts. The problem was that I barely knew him. There were too many missing pieces.

I watched his hands sliding deftly over nuts and bolts and gears. I liked the way he moved, confidently, slowly, as if he'd never drop a bolt by accident.

I fantasized that he'd dropped it on purpose, to get me to climb up.

Glancing down, he smiled, and breath caught in my throat. I forgot all about puzzle pieces, and just enjoyed the lighter-than-air moment. Maybe that was the point, I decided—not to overanalyze, but to enjoy the temporary rebirth of a part of myself I had thought was lost and gone forever.

Yet in the back of my mind a voice warned that it was going to be hard to go back to the basement after this, difficult to be satisfied with life behind the chain-link fence.

"Hand me that gear oil. The red can by the toolbox," he said.

I scooped up the oilcan and was up the tower like a rocket.

After that we were a precision surgery team. Wrench, grease gun, screwdriver, rag, knuckle buster, pipe wrench, oilcan, rag, bolt, socket set, small soft-sided nylon bag with some kind of jars inside, crescent wrench, larger screwdriver, wrench, and . . .

The windmill was done, successfully doctored by the crackerjack team of Zach and Lindsey. I was vaguely aware that we'd been there a long time, and I wasn't going to make it to the riverbed today, but somehow that didn't matter.

Zach gave the windmill a pat as he tightened the last bolts on the bonnet. "Good as new," he said, swinging his legs around so that they dangled beside the ladder. "No Bales brothers windmill service needed around here. This old girl will go a few more years."

"Congratulations, Doctor," I joked, standing back from the tower. "Drop the tools down and I'll put them away." One thing I'd learned from years of hanging around my father's woodshop was that tools should always be stored in the proper place.

"Sure." He pitched several tools off to the side, where they landed safely in the grass. I put them in the box. Zach was surprisingly organized. One more thing to like about him.

"I love a woman who knows her tools," he said. I found him watching me from the top of the windmill tower. The amber glow of the setting sun silhouetted his form, so that I couldn't see his expression.

Ignoring the twitter inside me, I finished putting away the screwdrivers and wrenches and returned for the bigger stuff, which couldn't be tossed down from the tower. "Hand down the socket set and the bag with the jars in it," I said, climbing a few steps and reaching toward him.

"Come up and get them." He was occupied with wiping the grease off his hands. His face was hidden beneath the the cowboy hat, so I wasn't sure I'd heard him at first.

"What?"

"Come up and get them," he repeated, patting the empty spot on the platform beside him.

"Ummm . . . no." Bracing my hands on my hips, I tried to appear flirtatiously stubborn, yet firm. But deep inside I knew I was already sold. I was going to climb the windmill tower and sit up there with him. It could have been five hundred feet in the air, and I probably still would have done it.

"You're missing the sunset."

"I can see it from here."

"I've got drinks up here." He held out the nylon bag with the jars inside, which I now realized was a soft-sided cooler of some sort. "Cold drinks."

"Well"—*pretend to think about it*—"in that case"—*pretend to think some more, act charmingly coy, gaze at sunset. Gorgeous sunset*—"all right, then." Grabbing the bottom rung of the ladder, I started upward one step at a time, keeping a white-knuckled grip on the rails. The tower seemed to sway beneath me as I neared the top, and I stopped two rungs below the platform.

My head whirled and I felt sick. "I don't think I can do this."

Zach's hand slipped over mine easily, naturally. "One more step," he coaxed.

"Two," I corrected, letting my head sag between my arms.

His chuckle slipped over me like warm water. "All right, two. The view is worth it. Trust me."

Trust me. The words repeated in my mind. Once again I stood at the dividing line between fear and faith. Zach's hand drew me across, and I climbed the last two steps, then inched onto the platform beneath the motionless windmill fan. Zach held tight, the circle of his fingers warm and solid as I scooted to the front of the tower, where the ground beneath dropped off so sharply that it felt like we were flying.

"Wow," I breathed, taking in the valley and the layered violet of the far hills. Overhead, the sky was painted with an array of colors only God could have imagined. "I don't think I've ever seen anything so amazing."

"Me either." Zach leaned close, his body warm against mine, his gaze capturing me with a power that made everything else fall away. I closed my eyes, and his lips brushed mine, lightly at first, then with more intensity, with a deeper passion that sent my mind swirling. All the thoughts, worries, fears, questions were swept into the torrent of desire and disappeared like leaves in a gale—small, unimportant things that could not withstand the power of the storm. Pressing into him, I lost myself in his kiss, felt the steady drum of his heart beneath shirt and skin, imagined that my heart was now beating in time. Two moving as one.

When our lips parted, I caught my breath like a dreamer awakening too suddenly. He blinked hard, as if it were a mystery to him, too, as if he were surprised by the awesome longing, the electric desire and invisible connection. His fingers traced the outline of my cheek, brushing away a stray strand of hair, skimming my shoulder and the curve of my arm to where my fingers clenched the cool metal frame of the windmill tower.

A low chuckle made him smile. "Holding on?"

"I think I'd better," I breathed, and we sat gazing at each other for a few minutes before he finally cleared his throat and turned away, seeming embarrassed, or maybe just uncomfortable with the intensity of it all. I should have been, too. I should have been stunned, and afraid, and worried that I was starting something I couldn't finish. But at the moment all I felt was contentment. There was no room for anything else.

Reaching into the cooler, he brought out two glass soda bottles, pried off the caps on the edge of the windmill head, and handed me one.

"Wow, Dublin Dr Pepper," I said, still so light-headed that the presence of real Dublin Dr Pepper in a glass bottle seemed miraculous.

Zach raised a brow. "You're easy to please."

Me? Easy to please? I couldn't recall anyone ever saying that to me before. Not once in my entire life. "Thanks," I said, unable to imagine anything that could make the moment more perfect. "It's been a really great day."

"Yes, it has." He raised his Dr Pepper in a toast. "Here's to tilting at windmills."

"Absolutely." I tapped my bottle against his. The sentiment seemed particularly appropriate for the two of us, sitting atop a tower at the edge of earth and sky. Together we raised our bottles in a salute to the setting sun, in honor of impossible dreams, and tilting at windmills.

We sat quietly for a long time, watching the day surrender and the first evening star twinkle to life overhead.

"I guess it's time go," I said, facing the fact that it was getting dark, and we should head back before everything turned pitch-black.

Zach seemed surprised or disappointed, I couldn't tell which, so I added, "I mean, shouldn't we get back to the road while there's still some light?"

He squinted speculatively. "Afraid to ride across the pasture with me in the dark?"

I couldn't help smiling. "Zach, I'm afraid to ride across the pasture with you in the broad daylight. You drive like a maniac."

He chuckled, raising a boot and bracing it beside himself. The platform shook as he shifted toward me. I grabbed on with both hands.

"I'll have you know," he said, "that driving on this caliche soil is an art. One minute it's mud, the next minute it's loose gravel, and after a rain it has all the traction of axle grease. What seems like maniacal driving is really just years of training and experience in action."

I rolled my eyes at the lame argument. "You are so . . . " I didn't finish the sentence. He was going to kiss me again, and it seemed like a fine idea, so I raised my lips to his, taking the offensive for the first time in years. Zach seemed impressed. His hand slid into my hair, and his lips played hard on mine. I clung to the tower as a heady swirl of passion spun through my senses, whisking away all the normal frames of reference.

When our lips parted, he studied me for a long moment. There was a question in his eyes, but in the end he didn't ask it. Slipping his hand over mine, he loosened my grip, lifted my hand and kissed it, and pointed toward the horizon with our fingers intertwined. "There," he whispered. "Right there." I followed his line of vision as a gigantic orange moon lifted from the hills just off the tips of my fingers.

"How did you know where it would come up?" I asked.

"Years of experience," he answered against my hair, then chuckled and added, "Pop used to do that to me when I was a kid. For years he had me convinced that the moon wouldn't come up until he called for it. It worked for me, because I was sure he hung the moon, anyway."

I smiled at the image of Pop as a younger man and Zach as a boy. "You're lucky to have grown up so close to your grandparents. My dad's mom passed away when I was fairly young. I always wished we lived near my mom's folks. Sometimes I feel like I'm only giving Sydney half a life, because I can't give her that grandparent relationship." It was a surprisingly honest admission, one I'd never shared with anybody, not even my twin sister. "She barely remembers my mom, and my dad's not really the touchy-feely type. There's no family on Sydney's father's side. Not that he keeps in touch, anyway." I left out the fact that, until this summer, Sydney hadn't had her father, either.

"I can tell she's got a great mom." Zach gave my hand a squeeze. "Some kids don't even get that much." The way he said it made me turn and look at him. It sounded like he was speaking from experience. A flicker of pain crossed his face.

"What's your mom like?" I asked, and he raised a brow at the question, seeming to think it came out of the blue. Nudging him on the shoulder, I added, "Come on, spill. I'm trying to figure you out, in case you haven't noticed. You can tell a lot about a man by how he feels about his mom."

He frowned thoughtfully, as if he were giving the question deep consideration, then answered with, "She's great."

I shoulder-butted him harder, which rattled the tower. Gasping, I renewed my choke hold, reminding myself that twenty-some feet in the air was not the place to get playful.

Grabbing the tower, Zach stiffened his arms, imitating my death grip.

I sneered at him, only half-kidding. "You know, you make a joke out of practically everything. You're hard to get to know. Did anybody ever tell you that?"

"My mother," he answered, and I couldn't help it—I laughed.

"You are impossible. Don't you ever get serious about anything?"

He shrugged in a way that said, *What can I say—this is me.* "Sometimes you can either laugh or cry, and it's better to laugh. My mother used to also say that, by the way."

I blinked, surprised. "My mother used to say that, too. She used it a lot on me, because I was such a whiner."

"A whiner?" Drawing back, Zach eyeballed me. "You?"

For an instant I thought he was kidding, and then I realized he really meant it. Zach could not imagine why anyone would classify me as a complainer.

I felt lighter than air. Zach liked me just the way I was. A rush of warm, soft emotions wrapped around me, and I snuggled in. My eyes teared up. Ever since Geoff left, I'd felt worthless, unattractive, rejected. Even though I'd told myself over and over that Geoff was a self-centered jerk, that the divorce was his fault, that he'd put his career before Sydney and me, deep down I was convinced that I was *really* responsible. Geoff didn't love me because I wasn't worth loving.

Now suddenly I felt special. I felt admired and accepted and affirmed. I felt a connection to Zach that I couldn't describe. It was like magic. There was no scientific explanation for it. It was just there.

"What?" Zach said softly, perplexed by my emotional reaction.

I started to tell him what I was thinking, but some practical part of me warned that it would be completely inappropriate, considering that we barely knew each other. "That's the nicest thing anybody's said to me in years." I sniffed.

He chuckled low in his throat, a warm, resonant sound, and peered over the edge of the windmill tower. "You've been hanging around with the wrong people."

"I think I have," I admitted, studying his profile, memorizing the contours of his face in the moonlight—the strong nose, the chin with a slight cleft, the downward sweep of dark lashes, the high cheekbones, the way his dark hair curled over the top of his ear, the way his lips were parted slightly, undecided between a smile and a pensive frown. I wanted to know what he was thinking. I wanted to know everything about him. I'd never felt that way about anybody before.

"Zach, thanks for today," I said quietly. "I know you probably had other plans."

He threaded his arms around me, and I leaned into him. "Not a one," he whispered against my hair. "Nothing that mattered."

"Me, either." The words couldn't have been more true. Nothing else mattered right now but being with him.

Zach and Lindsey, tilting at windmills. The only two people as far as the eye could see.

FIFTEEN

⟶◆◆⟵

A STORM CAME IN SOMETIME LATE AT NIGHT. ZACH HAD POINTED out the distant lightning as we stood together in front of my cabin. He'd escorted me home, which wasn't strictly necessary, since I'd picked up my car at the horse barn. But, as thunder rumbled far off and a blanket of clouds narrowed the sky, I was glad he was there. Part of me wanted to invite him in, and part of me knew that probably wasn't a good idea. Things were moving too fast already, and my head was in a spin. The ground under my feet felt soft and shifty, like puffy cotton, and I knew that if we went into the cabin, almost anything could happen, and probably would.

He seemed to sense that, and stopped on the porch, leaning against one of the stone pillars with Mr. Grits at his side. "Looks like we'll have a gully washer before morning," he said, squinting into the distance. He'd left his cowboy hat in the truck, and a few strands of straight, dark hair fell over his forehead. He looked like Jeremiah Truitt, from the picture above the fireplace.

"It's a long way off. How can you tell it's coming here?" I made idle conversation, trying to delay his leaving.

"It's coming from the southwest, probably somewhere around San Angelo or Menard right now." Glancing at his watch, he ran some mental calculations, then added, "It'll be here about one a.m. Two, maybe three inches of rain and some pretty strong winds on the leading edge."

Leaning off the porch, I surveyed the flickering thunderheads on the horizon. "You can tell all that just by looking?"

"No, I heard it on the radio after I dropped you off at the horse barn." Without waiting for a retort, he kissed me on the forehead, said, "Good night, Lindsey. Don't get out on the roads first thing in the morning. It'll be muddy," and headed for his truck whistling an off-key rendition of "My Heroes Have Always Been Cowboys."

"Good night, Zach," I whispered, hugging my arms around myself and watching until he climbed into the truck and disappeared around the bend. With a sigh, I went inside, ate a late-night snack of Moon Pies and soda, fed Mr. Grits, took a bath, and headed for bed, hoping I could drift off to sleep before the storm rolled in.

The wind singing against the window wells lulled me away as soon as my head hit the pillow. I didn't have time to analyze the evening, or consider what it meant, or wonder why, even with Zach far off, I still felt him near me.

I dreamed of the Lover's Oak, lofty and proud, its branches stretching over a carpet of Indian blankets. Among the flowers sat row upon row of old-fashioned church pews, filled with townsfolk in historic dress—men in coats and tails and women in brightly colored dresses and bonnets. A wedding was in progress, but I couldn't see the bride and groom from overhead. The wedding march began, and in the front row the Blum sisters, Mr. Grits, and a giant jackrabbit stood at attention. . . .

When I woke in the morning that was the last thing I remembered. I lay drifting between the conscious and subconscious, trying to decide what the dream meant. Then I remembered everything that had happened the day before—Zach and me kissing under the Lover's Oak, the two of us rescuing Sleepy, then sitting atop the windmill tower. Suddenly last night's dream didn't seem so strange. Compared to yesterday's reality, giant jackrabbits weren't much of a stretch.

Staring hard at the ceiling, I tried to divine whether it had really happened, but even as my mind was sorting out dreams from reality, my body remembered. I touched my lips and felt him there, closed my eyes and basked in the warmth of his arms around me, shivered as an electric attraction crackled between my body and his.

But the memory was short-lived. Thunder rumbled somewhere in the distance, chasing away my sunshine and rainbows, causing me to open my eyes to the realities of the day. It was raining. I was a thousand miles from home. Sydney was far away in Mexico. And now I was carrying on an ill-advised romance with a man I barely knew.

It was more than I could bear to ponder, lying in the gray morning light of a rainy day, so I got out of bed, dressed, flipped the light switch, and realized that on top of everything else, the power was out. Peeling an orange from the bowl on the counter, I wandered around the shadowy cabin, feeling lost and lonely. No doubt horse psychology class was rained out. I was surprisingly disappointed about that. I wanted to show off my new skills. As it was, I wouldn't even be able to answer Sydney's e-mail. Even if the rain tapered off, everything outside was wet and muddy, and climbing the hill to my communications post would be almost impossible.

I checked my watch. Seven o'clock. Too early to drive to the ranch house and . . .

See if Zach happens to be there . . .

No. I reprimanded myself. I wasn't going there to look for Zach; I was going to use Jocelyn's computer to e-mail Sydney, make sure she was all right after Geoff's crew party last night, and see if Geoff had answered my note about the fossils. Just business. If the day stayed wet and rainy, I might hang around Jocelyn's office and post some discreet inquiries on palentology chat boards, maybe do some snooping through the online sites that advertised fossil auctions all over the world.

. . . or see what Zach does on a rainy day, when it's too wet to work.

God, I was hopeless. Hopelessly preoccupied, smitten against my will. It was as if I'd consumed some mind-altering substance the moment Zach kissed me under the Lover's Oak, and even now, in the fresh light of morning, I couldn't shake its effects. The memories of last night were swirling around and around in my head, and if I didn't do something, I was going to go crazy from reliving it, then analyzing whether it was a good idea. The more I obsessed, the more real the desires became. They were like a chocolate craving after an eight-year diet: physical, mental, emotional, and powerful in a way that was disconcerting.

What I needed was a distraction, but there was nothing to do in the cabin except read old magazines by the window light and think about my life. I felt as if I were trapped in a cell filled with unfamiliar surroundings and foreign emotions—someone else's life, not mine. A pang of homesickness went through me, and I thought of the comfortable safety of my apartment back in Denver. On a normal day Sydney would just be waking up about now. We'd eat breakfast at the bar in the kitchen, talk about what she wanted in her lunch for summer day camp, maybe walk out onto the balcony and say hi to Mrs. B., our next-door neighbor, who kept Sydney stocked with cupcakes and homemade chocolate-chip cookies.

I missed our normal morning routine. I missed its continuity, its predictability. Reliving the images, I felt the rainy-day blues creeping up on me. I had to fend them off before I fell into what my mother called a blue funk. I'd been in one for the last three weeks, and I couldn't let myself go back.

Putting on one of the rain slickers from the hook by the door, I slipped the leash onto Mr. Grits and headed for the car. Where I was going, I didn't know. Somewhere, anywhere but here for an hour or so, until it was late enough to go by the ranch house to use the computer.

I ended up driving to the riverbank. The rain had slacked off, and it seemed as good a time as any to further investigate the fossil site. Fossils were often easier to spot when the rocks were wet and slick, the striations and textures clearly visible. Overhead, the sky was clearing slightly, allowing faint sunbeams to probe the dingy morning gray as I circled the field above the river. The water had risen and was running surprisingly fast, covering even the rock shelf and the trackway by several inches. Opening the car door, I stepped out to get a better look. My foot sloshed through the thick grass into an underlying puddle of water, and I had, quite literally, a sinking feeling. I stood staring down at my foot, becoming aware that if my shoe was in the mud, so was the SUV.

"Oh, no," I muttered, sensing that the day was about to go from bad to worse. Leaning out the door, I watched mud ooze up around the tires. What had yesterday been a grassy slope was now a quagmire, well hidden beneath a thick layer of grass that did nothing to support a two-thousand-pound vehicle.

Climbing back in the door, I shifted the Jeep into gear, and slowly pushed on the gas. The car rocked forward, and my hopes leaped up. Thank God for four-wheel drive. When I made it back to the cabin, I was going to stay there until the weather cleared.

Please, please, please, please, I prayed. *Out, please . . .*

All four tires started to spin, and I punched the gas harder. Wet clumps of cream-colored mud showered the windows and pelted the roof. Mr. Grits hopped out of the passenger seat and onto the floorboard, looking up at the ceiling.

The Jeep went nowhere. Letting off the gas, I let it rock back, then race forward, back, then forward, back, forward, and down, down, down. In less than sixty seconds I had it mired up to the axles, hopelessly stuck. Outside, it started to rain again. Things weren't going to dry up anytime soon.

Turning off the key, I let my head fall back against the seat and tried to decide what to do next. I could walk back to the cabin, but I would be marooned there until someone finally came to check on me. Who knew when that would be? The main house was probably two or three miles' distance on the road, and the road was a muddy mess. Zach was right: The soil here, when wet, had the consistency of axle grease.

Now I remembered the other thing he'd said to me just before he left last night: *Don't get out on the roads first thing in the morning. It'll be muddy.*

Why hadn't I listened? What was wrong with me lately? Why did I make one impulsive move after another? Now I was stuck in the mud, miles from everyone and everything. Meanwhile Sydney would be waiting for my e-mail. She'd think I'd forgotten. What if the party hadn't gone well last night and she was lost and lonely and needed to talk? What if Geoff and Whitney were passed out somewhere, hungover, and Sydney was wandering around the house alone, or worse yet, with some of Geoff's shady crew members . . . ?

I stared through the window at the falling rain, and my eyes filled up with tears. I wanted my daughter back. I wanted my life back. My nice, comfortable life with the quiet apartment, the friendly neighbors, and no big questions. No custody issues, no romantic fascination with cowboys, no smelly stray dog, no Jeep stuck in the mud.

That isn't going to happen, Lindsey, I told myself. *Stop wallowing in self-pity and do something.* Gathering my resolve, I pulled up the hood on my slicker, grabbed the dog's leash, and got out. My tennis shoes sank ankle-deep in mud as Mr. Grits splashed to the ground beside me, happily wagging his tail and sneezing as we slogged up the hill toward the road. A trickle of water ran into my hood and dripped down my spine, and I bent against the rain, focusing on the soggy ground, alternately sniffling and giving myself a pep talk. Bad side—I was wet, cold, stranded, and had no way to get in touch with Sydney; bright side—the day had to get better from here. There was nowhere to go but up.

Mr. Grits barked and pulled on the rope, and I looked up. Water rushed down my neck in torrents as I squinted through the rain, sighting the first good omen of the day. Two pickup trucks were headed in my direction, and the one in the lead had Zach at the wheel.

He pulled up and stopped, gaping like he'd just seen the Loch Ness Monster crawl out of the river. "Lindsey?" he said, leaning across the seat and peering through the passenger-side window. "What are you doing out here?" Observing my Jeep, and then me again, he added, "Did you get stuck?"

I was going to answer with something witty like, *Oh, I was just out for a swim,* but to my complete horror, I sniffled, said, "Yes," and started to cry.

Zach immediately threw the truck into park, slid across the seat, and opened the passenger-side door. "Here," he said, patting the seat. "Hop in." I wasn't sure if he was talking to me or the dog. Mr. Grits climbed onto the floorboard, and I climbed into the seat. It was a tight fit, but it didn't matter, because both of us were equally glad to be out of the rain. Zach looked like he'd been in the weather as well. He had on a wet gray cowboy hat, a tan canvas slicker, and mud-spattered jeans tucked into the tops of boots that were caked with mud and grass. He seemed completely comfortable that way.

The other truck pulled alongside us, and he lowered the window enough to talk. Dan eyed me suspiciously from the passenger side, and from the driver's seat, Jimmy checked out my Jeep with admiration. "Man, that thing's stuck up to the hubs. Bet that took some doing."

Zach had the good grace to answer before I broke down again. "We'll bring the tractor down here and get it out after the rain stops," he said, and I felt better already. "Y'all go on down and get started fixing the water gap. I'll be there in a minute."

Jimmy said, "Yes, sir," and Dan grumbled something, still scowling at my Jeep, or me, or both. The two of them drove off in a spray of mud.

Rolling up the window, Zach took off his cowboy hat and set it on the dash. He studied me, clearly at a loss. "Lindsey, what happened? What are you doing down at the river?"

Pushing my hood back, I wiped my eyes, feeling foolish and pathetic. I considered explaining about the fossils, and Collie's newspaper article, and why I really came to the Jubilee Ranch, but I was teetering too close to the end of my rope to go through all that. "It's a long story." My voice was choked and small, tears still obvious in it. "Is there any way you could give me a ride to the ranch house? Jocelyn said I could use her computer there. I always check on my daughter by e-mail in the morning."

He scrubbed his forehead with his thumb and forefinger. For a moment I thought he'd say no, and I was going to be disappointed in more ways than one. "The power's out at the house, and as usual the phones are messed up."

"Oh . . ." I muttered, looking down at my hands, knowing that I was making a bigger deal of this than it was. Zach probably thought I was an emotional basket case. "Well, that's OK. It can wait until later."

Tapping his thumb against the steering wheel, he studied me for a long moment. "Lindsey, what's going on?" he said with the same bedside manner he used when he talked to Mr. Grits. It seemed as if next he would check my ears and teeth to see what was ailing me.

Pulling in a breath and letting it out, I pushed strings of wet hair away from my face, wiped my eyes again, and pressed my fingers against my temples. "Just ignore me. I'm having an off-kilter day. It's raining, and I miss my little girl, and I was stuck in the cabin with the power out, and I got a little crazy." Zach didn't answer, and I didn't glance over to check his reaction. If he had any doubts about my being a therapy patient, he was probably fully convinced now. The rest of the Sydney story oozed out of me like thick, black ink. "She's never been gone for the summer before. She's never spent any time away. All of a sudden her father has remarried, and out of the blue he wants to exercise the joint custody, and now she's gone to Mexico until school starts. Her dad was having some big party last night with his crew, and I have this horrible image of Sydney running around some grown-up fiesta with everyone drunk, or stoned, or God knows what else. Geoff's crew members aren't the most savory people, and he doesn't get the fact that, even though Sydney talks like an adult sometimes, she's just an eight-year-old girl." There, I'd done it. I'd dumped my whole pathetic story, identified myself as a divorced-mom-with-major-baggage. Now it was time for him to politely backpedal, then run the other direction.

I felt relieved, let off the hook the way I had when Sleepy increased the distance between us in the horse corral. Jocelyn was right about me. I was a serial offender. Once again I was committing willful injury to a potential relationship.

Zach was silent for a long time, and when I looked up, he was staring out the window, concentrating on some point far in the distance, thinking. Probably figuring out how to let me down easy. An eternity of silence passed. I wished he would just get on with it. Make his excuses and be done. He seemed far away, as if he'd forgotten I was there. Maybe he hadn't even been listening to my big information dump. Maybe his mind was on something else altogether.

In which case, he wasn't a fit relationship partner, and my problem was solved, either way.

He turned slowly to look at me, his eyes reflecting the brooding sky outside. "That has to be hard." I had the distinct impression he'd been about to say something else. "Having Sydney gone, I mean."

"It is." As I had last night, I sensed that he didn't just hear what I was saying; he heard what I was feeling, as if there were some invisible connection between us. "It's like someone ripped out my heart, and it's walking around outside my body, and I have no control over what's happening to it. I can't think. I can't function. I can't . . . breathe." I couldn't believe I was telling him all of this. I couldn't believe he was listening.

"Is that why you came to Texas—here to the therapy camp?" His chin came up, his eyes narrowing slightly. He knew there was more to me than I'd been letting on, and he was waiting to see if I would tell him the truth.

I met his gaze, and knew I couldn't lie anymore. "Zach, I have a confession to make." An invisible fist clenched in my chest, squeezing everything. What was he going to say when I told him the truth? Then again, if I really wanted him to run away, why did I care? Maybe because I didn't want him to run away? "I came here . . . for something other than horse therapy. I mean, I came to Texas in the first place just to get away from home and visit my sister, but when I got here, Laura had this idea of my helping Collie with an article"—taking a deep breath, I came out with it—"about the stolen dinosaur tracks. I'm not really a writer. I'm a lab supervisor for a museum in Colorado. I specialize in archaeology and paleontology. Jocelyn and Collie were hoping I could help find the people who took the fossils."

Zach nodded, his face impassive, giving little hint of his feelings. If this were poker, he would have been good at it. "That explains a few things"—he glanced speculatively toward my mired Jeep—"like you visiting with Melvin in town, and being down here at the river this morning. But then, why the horse psychology class?"

Biting my lip, I tried to decide if the whole truth would cause serious trouble between Jocelyn and him. I wished he would look at me, react, give some indication of what he was thinking. He seemed to be calmly taking it all in, maybe waiting until he had all the facts before he exploded. The funny man didn't look so funny anymore. There wasn't a hint of the usual humorous twinkle in his eye.

I puffed out a breath. Jocelyn and Collie were probably going to kill me for telling him. What if he blew the whole plan right out of the water? "Don't get mad," I prefaced, "but the horse psychology class was . . . a cover. Jocelyn didn't want to upset Pop, or you, and she didn't want any of the ranch hands to know why I was here. She and Collie think the theft was an inside job."

"Great." He drummed the steering wheel with his palm heel— the first hint of brewing emotion. "We've been over that. I told her to leave it alone. That's just what Pop needs now—to find out Jocelyn's investigating his help. Pop's got enough problems already. He doesn't need anything else to happen." The depth of his feelings for Pop were clear in that last sentence. Zach's face was dark with worry and grief. It was obvious how much he loved his grandfather, and for him, nothing else mattered but Pop's well-being.

I laid my hand on his arm. "We're keeping it quiet, Zach. Jocelyn knows Pop's health is fragile. But if there's somebody working here you can't trust, don't you think you should find out about it before something else happens?"

His jaw tightened in response. Clearly his mind was made up. "If something else happens, we'll deal with it then. I told Jocelyn that already. Pop's not the addle-brained idiot she thinks he is. He's going to find out what's going on eventually, or else Dan will figure it out and tell him. Pop doesn't need that kind of excitement. The tracks are gone. The damage is done. Jocelyn should leave it alone and let Pop recover in peace."

"Just let it go a few more days. Don't say anything to Jocelyn," I pleaded. "I'll be discreet. I'll make sure no one figures out what's going on. I'll even take more horse psychology classes." The last part was a feeble attempt to lighten the moment. To my surprise, it won a faint smile from Zach. "Come on, humor me." I made a puppy face at him. "I'm having a bad day."

"Good Lord, those eyes," he muttered, shaking his head at me. "All right."

"Thanks!" Leaning across the seat, I gave him an exuberant hug. The next thing I knew, we were kissing and my heart was thundering like a racehorse bolting from the starting gate.

By the time the kiss was over, I couldn't imagine how I could ever have thought of this as a bad day. Today was a wonderful day. Sunshine and rainbows, regardless of the weather. It wouldn't have mattered if I got ten Jeeps stuck in the mud, as long as Zach came to rescue me every time.

"Tell you what"—he put the truck in gear—"I'll drop you by the cabin to clean up, and then let's run on into San Saline. They have high-speed Internet at the library, and when we're done, we can grab some lunch at the café over there."

A lump formed in my throat again, but it was a happy-tears lump, the kind you feel when someone gives you an unexpected gift. "You don't have to do that. I'm all right now. I promise."

"I want to," he said, reaching over and mussing my hair in a way that was both familiar and sweet. "Besides, it'd be good if I got on-line today and cleared up my e-mail from work, maybe checked in with the kid who's house-sitting my place in Austin. The rain's supposed to stop pretty soon. Once things dry out a little, I've got some more windmills to check. I'm on a mission to eliminate the need for the Bales brothers before I leave here." Glancing sideways at me, he raised a brow playfully. "You might want to come along."

"I might," I said, smiling back at him. "You know what? I just might."

SIXTEEN

Dear Sydney,

Mommy misses you. Sorry I didn't get to send a very long e-mail yesterday. I was borrowing the computer in the local library, and the power kept blinking on and off. I think the power company must have been trying to fix some lines around town. Anyway, I'm sorry your dad's crew didn't get to come over last night.

I didn't comment on the rest of what she'd said about one of the crew members having been thrown in jail for brawling in some bar, and Geoff spending his evening at the police station, no doubt bribing the officials to drop the whole thing. I didn't want to think about that. If I did, I'd go crazy worrying about the fact that Geoff planned to have his party tonight, now that none of his crew members were in jail.

Anyway, if they come tonight, be a good girl and stay out of the way. Grown-up parties are for grown-ups, sweetheart. You go on to bed early and let the grown-ups have their get-together, all right?

I hope you had a good day yesterday. Did you like the pictures of the running horses and the big white dog? Isn't he funny-looking? It's the middle of the night, and he's sleeping by the door. He snores worse than

GRANDPA DRAPER. THERE ARE COYOTES HOWLING OUTSIDE, AND
IT ISN'T BOTHERING HIM ONE BIT, BUT IT'S KEEPING ME
AWAKE. . . .

I knew it wasn't the coyotes or the snoring dog that was keeping
me awake, but I couldn't tell my daughter that. My mind was in
hyperdrive, reliving the last two days with Zach over and over again
as I tried to distract myself by writing tomorrow's e-mail to Sydney.

THE DOG HAD A BIG ADVENTURE THE OTHER DAY. HE'S A BIT
OF AN OUTLAW, I THINK. HE MADE A GREAT ESCAPE AND WE HAD
A WILD CHASE THROUGH THE PASTURE IN A PICKUP TRUCK. FI-
NALLY HE STOPPED UNDERNEATH A TREE. . . .

Where I kissed Zach Truitt while the Blum sisters looked on. By
now, word was probably all over the county.

IT'S A FAMOUS TREE, AND YOU WOULDN'T BELIEVE HOW BIG
IT IS. WHEN YOU'RE UNDERNEATH THE BRANCHES, THE SHADE
IS THICK AND COOL, WITH BITS OF SUNLIGHT STREAMING
THROUGH. THE BRANCHES START HIGH OVERHEAD AND SCOOP TO-
WARD THE GROUND, SO THAT ON THE ENDS THEY TOUCH THE WILD-
FLOWERS. IT WOULD BE A GREAT TREE FOR CLIMBING. THERE'S
A LEGEND THAT IT'S A MAGIC TREE, AND PEOPLE AROUND HERE
REALLY BELIEVE IT. DOESN'T THAT SOUND LIKE SOMETHING
FROM ONE OF YOUR STORYBOOKS? SORT OF LIKE THE MAGIC TREE
HOUSE, WHERE JACK AND ANNIE HAVE BIG ADVENTURES . . .

Except in this case, Zach and Lindsey ended their adventure with
a kiss, and not just any kiss. My body flushed as I snuggled into the
memory—Zach and I chasing Mr. Grits through the pasture, kissing
beneath the branches of the Lover's Oak, driving back to the ranch,
sharing a private lesson in horse psychology, our hands moving together over Sleepy's sleek silver hide, his velvet muzzle beneath my fingers. Trust. Faith. Fear. Freedom. Climbing the windmill tower. Dublin

Dr Pepper. Zach's lips touching mine. His heartbeat. His smile. Watching the sun descend, the sky catch fire, then turn dim, the stars come out, the moon rise, heavy and orange and full. Sitting and talking for hours. Zach rescuing me from the mud yesterday, not saying a word about how idiotic it was to have gotten stuck like that. The way he listened as I talked about Sydney, not offering the usual trite comfort lines or pat solutions, just holding my hand in a way that eased the lonely ache in my body and soul. He'd spent the morning taking me to the library to use the computer, sat there thumbing through a copy of *Lonesome Dove*, patiently waiting in a chair that was made for someone much smaller than he was, as the power blinked on and off, repeatedly losing my message before I could send it to Sydney. He never seemed frustrated, or urged me to give up so he could get on with his day. He just skimmed his book, chatted with the librarian—the only other person in the library on such a day—and finally resorted to experimenting with the balance point of his undersized chair, tipping back onto two legs like a little boy bored at school.

When the electricity finally seemed to be recovering, he moved to the computer next to me, and we sat side by side checking e-mail. Afterward, we had lunch at the Sale Barn Café, where everyone knew Zach and was interested in me, and then we took a tour of San Saline. By the time we were finished, things had dried out and the sun was high and hot as we headed back to the ranch. We performed minor operations on three windmills, drove the tractor down to the river to pull my Jeep out of the rapidly drying mud, washed the mud off with the pressure washer at headquarters, then went back to Loveland for more windmill oil and supper at the Big Lizard, where we sat by the river in the moonlight, talking for the longest time before he brought me back to the cabin.

Only later did I realize that, all day long, the conversation had focused mostly on me, my life. We hadn't talked about Zach's past, not the more recent parts anyway, except that he traveled a lot for his job, and he had a home outside of Austin where he lived when he wasn't traveling. He hadn't mentioned the divorce, or why he was no longer Becky's brother-in-law.

Why?

Of course, there were things I'd omitted from my personal history, as well. How deeply I'd been in love with Geoff. How devastated I was when he left. How afraid I was of everything. I'd revealed that I was investigating the stolen tracks, but I hadn't told him that Melvin had shown me a perfectly preserved femur, and I suspected there was something big somewhere on the Jubilee Ranch—his home, which he didn't want changed by horse psychology camps or, undoubtedly, the discovery of a major fossil site along the river.

It was wrong to keep that secret. Alone in the dark of midnight, I could see that clearly enough. If he found out by accident, he might think that the romance was part of some sleazy plan. My way of distracting him while I snooped around the ranch. Today when I saw him, I'd tell him about Melvin's discovery. Somehow I'd show him that this—whatever it was between us—was as far from my plans as the sun is from the earth. What was happening was a matter of pure gravitational pull. I was terrified of getting burned in the end, but when we were together, I couldn't stop myself from dancing closer and closer to the flames.

If I told him all of that, would he reveal the parts of himself he had so far kept hidden? If he did, what would they be? Then again, what if he didn't. . . . ?

Rubbing my eyes and blinking away the sleep, I left off the analysis of Zach and returned to my e-mail to Sydney. I was finally getting tired, sheer exhaustion slowing the whirling in my head and extinguishing the sparks floating through my body like drift from a Fourth of July sparkler. As soon as I finished writing, I'd turn in.

I'd sleep in the bedroom where Jeremiah and Caroline's picture hung on the wall, where they once shared a lovers' bed. The thought of it brought an emptiness, a hollowness to some deep, needy place inside me—a place I'd tried for so many years to ignore. I wanted to love. I wanted to be with someone who loved me more than anything. I wanted to ride the sky-high gondola across the Royal Gorge and see what was on the other side. I didn't want to be alone and afraid, insulated behind a chain-link fence the rest of my life.

Common sense told me that I shouldn't be looking for a solution a thousand miles from home with some cowboy veterinarian I barely knew.

I focused on the computer screen again. On a story I could write the way I wanted to. Real life was so much more complicated.

I think I am in love.

I sat staring at the words, wondering if my fingers were in need of an exorcism. How was it possible that I could have typed those six little words? How could I have thought such a thing?

Yet there it was in black and white. *I think I am in love.* At the end of the line, the cursor sat blinking, demanding more, insisting on further analysis. *I think I am in love . . . and, and, and?* And what? What could possibly come after that? Perhaps some unrealistic Hollywood description, like:

When I'm near him, I feel like a completely different person. I feel free, alive, ecstatic. He makes me laugh. When he smiles, I catch my breath. When he touches me, I can't catch my breath. When he kisses me, I feel like I'm soaring, like nothing matters but that moment. I feel as giddy as a teenager, as if my entire body is full of giggles and butterflies. Sweet sixteen and never been kissed. Never been kissed like that . . .

Sitting back in my chair, I studied the words, shaking my head at their foolishness. I wasn't a teenager, or some dewy-eyed starlet in an old movie. I was a grown woman—a combination of Control Freak Lindsey, and Mommy Lindsey, and Archaeologist Lindsey, and Romance Lindsey, and Practical Lindsey, who should have been able to think things through more clearly than this.

I started typing again, my emotions flowing from the keyboard like an artist's self-portrait, rough and honest and freehand.

When I'm with him, I feel like a completely different person. I like the way this person feels. And then I wonder—is this the person I really am?

How can you know for certain what parts of yourself are authentic and what parts you've invented to make life bearable?

Stopping, I stared at the cursor, reading, thinking, afraid to put the most important question into print, until finally I broke down and typed it anyway, so that I could see how it looked.

What if this is real? Sometime between grits in the morning and Dublin Dr Pepper at night, I fell in love. Really in love. True story.

The cursor demanded more.

And now, and now, and now?

I had no idea. Until today, I would have never considered that love at first sight was even possible, though that was the way my father told the story of falling for my mother. They met at a party for returning soldiers, they danced all night, and he knew. He wrote home and told his mom he'd met the girl he was going to marry. I'd always thought that story was fiction, something he made up to make life sound more glamorous than it really was. A funny little anecdote to tell at neighborhood barbecues and Christmas parties at the army base. Now I wondered.

Maybe the legend of the Lover's Oak really is true. Maybe it's—

By the door, Mr. Grits let out a deafening bark, and I jerked halfway out of my chair, the laptop sliding down my legs and clattering onto the floor. Mr. Grits scrambled to his feet and barked again as I untangled myself and reached for the computer.

"Please don't be broken," I muttered, pushing up the screen and waiting to see if the computer was dead, or had just gone into sleep mode when the screen snapped shut.

The dog growled ominously, and I forgot all about the computer. I'd never heard him make that sound before. Setting down my laptop, I moved closer to the dog, my heart rocketing into my throat as he snarled at the door, his jowls drawing back so that his long canine teeth flashed in the dim light.

"Mr. Grits?" I whispered, afraid of him, or whatever was outside, or both. I looked for a weapon and settled for a flashlight and an old walking cane from the hall tree.

Mr. Grits glanced at me, whined, then growled at the door again.

"What's the matter, fella?" I stood looking at the old iron doorknob with the skeleton key still in the lock. Slim protection if there really was something out there.

The high squeal of vehicle brakes said *someone*, not *something*. Shifting to the window, I saw headlights moving through the trees, traveling the road to the fossil site.

Slipping into my shoes, I turned the lock with shaking hands and carefully opened the door. Mr. Grits squeezed past me, bolting out before I could catch him.

"Mr. Grits!" I hollered, but he only bayed and kept running, his bark echoing into the night again and again, and then silence. Flipping the flashlight on, I dashed after him, calling his name. Halfway down the driveway, I slid to a stop, scanning the trees with the beam, listening.

Somewhere near the river, brakes squealed again, the dog bayed, and I heard a vehicle grind gears and come back in my direction. Headlights passed through the trees, then disappeared for a moment behind a grove of cedar before a dark-colored truck bounced onto the road and vanished around the corner. Within moments the night was as silent as if nothing had happened.

Shivering, I made a circle with the flashlight beam, suddenly feeling exposed and vulnerable. If they were thieves, obviously Mr. Grits had scared them off. "Mr. Grits . . ." I called. His answer came from near the house. When I walked back, he was sitting in the shaft of light from the front door, looking at me as if he couldn't imagine why I was running around in my pajamas in the dark of midnight.

Puffing out a long sigh, I reentered the yard and closed the gate, exhausted mentally, physically, and emotionally. I tried not to think about what sorts of creatures might be moving around in the trees as I stood on the porch with Mr. Grits, listening to make sure the night was again free of human sounds. Finally I went back inside, locked the door, and checked the laptop, which was sitting on the fireplace ledge, the screen saver displaying a cityscape of Denver. The machine seemed to be undamaged, but my letter was gone, which was fine. Since I wasn't hooked up to the Internet, there was no chance of my ramblings having accidentally been sent into cyberspace. It was just drivel, anyway. Foolishness. Wishful thinking and impractical notions. I was better off never seeing it again.

But climbing into bed, in the room where Jeremiah and Caroline had lived, and loved, and created a family, I thought about the words and felt the painful loneliness again.

I think I am in love. . . .

Is this the person I really am?

With questions, no answers, I drifted off in the arms of a prayer. *Please, God, if this is real, send me a sign. If not, take away this terrible longing. . . .*

Deep in the night, I dreamed of Sleepy, dressed in a fine cowboy saddle, black leather with glimmering silver studs. His long white mane floated in the breeze, cascading in slow motion as he tossed his head and reared high onto his hind legs, pawing the air. On his back, I did a parade wave in fringed leather gloves, then tipped my hat to the crowd of admirers lined along the open prairie. My father was there, and Laura, Collie, Melvin and Vanita Blue, and Pop Truitt holding the hand of Sydney. My mom was there, waving to get my attention. She smiled when our gazes met. I wanted to run to her and ask where she'd been, but she was busy talking to John Wayne—

the older John Wayne, weathered and leathery, the way he looked in *Rooster Cogburn,* my father's favorite movie.

Beside me a horse nickered, and I realized I wasn't alone. I turned to find my sidekick atop a pinto, his grin unmistakable, his frosted green eyes out of keeping with the Hollywood Indian garb. "Here's to tilting at windmills," he said, and his horse reared high in the air, then leaped forward. Sleepy followed, and together we streaked across open prairie toward the dawn.

The sound of a music box tugged me from my sleep, and I jerked fitfully, opened my eyes to the blurry image of the room, then closed them and drifted somewhere between dreams and reality.

I saw Caroline Truitt standing at the window, swaying to the tinny rhythms of the waltz. She heard me moving in the bed, turned, and smiled. "Welcome home," she said, and held out her hands, beckoning me to dance. I reached toward her, but she wheeled away, and I knew she was talking to someone else. Jeremiah filled the doorway. He took her in his arms and swung her around the room, and she threw her head back, her laughter floating with the music. . . .

My body jerked, and I sat up in bed, realizing I was laughing, my mind still spinning from the imaginary dance. Mr. Grits was sitting in the doorway, watching me with his face tipped to one side, and his brow raised in curiosity.

"I've lost my mind," I admitted, surveying the room. "Don't tell anybody." The cabin was awash with light, testifying to the fact that I'd slept later than I'd intended to.

Jumping out of bed, I checked my watch on the nightstand: seven fifty-one a.m. Horse therapy class started at nine thirty. If I didn't hurry with my hike up the mountain and e-mailing Sydney, I'd be late. Surprisingly, I didn't want to be. I couldn't wait to show Jocelyn, and the professor, and all the college kids that I was not a horse psychology failure, after all. Today the professor would have to write about somebody else on his little notepad.

I rushed through bathing in the little bathroom on the back porch. The old galvanized-metal bathtub was awkward, but quaint, and the tiny bathroom functional, if not luxurious. The Spartan nature gave me an awareness of all the unnecessary things that cluttered my life. Here, I didn't bother with a hair dryer, just left my hair in long, dark waves that reached to the middle of my back, but would dry shorter. Here, it didn't matter if straight hair was more stylish, or if "up" hair looked more fashionable for giving tours at the museum. Here, I could be myself.

Is this the person I really am? The question whispered through my mind as I slipped on jeans and a T-shirt and stood staring in the bedroom mirror.

Is this the person I really am?

Who am I really?

Mr. Grits saved me from my impromptu analysis by whining and scratching at the door in the other room.

"OK, OK, I'm coming. I'm coming," I muttered, slipping the laptop into the backpack, hefting it onto my shoulder, then grabbing the dog rope. "I bet you really need a restroom break by now."

Whining again, Mr. Grits lifted a paw and scratched the door.

"Hang on," I said, reading the carved words on the door frame as I untangled the rope. *Ende gut, Alles gut.*

What did that mean?

"We're going to have to ask somebody what that says." Slipping the rope into place, I reached for the door. As soon as it was open far enough, Mr. Grits bolted through, dragging me out so fast that I barely had time to catch the handle and pull it shut.

We were up the mountain in record time, Mr. Grits running, and me half jogging, half skiing behind him.

When we reached the bench at the top of the hill, I dropped the rope and let the dog roll in the wildflowers while I set up the cell phone and computer, anxious to read my latest e-mail from Sydney and know that everything was all right after Geoff's party for his crew.

I held my breath as the e-mail came up.

There was only one note from Sydney, written early in the morning after the party. The picture of the horses was cool, she said. She wanted to keep the dog, and she was sure he'd do fine in an apartment. She was bored this morning because Whitney was still asleep after the party. She couldn't swim because the housekeeper was busy cleaning up the mess and couldn't watch her. She missed her friends back home in Denver, and she missed me. She guessed maybe she'd go back to bed awhile. She signed it, *XOXOXO, Sydney Anne Attwood*. Her full name, as if this were an official document. A communiqué to a stranger, or a foreign dignitary.

I sat staring at it, feeling my little girl slipping through my fingers. Sydney Anne Attwood signed her letters with Xs and Os, like a teenager. Probably something she'd learned from Whitney. But there was another thing that bothered me, aside from the new signature and the full name. There was a lack of details that was not Sydney's usual style, as if she were hiding something, or there were facts about the party she thought she shouldn't tell me.

Was it real, or was I imagining it? Was she trying to protect her father, or could it be that someone had edited her e-mail, making things sound better than they were?

"Don't get paranoid, Lindsey," I muttered as I answered Sydney's note. I talked about horse psychology class, and Mr. Grits, and the magic tree—gave her a condensed version of the e-mail that had disappeared the night before. This one said nothing about Zach Truitt, or the kiss, or the soul-searching questions of love and destiny.

Pushing the send button, I sighed, once again feeling the ache of separation, wishing I could squeeze myself into the tiny electronic words and fly to where my little girl was.

I tried not to think about it as I composed an e-mail to Collie, describing day one of horse psychology class. I glossed over the fact that I'd failed to actually catch my horse during class, and that Zach had to help me later. Instead I talked about how Jocelyn worked with the different students, and how each of us learned lessons about our own hang-ups and relationship-building skills (or lack thereof). I finished by describing the complete sense of elation I felt when I'd finally captured Sleepy and led him to freedom. If Collie talked to Jocelyn, she would get a different story, but I thought my version would look much better in *Family Circle* magazine.

When I'd finished my e-mail to Collie, I wrote a quick note to Gracie at the sheriff's department to report the suspicious vehicle by the fossil site last night. It wasn't much to go on, I told her, perhaps not related to the thefts at all, but it seemed as if they left in a hurry when they saw that someone was in the cabin. She might at least want to come by and see if the vehicle left any tracks. Even though things had dried out surprisingly well since yesterday's rain, the soil was still damp enough that some tire imprints might have remained.

I moved quickly through the rest of my e-mail list, deleting spam and junk messages, answering one from my boss at the museum, who was worried about me and wanted me to take all the vacation time I needed; and my neighbor in the apartment building, who knew the entire custody saga, heard me sobbing at night through the ventilation system, and wanted to make sure I hadn't driven off a cliff somewhere between Denver and Texas. Sydney's third-grade teacher had even checked in, just to see how the summer was going. She hoped everything was all right with Sydney's visit to her father's house.

I answered them all quickly.

EVERYTHING'S FINE. THANKS FOR CHECKING IN. I'M ON A RANCH IN THE TEXAS HILL COUNTRY, HAVING A LITTLE VACATION AND HELPING TO RESEARCH AN ARTICLE FOR MY SISTER'S MAGAZINE. SYDNEY E-MAILS ME EVERY DAY TO TELL ME WHAT SHE'S BEEN DOING. I MISS HER, BUT IT SOUNDS LIKE THINGS ARE GOING ALL RIGHT THERE. SEE YOU SOON, LINDSEY.

I left it at that. No point dredging up all my fears and worries about what might or might not be happening in Mexico. It was hard to know how much of that was real, and how much of it was the product of my separation anxiety.

There was one more entry at the end of the page. The subject line stopped me from deleting it as spam. *Dinosaur Tracks?* Opening it, I scrolled through the paragraph quickly, my eyes skimming the text, my mouth hanging open. They were questions from Geoff about the stolen fossils—how large were they, what composition of rock, what size and type of tracks, exactly? Apparently my e-mail had piqued his interest. He had already started putting the word out on the market, as if he were a buyer—to see if he would get any bites. Something that big would be bound to turn up, he said.

I stared at the e-mail, at his electronic signature, torn between answering it and deleting it. Three paragraphs of questions about dinosaur tracks, and not a thing about our daughter. Just one little line at the bottom.

P.S.: SYDNEY'S DOING FINE. DON'T WORRY IF YOU DON'T HEAR FROM HER THIS MORNING. SHE'S SLEEPING IN.

His attempt at peacemaking, perhaps, but not a very good one. Our daughter's first visit deserved at least a paragraph or two. He owed me that much for having raised the little girl he now claimed he wanted so badly, the one who sat home day after day, waiting for a little of his time.

Closing my eyes, I breathed slowly in and out, stifling the urge to spill that bitterness onto the screen and send it to him. I imagined myself back at horse psychology class as Jocelyn corrected one of the college kids when he threw the halter at his horse, causing it to run away. *Angry outbursts are unproductive in a relationship. Do you see how lashing out only separates the parties involved? If you're not getting what you want, you have to try a different approach . . .*

Maybe the dialogue about fossils could be a bridge between Geoff and me, a way to build the trust we needed to raise our daughter in this uncertain world of custody and visitation.

Taking a deep breath, I answered the note with more facts about the fossils, then added at the bottom:

THANKS FOR LETTING ME KNOW ABOUT SYDNEY. I JUST WANT HER TO HAVE A GOOD SUMMER.

I paused with my fingers above the keyboard.

And a good life, I wanted to add. *I don't want her to grow up wounded and torn. I want her to be whole. Happy. That's all I want.*

I pushed send without adding the last part.

One step at a time. It's all about trust.

The e-mail went through, sent and gone, and I logged off the Net, then sat there for a moment letting the cool morning breeze smooth my emotions like water over sand. In the valley below, the horses raised their heads and began moving toward the gate. Standing up, I shaded my eyes, spotting Zach near the corral, sitting bareback atop a brown-and-white-spotted horse, just like in my dream. My hero.

He looked my way, and I waved madly, mindless of the fact that I was standing on the edge of a cliff. Every ounce of anxiety left me, and a warm flush traveled my body from head to toe. I felt as if I could sail off the mountain and flutter through the air like a butterfly.

"Good morning!" I called. It was silly, I knew, since he couldn't hear me.

My cell phone rang on the bench, and I jumped, then picked it up as Zach waved, and tapped his ear, then held his hands up helplessly. I considered hollering something about tilting at windmills, but I thought better of it and answered the phone. Collie was on the other end.

"Hi, there!" I said, sounding far too cheerful.

"Hi . . . yourself," Collie replied hesitantly. "How are things going?"

"Great!" I chirped, fanning the heat in my face, trying to return to earth. Zach was coming across the pasture on the spotted horse. At a full gallop. Bareback. Straight toward me. It was hard to stay calm.

"Wow . . . uhhh . . . really?" Collie sounded incredulous. "So . . . what's going on?"

"Well . . ." *I went on a wild dog chase, I kissed Zach under the Lover's Oak, I mastered horse psychology lesson number one, I learned how to fix windmills, and I developed an affinity for Dublin Dr Pepper. I got my Jeep stuck in the mud, visited the library, toured San Saline, and learned how to pull a vehicle out of the mud with a tractor. I think I may have fallen in love. . . .* "Not a lot, really."

"Oh." Collie sounded disappointed, or worried, I couldn't tell which. "By the way, I put a notice in the paper for the lost dog. Maybe someone will call about him. Anything new on the stolen tracks?"

"Not much to report," I admitted, feeling guilty for having spent all day yesterday making goo-goo eyes with Zach, even after the weather dried up and I could have been down at the track site. "I'm going to dig into it more today—no pun intended. I still need to get the copies of Caroline Truitt's journals from Pop." *I should have done that yesterday, but I was too busy fixing windmills.* "Something strange happened last night, though. I was up late"—*thinking about Zach*—"and a truck went by, headed for the riverbank. I'm not sure who it was, but it seemed like they left in a hurry when they heard the dog."

"That doesn't sound good." Collie paused, like she was writing down something. "Did you get a look at the truck?"

"Not really. Dark colored. Black or blue, maybe, with squeaky brakes and no tailgate." Like Jimmy Hawthorne's new truck, I realized. I didn't want to say that to Collie. The grumpy ranch foreman, Dan, also drove a dark-colored pickup truck with no tailgate. Probably so did half of the county. "It isn't much to go on, but I e-mailed the details to Gracie."

"Good. Listen, be careful."

"I will." Below, Zach disappeared into a brush-covered creek bed, then came out the other side, waving his hat, because he knew I'd be watching. I waved back, giggling.

Collie heard it, of course. "Lindsey?"

"Sorry." *Get a grip. Calm down.* "Anyway, I'll see what I can find out about the fossils today, and report back. I e-mailed Geoff, and he said he'd put the word out on the market. Something might turn up there, as well."

"You e-mailed *Geoff* for help with the fossils?" Collie choked on the idea. "Really?"

"Yes, really." Zach moved into the shadow of the cliff, and I inched forward so that I could watch as the spotted horse slowly picked a path through the loose rocks below. "If anyone would know where to find black-market fossils, it's Geoff. Besides, I'm trying to approach things from a psychological perspective—make peace, build trust, work with each other, not against each other, all that stuff."

Collie chuckled. "Sounds like you learned something in horse therapy class."

"I was a washout, actually. I sent you an e-mail about it a few minutes ago. I was the only one who couldn't catch my horse, and then . . . " My concentration wavered. Zach was almost directly below me now. What was he doing? "Zach." I realized I'd said his name out loud, with a little jitter of vocal excitement. I finished lamely, ". . . helped me out."

"Really?" Now Collie was interested. Much more interested than she'd been in the fossil hunt. "Zach helped you with horse therapy class?"

"It was no big deal. We were headed out to fix a windmill." I dropped my face into my hand. *Shoot. That was stupid.*

"You and Zach were out fixing windmills. . . ." Collie trailed off suggestively, the way only a girlfriend can do. The way that lets you know you've given out too much information, and she's figured out your secrets. "Something I should know about?"

"No." Below, Zach stopped the horse and tipped his hat back to look up at me. Sitting down I scooted to the edge of the cliff on my rear end. Safety first.

He pointed to the cell phone, made the *naughty, naughty* sign with two fingers, reminding me that all electronic devices were forbidden in Jocelyn's horse psychology program.

Giggling into the phone, I shrugged with my palms up. Down there, bareback on the spotted horse, Zach looked very much like Tonto in my dream.

"There *is* something I should know about," Collie concluded.

"No, there's not," I rushed out. I wasn't ready to bring Collie or anyone else in on this thing, this . . . whatever it was between Zach and me. "I had a funny dream last night, that's all. It just came back to me. I was the Lone Ranger on my horse psychology horse. You were there, and Laura, and my mom and dad, and John Wayne." And Zach as Tonto, but I left out that part.

Collie gasped. "You had a John Wayne dream?" Covering the phone, she repeated to someone else, "She had a John Wayne dream."

It suddenly occurred to me that she'd been repeating almost everything I said. "Collie, is someone there with you?"

"Laura." Collie was trying very hard to sound nonchalant. "She says hi and she loves you. I came to her office to go over some things for the article before all her staff gets here this morning. We thought we'd call and see how research on the fossils was coming along."

"Oh, give me a break." I lowered my voice, even though I was pretty sure Zach couldn't hear me from below. The last thing I wanted was for him to think I was girlfriend-talking about him on the phone. "You two are scoping me out, big-time." All of a sudden it all started to make sense. The picture was disturbingly clear. "Listen, Collie, if you two have some crazy idea about Zach and me, just let it go, all right? Please? He drove me around the other day because my Jeep had a flat tire . . . well, and yesterday because my Jeep was stuck—long story. He helped me with my horse psychology horse, and I went along with him to fix some windmills. That's all. End of story."

Laughter poofed through the phone. "Was that before or after you kissed him under the Lover's Oak?" The last word broke into a torrent of giggles, and I could hear Laura cracking up in the background.

I dropped my face into my hand, my skin on fire with embarrassment that was probably visible, even from the bottom of the cliff. "Collie . . . I'm warning you . . ."

"Those Blum sisters get around," Collie gasped out between raucous giggles. "And you had a John Wayne dream. I had John Wayne dreams when I met True, and Laura had John Wayne dreams when she met Graham. I knew right then that she was in love. A John Wayne dream is a serious sign."

"Oh, Collie, for heaven's sake, that's—"

"Have a good day, girlfriend. Have *fun* for a change."

"Collie—"

"Love you."

"Collie, you tell Laura that—"

"Laura loves you, too. 'Bye." *Click*. She hung up, and the line went dead.

Rubbing my eyes, I set the phone down, trying not to consider the implications of Laura, Collie, and the Blum sisters all being in on my fledgling . . . whatever . . . with Zach. I leaned over the cliff so that I could see him.

"Morning." His voice echoed against the rocks, . . . *orning, orning, orning*.

A rush of giddiness danced over me like goose down, tickling my skin. "Hey, you!" I called, and the echo repeated: . . . *ey-oo, ey-oo, ey-oo*. He looked good down there, bareback on the painted horse. I felt like Rapunzel in the tower. I wished I could let my hair down and pull him up.

Cupping a hand to his mouth, he hollered, "Lunch at the Big Lizard?" The echo repeated: *izard, izard, izard?*

"Sure," *ur, ur, ur,* I answered.

"Meet you there at noon," *oon, oon, oon*.

"Sounds great"—*ate, ate, ate*. "See you"—*ooo, ooo, ooo*.

Oooh, oooh, oooh. There was nothing I wanted to do more than meet Zach for lunch at the Big Lizard Diner. Except possibly jump off the cliff right now and have him catch me.

Barring that, lunch would have to do.

Down below, he waved his hat, spun the horse around, and headed back toward the barn. I watched, feeling wistful.

The day was shaping up very well, indeed.

SEVENTEEN

D AY TWO OF HORSE PSYCHOLOGY CLASS WAS AN ENTIRELY DIFFERENT experience than day one. I was a star, a leader. Sleepy came to me like an old friend. I stroked his fur, rubbed his muzzle, felt his breath on my fingers, imagined my hands and Zach's intertwined, bridging the barriers of fear.

I talked to Sleepy as if he were a person, an extension of Zach. "Hold still, wait, wait. Give me a minute," I crooned as I tried to untangle the halter and put it on while keeping the rope off the ground, which was still slightly damp from yesterday's rain.

Sleepy sighed, blowing a spray of horse snot on my pants. I didn't care, really. I was completely comfortable and at ease. Sleepy knew that, and so he was relaxed, as well.

I began to see the magic of Jocelyn's horse psychology school. You couldn't put on airs with a horse, as we so often do with people. Horses look through the masks we wear and the things we say. They see who we really are. They gauge our intentions in a thousand invisible ways that have nothing to do with the words we say. They shy away from the barriers of fear, self-centeredness, jealousy, anger, impatience. They are drawn in by kindness, understanding, concern, openness, love.

The thing is, so are people.

I got it.

Right there in Jocelyn's horse corral, with the flies, and the dust, and the milling college kids, and the professor scribbling in his notebook, I had an epiphany.

Trust is the invisible string that binds a relationship. Fear is the knife that severs it. Fear manifests itself in many ways—fear of being alone, fear of losing control, fear of being hurt, fear of loving too completely, fear of being unloved, fear of the future. The list went on and on.

There is no way to mix faith and fear. They repel each other like oil and water.

Jocelyn nodded approval as I led Sleepy to the second corral. She knew I got it. "Good work, Lindsey," she said as I tied Sleepy to the railing, lifted his feet, and began cleaning them, as Jocelyn had shown us at the beginning of the lesson.

"Thanks," I said. It was work, this learning to build relationships, not to mention picking up the feet of a thousand-pound horse and chipping out cakes of compacted muck and horse poop, but today I was doing a good job. I was a crackerjack student.

Halfway through class, I started handing out free advice.

Madison, the blonde who'd had so much trouble the day before, was having difficulty picking up her horse's feet today. She was sure that the horse had decided again not to like her.

"See? He's trying to kick me!" she squealed.

"He's swishing at flies," I said, like the old pro I was.

Crossing her arms, she gave me a murderous sneer and tossed her ponytail with a bobble-head maneuver that said, *Who do you think you are?* "He doesn't like me. I swear, if I get a bad grade in this class, my dad is *so* gonna be at the dean's office."

On the fence, the professor wrote furiously on his notepad. *Bratty society girl, obviously a victim of parental overprotection. Classic case of chronic overindulgence. Suffering from ego dependence. Unprepared for life in real world. In lay terms, spoiled . . .*

I moved closer to Madison. Having just figured out the meaning of life, I was inclined to share it. "Horses don't like or dislike people. They react only to trust, or the lack of it," I parroted Zach's mantra from the day before.

She vacillated, reluctant to listen to the strange, thirty-something lady in the discount-store T-shirt and the slightly out-of-style jeans.

"Well . . . hold his head." She waved her fingers toward the horse, or me, or both.

"That's against the rules." I was patient. Surprisingly so, for me. The old Lindsey would have told her to drop the royal attitude. "You have to do it yourself. All the work that really matters in life, you do yourself. Other people can't do it for you."

Frowning at the completely foreign concept, she slowly uncrossed her arms. "So . . . like, what do I do?"

"Try approaching him slowly," I advised. "Run your hand down his legs a little at a time. Lean your shoulder against his shoulder. Let him shift his weight around and get comfortable; then lift the foot when he's ready."

She did, and it worked. Madison successfully cleaned her horse's feet, and not long after that she was giving advice to Robert, the sheriff's deputy with the bad attitude.

Around that time I checked out of horse psychology class. I was such a whiz that I got to leave early.

Jocelyn complimented me on my performance, then told me that Pop had found his Big Lizard Bottoms box, containing copies of Caroline Truitt's journals and some photos of the tracks, and I could pick them up at the main house after lunch, when Pop returned from his domino game in town. "In the meantime," she said with a conspiratorial smile, "I know you have other things to do."

I wasn't sure whether she was talking about Zach or the dinosaur mystery, and I didn't ask. "Great! See you later." As I untied Sleepy from the fence, the college kids glared at me like I'd just set the curve on a test.

"Teacher's pet," one of them grumbled as he squatted with both hands wrapped around his horse's leg, tugging like a frog trying to pull up a lily pad.

I smiled pleasantly and said, "Try putting gentle pressure against his shoulder with your shoulder and rubbing your hand down his leg until he shifts his weight." Then I offered a thumbs-up, adding, "Good luck," before I took Sleepy out to the pasture, giving him a last pat and a bear hug before heading for my car.

The professor nodded and said, "Good work," as I slipped out the gate.

"Thanks." Masquerading as a horse psychology student was kind of fun, I decided as I untied Mr. Grits from the fence and loaded him into the car. Ranch life seemed to suit me. I liked the long, busy days close to the land, the company of the animals, and, of course, the rancher.

Giggling, I danced a quick little jig as I climbed into the driver's seat. Dan, the grouchy ranch foreman, watched me from the barn. As usual, he looked like he'd just bitten into a lemon. Refusing to let anything dampen my spirits, I waved. I was having a zippity-do-dah day, and nobody was going to talk me out of it. I couldn't remember the last time I'd felt such anticipation for whatever lay ahead. It was good to be operating without a strict plan, filled with enthusiasm and curiosity about what the day might bring. The possibilities seemed endless.

I checked the time, trying to decide what to do next. It was eleven o'clock, too early to meet Zach at the Big Lizard, but there wasn't enough time for exploring the track site, either. The best idea was probably to go into town and find Melvin Blue. I wanted to make some field notes about the dinosaur bone in the closet, snap a picture or two, and take some measurements. I needed a more detailed look at his pretheft picture of the Jubilee tracks, so that when I picked up the Big Lizard Bottoms box from Pop this afternoon, I could go to the riverbed with a before picture in my mind. Caroline's field notes and Pop's old pictures of the site would also be helpful in that task.

I should have done all of that yesterday, I reminded myself with a small measure of guilt. This afternoon I needed to stick to business. I had to avoid becoming all light-headed and moony over Zach Truitt and getting coerced into being his assistant windmill fixer, or anything else—at least until after my work was done.

But even as I lectured myself, as I tried to focus on calculations about the age of the stolen Acrocanthosaurus tracks and the dimensions of Melvin's dinosaur bone, and whether it could be from a tyrannosaurus, I found myself, instead, pondering lunch with Zach. I couldn't wait to tell him how well Sleepy and I had worked together. Zach would be impressed. He would wink and say it was because I had private lessons; then he'd grin in that slow, lopsided way that sent a glimmer all the way to my toes.

When I thought about that, the dinosaur mystery hardly seemed important, and all I wanted to do was spend the day fixing windmills. I fell into a daydream as I stopped the car, allowing a slow-moving line of cattle to cross the driveway. In my mind I was Rancher Woman, rescuer of trapped horses, defender of threatened fossil sites, dog trainer, windmill mechanic, and romantic lead in whatever cowboy adventure Zach was starring in today.

I wished I knew the script. . . .

A rumbling diesel engine broke into my thoughts, and Mr. Grits sat at attention as I glanced in the rearview mirror. A truck was speeding along the road behind me, kicking up a cloud of dust that obliterated the view for a half mile. For an instant, I imagined that it was Zach, but this truck was dark and his was tan. A dark-colored truck . . . like the one I'd seen in the woods last night.

Slowing the SUV, I pulled over in a grassy spot to let the truck pass, so I could see who was driving.

Dan, the ranch manager, passed by without looking my way—as if, out here in the middle of the prairie, he hadn't noticed my Jeep beside the road. The squeal of brakes cut the quiet air as he turned the corner ahead.

Suspect number two: grouchy ranch manager with latent resentment toward horse psychology camp. Feels position on ranch is threatened. Possible motive—revenge or sinister plot to blame fossil theft on presence of tourists on ranch . . .

What if it really was him at the fossil site the night before? Then again, what if the truck I saw by the river last night was there on some official ranch business, making a night check of cattle or trying to chase away those annoying coyotes? What if I'd given Gracie an erroneous report of a suspicious dark pickup prowling around the river in the dark?

The vehicle disappeared around a curve, and I pulled out again. Dan could be the insider Jocelyn was worried about—someone who would have known the ranch schedules, and could have told the fossil thieves when the cabin by the river would be empty.

But if he knew I was in the cabin last night, why would he come down to the track site? Was he trying to frighten me off? Or was he just a harmless old coot, completely uninvolved with the fossil theft, just resentful of the tourists invading his territory? A dark truck and squeaky brakes weren't much to go on. I'd have to try to ferret out more information.

Pondering the mystery, I drove to town. By the time I reached Melvin's store, I had decided that a few tactful questions about the sour-faced ranch manager might be in order. I phrased and rephrased them in my mind as I parked in the shade, cracked the windows to give Mr. Grits some air, and headed up the steps to the store.

There was a note on the window that said, *Back at one*, so I drove over to the Big Lizard to see if Melvin was there having an extended lunch.

Vanita met me at the door to the dining car, which at the moment was full of old folks playing dominoes. I wondered if Pop was in there somewhere.

"Come on in. Lordy, these flies are terrible." Vanita gave me a little hug around the shoulders, pulling me into the coach and squeezing us through the doorway area, which was crowded with extra domino players and chairs. "Well, how are y'all today?"

I glanced over my shoulder. *Y'all . . . who?* Did she know that I had more than one personality in here? "Great," I answered.

Glancing out the door, she knitted her dark brows, which were out of keeping with her graying hair. "Oh, I just figured Zach would be with you, considering that—" Popping her mouth shut, she snapped to attention, just short of saying too much, I had a feeling.

The domino players paused in their games and regarded me with interest. From the far end of the room, Pop waved, and said, "Hiya . . . uhhh . . . Lin . . . Lindsey."

I waved back, feeling like an exotic specimen in one of the glass cages at the zoo. Clearly the Blum sisters had spilled the news about the incident at the Lover's Oak.

"Actually, I was hoping to catch Melvin," I replied, and Vanita looked perplexed.

"Oooh. About the bones in the closet?"

I jerked back, wondering if anyone else had heard. Fortunately, the domino players had returned to their games, all except for the Blum sisters, who were eagle-eyeing us from three booths away. "I wanted to take some measurements," I said.

The Blum sister on the right gasped and whispered to the Blum sister on the left, who blinked in astonishment.

"Why, sure," Vanita replied, shooing me toward the exit. "You go right ahead. The door's open over there. I'm keepin' an eye on the store while Melvin's gone to San Saline. Luckily we don't have too many customers this time of day."

"Thanks." I wondered when, exactly, rush hour started at the Over the Moon. "If Zach shows up, tell him I'll be back in a minute. We're supposed to meet for lunch."

Looking pleased, Vanita nodded as she held open the screen. "Oh, I know. He called while ago." Her tone made me wonder if Zach was up to something, but I didn't ask, because the Blum sisters were listening in. They had enough ammunition already. In the third booth on the left, they were retelling the story of the infamous dog chase. I heard it while trying to squeeze past Vanita in the doorway.

". . . thought maybe it was some kind of a drunk, driving across the pasture like that. Looked like one of them four-wheel-drive commercials. And I said to Iris, 'Iris, we'd better see what's goin' on down there. Might be some joyriding teenager's made off with the Jubilee Ranch truck, and we need to call the county sheriff.' So Iris and I loaded up and we drove down there, we did, and there they were. That pretty girl with the dark hair and Zach Truitt, parked smack-dab under the Lover's Oak. Wasn't no little chitchat going on, either, let me tell you. They were wrapped around each other like lizards on a beanpole. Full-frontal kiss . . ."

I let the door slam behind me, cutting off the rest. Good God, what a mess. By the time the Blum sisters got through with the story, there was no telling what everyone would be thinking about Zach and me.

On the other hand, it was kind of fun being a local celebrity, the topic of small-town scandal and speculation. But there was a part of me that worried I might be enjoying this too much. I had a daughter, and a job, and a real life waiting for me a thousand miles away. Getting involved with Zach Truitt was only going to make it that much harder to go home again.

Crossing the parking lot, I hummed the theme to *The Sound of Music,* blocking out the negative thoughts. *Live for today,* I told myself. *Enjoy what is, for a change, without worrying about what might be.*

I mentally practiced my new motto as I was working in Melvin's storeroom, bumping into shelves laden with old peanut jars containing every possible type of screws, nails, nuts, and bolts. An artificial Christmas wreath fell on my head and deposited a fine layer of dust as I moved around the fossil, carefully taking measurements and jotting them down in a notepad. Pushing the plastic wreath aside impatiently, I finished my work, then gently covered the specimen and backed out the storeroom door, closing it softly, having a vision of peanut jars falling on the valuable fossil.

When I turned around, the Blum sisters were on the porch, peering through the dusty glass like goldfish in a bowl, right beneath the words BAIT and AMMO. They jumped, and I jumped.

Catching my breath, I proceeded to the door.

The sisters met me there, pretending to be looking at a display of fishing poles. "We thought Melvin might be back," one of them said.

"He doesn't seem to be here," I answered sweetly as they peered past my shoulders toward the storeroom like a couple of savvy old hens eyeing the corncrib. Flipping the lock on the door, I pulled it closed, and added, "I think he'll be back around one." Then I trotted off down the steps.

Behind me, the Blum sisters tried the door and snorted in frustration, one of them whispering to the other, "I'm sure she's with the FBI. Vanita said *bones.* I heard her. . . ."

Chuckling to myself, I scurried off, expecting the Jubilee Ranch pickup to be at the café. I was unprepared for the level of my disappointment when it wasn't. I found myself lingering by my Jeep watching the dog, who was still sound asleep in the front seat, drooling on my upholstery. Gazing up and down the highway, I wished Zach would materialize from the heat waves. It was five minutes after twelve. He was late. Heroes weren't supposed to be late.

"C'mon in and play a round of forty-two with us," Pop hollered from the dining car window. "Zach got held up this mornin' with some important call from his work. Been on and off the phone tryin' to straighten out some mess in Fedora, Texas. He'll be here directly, I reckon."

"All right," I called, and gave up my lonely vigil to enter the Big Lizard.

The next thing I knew, I was engrossed in a life-or-death domino tournament with Pop, Dandy Roads, and another old gent named Ham, who I gathered had once been the vet in town, Zach's idol and inspiration for a career in veterinary medicine. He patted my hand and told me what a fine young fellow Zach was, and how he sure wanted to see Zach finally settle down and be happy, preferably in San Saline, which didn't have a vet since Doc Ham retired. Doc Ham was none too subtle in his matchmaking, and I was glad when the domino competition became intense enough that Dandy Roads told him to hush up and concentrate.

The game was Pop and me against Dandy and Ham. I was relieved that most of the morning domino crowd had cleared out, because I hadn't played dominoes since summer camp in the seventh grade. Under pressure, I brushed up my skills quickly. Fifteen minutes passed without my even noticing.

Vanita came by at twelve twenty, brought me a glass of tea, and told me Zach had just called and he would be there in five minutes.

"No problem," I said, and made a startlingly brilliant domino play.

Pop was impressed. "Pretty . . . and smart." He wiggled a bushy eyebrow at me. "Just my kind of gal."

Doc Ham scoffed. "You cain't have her, Pop. She's already taken.

Didn't you hear? Her and Zach was down under the oak tree last evenin' wrapped around each other like lizards on a beanpole."

Shaking my head, I covered my eyes with my hand.

"Ham!" Vanita scolded. "Mind your manners. She's a guest."

Doc Ham cleared his throat irritably. "Well, not for long. It's only a matter of time before—"

"Willard Ham!" Vanita scolded again, popping the top of his baldhead with her dishrag, leaving behind bread crumbs, coffee grounds, and a little red mark.

Bracing an elbow on the table, he wagged his chin indignantly, rubbing his head. "They *been* together under the *Lover's Oak*. Like lizards on a beanpole. You *know* what that means."

"Hush now," Vanita muttered, then turned as the doorbell jingled. "Well, hi, Zach, there you are."

Everyone looked up, and Pop peeked at Willard's last two dominoes, then winked at me.

"Ready?" Crossing the dining car with a long, unhurried stride, Zach smiled the exact lopsided smile I'd been waiting for, and stood above the table.

I resisted the urge act giddy right there in front of everyone. "Well . . . you know, now I'm sort of engrossed in a domino game with three handsome men."

Pop's lips twisted sideways beneath his gray mustache. "Got good taste. I like that in a woman."

Zach leaned against the booth, and his nearness went through me like a bolt of electricity. He touched my hair, and I felt myself moving closer. "You've got tinsel in your hair," he teased, pulling out a long strand of silver that must have come from the Christmas wreath in Melvin's closet.

Employing supreme restraint, I managed to play a domino before I answered. "Yes, well, that must be a piece of my halo showing, because otherwise I'd be *mad* at you for being *late*."

"Spunky, too," Pop commented, and Zach chuckled. The deep, resonant sound was more than I could resist. I loved his laugh.

"All right, I give," I said, passing my dominoes over to Pop and standing up. "I'm about to starve to death."

"If you're nice, I'll let you have a snack on the way," Zach said, then turned to Vanita. "Everything ready?"

Pressing her lips together, Vanita fended off a self-satisfied grin. "By the door. In the picnic basket."

"Picnic basket?" I questioned, glancing toward the exit, where a huge basket was, indeed, waiting on one of the tables. "I thought we were eating here."

Zach leaned close to my ear, so that I felt the warmth of his breath against my skin. "I had something more private in mind."

He needn't have whispered. Everyone at the table heard. The old men chuckled, and Vanita shushed them. I realized this was all part of a plan, and everybody knew about it all along. Everyone but me.

EIGHTEEN

———◦◆◦———

I QUICKLY FORGAVE ZACH FOR BEING LATE FOR OUR LUNCH DATE. AS it turned out, he had been busy planning a picnic for the two of us. He'd even arranged for Pop and Doc Ham, who'd ridden to the café together, to take my SUV back to the ranch and put Mr. Grits in the dog kennel, where we wouldn't have to worry about him. Pop and Doc Ham drew straws for the pleasure of driving the dog back to the ranch, and Doc Ham won—or lost, depending on how you looked at it.

We left them finishing a cutthroat domino game with Dandy Roads. Zach shook his head as the domino discussion rose in volume, following us out the door. "Sorry you got roped into a game with those old reprobates. Although it looks like you were pretty good at it."

"Actually, it was kind of fun," I admitted as we checked on Mr. Grits, then climbed into the Jubilee Ranch truck and headed out. "Pop said you'd been tied up all morning with phone calls from work."

Frowning, Zach waited for a UPS truck to turn off into a driveway outside of town. "We've got an Exotic Newcastle Disease scare at a commercial poultry facility in Fedora. It looks like the area manager and the state vet have it contained at this point, but I'll have to make an overnight trip to west Texas."

I felt a sharp pang of disappointment. "I wish you didn't have to go," I said as we turned onto a back road, heading for some special place Zach had in mind.

"Yeah, me too," he agreed. "Technically, I'm on leave for a couple more weeks to take care of Pop, but things come up. We've got one vet out with a slipped disk and another on paternity leave, so I'm it for this little junket to Fedora. I'd ask you to ride along, but the only hotel in Fedora is so bad the truckers don't even stay in it, and it's a long way from Fedora to anywhere else. I'm just going to get the inspection done as quickly as possible and head home." Pausing, he tapped his thumbs on the steering wheel contemplatively, and for an instant I thought he was going to ask me to go along, even though there was no decent hotel in Fedora. Then he finished with, "Not much fun."

"Not like fixing windmills." For a fleeting moment I considered offering to go, in spite of the problem with accommodations, but an overnight trip brought up all kinds of issues. Besides, I needed to be here, studying the track site and watching to see if the mystery truck came back.

"I do know how to show a girl a good time, don't I?" He grinned wickedly beneath the straw cowboy hat as we pulled off the road and drove across a cattle guard into a pasture.

"Yes, you do," I said, smitten anew.

Beyond the cattle guard the road faded quickly, and we jounced along a dry creek bed that looked a little like the surface of the moon. The back end of the truck bumped over a rock, and I popped out of my seat like a Super Ball, caught myself against the roof, and landed practically in Zach's lap.

He set me upright again. "Whoa, there, little lady, you all right?" He did a pretty good John Wayne impression.

"I think I need a visit to the chiropractor. I don't know if I'm cut out for all this cowgirl stuff."

"Could have fooled me." His grin made my heart flutter. Before I could answer, he stopped the truck, killed the engine, and said, "We're here."

"We are?" Leaning close to the front window, I peered out skeptically. We were parked at the base of a small mountain, an old volcanic cone that rose from the surrounding flatland like someone had dropped it there by accident. The terrain around it was rocky and bare. Not an ideal spot for a picnic. "Where are we eating?"

"Up there." Zach pointed toward an ancient volcanic deposit that had worn smooth over time.

"Up there?" I echoed doubtfully, craning to look out the top of the window. "*Way* up there?"

Stepping out, he grabbed the picnic basket from the backseat, then extended a hand. "Come on. You'll love the view."

Slipping my fingers into his, I slid out the driver's side. "I'll need more than a chiropractor if I go up there. I'll need CPR."

Zach raised a brow. "Don't forget—you're with a highly trained medical professional."

"Geez." I groaned at the lame joke. "You are so bad."

He chuckled low in his throat. "Not usually. You just bring it out in me."

I shook my head, wondering how that could be true. I'd never been the type to bring out the *bad* in any man. "You don't get out enough."

Catching my gaze for a moment, he shrugged ruefully, and I had a sense that his life was much like mine. Could it be that the last few days were as much a change for him as they were for me?

Winding through a thick stand of cedar, we crossed the distance to the bottom of the hill. "Are you sure there's a way up?" I said, shading my eyes and doubtfully surveying the boulder-strewn slope.

"I'm sure." Confident as usual, he started out ahead of me with the basket. "There's a goat trail all the way up."

I followed, because I didn't have much choice. I tried not to think about what it was going to actually be like when I got to the top and looked down. Then again, I would be with Zach, which was all that seemed to matter.

"The trouble is . . ." I puffed, my breath coming in short gasps as the trail turned steep and rocky, "I'm not a goat." I couldn't believe how out of shape I'd let myself get during these last few months of worrying over Sydney's custody case.

Ahead, Zach laughed. "Come on," he said again. "You'll love the view."

Bracing my hands on my hips, I sucked in air, watching him move easily up the trail, his strides, graceful, strong. I didn't hurry to catch up, just stood enjoying the moment, admiring the way he moved. Actually, I loved the view already. . . .

We spent the afternoon at the third-highest point in San Saba County. The scenery was breathtaking, the food excellent, and the company absolutely perfect. By the time we finally returned to the Jubilee so that Zach could leave on his trip, I felt like I could have floated down from the mountain.

He kissed me one last time behind the corner of the barn at ranch headquarters. I hung on a moment and so did he. It seemed that if he left, something would change, and I didn't want it to. I wondered if he felt the same way.

"Be careful," I said, with an odd prickle of sadness in my throat, feeling like this was the end of my Cinderella fantasy.

"I will." Checking his watch, he frowned reluctantly, the carefree cowboy looking much more like a USDA veterinarian with obligations. "I've already got my things in the truck. I'd better head out." He motioned vaguely toward a brown pickup, which I surmised was what he drove when he wasn't in the Jubilee Ranch monster truck. "I'll be back late tomorrow afternoon." He kissed my hand before breaking the bond of our intertwined fingers, then touched my cheek, turned, and left.

"I'll be here," I replied softly, watching until he had climbed into the truck and driven out of sight.

I wandered by the stone water trough with the goldfish inside. Stopping to watch the fish swim in and out of the dappled sunlight, I touched the water's surface and thought about our first meeting there—a day that began with the insanity of my all-night drive from Colorado, and ended in a place I could never have imagined, with me romanticizing about, of all things, a cowboy.

A lot can happen in a day, my mother would have said, in her ever-cheerful Pollyanna way. *Keep your chin up. All things are possible.*

Are they? I wondered as I headed for the ranch house.

Pop Truitt was waiting on the porch, and my Jeep was parked in the drive with the back hatch raised. Mr. Grits popped his head over the passenger seat and whined at me when I looked inside. "What are you doing in there?" I asked.

Pop hobbled toward the gate to meet me. "We tried to convince him to go in the dog kennel, but he wasn't willin,' and Ham and me . . . well, we figured our steer-wrastlin' days was over, so we just let him stay in there. I opened the back door so he could get some breeze. He got out, did his business on the grass, took hisself a drink out of the flowerpot, then got back in again. I just been sittin' out here keepin' an eye on him since Ham left."

"Thank you," I said as the dog poked his head out the window, greeting us. "I'm sorry he was so much trouble."

"Wasn't no trouble," Pop insisted. "Jocelyn won't let me do anything but hang around the house anyhow. Every time I try to pick up somethin' heavier than a domino, she squeals like I just committed dadgum grand larceny. Why don'cha just put that feller in the dog pen over there, let him stretch his legs while you and I talk? Got some iced tea in the fridge."

"Oh, I really just came to—"

Mr. Grits stumbled sideways, hitting the GPS and causing Gertie to begin giving directions to get from Texas back home to Denver. Before the dog could go into panic mode, I opened the door and took him out of the car.

Sticking his head into the car, Pop gave the dash an uncertain frown. "Well, what in the world? I never."

"Maybe it would be a good idea if I put the dog in the kennel, just for a minute," I said, silencing Gertie as Mr. Grits tugged at the rope.

"Reckon so," Pop agreed and we walked Mr. Grits to the kennel. "That car always do that? Doc Ham said it was a-talkin' to him all the way back from town. I thought old Doc had finally gone plumb over the fence." He glanced back at the car like it might be possessed. "Guess not."

"It's a GPS," I replied, and Pop delivered a cross-eyed frown through his Coke-bottle glasses, so I explained, "Global Positioning System. I bought it with the car."

"On purpose?" Pop asked, and I chuckled.

"Well, now that you mention it, it is pretty annoying. It keeps you from getting lost, though."

Pop raised an incredulous brow. "Think I'd rather be lost."

Laughing together, we secured Mr. Grits in the shady dog kennel and walked toward the house. I could see where Zach got his sense of humor.

Pop moved his lips beneath the gray mustache, chewing on a thought. "That's what's wrong with the world these days. Folks think everything's got to be planned out, guaranteed, and insured. Don't nobody ever want to take a risk."

Frowning, I considered the unpredictable events that had led me to the Jubilee Ranch. The last few days I'd been learning to take risks. So far the risks had paid off, but where this would eventually lead, I couldn't imagine. "Guess so," I agreed.

Pop leaned on my arm as we walked slowly up the steps. "All the best things in life start with a risk." We stood for a moment on the porch while Pop caught his balance and his breath. His eyes were wise and thoughtful. "When I was a young pup . . . " He stopped to check his watch, then said, "Hang. We'd better get on inside. It's time for the gardening show on the Home Shopping Network."

"Oh . . . all right," Bemused by the switch from "life's an adventure" to gardening on TV, I followed Pop inside, where he offered me iced tea and gave me a tour while the Home Shopping Network blared through the rooms.

By the end of our visit, I knew all about the history of the main ranch house, I'd heard several potentially embarrassing stories about Zach's childhood, and I'd been introduced to a half dozen new gardening tools on the Home Shopping Network. I waited by the player piano in the front parlor while Pop retrieved a box of documents about Big Lizard Bottoms.

On the piano among other photos, there was one of Zach holding a little dark-haired girl, perhaps four or five years old. She was smiling softly at the camera with her head tucked under his chin. A tender moment between cowboy and child. I touched the photo, wondering who she was.

"That's Zach's daughter, Macey," Pop said as he returned to the room, carrying a wooden box with fading blue paint.

Pulling my hand away, I felt the blood drain from my arms and legs, and my body went cold. Zach had a daughter? I read the date on the photo and guessed at the age of the little brown-eyed girl in ponytails that reminded me of Sydney's. Four, maybe five years old then. She would be nine or ten now, just a year or two older than Sydney. *That's Zach's daughter.* The words repeated in my mind, re-painting reality with broad, careless strokes. Zach wasn't who I thought he was. He was someone's father. How could he have kept such a secret, after I'd poured out the entire saga of Sydney, sniffling and sighing about how much I missed her and how worried I was about the custody issue? All he'd said was, *That must be hard.*

We'd talked about everything from our childhoods to the difficulty of watching our childhood icons—my father and his grandfather—suffer the ravages of time. I'd told him about Sydney's daily e-mails, how much she liked the picture of the horses, and how she wanted to keep the dog, and he never brought up the little girl in this picture. His *daughter?*

How could that be?

"This place sure was full of laughs when she was livin' here." Pop reached out affectionately, swiping dust off the picture frame. "Course, she's probably growed quite a bit by now. We don't see her anymore since the divorce."

"Oh," I said, not trusting myself to respond further. Zach had a daughter he hadn't seen in years? One who used to live here at the ranch with him? "I . . . I guess I'd better go," I stammered. I wanted to turn and run, dash out the door of the big stone house and forget everything I'd learned here. Forget the image of a little dark-haired girl living . . . where now, exactly? Yearning for a father who never came to visit. Just like Sydney.

"Well, I didn't mean to go into all that. These days I get to rattlin' on and sometimes I don't even know why." Handing me the box, Pop stepped back and eyed me quizzically. "You all right? You look white as a fresh-painted fence."

I nodded vaguely, gripping the box so tightly that the wood pinched my fingers. The weight seemed slight compared to the heaviness of Pop's revelation. The idea of Zach as some kind of a deadbeat dad, a chip off the same block as Geoff, was more than I could bear. Could that be who he really was? I'd let myself fall for him without knowing even this most basic thing about him—he had a daughter. I didn't know, because he kept it to himself, hid it behind easy smiles and innocuous talk about his childhood on the ranch, his college years in vet school, his job.

What if he wasn't the larger-than-life cowboy hero I'd painted in my mind? What if he was just one more father, like so many—like Geoff—more concerned about moving on with his own life than raising his child?

"It's just the heat," I muttered, realizing that Pop was watching me with growing concern. "I'd better go."

We stumbled through a quick good-bye, and I rushed down the walkway, loaded the box in the back of my SUV, grabbed the dog, and sped off without thinking of where I was headed.

I ended up at the riverbank. Parking above the track site, I let the dog out and started walking, trying to catch my breath as Mr. Grits trailed along beside me, looking worried. Air formed a knot in the top of my chest, and tears welled in my eyes. I wiped them away impatiently. I wasn't going to cry. I wasn't. There wasn't any reason to cry. What was I crying about? I'd known all along, in some practical, rational part of myself, that this grown-up fairy tale was all smoke and mirrors. Sooner or later the stroke of midnight would slash through the illusions, the coach would be a pumpkin, my glass slippers worn-out Birkenstocks, and I would be just another lonely single mother spending Friday nights with the prime-time lineup and a bucket of ice cream.

But no matter how unrealistic it was, I didn't want to give up the fantasy. I wanted to believe in magical trees, and love at first sight, and someone, somewhere out there, waiting just for me. My soul mate, brought into my life at exactly the right time. I wanted to have faith in divine providence. I'd floated so far off the ground the last few days that there was no way to land softly back on earth.

There has to be an explanation, I told myself. I was making assumptions about Zach, based on sketchy information from Pop and my own suppositions. Zach deserved more than that, didn't he? The real Zach couldn't possibly be so different from the man I saw looking at me on the windmill tower. The one I wrote giddy love notes about on my computer.

But what if I was seeing only what I wanted to see? What if I was fooling myself? What if I was so desperate, so lonely and depressed with Sydney gone, that I was willing to jump at any remote possibility of love?

Take a chance, a voice inside me whispered. *Take a chance. Take a leap of faith.*

Don't be a fool, another voice said. *You've been fooled before. Pack up and go home.*

The two fought like angel and devil on my shoulders as I walked along the water's edge with Mr. Grits. Finally I stopped, stood still, closed my eyes, and just listened to the water passing, the trees shifting in the breeze, the grass rustling as some tiny creature scurried about collecting seeds. I tried to think rationally. Stay or go? Go or stay? Take a chance, or play it safe?

Mr. Grits splashed into the water, and I opened my eyes, watching him track the movement of a tiny perch. The fish darted toward shore, then back to the shallows, and I saw something that swept every other thought from my mind. Polished smooth by the kiss of the water, it lay only inches from my foot, rocking slightly in the tide. A partial caudal vertebra, sleek and unmistakable, cutting a swath of dark brown among the cream-colored fossils of snail shells and sea urchins. Squatting down, I plucked it from the water and turned it over in my hand. It was hollow, the fragmented fossilized bone of a meat-eating creature, large enough to be part of Melvin's dinosaur. Laying it carefully on a rock, I checked the area, but there was nothing more. This one small piece had been carried from somewhere upstream, deposited among the rocks only inches from where I stood.

It was a sign. I wasn't meant to leave yet. Picking up the vertebra, I hurried back up the riverbed to my car, took out the wooden box of Pop's ranch history mementos, sat down in the grass, and began to read.

I lost myself in the life of Caroline Truitt. Even though the pages were copies, produced at some time in the past when Xerox machines used slick paper and left a haze of gray, I imagined that I was reading the original journal, the one that was now somewhere in the county museum. In my mind the paper was crackled and yellow, and the drawings of plants, animals, the cabin by the river were sketched in faded pen and ink. In fine loops of handwriting with the occasional inkblots of an old-fashioned pen, Caroline recounted her life, her love, and the founding of the Jubilee Ranch.

She wrote on the first page:

It began with an unlikely meeting on a street corner in New Orleans. He was lost, wandering around Esplanade, carrying directions to an office somewhere near the water. I lingered, I must admit, out of sympathy and some fascination for his dark skin and hair. He cut a fine figure, and when finally he became bold enough to ask my assistance, I could see that he was from some completely foreign place . . .

The story went on from there. Eventually Caroline discovered that her foreigner was a Texan, the lowest form of white man, according to her father. And on top of that, Jeremiah Truitt was part Kiowa Indian, a hero of the battle of San Jacinto when he was only fourteen years old, now homesteading a land grant in what was still a wild, untamed region of Texas. He'd come east to buy a horse, a Thoroughbred stallion to lend some height and stride to his herd of sturdy mustang mares. He hadn't intended to find a bride, but a week later, Caroline Portelieu Truitt left with him on a ship, against the wishes of her parents, to the horror of friends, and to the complete dismay of professors at the women's university, where she had been studying ornithology.

She wrote next to a sketch of a seabird diving for a fish:

To my mind, it is a far better thing to experience life than to read about it in a book. I am in love, blindly so. I would follow him to the end of the earth if he wanted it, though my father assures me that Texas is somewhere close. He says the Texans are fools and rabble-rousers who will soon be taken over again by the Mexicans, by which course we'll all be put in chains. I am not worried in the least. In fact, it is another case that worries me more. What if this is my one chance in all the world to fall truly, deeply in love, and I fail to take it?

Caroline told of a difficult journey by sea, then land, of founding a ranch in a dangerous country, of falling more deeply in love each day with a husband she adored, but barely knew. In her first four years at Jubilee Ranch, the time the initial journal spanned, they lost babies and crops, and from time to time each other, but they always found each other again. In her quiet time she contented herself with her writings, where she cataloged strange plants and animals, and the awesome relics of mysterious dragons that walked the river basin in ancient times, long before Caroline Truitt set foot on the untamed hills of Texas.

NINETEEN

W HEN I FINISHED READING CAROLINE'S JOURNALS, I SAT FOR A
long time thinking—not only about the fossil sites she had
sketched and identified, but about her life, and my life, and the
similarities.

Caroline was convinced that there was something big on Jubilee
Ranch. *A fossil of epic proportions,* she called it. In her journals she
wrote about a meeting with neighboring Comanche Indians, who
spoke of the stonelike remains of a gigantic creature with long black
teeth and sharp claws, which ancestral legend claimed had once lain
exposed near a salt flat by the river. The bones were buried by a flood
and a resulting landslide. Caroline had spent her life, in between
ranching and raising children, trying to determine the exact location
of the salt flat, but her attempts were unsuccessful.

The recent appearance of Melvin's dinosaur bone and now the
fragmented vertebra made me suspect this spring's rains or perhaps
another landslide had reexposed the salt flat. Most probably it lay
somewhere upstream, the fossils at least partially open to air and
water, waiting to be found. As exciting as that possibility should have
been, it was the private parts of Caroline's journal that drew me back
again and again.

I thought about the courage it must have taken to leave behind
everything—home, family, friends, security—and board a ship with
a man she barely knew. To move to a far-off place, with wild animals
and hostile native peoples. I tried to imagine birthing babies miles

from the nearest doctor, and raising children when there were no guarantees of survival. Caroline had buried two children and raised four. She grieved the lost ones in long, painful passages, her writing trembling between inkblots as she paused to weep, or think, or gather strength. She taught local children to read, worked cattle alongside her husband, milked goats, involved herself in Texas politics, and struggled to raise crops in the pale, rocky soil of the hill country. She gave the town of Loveland its name, and selected its location, near the Lover's Oak, which the Comanches had for years revered as a matrimonial site. She never questioned whether she should have boarded the boat with Jeremiah Truitt at just twenty-three years old. She never wondered if she should have stayed in the civilized world and lived an easier life.

She died at thirty-eight, when she came in from the field, lay down to rest, and never woke up. Her final journal entry ended with a few lines written by a neighbor's wife, who described Caroline's passing as peaceful. The doctor in New Orleans wrote a letter to her husband, saying that Caroline had a weak heart, which she had known about since childhood. She never told anyone, not even her Jeremiah.

As if somehow she knew she would be passing soon, she wrote in the final pages of her journal:

> *My only fear has been failing to really live. And I have lived entirely, every moment in this wild and delicate place. What more would there be for me to do, if I lived to be one hundred? One bold year is worth a dozen timid ones.*

The last line of the journal, written by the neighbor, said:

> *She lived on the Jubilee Ranch for fifteen years. She was buried beneath the Lover's Oak, without a marker for mourners to gaze down upon, as was her request. The tree, she said, would mark her very well. It was ever reaching upward to God.*

Mr. Grits nuzzled my hand as I closed the journal. Stroking his fur, I lay back in the grass and stared into the sky as the clouds blazed red and then dimmed among the branches.

My only fear has been failing to really live.

I have lived entirely, every moment in this wild and delicate place. . . .

These past few days, I felt as if I had lived entirely. I couldn't remember when I'd ever been so alive. Perhaps when I was fresh out of college, traveling the world with Geoff, hunting for buried treasure in exotic locations. Sometimes the locations were dangerous, but I was never afraid. I was young, and in love, and doing what I wanted to do. I felt that, if something happened to me, I would die happy.

And then I grew up. One simple line on a pregnancy test accomplished what childhood and college, endless lectures from my mother, and four years of marriage could not. I opened my eyes and saw that the world is filled with risks, and the risks weren't just about me anymore. Geoff left, and I learned that life can change in an instant. It can flip over like a box of Styrofoam peanuts, and you're left scrambling to gather enough insulation to survive, before it all blows away. After that, you sink down into what's left, like a fragile glass vase with a crack in it, trying to avoid further damage.

One bold year is worth a dozen timid ones. . . .

I'd lived more in the last few days than in months of my normal life. I didn't want that feeling to stop. I wanted to stay here, in this wild and delicate place. But part of me knew I couldn't. I had a daughter and job and a home to return to, a thousand miles away. With Sydney's life a chaotic jumble of custody arrangements, new parents, part-time houses, she didn't need the added confusion of my dating—long-distance or otherwise. I couldn't have her building her hopes on some unpredictable, improbable situation with a man who kept the most important parts of himself a mystery, who had a daughter he apparently never saw and didn't acknowledge.

But Sydney isn't here, a voice whispered in my head. Sydney was thousands of miles away, for weeks yet. What if I was jumping to all the wrong conclusions about Zach, based on sketchy information from Pop? What if I was using that as an excuse to run away from another potential relationship?

But if I stayed, if I let myself become more deeply involved, was I setting myself up for another painful fall?

It is another case that worries me more. What if this is my one chance in all the world to fall truly, deeply in love, and I fail to take it? Caroline was in my head now, too. Another voice, one that was willing to risk it all.

What if this is my one chance?

Overhead, the sky turned dark and the branches became shifting shadows against dusky blue velvet. Somewhere along the river a coyote yipped, and Mr. Grits lifted his head, growling. Sitting up, I grabbed his fur to keep him from taking off after the sound.

"Ssshhh. We'd better go," I whispered.

Grateful for the reprieve from my own questions, I took Mr. Grits to the car, then went back to gather the journals. I stood for a moment, gazing toward the riverbank with the box in my arms. Even though I'd spent the afternoon analyzing all the reasons for leaving, I couldn't imagine never coming back here again. If I left now, I'd always wonder what was hidden along the river. I'd always wonder what might have happened between Zach and me.

I'd always know that once again, I'd chosen fear over faith.

The two were at war inside me as I drove back to the cabin. On the hillside, the coyotes had started into a full-scale chorus by the time I'd brought in Mr. Grits and Pop's box. Shivering at the sound, I locked the door, feeling lonely and vulnerable. I hoped the mystery truck didn't come back tonight.

My nerves were on edge as I fixed a supper of ham sandwiches and instant grits. I ate on the table, and the dog ate on the chair. I didn't put his food in the bowl by the door because I didn't want to be alone.

The cacophony of the coyotes and my own whirling thoughts kept me up late, even though my eyes were burning, and I was physically exhausted and emotionally drained. The dog, either sensing my disquiet or sharing it, moved restlessly between sitting by the window and leaning against my chair with his head on my arm.

I stroked his fur absently, sailing on a sea of conflicting desires, until finally I pulled out Caroline's field journals, old pictures of the trackway, and a topographic map of the ranch. Spreading them on the table, I spent an hour comparing Caroline's notes and drawings to the modern map. Sometime between listening to the sounds of the night and trying to plot the locations of Caroline's fossil sites, I fell asleep with my head on the table.

I awoke hours later with a sinus headache and my spine feeling like it had been put in a vise. Groaning, I stood up and wandered off to the bedroom, slipped into my pajamas, and burrowed beneath the old quilt, not wanting to think, or wonder, or worry anymore.

Hush up now. Sleep. I felt my mother in the room, her presence so real that I sensed her fingers smoothing tangled strands of hair away from my face. *Things will look clearer in the morning.*

I hoped that was true. I hoped I'd awaken and know what I was supposed to do. I hoped there would be a sign.

Deep in the night, I once again fell into bizarre cowboy dreams. I was in an old movie theater, the fancy kind built in the thirties and forties. On the screen, John Wayne and Katharine Hepburn were traveling down the river in *Rooster Cogburn*. They were arguing, but someone had turned down the sound so that I couldn't hear the words. Then I was on the screen, standing on a butte high above the riverbank. I could see that the river was rough and angry around the bend, littered with rocks. Cupping my hands, I screamed at the raft, but the passengers couldn't hear me.

Suddenly it wasn't John Wayne below; it was Sydney, all alone, being swept away by the current. She called out, and I tried to run to her, but my legs wouldn't move. I was on top of a windmill tower, and there was no ladder. I dove off, fell and fell like a cliff diver until I hit the water and plunged below the surface. I drifted downward into a cool, deep pit, where the sand was white with salt, and the bones of ancient creatures lay glittering like pearls in a giant oyster. Overhead the raft passed by, two dark-haired girls looking over the edge—Sydney on one side, and Zach's daughter on the other.

Jerking upright in bed, I called Sydney's name, fighting the tangle of the quilt and scrambling to the edge of the mattress before I came to my senses.

"It's all right." I gasped, falling back against the pillows and throwing my hand over my eyes to shut out the morning sunlight. "It's all right. It's all right."

I lay still, getting my bearings, letting my surroundings sink in, remembering the turmoil of the day before. In the bright glow of morning it seemed foolish—sitting at the riverside, crying, and analyzing, and making decisions based on something Pop said in passing. The most logical course of action was to stay a few more days, get serious about investigating the stolen tracks, and take some time to talk to Zach. There could be all kinds of extenuating circumstances separating him from his daughter.

But what kind of extenuating circumstances could justify abandoning a little girl, not seeing her or talking about her?

In my mind there were none. A parent who left a child behind after a divorce was self-centered, immature, cruel, unfeeling—everything that Geoff embodied. I couldn't imagine ever being in love with such a person.

But I couldn't imagine Zach doing such a thing. Then again, if there was some logical reason he no longer saw his daughter, why wouldn't he have mentioned it when we were talking about my custody issues with Sydney?

The debate raged in my head as I dressed and climbed up the hill to e-mail Sydney and see if Geoff or Gracie had sent anything new about the stolen tracks. Leaving my computer on the picnic bench, I stood for a long moment, gazing at the horse herd and wishing Zach would appear at the gate. From time to time the horses lifted their heads and looked toward the barn, but no one came. Whoever was supposed to feed them this morning was late.

The vast stretch of country below suddenly seemed empty, and I felt the painful sting of loneliness. I wanted Zach to streak across the prairie at a gallop and make me feel like I could soar off into the blue.

Finally I turned away and walked back to the bench, connected the computer to the cell phone and dialed, then waited while my e-mail window opened. My mind drifted as I worked my way down the list, deleting spam, and answering a work-related question from my boss at the museum. The bottom of the list scrolled into the window, and my pulse ratcheted up. There was nothing from Sydney. I scanned again. Nothing from Sydney or Geoff. Sydney never missed a day. Sometimes she e-mailed two or three times, but always at least once, in the evening, when she was sitting up late, lonely and sleepy, missing her mom and the normal bedtime routine.

A burst of fear rocketed through my body. Something was wrong. I searched my old mail list, my recently deleted mail, my filing cabinet, hoping that some computer glitch had rerouted her e-mail— that I would find it, and it would say she was fine, and she'd had another busy day with Whitney and the housekeeper. But there was nothing. Staring at the screen, I tried to decide what to do.

I e-mailed Geoff, hoping he might be online.

ARE YOU THERE? I DIDN'T GET AN EMAIL FROM SYDNEY TODAY. I'M WORRIED. IS EVERYTHING ALL RIGHT? PLEASE LET ME KNOW.

—L

I waited, watching the minutes tick by on the bottom of the screen. Two minutes, three, four, five. Long enough for him to answer if he was at his computer. Nothing came. Disconnecting, I picked up the phone and dialed his number, even though I knew that at this time of day I would get the housekeeper or Whitney, either of whom would give me the brush-off, and remind me that I was to call Sydney only once per week, at the specified time. I didn't care who answered. At least I would know that Sydney was all right.

The phone made a series of electronic tones, then clicked in my ear, *tick, tick, tick,* as my desperation whizzed through the atmosphere, to some satellite and back, to a relay tower, down mile after mile of foreign phone lines in Mexico, until finally it reached Geoff's house. The connection came up busy. I called again and again, but the result was the same. Busy signal. Finally I tried the operator, had her dial, with the same result. Perhaps a problem in the phone network, she said. I should try again later. I shouldn't worry. Foreign networks often went down, and that would affect both Internet and phone service.

The operator's reassurances helped calm my panic. She was probably right. Some foreign phone systems were unpredictable—I knew that from experience—and a problem with the telephone system made sense, considering that I couldn't reach Sydney and Geoff via e-mail or phone.

I tried one last time, then packed up my things and headed down the hill with Mr. Grits walking ahead of me, surprisingly subdued. Even that bothered me. It was as if the dog knew something I didn't. "Stop it," I muttered to myself, and the dog looked over his shoulder. "Go on," I told him, sounding as uncertain as I felt. Stop, go, stop, go. I didn't know what to do next.

I decided to take Caroline's field notes and the map to the river, as a distraction. I drove down to the riverbank thinking about Sydney, wondering what she was doing and hoping that by the time I came back, the phone lines to Mexico would be functional.

For the better part of two hours I explored the riverbed with the map and a small gardening spade and claw from the cabin. They were poor substitutes for a rock hammer and air scribe, but good enough for moving the soil and slivering off some rock samples in areas I thought might correspond to sites on the map. Unfortunately the map was old, and Caroline's notes even older. The river had changed over the years. Landmarks had washed away, rock formations had weathered, and overhanging bluffs had tumbled into the water.

After two hours I was right back where I'd started from, at the site of the stolen tracks. I'd found nothing, not even a disassociated fossil like the vertebra fragment. Except for the vandalized site and a trackway a short distance up the river, most likely made by a Pleurocoelus, there was nothing.

I walked back to the car, feeling that, among other things, I was now a failure at paleontology. In the old days I had an innate sense of where to dig. I had "the luck," as Geoff called it. It frustrated him, because he was methodical and scientific, while I operated on intuition. We were both equally successful, and, in fact, my percentage of digs to FSO, found significant items, was a little higher than his. Geoff was the type to keep percentages. Everything between us was a competition, which, for some reason, was all right at the time. Now it seemed immature and a little twisted. Love wasn't about competition and self-promotion. It was about caring so much about somebody that you wanted to be happy together, or not at all.

I started thinking about Zach again, about how I felt when I was with him, how he did little things that made me laugh, how I liked the way he walked, the sound of his voice, how he coerced me into doing things I wouldn't normally consider. It was as if he knew me better than I knew myself—as if he saw through all the masks, and the worries, and the fears, and found the most authentic part of me.

Is this the person I really am? My own question haunted me. *How do you know what parts of yourself are authentic, and what parts you've created to make life bearable?*

When I slipped my hand into Zach's, all the conflicting voices in my head fell away, and nothing mattered but being with him.

If that wasn't love, what was? But how could I possibly be in love with a man I didn't really know, who'd hidden a deep and integral part of himself, something as important as the existence of a daughter? If Zach felt for me what I felt for him, how could he possibly do that?

The answer was simple, yet it struck me like an unexpected slap. Zach didn't feel what I felt. The connection I perceived was one-sided, the result of a lonely heart that wanted to believe there was a soul mate out there for me, and that finding him would be as easy as taking an unexpected trip to Texas. To Zach I was a passing infatuation, something to do while he was spending time at the ranch, a pathetic divorcée who needed a little fun and a dose of cowboy charm.

The idea stung, and I was glad when Mr. Grits barked at a truck coming up the gravel road. A dark truck, the one belonging to the grouchy ranch manager. Tucking my tools, the map, and the wooden box in the back of the SUV, I closed the hatch and moved to the driver's-side door, trying not to look like I'd been caught trespassing. Through the glare on the windshield I could see two cowboy hats. My pulse fluttered, and I found myself hoping one of them would be Zach's. He'd said he wouldn't be back until late in the day, but maybe he'd returned early. Maybe he'd been thinking about me, and he couldn't wait to return. . . .

The truck hit the grassy clearing and sped up, and for a minute I thought it had to be Zach driving, speeding up to tease me. Either that, or the driver was going to hit my SUV. I backed away a step, unsure.

At the last instant the truck did a one-eighty, the rear tires fish-tailing and kicking up loose grass. Jimmy Hawthorne leaned out the window and grinned at my wide-eyed look. "Scare ya?"

"A little," I said, trying to act casual. "You practicing for a career in cowboy stunt driving?" I peered into the truck. Dan, the sour-faced ranch manager, squinted at me from the passenger seat, glancing suspiciously toward the river and back at my vehicle.

"I drive down at the dirt track on Friday nights," Jimmy informed me. "I was seein' what this old baby can do, in case I want to buy 'er from Dan. She's got an old V-eight in 'er. Lotsa power."

"Oh," I replied hesitantly.

Jimmy revved the engine. "So Jocelyn wanted us to run by and check on ya. She was worried something might of happened." I blinked in confusion, and he added, "Because you weren't at horse class."

"Oh, my gosh." I glanced at my watch. In the morning turmoil I'd completely forgotten about horse psychology class. "I . . ."

In the passenger seat, the ranch manager craned to look out the back window, suspiciously surveying my Jeep, then glancing toward the riverbed again.

I stumbled quickly into an excuse. "I wasn't feeling well this morning, and I went for a walk down the river, and . . ." *What? Think of something.* "I got a little lost."

Jimmy's eyebrows drew together. "Well, you can always just follow the river back."

Duh. "Yes. That's what I did finally. Don't know why I didn't think of it sooner."

"Looks like you finally found your way to your Jeep, at least." Jimmy smiled good-naturedly.

Dan sneered at me suspiciously. "Guess you'll be headin' back up to the cabin now."

"Yes, thank you. If you see Jocelyn, will you tell her I'm sorry for missing class?" I tried to sound pleasant and nonchalant. " 'Bye."

Watching the truck drive away and disappear into a cloud of dust, I mentally weighed a new theory. Suspect number one and suspect number two together. Returning to the scene of the crime, suspicious at having found someone snooping around.

When they were gone, I loaded up Mr. Grits and drove back to the cabin, then grabbed my backpack and climbed the hill to try my e-mail again. More spam, but nothing from Sydney or Geoff. I called the phone number, but the result was the same: a busy signal, no answer or answering machine.

Don't panic, I told myself. *If the whole day goes by and you still can't get in touch with them, then you can panic.* Knowing Geoff, he'd probably taken a sudden trip to the coast, or forgotten to pay his phone bill. Maybe he was actually spending some time with Sydney and took her to see some of the sights in Mexico City.

As plausible as those possibilities were, I knew I wouldn't relax until I heard my daughter's voice. After I spent an hour trying the phone and e-mail over and over, a viciously creative part of my mind started inventing scenarios about earthquakes, sudden volcanic eruptions, summer hurricanes, and foreigners being kidnapped for ransom.

When I began envisioning ransom notes and how I would gather the money to pay, I decided it was time to go somewhere else. Returning to the cabin, I nibbled at lunch, thumbed through magazines without looking at the pages, and paced the room like a lion in a cage. Finally I went up the hill one more time and again tried to contact Geoff or Sydney. No luck.

When I returned to the cabin, there was something on the door.

A note, with my name at the top. Panic exploded like a string of Black Cats in my throat, propelling me onto the porch.

Please don't let it be about Sydney, I prayed. *Please, please, please.* I pictured Jocelyn or Collie or Laura trying to track me down after having received some tragic news about my daughter.

Ripping the note off the door, I opened it with trembling hands. The contents were cryptic, just a hurried scrawl telling me to drop by the main house when I returned to the cabin. The handwriting was a woman's—probably Jocelyn's. *Drop by,* it said, not *ASAP,* or *urgent,* or *emergency.*

For what seemed like the thousandth time that day, I admonished myself not to jump to conclusions. Walking to the car with Mr. Grits, I tried to breathe deeply, settle down, get real, but I was edgy and exhausted. I couldn't shake the feeling that something was wrong.

Driving to the ranch house, I rolled down the window and let the warm afternoon air wash over me, lifting the dampened hair from the back of my neck, soothing the knotted muscles. I wished I could go to sleep, roll the clock back twenty-four hours, and reenter yesterday. I wanted to be back on the mountaintop with Zach. When he drove me back to the ranch, I wouldn't go into the house. I wouldn't see the picture of him with the little dark-haired girl. I'd wake in the morning, and read e-mail from Sydney, and far below on the prairie Zach would be gliding through the waving grass astride the spotted horse. . . .

The mirage faded as I wound through the stand of trees near the ranch headquarters. Stiff in my seat, I peered ahead as the horse barn came into view. Jimmy and Dan were working with a horse out front. Dan was squeezing the horse's upper lip in his fist, and Jimmy was trying to put a syringe in its mouth. They didn't look up as I passed by.

At the house, Pop was entertaining company on the porch, sipping lemonade with Jocelyn, Collie, Laura, and a man who needed a haircut. They turned as I drove up, and from the body language I realized they'd been waiting for me. My mind hopscotched, trying to reconcile the shaggy-haired man's face with the location on Pop Truitt's porch. On the other side of the table someone stood up—a little girl with long sandy-brown hair in uneven pigtails.

Throwing the SUV into park and killing the engine, I gasped, shoved the door open, jumped out, and started running. "Sydney!" I screamed, even though I couldn't believe my eyes. I knew I would awaken any minute, and my daughter, my little girl, wouldn't be dashing across the porch and down the steps, her hair streaming out behind her. "Sydney! Sydney!"

TWENTY

━━━◆◆◆━━━

I HELD ON TO SYDNEY AND CRIED AND CRIED. I DIDN'T CARE WHO saw. My soul was filled with a rush of gratitude that spilled over into every part of my body. The warmth of my daughter's arms around my neck, the smell of her hair, the sound of her muffled voice singsonging, "Mommy, Mommy, Mommy," enveloped me, lifted me, transported me until I didn't know where I was. It was as if a part of my body, an arm or a leg that had been torn off, had suddenly returned, and I didn't have to be in pain anymore.

Please, I prayed, *please let this be real. If this is a dream, I don't want to wake up.* Waking up with my arms empty would be more than I could bear now.

Holding Sydney away from me, I checked her over, from uneven pigtails to toes peeking through Mexican leather sandals that were too small for her. Her skin was caramel brown from hours in the sun, little freckles standing out over her pert nose and touching the long fans of dark lashes when she blinked. Her hair was lighter, either from the intense Mexican sun, or Whitney had highlighted it during one of their games of beauty shop. Flyaway strands of burnished gold escaped her sandy-brown pigtails and flitted around her face as she smiled shyly, and said, "Hi, Mommy." There was a hole in her smile where an upper front tooth had fallen out. She hadn't mentioned that in her e-mails. Perhaps she knew I'd be sad about having missed the event. Her baby smile was gone forever now. Soon the grown-up teeth would come in, and she would start looking like a big kid. I wondered if the tooth fairy had remembered to come to Mexico.

"Hi, yourself, pea pod." I used the silly endearment that had been handed down from my mom. "You look so good." She didn't really. Her hair was a mess, and there were dark circles under her big brown eyes. Her gaze flicked uncertainly over me, as if I were someone she didn't know very well. The expression gave my heartstrings a painful twist. Three and a half weeks was a long time in the life of an eight-year-old.

"How's my little banana girl?" I said, making a joke about her favorite food to remind her of our life together. Sydney ate bananas on everything—cereal, pudding, peanut-butter sandwiches. She dunked them in chocolate milk and lemonade, and never approved of a sack lunch that didn't have at least two bananas in it.

She rolled her eyes thoughtfully, her tongue poking out through the new hole in her teeth. "Good," she said finally, then leaned close to me and whispered, "Whitney left and went back to England."

"What?" I'd been so overjoyed about seeing her, I hadn't yet begun to wonder what she was doing here. Now the still, small voice of my conscience reminded me that I shouldn't pump her for information. Dozens of divorce books and self-help articles had warned me not to use her loyalties in a tug-of-war between her father and me. "It's OK. We can talk about it later." I glanced toward the porch, where everyone, including Geoff, was allowing me to have my reunion with Sydney in relative privacy.

Following my line of vision, Sydney lowered her voice. "They had a big fight." Her eyes were wide with an unhealthy amount of interest in what was clearly an adult situation. She was gauging my reaction, so I tried to appear impassive as she fed out more information. "Then the police came, but it wasn't a do-mes-tic distur-bance call. They made us go straight to the airport, and we didn't even get to pack our suitcases. I had to leave all my stuff that I bought. Dad said Melicha would pack it up and send it to our house in Colorado."

I stood silent for a moment, too stunned to reply. *Domestic distur-*

bance call? Where had she learned that phrase? What had my daughter been exposed to in Mexico?

"Mom?" Sydney's dark brows twisted into a worried knot. "It's OK, isn't it?"

No, it's not. It's so far from OK, you'd need a rocket ship to get to OK from here.

"Of course it's OK, honey. I'm just so glad that you're here, I can't even think of what to say. Give me another one of those great hugs. Oh, I have missed your hugs." I took her in my arms and lifted her up as though she were a toddler, even though she was too big for it now. And even though she was too big for it, she wrapped her arms and legs around me and hung on. Her chest deflated as if she'd been holding her breath for a long time and could finally let go. I felt her heartbeat against my mine, the hurried rhythms slowly lengthening into sync.

Carrying her toward the porch, I glared at Geoff. *You rushed our daughter out of Mexico with only the clothes on her back? You let her learn words like* domestic disturbance call? *What is wrong with you? How could you do this? She is an eight-year-old child. She needs a father, not an oversize teenager playing some bizarre game of international house with his college-age girlfriend . . . wife . . . whatever.*

Geoff blinked at me with a hopeful look that said, *Hey, look, I brought Sydney for a visit. Isn't that great?* I wanted to wrap my hands around his razor-stubbled neck and squeeze that look off his face.

But underneath the happy-hippie facade there was something that tugged at me, even though I didn't want it to. Geoff looked ragged, his overly long hair hanging in shaggy brown curls around his face, his eyes bloodshot around the brown centers. Deep, worried wrinkles fanned across the tops of his cheeks, which had been polished to the color and texture of leather by the sun and blowing sands of Mexico. He needed a shave and a bath and, judging by the sagging curve of his shoulders, some sleep. Sitting on the porch chair in his wrinkled hiking shorts, the Moroccan-style sandals I'd always jokingly called his Moses sandals, and a loose-fitting Hawaiian shirt with an annoyingly loud print of beer bottles, beach chairs, and margarita glasses, he seemed out of place, uncomfortable, and depressed. He looked like a teenager who'd just wrecked the family car and was waiting for the lecture.

In all the years I'd known Geoff, I'd never seen him like that. Geoff was always confident, the life of the party, with an easy laugh and an invisible charisma that drew people to him. He was a consummate salesman, equal parts idealist and shyster. But today he appeared to have run out of things to sell. He seemed to have deflated to half his normal size.

Frustrated by the rush of sympathy, I stopped in the gateway, hiking Sydney's knobby legs up onto my hip bones. She wrapped herself tighter as if she'd never turn loose again. Closing my eyes, I leaned against the gate and drank her in like water.

When I looked up, Laura was coming down the steps with a nervous frown. Geoff still hadn't moved. He'd probably seen the murderous glare on my face, and was afraid to. Nobody on the porch had reacted, except for Laura, the designated emissary and family peacemaker.

Laura looked like she was afraid I'd toss Sydney into the SUV and make a run for the state line.

"Lindsey, don't make a scene," she ground out, like a ventriloquist, holding a false smile and speaking through clenched teeth. Giving me a one-armed hug, she patted Sydney's back so that from the porch it would look like a perfectly pleasant sister-to-sister greeting. Against my ear, she whispered, "Just be calm, all right?"

I focused on my sister. Sydney wiggled out of my arms, and to my complete horror she trotted back to the porch and climbed into Geoff's lap as if she needed to protect him from me. I felt like I'd lost her all over again. "I *am* calm." *Deadly calm.* "What is he *doing* here? My God, I've been going out of my mind all morning, wondering where my daughter is."

Laura lifted a hand helplessly, then clamped it to the top rail of the fence, conscious of her body language and the audience watching. "I don't know, exactly. It sounds like his wife left him and he had some kind of trouble with his visa, not necessarily in that order, although her father is apparently some kind of a British ambassador to Mexico, so it's certainly likely that the two events are related."

"Leave it to Geoff to be well connected," I growled, rekindling the urge to strangle him. Anger and resentment crackled through my body like a fuse carelessly lit, the flame heading for something big.

Sensing it, Laura shifted nervously, smoothing a hand up and down my arm. "Don't do anything hasty, all right?" She leaned down to catch my attention, her blue eyes so like my mother's. "The main thing is that Sydney's here. He could have taken her anywhere, but he brought her to you." My sister was the voice of moderation, as always. She was, after all, the sweet and sensitive twin.

"Thank God for that." I let a long breath slip through my lips, then another, slowly feeling a little less like the evil twin, and a little more like the new Zen Lindsey who'd learned that relationships take time, and when you are dealing with someone more powerful than yourself, love, patience, honesty, trust, and kindness are the only tools that work. This summer Geoff had the power. He had custody of Sydney for six more weeks, and he could drag her all over the world and into all his marital problems, if he wanted to. I puffed out another cleansing breath, like the ones I had learned years ago in Lamaze class. Giving birth to a new relationship with Geoff was going to take some effort and lots of mental pain management. To help the process along, I visualized Sydney safely back with me for the rest of the summer. "How did they get here? When? Has he said anything about sending Sydney home with me?"

Laura shrugged. "He hasn't said anything about his plans. He seems kind of . . . lost and disoriented. They phoned my house from the airport around eleven o'clock. Graham happened to be home for lunch, and he took the call. He contacted me, and we picked them up. Then we drove here. That's about all I know."

"They flew all the way from Mexico without telling anyone?" My anger ratcheted up again. I pictured my exhausted daughter stranded for hours in some airport while Geoff called around for a ride.

"Lindsey . . ." Laura admonished.

Breathe, breathe. "OK, I'm calm." I checked the crowd on the porch again. "How did Collie get here?"

"I picked her up for moral support. I was afraid you might—"

"Pop a cork?"

"Exactly."

"Well, I'm not. I want to take Sydney back to Colorado, and reaming Geoff out won't get me what I want." Laura drew back, surprised, and I added, "I learned a few things in horse psychology class."

"I was hoping you would," slipped from her mouth, and then she slapped her fingers over her lips as in, *Did I say that out loud?*

I wagged a finger at her. "You and I can talk later. I know you and Collie sent me here as a setup."

"No, we didn't," Laura rushed out, blinking innocently and pulling her lips between her teeth.

"Well, it doesn't matter now. The psychology class was helpful." Squinting toward Geoff again, I started toward the porch. "Especially now that we're dealing with a horse's butt."

"Lindsey . . ." Laura warned under her breath, hurrying to catch up with me with her petite steps. "Be good."

She needn't have bothered with the reprimand, because Sydney ran interference, hopping off Geoff's lap and catching me on the stairs. "Can we go swimming now?" Grabbing my hand, she put on her puppy face. "Pleeease. Miss Jocelyn said I can swim at the river, and Dad said as soon as you got here we could go. Can we go? Pleeeeeease?"

I scratched my head, trying to decide what to do. On the one hand, Geoff and I needed to talk. On the other hand, this wasn't the place. "What would you wear to swim in?" I asked, loudly enough for Geoff to hear. "You don't have any suitcase or anything."

"She's . . ." Geoff paused to clear his throat. His voice was gravelly and raw. "She's got a swimsuit on under her clothes."

I widened my eyes at him over Sydney's head. *You brought my daughter all the way from Mexico in her swimsuit?* I pictured her skin chafed and raw from a night in tight elastic. Not only had she arrived without clean underwear, she didn't even *have* underwear.

"I was swimming when the police came," Sydney said cheerfully, as if all of this were perfectly normal. "Anyhow, now I won't have to change clothes to swim at the river." Her smile added, *Cool, huh?*

"That's true, honey." *Calm down, calm down*, Horse Psychology Lindsey whispered in my head. *You have to work with Geoff's stupidity, not against it. It is too big to conquer by brute force.* I smoothed a hand over Sydney's hair. "Tell you what. Why don't your dad"—I swallowed hard, trying not to choke on the word—"and I take you?" I needed to talk to Geoff alone. If he was planning to traipse around the world after his escaped wife, I didn't want him taking Sydney along.

Collie and Laura quickly took the hint and stood up. "We'd better be getting home," Collie said, making a show of checking her watch. "We left the guys at my house watching Bailey, but True was dying to head out to the pasture and show Graham his new cedar-eradicating machine. There's no telling where they are now, and what they've done with my daughter."

I forced a laugh. *Bet she has clean underwear on.* "You know, I have to see her before I leave."

Laura, Jocelyn, and Collie all drew back at the word *leave*. It felt wrong on my tongue. A strange reality, but what else was there to do now? My days on Fantasy Island were over. It was time to focus on Sydney.

"Oh, listen, Sydney and Geoff can bunk at our place," Collie offered. "Laura and Graham brought clothes to stay overnight, because some friends of ours are having a big anniversary bash tomorrow and renewing their vows. Bailey's the flower girl—no telling how that will work out, with a toddler—but if you come over, you can see her in her flower-girl outfit. We could get some pictures of her and Sydney. Who can say when we'll get the chance to do that again?"

"Oh, I don't know." I hesitated. "Sydney doesn't even have clothes with her. I should probably . . ." What? Toss her in the car in her swimsuit, exhausted, and make her ride fifteen hours, back to Colorado? Sydney needed a good night's rest, and I needed time to straighten out Geoff's mess.

"Tell you what," Laura rushed in like a wide receiver taking Collie's pass. "I'll pick up some things for her at the dry-goods store in San Saline and bring them out in the morning."

Collie nodded. "See? Problem solved. I'll get some rooms ready for Geoff and Sydney, and they can come on over when they're ready. One thing about living in a restored schoolhouse—we have plenty of bedrooms."

"They can stay with me tonight." The words were out of my mouth before I even thought about what I was saying. The truth was that I didn't want my little girl to be anywhere but with me. If I had to take Geoff in the bargain, I would. He could sleep on the doormat with Mr. Grits. "There are two upstairs bedrooms in the cabin. There's plenty of space. It's just for one night, anyway. That is, if it's OK with Jocelyn and Pop."

"Course it's OK," Pop answered without waiting for Jocelyn. Reaching toward Sydney, he opened and closed his fingers, palms up. "C'mon in here for a minute. As I recall, there's some old floatin' tubes in the storage room. Let's pull one out and we'll hop down to the barn and air it up. Nothin' more fun on the river than floatin' the rapids."

"Cool!" Sydney cheered, and slipped her hand into his. She followed him into the house, her short-legged steps a perfect companion to his slow shuffle.

Jocelyn watched them go, then turned back to Geoff and me. "Anything you need, just let me know. The swimming hole is just upriver from the track site, so you shouldn't have any trouble finding it. It's a beautiful afternoon. Enjoy." Hands folded calmly in her lap, she looked every bit the benevolent therapist observing the drama of human interaction through a pleasantly impassive face. I could only imagine what she was thinking about Geoff and me: *Dysfunctional divorced couple. Mother displaying serious abandonment issues, latent resentment. Father afflicted with Peter Pan syndrome. Daughter acting in inappropriate role as peacemaker. Big mess.*

Jocelyn glanced toward the driveway, and it occurred to me that she was watching for Zach. Zach, who would be showing up anytime. I'd lost sight of that for a minute. When he came home he was going to find me hanging out at the cabin with my ex-husband. Worse yet, when Geoff saw Zach and me together, he was going to add up two and two. Worst of all, if Sydney saw any hints of romance, she would start building one of her pipe dreams about her mom finding a soul mate—another phrase she'd learned from Geoff and Whitney. *Soul mates*—life's plan and purpose, according to Whitney. It was impossible to be happy without one, and Sydney wanted me to be happy. Aside from that, her best friend had a great stepdad, and she wanted one, too. Every time she saw me acting even remotely friendly with a man, she fell into a blended-family fantasy, and then when nothing happened, she was crushed. She'd already had her emotions tied up in enough romantic drama this summer. She didn't need me adding more.

I'd just have to make sure there weren't any hints of romance. My biggest complaint against Geoff, and my most convincing reason for getting him to leave Sydney with me, was his inappropriately involving her in his unstable relationship with Whitney. I couldn't let myself be guilty of doing the same thing. Sydney's well-being had to come first, at least with one of us. I had to talk Geoff into letting her go, and then take her back to Colorado before he changed his mind. As soon as we got home, I was going to see the judge about the custody agreement. With Geoff single, unstable, and now homeless, there was no way he should be taking care of an eight-year-old child.

Even though the decision was clear in my mind, I continued nervously checking the driveway as we said good-bye to Collie and Laura, and then waited for Sydney and Pop to come back. When she returned, Sydney had a gigantic black inner tube, an olive-drab army life raft, an old-fashioned orange floatation vest, a box of old clothes that Pop said she and Geoff could borrow, three towels, and a stringer of plastic fish with squirty mouths.

"Tomorrow morning I'll take you fishin' and we'll catch some real ones," Pop told her as we opened the back hatch of my SUV to cram everything in. "That is, if you can get up early."

No, no, no, I thought. *Don't encourage her to hope for things that aren't going to happen. Don't make promises we can't keep.* "We'll see," I interjected, playing the killjoy mom. "We'll probably be leaving in the morning."

Sydney completely ignored me, or else she didn't hear. "I can get up early," she said brightly. "Really early. Dad always sleeps late when he doesn't have to go to work, so we can fish for a long time."

"We'll see," I repeated. The situation was slipping out of control, so I hustled Sydney toward the backseat as Geoff headed for the passenger-side door. "Guess we'd better go. Sydney, tell Pop thank you for all the great stuff."

Sydney not only told Pop thank you, she ran back and hugged him, her face disappearing into the folds of his shirt just above his belt buckle. "Thanks, Pop!" she chirped into the fabric, then unwrapped her arms and ran back to the Jeep, yanking up the door handle, which turned out to be locked.

"Here, I'll get it." On the other side of the car, Geoff opened the passenger-side door and punched the unlock button. He and Mr. Grits spied each other at exactly the same moment. Jumping out of the floorboard, the dog let out a booming, "Bar-bar-bar-ooo!" and Geoff scrambled backward, landing on his rear end in the grass. "Holy . . . What the . . . Son of a . . . Sweet Jiminy Cricket, what is that?"

Diving across the front seat, I grabbed a handful of dog hair just in time to stop Mr. Grits from bailing out the door to tackle Geoff. "It's all right." In my excitement over seeing Sydney, I'd completely forgotten the dog was in the car. "He's all right. You just surprised him when you opened the door."

"I surprised *him*?" Geoff coughed, raising his hands palms out, afraid to move. "What in the world is that, a yeti?"

I laughed, in spite of the fact that I was determined to detest Geoff's company. Seeing him on the ground on his rear end was deeply satisfying. "It's a dog. Part Great Pyrenees. A sheepdog."

Standing up slowly, Geoff kept his hands in front of himself like a suspect under arrest. "Well, tell it I'm not a sheep, OK?" He sidled to the back door, eyeing the dog. "Where'd you get that thing?"

"Long story." I turned around as Sydney bounced into the backseat and reached out to pet Mr. Grits. "Careful. I don't know how he is with . . ." I needn't have bothered. As soon as Mr. Grits spied Sydney, he forgot all about Geoff and me. Spinning slowly around, he whacked me in the face with his bushy tail, then proceeded to cram himself through the space between the front seats, so he could sit in the back next to Sydney. Geoff quickly vacated the area and moved to the front.

When everyone was finally situated, we waved good-bye to Pop and headed for the river. Geoff and I sat silent while Sydney and Mr. Grits bonded. It was surreal in a way, all of us in the car together, bumping slowly along the dirt road. To a casual observer, watching from a distance through a long-range lens, it would have looked like the perfect scene—Mom, Dad, dog, daughter in perky pigtails, driving to a charming vacation destination with swimming equipment in the back.

Only it was anything but perfect. Geoff faced out the window so he wouldn't have to look at me, and in the rear seat Sydney began cheerfully telling Mr. Grits about the harrowing trip out of Mexico. Police cars, a mad rush at the airport, a rickety plane that had to toss off cargo because it was overweight for takeoff. Two plane changes in tiny Mexican airports, where Geoff scrambled, begged, and bribed to get them onto flights, an argument with customs officers who didn't believe they had no luggage. An hour in a locked, unairconditioned room waiting to talk to a detective, a walk across a border bridge in the middle of the night, a cabdriver who warned them not to talk to anyone, because they might get mugged. Another airport in El Paso, more layovers during which a nice man gave her Krispy Kreme doughnuts because she was such a pretty little girl, and finally a flight to Dallas, then Austin, where they tried and tried to call Aunt Laura's house, until finally they got Uncle Graham. Oh, and she was worried about Whitney, because after the big fight she left home without any suitcases, and Sydney hoped she made it out of Mexico and back to England all right.

I felt sick to my stomach. In the passenger seat Geoff got shorter and shorter, until he was barely there. Bracing his elbow on the armrest, he cupped his hand over his eyes and stayed that way. His head bounced up and down in rhythm with the SUV, colliding repeatedly with his palm. He didn't seem to care.

When we reached the riverbank, Sydney bailed out before I could stop her. Mr. Grits was right behind her, and they dashed across the grass through the uneven spray of afternoon sunlight and shadows. "Not into the water until I get there!" I hollered, opening the back hatch and struggling to untangle the tightly packed jumble of rubber and sun-bleached nylon.

Climbing out of his seat, Geoff stretched as if he had all the time in the world.

"Hurry up," I barked. Shades of the old, married days, when I handled all the practical details, while Geoff dreamed and played and amused himself. "She shouldn't be down there by herself. There could be snakes or something."

"She's got the yeti with her." He gave me a smile that was probably supposed to be cute and charming, but only served to make me want to choke him. "Anyway," he added, standing nonchalantly behind the Jeep while I pulled out flotation devices, flinging them intentionally in his direction, "you told her not to get in the water until we were down there."

I squinted at him, unable to believe how stupid that sounded. "Did it ever occur to you that she might *fall* in? Or that she might, just might, get tempted and disobey? She's an eight-year-old *child*, Geoff. She has to be watched every *minute*." Slamming the hatch shut, I stalked around, yanking tubes and towels and squeaky plastic fish out of the grass. "I can see you haven't learned much about *parenthood* in the past month." I headed for the riverbank as fast as was possible with a giant inner tube on my hip and a stringer of plastic fish wrapped around my legs.

Grabbing the army boat and the life jacket, Geoff followed. "Well, you know what, Lindsey? Not all of us are as perfect as you."

"Oh, come on, Geoff," I snapped, rapidly moving beyond the boundaries of self-control. "I never said I was perfect, but at least I never dragged Sydney halfway across two countries in her swimsuit and dirty clothes. Is everything she says true? Were you and Sydney thrown out of Mexico by the *police*?"

Geoff winced—the first time I'd seen him look regretful on Sydney's behalf. Ever. "Someone reported my team for a customs violation—trafficking in antiquities, something like that. All of us got kicked out of the country with no warning. They took our equipment, the fossils, everything. Some local official is probably making big bucks off our stuff right now."

"Were you trafficking in antiquities?" I was almost afraid to ask.

Geoff had the nerve to look shocked and offended. "Of course not. We were set up, plain and simple. The dig was completely legit. No problems with the local police. No problems getting permits to dig. Nothing. Then Whitney and I had a fight, and she left me. The next thing I knew, the police were at my house. Whitney's dad probably had something to do with it. He hates my guts, and he has a lot of pull down there. It wasn't my fault."

"Nothing is ever your fault." I threw the inner tube down, then snatched it up again. "My God, Geoff, you're lucky you didn't end up in a Mexican prison. Then what would have happened to Sydney?"

Geoff threw up his hands, boat and all. "How about giving me a break, Lindsey? The rest of us don't have everything mapped out, minute by minute, on a little spreadsheet. Some of us make mistakes. We screw up, and then we have to go back and try to fix things."

"Well, that's just great!" I whipped around so quickly that the inner tube collided with the boat and both of us bounced backward, which was probably good, because I wanted to slug him. "Sydney isn't a *thing*. She's a person. What if you screw up something that can't be fixed? What about that? My God, Geoff, she's not some fragmented piece of pottery you can try to fit into your life this way or that way until you figure out something that works for you. She's a kid. You only get one chance. You have to do everything right. You can't run some kind of daddy experiment with her and then give up when it doesn't work out." Tears rushed into my eyes, and I knew I was cutting close to the quick, removing scar tissue so near wounds, that they were starting to bleed again. "She's been waiting all her life for you to want her, and now that you've got her, you can't even be bothered to spend time with her."

Geoff stood stunned, staring at me with his dark eyes blank and his mouth hanging open, the army boat drooping at his side. In his flowered shirt and baggy shorts, his shoulders sagging, he looked like Charlie Brown right after Lucy tells him he's a blockhead.

I didn't wait for an answer. I could tell he didn't have one. He couldn't imagine what I was talking about. He'd finally stepped up to the plate after eight years, exercised his custody rights and taken his daughter for the summer. Wasn't that enough?

Tears clouded my eyes as I stumbled down the hill and stopped on the rocky ledge above the water. Below, Sydney had stripped off her travel-stained shorts and T-shirt and tossed them over a tree limb, where the wind stirred them gently, giving them a life of their own. She stood at the edge of the water in her swimsuit with the big white dog, the two of them a greeting-card photograph, a perfect portrait of summer, and silence, and childhood. A representation of softness and innocence, two creatures shedding the cares of the world like old clothes and losing themselves in the dance of sunlight on water.

Turning, she smiled up at me, and hollered, "Mommy, can I get in now?"

"Sure, honey," I called, suddenly wishing I could dive in with her and hide in the quiet below the surface. Standing the tube on end, I sent it rolling down the bank like a giant doughnut. "Here you go."

The tube bounced into the water, Mr. Grits barked, and Sydney splashed in after the toy, laughing as the dog plunged in with her. "Look, Mom, he can swim!" Scrambling onto the inner tube, she waved at me as she drifted into deeper water. "C'mon, Mommy, come do seesaw with me."

Shaking my head, I laid my towel on the rock ledge and sat down, calling, "No swimsuit. Sorry."

She turned her attention up the hill, beckoning past me. "C'mon, Dad. It's not cold." Throwing her hands over her mouth, she squealed, and the next thing I knew Geoff was careering down the hill in a barefoot run. Stripping off his shirt, he tossed it on the grass without slowing down.

"Yoweee!" he screamed when he left the grass and hit the rough rock shelf above the water. "Yow, yow, yow! Ouchy feet! Look out, here I come!" Bailing off the rock shelf in one huge jump, he landed in the water, hooked an arm over the tube, and bounced Sydney into the air. She flew up, laughing and kicking, and hit the water in a cannonball that made me rise partway before she came up laughing and sputtering and begging him to do it again.

Sitting back down, I pulled my knees to my chest and rested my chin, watching them play inner-tube seesaw over and over as they drifted slowly down the river, while Mr. Grits ran along the shore, yapping like a puppy. It was, I knew, exactly the kind of moment Sydney had dreamed of all those nights she lay awake imagining the father she'd seen only in pictures.

How could I deny her that?

In one quiet instant, before they drifted, laughing and jostling, around the bend, I realized something with startling clarity: Geoff could give her things I could not. I could keep her safe; I could teach her to be practical, to plan, to pay bills, have a real job, get up and go to bed on a regular schedule. I couldn't teach her to shed her cares, no matter how bad they were, run down the hill barefoot, and plunge into the water without knowing how deep it was. I couldn't teach her to be bold, to meet life head on and embrace the possibilities. I couldn't give her the courage to tilt at windmills, because I didn't have it myself.

Letting my eyes drift closed, I listened to the two of them laughing just beyond the trees. They'd pulled the tube out and were coming back to the swimming hole again, where the rapids started. . . .

My mind floated away, back to Zach and me sitting on top of the windmill tower, drinking Dublin Dr Pepper and watching the day fade. I felt his body warm against me, his lips touching mine, the light stroke of his fingers through my hair. The kiss was long and slow, and when it ended I looked into his eyes, those incredible silvery-green eyes, and everything else fell away. I didn't want the moment to end. I wanted it to go on, and on, and on.

I like a woman who knows her tools, he said, and I laughed. The motion jerked me from my dream, and I frantically scanned the river, afraid for just an instant that Geoff and Sydney were part of the dream, too. Somewhere out of sight I could hear the faint sound of Mr. Grits barking enthusiastically. Sighing, I relaxed again.

"Good daydream?" The voice from behind surprised me, and I bolted upright, twisting around, though I didn't need to.

"Zach," I said. He was sitting on the spotted horse, with a saddle this time. The horse had its back foot cocked, resting. I wondered how long they'd been there. Standing up, I started toward him. "What are you doing?"

"Watching you." He grinned, and all the old feelings came back in a rush so powerful it stopped me where I stood.

"When . . ." I blinked hard, trying to clear my head, listening again for the sounds of Geoff and Sydney, trying to be sure they were real, really here. I wanted them to be, and then I didn't, and then I did again. It was all so complicated now. "When did you get back?"

Zach dismounted in a casual way that told me he had no idea my daughter and ex-husband were just beyond the bend. "A little while ago. No one was at the house, so I thought I'd get this colt ridden. He needs it. I thought you might be down here."

"I was . . . I am . . ." Shaking my head again, I tried to clear the fog. "I mean, I'm here, but . . ."

A high-pitched squeal from the riverbed spun me around, and my two realities collided with five excited words: "Oh, my gosh, a horse!" Sydney was up the hill before I had time to think, standing there dripping in her bathing suit between Zach and me, jittering up and down, looking at the horse.

I took a breath, swallowed hard. *Be calm. You have to handle this well. Don't tip Sydney off to anything romantic.* I laid a hand on Sydney's shoulder to calm her down. "This is my daughter, Sydney. Sydney, this is Za . . . Mr. Truitt, or Dr. Truitt, I guess it is, really."

"Zach," he corrected, offering his hand to shake Sydney's in a very grown-up fashion. "Or Mr. Zach, or Dr. Zach, as you prefer, madam. Nice to meet you, Miss Sydney."

He smiled, and Sydney was thoroughly charmed. After all, he did have a cowboy hat and a horse. "It's just Sydney," she said, shaking his hand. "Is this your horse?" She sidestepped him slightly to get a better look.

"Well, more or less." Zach turned his attention fully to Sydney, holding the horse steady as she touched its nose. "Like this," he said, slipping his hand over hers and turning both palms up, so that the horse sniffed, then nuzzled her outstretched fingers. In my mind I saw Zach and me stroking Sleepy's silver hair, our hands intertwined, our bodies close, moving beyond the barriers of fear. "And never with the fingers sticking up, because he might bite one accidentally, and that hurts," Zach was saying, and Sydney hung on every word.

"Can people ride him?" Sydney asked, covetously eyeing the saddle.

"Sydney!" I scolded.

Zach's good-natured laugh slipped over me like warm honey. "Well, not this colt, because he's a little young and rancorous yet, but in the morning I'll saddle your mom's horse and you can take a ride. How about that?"

Sydney's eyes widened until the rest of her face seemed to disappear. "Really? Cool! Oh, my gosh. Cool!"

No, no, no! I thought. *Don't promise her things that aren't going to happen, that can't happen.* "Oh, well, I think we're supposed to meet Collie in the morning to take some pictures," I said.

Sydney didn't hear me, probably because she didn't want to. She only had eyes for Zach, the horse guy. "*Mom* has a *horse?*"

"Sure, she does. Everyone gets a horse to care for while they're staying here," Zach answered, winking at Sydney. "Tell you what—after you finish taking pictures with Collie, then I'll saddle Sleepy and we'll go for a ride."

Vibrating in place, Sydney fanned her hands like a crazed teenager at an Elvis concert. The spotted horse snorted and backed to the end of his reins.

"Dad!" Sydney hollered, turning around. "Mom has a horse named Sleepy!"

Oh, God. I glanced over my shoulder, and Geoff was coming up the hill in his wet shorts with his beach-bum shirt hanging unbuttoned. My worlds collided again in an even bigger way, a full nine on the Richter scale. "Zach," I heard myself say mechanically, "this is Sydney's father, Geoff Attwood. Geoff, this is Zach Truitt. He . . ." *Taught me how to fix windmills and tame wild horses, and made me feel alive for the first time in years.* "His family owns the ranch."

Zach and Geoff looked equally confused. Zach reacted first, offering his hand with a cordial, even slightly friendly greeting. "Nice to meet you, Geoff."

"Likewise," Geoff returned, then slanted a gaze from me to Zach and back, like he was surmising that we were more than casual acquaintances.

Sydney was completely oblivious to the goings-on around her. "Mr. Zach's going to let me go riding tomorrow. On Mom's horse."

"Oh, well . . . I don't think we'll be here long enough to do that," I interjected, and Sydney turned to stare at me, openmouthed and ashen faced, shivering because the sun had faded and the evening air was getting cool.

Worse than her expression was Zach's. He looked completely confused, blindsided.

Geoff surveyed the circle and broke the stalemate by ruffling Sydney's wet hair. "Why don't we just wait and see," he suggested. "In the meantime, looks like we'd better get some clothes on and pick up the swim things, huh?"

"All right," Sydney agreed glumly, giving Zach and the horse one last, forlorn glance before she turned away and followed her father down the hill.

"I'm sorry about that," I said to Zach when they were gone. "I didn't realize ... I didn't know ... they were coming. Geoff had some kind of breakup with his wife and trouble in Mexico, and he and Sydney showed up here completely unexpected. Sydney's caught in the middle of Geoff's mess, of course."

Zach nodded, and for an instant I had the feeling that he understood all too well. "At least she's back safely. That's what matters, right?"

Tears pressing my throat, I swallowed hard. "It's such a screwed-up disaster. All of a sudden, she's using words like *domestic disturbance* and *customs violation*. The Mexican police hauled her to the airport in a patrol car." Combing my fingers into my hair, I pulled until it hurt, trying to smooth away the images. Half of me wanted to tell Zach the story, slip into his arms, be comforted, and forget everything. Half of me knew I couldn't let that happen. "She shouldn't have to go through all this. I just want to take her home and let her enjoy the rest of her summer." Tears spilled onto my cheeks as I looked over my shoulder and watched my daughter put on the filthy shorts and T-shirt. "I just want her to have a normal life."

Squinting down the hill, Zach smoothed a hand up my arm, onto my shoulder. "It looks like she's doing fine now." He nodded toward the river as Sydney's laughter lifted the air. His hand slid into my hair, and I wanted to lean against it.

"She's not fine." *What would you know about it?* the bitter voice of Divorce Lindsey spat in my head. *What would you know about raising children? You aren't even raising your own.* Opening my eyes, I jerked away. "It isn't fine. I can't do"—waving my hand vaguely, I indicated the ranch, the horse, him—"this. I have to take Sydney back to Colorado, petition the judge, and see what can be done about the custody arrangements. It's bad enough that her father inolves her in his screwed-up love life. I can't do it, too. I can't be like him. She deserves stability. I have to go home, Zach."

Zach looked down at the ground, watching the toe of his boot scrub a bare spot in the grass. The brim of his hat concealed whatever he was thinking. The moment seemed to stretch on forever, until there was a chasm of silence too big to cross.

Say something, I thought. *Say something that will change it all. Tell me about Macey. Tell me about your daughter. Make me understand. Tell me who you really are.*

But he didn't.

"Good-bye, Zach," I whispered, an ache starting in the deepest part of me and spreading through my body, burning away hope like flash fuel, gone in an instant, leaving everything hollow and blackened. "Thanks for understanding."

"The thing is, Lindsey . . ." Turning from me, he gathered the reins, and I knew he was leaving. This was it. The end. "I don't understand."

TWENTY-ONE

SYDNEY SPENT THE NIGHT IN THE DOWNSTAIRS BEDROOM WITH ME.
I was glad when, after an impromptu supper of sandwiches, she
was too tired to chatter on about horses anymore. I helped her
shampoo her hair and dress in one of my old T-shirts, then sent her
off to bed while I washed out her clothes and swimsuit in the tub.
Hopefully in the morning Laura would show up with something
else for her to wear.

When I came out of the bathroom, Geoff was waiting with the
box of old clothes Pop had sent along. He smelled like sweat and fish
water—a little like the dog, actually. "Night," he said, making it clear
that he didn't want to talk after his bath, which was fine, because I
didn't either.

With Sydney safely tucked away, my mind turned to the scene
with Zach. It replayed in my head over and over, the picture becoming sharper each time, like a movie coming into focus. The
tragic ending, the classic black moment, getting darker and darker
and darker. Only this wasn't a movie. This was real life. No magic solution would leap out of some director's imagination and save us
from reality. Zach was going to return to his life, and I was going to
return to mine, and the past few days would be nothing more than
a memory that didn't really fit anywhere. Life would go on in a million tiny ways, just as it had before I'd come to Texas.

So why did I feel as if I were suffocating on the thought of returning to my normal routine? I had the one thing I wanted more

than anything else in the world. I had my daughter back with me, safe. Why wasn't that enough? Being her mom, raising her and seeing her safely through her childhood was my reason for everything, my mission. My calling.

Yet, lying there in the dark, her body curled against mine, I felt more alone than I'd ever been in my life. Tears seeped beneath my lashes, and I rolled away from her, burying my face in the pillow so she wouldn't hear me crying on her first night home.

When I fell asleep it was deep and dreamless, and in the morning I awoke to the sound of something hard clomping on the stairs. Dragging one eye open, I lifted my head, then let it fall back, waiting for the room—and the realities of the day—to come into focus.

Sydney dashed in searching for something, checked the closet and under the bed, then headed for the door again.

"Hold it," I said, blinking the grog from my eyes. "What in the world have you got on?" She looked like a miniature Annie Oakley, wearing a hot-pink Western shirt with a baby-doll-pink yoke and fringe under the arms. She had matching pants, with fringe in a horseshoe shape around the rear end and down the legs, and big bell-bottoms that flared over pointy-toed white-and-gold cowboy boots, straight out of the 1970s. She'd completed the outfit with a tooled leather belt to hold up the pants, and a huge belt buckle that read MICKEY MOUSE CLUB. I blinked again, trying not to laugh. "Where did you get all that stuff?"

"In the box that Pop gave us. He said some of it was Jocelyn's when she was a little girl." Bracing her hands on her hips, she twirled around, displaying the latest in hoedown fashion. "Isn't it totally cool?"

"Totally," I replied, swinging my legs over the side of the bed. "With that outfit, you definitely need braids." Her hair was hanging around her face in long cornrows from her having slept on it wet. "Run out to the car and get a couple of your hair bands from the glove compartment, and I'll fix it for you. Pink ones would be good."

"The dog's got my pink ones." Crossing her arms over her slim chest, she tapped a boot on the floor and pretended to be miffed. "Those were my favorites, too."

I felt my lips tugging into a smile. Sydney loved to make people laugh. She had a great sense of humor, which, as much as I hated to admit it, she got from her father. "I guess you could ask for them back."

Her nose crinkled on one side, and her mouth twisted into a grimace that revealed the missing front tooth. "Eeeewww!" she squealed, then spun around and dashed for the car.

By the time I'd put on my sneakers and found my hairbrush, she was back, carrying two purple fliggies with glittery Powerpuff Girls orbs on the ends. It felt good, sitting beside her on the bed, brushing her long hair, enjoying a quiet morning moment. Just like the old days.

"I like the way you do it," she said, closing her eyes and leaning into my hand. "Whitney pulls too hard and it hurts sometimes, but she knows all kinds of cool French braids." Sitting up straight again, she flicked a glance at me and added self-consciously, "But I like the way you do it best."

Finishing the first braid, I rested my hands before starting on the second. For an instant I imagined all the weight on those small shoulders—two families, divided love, torn loyalties, guilt, and a desperate need to make everyone happy. "Sydney," I said softly, resting my chin on her head and hugging her, "it's OK for you to love Whitney, and it's OK for you to love your dad. There are going to be different things for you to like about each of the special people in your life. You don't have to be afraid that you're hurting me by having feelings for them, all right?"

"All right." Gazing thoughtfully toward the window, she sighed as I started on the second braid. "Mommy, it'd be better if you—" Springing suddenly from the bed, she dragged me, holding the end of the braid, across the room. "Pop's here!" she squealed. "Pop's here to go fishing."

"Hold still." Finishing her hair, I fastened the fliggie as Sydney vibrated in place. "There. Done," I said, glancing reluctantly out the window. If I let Sydney go fishing now, next she'd want the horse-back riding lesson. With Zach.

Sydney beat me to the punch. "And, after that, can I go ride the horse, Mommy? Pleeeease, please, please?"

"Honey, I—" Pop honked the horn outside. "We'll see how the day goes."

To Sydney, of course, that was almost as good as a yes. "Oh-kay!" she chirped, and bounded toward the door, the Powerpuff Girls fliggies bouncing in strange contrast to the retro cowgirl outfit. I hurried after her into the living room.

Geoff was sitting at the kitchen table, gaping sleepily toward the front door, which was hanging open in the wake of Hurricane Sydney. "*What* was *that*?"

"Anybody's guess." I leaned out the door as Pop stole my daughter and the dog, without even asking. Waving out the truck window, he took off, not stopping to tell me where they were going or how long they'd be.

"Great," I muttered. Barely sunrise, and the day was already filling up with complications. One of whom was sitting at the kitchen table. I turned to face him. "Geoff, we need to —" My mouth fell open on the word *talk*, and a puff of laughter blew past my lips. He was wearing a red checked 1960s Western shirt with big blue-and-silver flowers on the yoke, and a pair Roy Rogers jeans with three-inch cuffs at the bottom. He looked like a cross between Howdy Doody and Mr. Green Jeans. "Been shopping in Pop's box?"

Geoff rolled his eyes. "It was the only thing that fit. My shorts are still wet from last night, and my shirt smells pretty rank, so it was this or nothing."

"Good choice," I said, motioning to the clothes.

We stood for a moment rebuilding our defenses after the rare moment of levity. Geoff picked a plop of dried-up grits off the table, and I leaned against the door frame with my arms crossed.

Rubbing his head, he looked exhausted despite the night's sleep. "Can we have a little breakfast before we start ripping each other apart?" he said finally. "I need some coffee."

"All right," I agreed, determined to be more diplomatic than yesterday, when I'd lost it down by the river. "I've got oatmeal, toast, bagels, and instant grits."

He shrugged, like it didn't matter what he ate. "Bagel, I guess." He stared out the window while I toasted bagels and poured coffee, then brought everything to the table. We ate in silence, then sat looking into our coffee mugs like some magical answer might appear there.

"I heard what you said to Sydney in the bedroom," Geoff said finally, his attention still focused on his cup. "Thanks."

"You're welcome," I replied, trying not to sound grudging. "This is a difficult situation, but I don't want her to struggle with it any more than she already has. I don't want her to feel guilty for loving you . . . or Whitney."

Geoff collapsed like a scarecrow falling off the pole. His head fell into his hands, and he spoke into the tabletop. "I really screwed up this time."

I blinked, taken aback. Never, ever, had I heard Geoff admit such a thing without quickly adding that it wasn't his fault. Sitting there crumpled over the table, he looked like a broken man. "Listen, Geoff, I don't know what's going on between you and Whitney, and I don't need to know. It's your business. But it's not healthy for Sydney to be involved in it, emotionally or otherwise. I want to take her home for the rest of the summer. When you've got it straightened out, with Whitney or without her, you can come back and tell Sydney how things are going to be."

Geoff shook his head, his fingers combing into his shaggy brown hair. "I don't know how things are going to be. I can't predict that."

"You have to," I insisted. "She can't live her life spending summers with the stepmom-slash-girlfriend of the month, while you go to work. If you want to be in her life, you have to *be* in her life. You have to take care of her, spend time with her, provide her with a consistent, predictable environment that doesn't include domestic disputes and trips to some foreign airport in a police car." The words rolled out of me like water through a dam, and once I'd started, I couldn't stop.

Geoff sank lower into his hands, his head drooping between his shoulder blades. "You're right. She should go home with you. She should be with you. I shouldn't have taken her away." The words I'd longed to hear, but now I realized they were wrong. Now that he didn't have Whitney to fall back on, now that his life was a mess and the pressure was on, he wanted to drop Sydney back in my hands like an unwanted puppy, while he limped off to lick his wounds in some far corner of the world. I could hear it in his voice, see it in his posture and the way he shifted toward the door—he was bailing out, and he wasn't coming back.

"You can*not* abandon Sydney again, Geoff," I said, gripping the edge of the table, my eyes burning and my heart pounding. "It's time to grow up and think about someone other than yourself. She's been waiting all her life for you to notice her, to pay attention to her, to *want* her. She needs her father. She needs you to love her."

"I do love her." His words melted into a sob that shook his shoulders. "But I've screwed everything up. I don't know how to do the whole domestic thing. I need to just go somewhere, be by myself where I can't hurt anybody. I'm not good for Sydney, and I'm not good for Whitney."

Slamming a hand on the table, I stood up so fast that my chair fell over and slapped against the floor like thunder. Geoff jerked upright. "Then figure out how to be better. For heaven's sake, Geoff, for once in your life, step up to the plate. Do the right thing. Grow up!" Throwing my hands into the air, I turned around and headed for the door. As I jerked it open, he sobbed out two little words that both explained things, and made the situation much, much worse.

"Whitney's pregnant."

"Great," I spat, pausing with my fingers on the latch. "That's just great." Slamming the door on Geoff and his revelation, I crossed the porch and started running.

I ran until I couldn't breathe, until all the anger, and pain, and anxiety were gone, and I didn't feel anything but aching muscles and burning lungs. Standing in the middle of the road, I doubled over with my hands on my knees, gulping in huge gasps of air. I stayed there for a long time, trying to catch my breath, waiting for the whirling in my brain to stop. When my body had finally recovered, I sat down on an uprooted tree beside the road and tried to think. What now? What did I say to Geoff now? I could only imagine how Whitney must be feeling.

No. I knew how Whitney was feeling. Abandoned. Betrayed. Desperate. I pictured her newly pregnant, finding out that Geoff didn't want to be a father. He must have confessed that fact to her. Why else would she have left?

I had to go back and talk to Geoff. Somehow I had to convince him not to repeat the mistakes he had made with Sydney and me. He had to see that this baby would need him, would yearn for him, just as Sydney had all these years. He had to know that Whitney would end up broken and afraid and bitter. He couldn't do it again. He couldn't run out on Sydney or this new baby.

Taking a deep breath, I stood up and started walking toward the cabin.

The rattle of tires on gravel stopped me before I reached the bend above the river. *Zach*, I thought, with an instant of hopeful euphoria that crashed back to earth like a paper airplane with crumpled wings. I wanted it to be him, in spite of everything. I wanted him to beg me to stay, convince me I could trust him with my daughter, tell me that the bridge between here and town had washed out, and I couldn't leave. Not today. Not ever.

I wanted him to rage with me about the fact that Geoff was going to run off to God knew where and leave not only my daughter, but also an unborn baby behind, fatherless.

But then, Zach would understand that all too well, wouldn't he?

Turning around, I watched the approaching vehicle, feeling a twinge of disappointment that it wasn't his. The pickup coming up the road was Collie's San Saline newspaper vehicle, with my sister at the wheel. Her blond hair waved a cheerful hello as she pulled alongside me.

"Out jogging?" Raising one brow and lowering the other, she surveyed my outfit. "In . . . your pajamas?"

I glanced down and realized I wasn't even dressed. "Things got a little . . . close in the cabin." Walking around the truck, I climbed in.

"You mean you and Goeff had a fight," Laura interpreted.

"A little one." Sighing, I brushed sweaty strands of hair from my face and rested my head against the seat.

Laura grimaced playfully. "Do I need to come help hide the body?"

I rubbed my eyes until they hurt. Until I couldn't see anything but flashes of color and light behind my eyelids. "God. What a mess."

"It can't be that bad," she soothed.

I nodded into my hand. *Yes, it can. Sydney's going to have a half sister or half brother she'll probably never know, her father's about to dump her, and I'm in love with a man I can't possibly stay with. How's that for bad?*

"Whitney's pregnant. That's what his marital breakup was about. Geoff's about to have another baby he doesn't want. Sydney's been telling me all summer about Whitney's treatments at some New Age infertility clinic down there. Now she's pregnant, and Geoff hadn't planned on that actually happening. He wants to cut and run. That's why he brought Sydney back to me. He's ready to take the easy way out, bail on the fatherhood thing and jet off to parts unknown." The truck swayed around a curve, and I felt sick. "It'll devastate Sydney."

"Talk to him. Make him understand how much is at stake here," Laura urged, sliding her hand down my arm and clasping my fingers. "Come on. Where's my got-it-under-control sis?"

"Lost." The word trembled into the air in a sigh of resignation. "Lost, lost, lost."

"No, you're not." Stopping the truck, Laura put it in park.

"I don't know where to go from here." None of the roads seemed to lead to happiness. Nothing seemed right.

"You don't have to go anywhere," Laura said softly. "Stay a while. Take some time to work things out with Geoff. Let Sydney ride horses and have a little fun. You and I and Collie can check out all the tearooms within a hundred miles, and I'll even go to antique malls with you." She shook my fingers to see if I was listening. "Stay."

Pulling my hand away from my face, I turned to her. "I can't stay. You know I can't stay. I have to get out of here."

"Why?" she pleaded. "Jocelyn said the cabin—"

"It's not the cabin. You know it's not the cabin." My voice boomed through the car, and Laura sat back, slapped by the vibration. "I can't do this whole vacation-romance thing with Zach, not in front of Sydney. I know you and Collie had some kind of scheme going here, but it's not going to work. I can't involve Sydney in a half-baked love affair with some guy I barely know."

Laura huffed an irritated breath. "Oh, for heaven's sake, Lindsey." Her lips pinched together, telling me we were about to degenerate into a sister-fight. "Sydney's already involved. The whole thing was her idea."

Blinking, I jerked away from her. "What?" I couldn't imagine what she was talking about. "What do you *mean*, her idea?"

"It was her idea," Laura repeated, raising a hand palm first, like she was going to serve up the truth because I was too stupid to figure it out. "This was the brainchild of your eight-year-old daughter. The one who understands a whole lot more than you think. The one who sees that you have your life wrapped around hers so tightly that neither of you can breathe. When she knew she was leaving for the summer, she e-mailed Collie and me and told us to do something with you."

"Do something?" I stammered, trying to grasp what Laura was saying.

"Yes. Do something." Laura was through mollycoddling me. " 'You've got to do something with Mom,' that's what she said. 'She needs somebody so she won't be alone all the times I'm gone.' For heaven's sake, Lindsey, your daughter feels guilty about having friends, going on sleepovers, spending time with her father, because when she's gone, you're alone. She sees that you don't have anyone but her, and she wants you to have a life."

"She is my life!" I sobbed, threading my arms around myself and rocking back and forth in my seat as the world turned upside down.

"Stop using her as an excuse!" Laura sounded like my mother

giving a life lecture. "Lindsey, you know and I know that there's something special between you and Zach. Collie saw it that first day she caught you two together in the barn. I heard it in your voice when you said his name on the phone. I can feel it in the part of me that knows you. I can feel you happy and alive for the first time in years." Leaning close, she tried to unclench my arms and take my hand again. "Come on, Lindsey, don't be so stubborn. Admit it. Collie and I were right—you and Zach are good together. He needed to get back into life; you needed to get back into life. It's perfect. Stay here awhile and see where it goes."

I stared out the window, my mind a mass of conflicting desires, swirling like a sea in a storm. Beneath it all there was an undercurrent, a black riptide that swept everything else away. Betrayal. I'd been betrayed by my twin sister, my best friend, even my daughter. I was everybody's pathetic charity case, who needed to be manipulated for my own good.

"It's not perfect," I ground out. "This is so far from perfect, it's not even in the same time zone. I can't believe you and Collie would involve Sydney. Good Lord, Laura, what were you thinking?" I didn't wait for an answer, just kept talking as the whole thing crystallized in my head. "I can't believe Jocelyn would go along with it. She's supposed to be a psychologist. And Zach . . . What did you do to convince him to help with romancing the stone? Or does he do this for every poor, pathetic single mother who comes to horse psychology camp? Is that some weird part of the therapy?"

"It's not like that." Laura clenched her hands on top of her head like a runner trying to get oxygen. Clearly this was not going as she'd planned. "Zach didn't know, and Jocelyn . . . well . . . Jocelyn thought Zach needed to find someone, and this was worth a try, that's all."

"Nice experiment." I shook my head, laughing ruefully. "You know what? Take me back to the cabin. I need to pack."

"Fine." Yanking the gearshift into drive, Laura stepped on the gas. "Go back home and live in that stupid apartment where you never bother to meet anybody interesting, and work in the basement of the museum, and lock your daughter in a closet so she'll never be hurt or disappointed. Keep a death grip on your mommyhood, and be lonely, and let time go by, and see how that works for you."

I winced at the picture of my life. "I have to put Sydney first," I defended, even though I knew Laura wasn't buying. "You can't possibly understand how that is. You're not a parent."

Laura exhaled a long breath, her lips tight around the flow of air. "Yes, well, I'm going to be in about eight months, and I hope I'll remember that to raise a happy child, you have to be happy yourself. Nobody wants to be around someone who's miserable."

I didn't even respond to the news of my sister's pregnancy, just leaned back against the seat, turned my face out the window, and watched Texas pass by.

When we reached the cabin, I opened the door and slid my feet to the ground. My legs buckled beneath me like wet spaghetti, and I held on to the door for a minute.

Reaching into the backseat, Laura grabbed a yellow sack and handed it to me. "Here are some clothes for Sydney."

"Thanks," I said, wrapping my hands around the bag. I hovered there, unwilling to end things with Laura and me in a sister-fight. "Could you give Dad a call and tell him Sydney and I are going to come by the farm today? Maybe you and Collie could stop over after the wedding, and we can get some pictures of the girls? I really want to see Bailey before I go back to Colorado."

"Sure," Laura muttered, tapping a finger on the gearshift, probably considering switching it into reverse and running me over.

"I'm sorry. . . ." *I'm sorry, I'm sorry, I'm sorry about everything. I'm sorry I can't take some fairy-tale leap of faith and move to Texas like you did.* "I hope Collie has enough material for the horse psychology article. I sent her a couple of e-mails about the class. She can call me if she needs anything more. I'm sorry I couldn't help her and Gracie find out who stole the dinosaur tracks." It was so much easier to talk about business than about the things that really mattered. "I was really hoping to help."

Laura shifted into reverse without looking at me. She was ready to give up and leave, and I was in the way. "Gracie's working on your tip about the dark truck, and checking into some information Geoff sent in over the Internet. She had some kind of a stakeout going last night. As for the horse psychology article, Collie finished it yesterday. It's done."

"It is?" I tried to lead the conversation into more neutral territory. If I could keep Laura talking long enough, things would soften up between us. She would understand why I had to go. "Why didn't you tell me?"

She cut a blue-eyed glare my way. "We didn't tell you because we didn't want you to run back home to your rabbit hole."

"Oh." Or maybe she'd never understand why I couldn't take the risk of falling for Zach. Maybe this was a decision I'd have to make on my own. It was, after all, my life, and I knew what was best for Sydney and me. Laura would have to understand that I loved her, but I couldn't live my life her way. "Congratulations about the baby. I'm really happy for you."

Moving her hands to the steering wheel, she glanced in the rearview. "No, you're not." The words knocked me back like a slap. "You're never really happy about anything. And the fact is, Lindsey, you deserve to be happy, but you're afraid to take a chance."

I stood silent, my arms hanging limp at my sides. What could I say to that? My sister, who knew me better than I knew myself, had me pegged. Afraid, afraid, afraid. Lindsey, afraid. Afraid of horses, afraid of heights, afraid of screwing up as a parent, afraid of failing in another relationship, afraid of being devastated all over again, afraid of losing control, even a little bit.

Laura let the car roll backward, so that I had to shut the door, then she drove away, giving me up as hopeless.

"She's right, you know." Geoff was standing on the path. His reading glasses were hanging at the end of his nose, making him look even more ridiculous in the outdated cowboy outfit. "Just because we fell apart doesn't mean things can't be different next time—for either one of us."

"What would you know about it, Geoff?" I stalked up the sidewalk and past him into the house, barely resisting the temptation to shove him into the flower bed. He was the last, last, last person in the world to be giving relationship advice. "After all, *you're* repeating all the same old patterns."

Geoff followed me into the house, but left the door open, so that a splash of light fell over the desk by the fireplace, where Caroline's journals and the maps, which had been in the wooden box, were now carefully spread out. I realized Geoff had been reading them. Angrily, I slammed the notebooks shut and crammed them back in the container, then clumsily tried to fold the map. "Leave this stuff alone, Geoff. It isn't yours."

"You found something here, Lindsey," he said flatly, his voice still coming from somewhere near the doorway. "I read—"

"I said, leave it alone!" Frustrated, furious, I threw the map on the table and turned to face him. It was just like Geoff to ignore all the family drama and try to use me to make a big find. He'd read Caroline's journals, snooped over the map, and probably also my field notes. My computer was open on the desk. No doubt he'd helped himself to those files, too. Over my dead body was he going to go digging around on this ranch. "Just leave it alone. There is nothing here. It's none of your business."

Folding his arms over the stupid cowboy shirt, he crooked his index finger and tapped it against his lips. "Come on, Lindsey." I could tell he knew everything. He knew about Caroline's dinosaur, and he meant to find it. "It's right there in black and white. I read it. I read the letter you wrote to Sydney."

"You had no right to—" Suddenly I realized he wasn't talking about Caroline's fossil. "The letter I wrote to Sydney? What are you talking about?"

He wheeled a hand toward my computer. "The letter—the one that went on and on about how you're in love. 'I catch my breath when he smiles. I've got butterflies when he looks at me. Is this the person I really am'—all that stuff."

"You had no right to read that!" I gasped, hitting the mouse, so that the screen refreshed. My letter was there, back from the abyss of cyberspace, now shining in electronic black and white. "I thought that was gone."

"Apparently not." There was laughter in Geoff's voice. "I assume you didn't send it to Sydney. I think I would have heard about that."

Hitting the delete button, I watched the letter disappear, then checked to be sure it was gone for good. Was Geoff accusing me of sinking to his level, of involving Sydney in things that didn't concern her? "Of course not. I would never send something like that to Sydney. I would never tell her that . . . that . . ."

"That you came to Texas and fell in love with a cowboy?" Geoff interpreted.

"No." I knew he was right. Even though it sounded ridiculous, especially coming from Geoff, dressed up as Howdy Doody, I knew he was right.

Clapping his hands together, he touched the tips of his index fingers to his lips, smiling. "Come on, Lindsey. You can't con a con artist." Before I could protest, he raised a finger to silence me, his brown eyes turning soft and crinkling at the corners. "What you decide to do about it is your business, but sitting here reading that, and the old journals, I realized something. I love my wife. When I'm with her, that's the way I feel—just like you described in the letter, just like in those sappy old journals. And while I was reading it, I thought, What if this is my one chance to be happy, and I let it get away?"

I closed my eyes, feeling all the ice between us melt like a glacier into the sea. When I looked up, our eyes met, really met, for the first time in years. "If you really love Whitney, Geoff, you should go after her. And you shouldn't wait. You should do it now, before all the resentments build up, like they did between you and me."

Geoff's gaze swept back and forth across the floor, his eyes slowly widening. "You're right. You're right. I need to go." Pushing off the door frame, he patted his pants pockets, looking for his keys.

"Geoff, you don't have a car."

"That's right. That's true." He paced a few steps into the cabin, then back toward the door. "I need plane tickets, and a ride to the airport, and some real clothes. Not necessarily in that order."

A horse nickered outside, and both of us glanced up. Geoff peeked through the opening, then went outside. Crossing the room to follow him, I half hoped and half feared it would be Zach.

What if this is my one chance . . .

"Hey, look at you!" Geoff said as I reached the doorway. He'd already crossed the yard and was standing by the fence, watching Sydney come up the road, mounted on Sleepy. She rode confidently in her pink cowgirl suit, holding the reins with one hand and gesturing and talking with the other. Beside her, mounted on a brown horse, patiently answering her questions and giving instruction, was, much to my surprise, Dan, the grouchy ranch manager. Mr. Grits was trailing behind them, occasionally glancing up as Dan told Sydney about Sleepy.

"But old Sleepy sure enough likes little girls," Dan said as they stopped in front of us. "You're a pure ol' natural cowgirl, Sydney." Leaning over, he grasped Sleepy's reins. "Slide on off the way I showed ya, now—with yer belly on the horse. There you go."

Patting Sleepy on the shoulder, Sydney moved around to the front and pulled his head down to kiss his nose. "Thanks, Sleepy," she said, then waved at Dan. "Thanks for letting me ride back down here, Mr. Dan, and can you tell Mr. Zach thanks too?"

Dan tipped his hat. "Yes, ma'am," he said, looking adoringly at Sydney. He didn't seem like a fossil thief now. He seemed like somebody's grandpa. Clearing his throat, he straightened in his saddle and tipped his hat to Geoff and me. "Hope we didn't hold y'all up. Pop had to cut the fishing trip a little short so there'd be time to ride, and then everyone left to get ready for the weddin' festivities in town, but Sydney, here, sure enough wanted to ride some more. Nobody'd said when she was supposed to be back, so we just headed this way on horseback. Figured if you come lookin' for her, we'd run into ya on the road."

"No, it's fine. Thanks for letting her ride." Stepping forward, I slipped a hand into Sleepy's mane. Memories rushed back like a swelling tide, and I leaned my head against Sleepy's, my heart aching. " 'Bye, Sleepy." With one last look, I started toward the house, trying not to listen as Dan turned the horses around and headed up the road while Sydney blew kisses to Sleepy.

"Hey . . . wait," Geoff called, and I glanced back to see him limping after the horses while trying to kick a piece of gravel out of his Moses sandals. "Do you have a vehicle near here somewhere?"

Turning around in the saddle, Dan pushed back his hat and squinted. "Well . . . back at the barn, I do, yes, sir."

Geoff pulled out his wallet and started leafing through it. "I'll pay you anything you want to drive me to an airport. Any airport. Whatever's closest."

Bracing both hands on the saddle horn, Dan stretched his neck back and surveyed Geoff critically, then looked at the wallet, softened, and said in a slow Texas drawl, "Well, all right. I reckon I can do that. If you'll just wait, I'll come back and git you in the truck in a little while."

"No. That's all right," Geoff rushed, motioning to Sleepy. "Will this thing get me to the truck?"

Dan's mustache tugged upward on one side and down on the other. "Reckon."

"All right," Geoff said, holding up a hand. "Don't leave. Wait just a minute. I'm coming with you." Jogging back to us, he kissed me on the cheek, then hugged Sydney, lifting her up and dropping her back on her feet. "You be good," he said, kissing the top of her head. "Be good for your mom. I have to go. I have to go after Whitney now."

Bracing her hands on her hips, Sydney tilted her head to one side uncertainly. "When are you gonna come back?"

"Soon," Geoff replied, and for the first time I didn't doubt that he meant it. "I promise I'll come see you in Colorado soon. But I said some things to Whitney that weren't right, and when you say things that hurt somebody, the first thing you need to do is say you're sorry. Does that make sense?"

"Uh-huh," Sydney muttered halfheartedly. "After you get back, can you come watch one of my soccer games?"

"Absolutely. I'd love that." Walking backward toward the horses, he gave her a sad smile. "I'm sorry our summer was such a mess. Next time we'll do better."

She pressed her lips together thoughtfully, then finally shrugged and said, "OK, Dad. Tell Whitney hi."

"I will. See you soon." Blowing her a kiss, he turned and jogged to the horses. He vaulted onto Sleepy's back with surprising agility, took the reins from Dan, and headed down the path of true love, bouncing along at a trot.

As they disappeared among the live oaks, I felt a stab of loneliness, a sting of jealousy, perhaps, because Geoff had the courage to hop on a horse and chase after a dream, and I didn't. "Guess we'd better get our things in the car and get going," I said finally, ushering Sydney and the dog toward the cabin. "It's time to go."

No sense putting off the inevitable any longer.

TWENTY-TWO

LEAVING THE JUBILEE RANCH WAS ONE OF THE HARDEST THINGS I'D ever done. As I stopped the car atop the hill and gazed back, I felt a part of myself being ripped away. Ranch Lindsey, and Horse Psychology Lindsey, and In-Love-with-Zach Lindsey were all staying behind. Like characters in a storybook who couldn't step beyond the pages, they had no place in the real world. It was probably for the best. Their lives were about fixing windmills, and taming wild horses, and climbing goat trails up mountains. They wouldn't have been happy in the basement of a museum, anyway.

Letting off the brake, I faced forward and allowed the car to drift over the hill. Jubilee Ranch grew smaller and smaller in the rearview mirror, until it was gone completely.

Sniffing, I wiped my eyes, straightened my shoulders, and tried to focus on the drive ahead.

Sydney slanted a glare in my direction from where she was sulking in the passenger seat. She'd been pulling a sullen act for the last half hour because she didn't want to leave, and because I made the dog ride in the backseat, rather than on the floorboard under her feet.

"What's wrong?" she asked, suddenly looking worried. She hated it when she caught me crying, and this last year she'd caught me crying a lot.

"Nothing," I said as we turned onto the county road and I hit the gas. "I had a good time here, that's all."

"We don't have to go." Hopeful brown eyes and a big pouty lip. "There's fun stuff to do here."

"No, honey, we have to go. We're going to stop by the farm and see Grandpa Draper, and then we're headed back to Denver. We have to get home."

"I don't go back to school for six more weeks, even."

Reaching over, I stroked one dark braid and straightened the strap on the new sundress Laura had brought her. We'd folded the cowgirl outfit and left it on the table at the cabin, along with the Big Lizard Bottoms box and a thank-you note.

"We need to get back to our regular routine," I said, falsely cheerful.

"Why?" Pulling away, Sydney crossed her arms, slouching in the seat. "It's boring at home, and I have to sit around in summer day care, and you're just sad all the time."

The picture of our lives settled in my stomach like a big, black wad of tar, growing larger and heavier as we drove away. "It'll be different when we get back," I promised finally. "I'll take some long weekends and we'll do things together—go hiking and stuff. Maybe we'll buy some new mountain bikes."

Sydney shrugged and crossed her arms, not happy because I wasn't telling her what she wanted to hear. "Can we keep the dog, at least?"

"We already talked about that." I'd had just about enough of the snotty cold shoulder. "Mr. Grits is an outside dog. He wouldn't be happy in an apartment. We may get some kind of a little dog, but we're going to drop Mr. Grits at the Hawthorne House on our way through San Saline. The lady there finds homes for lost dogs." Mr. Grits stuck his head between the seats at the word *dog*, and I stroked his fur. It was soft and supple after his swim in the river last night.

I hoped I could say good-bye to him without crying. If I cried, it would really set Sydney off about keeping him. I had to do what was best, and he belonged here, chasing goldfish and terrorizing jackrabbits.

Twisting sideways, Sydney sat picking at a loose piece of rubber by the window. We rode in silence as mile after mile flashed by, taking us away from the Jubilee Ranch, through the town of Loveland, where the Big Lizard Diner was full today, past the Over the Moon, where the OUT TO LUNCH sign was already on the door and Melvin's secret dinosaur bone lay hidden in the closet, past the tiny post office and the wedding chapel, and the Lover's Oak, where I kissed Zach Truitt while the Blum sisters looked on.

I didn't stop to read the sign one last time, or look at the tree, which I now knew was Caroline Truitt's final marker, her encouragement to others to look up and out.

Gripping the steering wheel, I turned to face forward and stared straight ahead, trying not to think about her words.

What if this is my one chance . . .

I didn't have Caroline's kind of courage. I couldn't take this chance. The risks were too great. I had a child to think about.

Sydney turned toward me as we sped along the open road. "I'm hungry. Can we get something to eat?"

I checked the clock. "It's almost lunchtime. Tell you what. Let's pull through the Dairy Queen in San Saline and grab some hamburgers. We can feed one to Mr. Grits before we take him by the Hawthorne House. He's a cheeseburger fan."

The idea seemed to cheer Sydney. Sitting up on her knees, she searched for San Saline, until finally it materialized on the horizon ahead.

When we reached the Dairy Queen, there wasn't a single customer inside, no cars in the parking lot, not even a worker's car around back.

"We may be out of luck," I told Sydney as we pulled up to the window. The bell made a *ding, ding*, and a waitress appeared, gesticulating wildly to someone out of view as she walked backward from the kitchen.

Through the partially opened glass, I could hear her as she came closer. ". . . carjacking the next thing that comes through here, I swear to God. Mama Hawthorne's gonna kill me if I miss the wedding lunch." She turned around, and I realized it was Becky. *Great.*

Throwing open the slider, she leaned out, breathless and wide-eyed. "You have to help. . . ." Taking on a look of recognition, she slapped a hand to her chest. "Oh, thank God. I know you. I'm so glad you came along."

"We'd like to ord—"

She fanned her hands back and forth in the air urgently, cutting me off. "No, no, wait. Listen. You have to give me a ride. Jimmy's folks are renewing their vows today, and the prewedding lunch starts in ten minutes. Everyone in town's already gone, and that stupid new truck of Jimmy's is broke down at the grocery store. Charlie"—she pointed to Charlie, who had come out from behind the fry grill—"rode here on a ten-speed bicycle. I'm so desperate I'd probably even try that, but I can't ride six miles in ten minutes, and it's all uphill anyway. I was just praying somebody would come along, and here you are. Thank God."

The barrage of words made it impossible to think, but I did realize one thing. She was talking about a wedding, a renewal of vows. Collie, Laura, Pop, and Jocelyn had all gone to a wedding. Zach had gone to a wedding. If I went there, I would have to face all the people I was running away from.

"I'm sorry but we're headed out of . . ." I paused, looking into Becky's desperate face. There was no way I could leave her standing there without a ride. I'd have to drive her wherever she needed to go. Hopefully I could drop her at the door and leave before anyone saw me.

"Please." Becky grabbed my arm. "Listen, I'm sorry about the other day. I was in a snotty mood, and I shouldn't of said things about Zach's ex. Jimmy was mad at me afterward. I do stuff like that sometimes, and I don't even mean to. Mama Hawthorne says I've got a mouth on me, and I like to stir up trouble. I'm sorry. I shouldn't of said anything."

"No, I'm glad you did." In her own weird way, Becky had helped save me from a disaster of my own making. "Hop in. We'll give you a ride."

Less than sixty seconds later, we were headed out of town with

Sydney and the dog in the back, and Becky in the passenger seat, working on an in-transit change from her Dairy Queen uniform to a skirt and high heels.

"Listen, I hope I didn't start up a problem between you and Zach," she said, panting as she tried to pull on a pair of panty hose.

"You didn't," I replied flatly, glancing in the rearview mirror at Sydney, who was listening to a CD with her earphones, while watching the crazy lady half-naked in our passenger seat.

Becky went on talking. "Because I heard that the Blum sisters saw you two kissing under the Lover's Oak."

"Don't worry about it," I said to cut her off. I didn't want to talk about it, especially not with Zach's ex-sister-in-law.

Becky paused to check where we were. "Turn left here. We'll take the shortcut."

"All right." I made the turn, then stepped on the accelerator, hoping to get the ride over with as soon as possible. "How far?"

"Two or three miles this way." Becky pointed ahead. "Turn in that gateway—there with the cattle guard. Just keep going all the way through. We'll come out almost where we need to be."

"Got it." Squealing around the corner, we rocketed onto a rough gravel road while Becky tumbled around, struggling with the panty hose like a magician in a straitjacket. "I'll have you to the church in a jiffy. You just worry about getting dressed."

I hoped that would shut her up and end the conversation about Zach, but, of course, it didn't. She finished with the panty hose and sat up in the seat, pulling on a long denim broom skirt. "Anyway, Zach's a good guy. He likes to play stupid jokes on people and stuff, but he's a good guy. What happened between him and Shawna wasn't his fault. They got married because she was pregnant, and he moved here to the ranch and everything, so she could be close to home. He really loved Macey a lot. He'd, like, stay home with her all the time, even when she was a little baby, because Shawna didn't want to give up rodeoing. Shawna had a good barrel-racing horse, and she was sure she was going to make the National Finals Rodeo. It's all she ever wanted to do. She never really cared about anything else. She was all into bright lights and glittery shirts. She only got married so she'd have plenty of horses and a place to live, and someone to stay home with the baby."

"What . . . what happened?" I felt reality shifting under my feet, turning, changing like one of those sand-and-water desk ornaments that flow into new patterns when they're flipped upside down. What could have possibly convinced Zach to give up his daughter to a woman like that?

Smoothing her skirt, Becky clipped on her seat belt as the road faded into little more than a cowpath through a pasture that seemed to go on forever. "When Macey was about four, Shawna got the hots for some bull rider up in Cheyenne. He was a big deal in rodeo, like he's on TV and stuff, and he was traveling the PRCA circuit full-time, and she figured that'd be great. She told Zach she wanted a divorce. When he tried for custody of Macey, she said at the hearing *in front of everyone* that Macey wasn't really Zach's. She'd had a thing with the bull rider before, and he was really Macey's father. He was a married man when he got Shawna pregnant, and so she told Zach that Macey was his. At the custody hearing she had the bull rider there, and they had DNA tests and the whole deal. It turned into one heck of a mess. Zach wound up in jail for the night, and Shawna and the bull rider left with Macey. There wasn't much Zach could do after that. He took a new job and moved to Austin and didn't come home very often until Pop had the heart attack. It's probably hard for him to be there where Macey used to live."

"Of course it would be," I muttered. And even harder to extend trust to another woman with a daughter who wasn't his. It was no wonder that, when I told him I was leaving, he was quick to walk away.

"What Shawna did was really wrong," Becky chattered on in the passenger seat. "It darned near killed Zach, and then when Shawna divorced the bull rider two years later, she gave the guy custody of Macey. We don't even know where she is now." Looking in the mirror, she finger-combed her hair, sucking air through her teeth, making a *tsk-tsk*. "But that's my family. One drama after another.

Somebody's always sleepin' with somebody's wife, divorcin' somebody, having someone's baby, getting arrested for DUI, or bringing guns to a family gathering. We don't have the best reputation. I'll tell you, Mama Hawthorne wasn't thrilled when Jimmy married me. I suppose she figured we'd fall into all that mess. But I've learned a lot from Mama and Papa Hawthorne. They fell in love all those years ago, and they never looked at another person. They just knew they were meant to be together. That's how I want to be."

"That's how it should be." I knew that much was true. If there was a chance, even the slightest possibility, that Zach and I could have that kind of love, I couldn't let it go this easily. Sydney was right. There was no reason to rush back to Colorado. No reason other than my fear of change and my paranoia over a situation in which I couldn't manhandle all the parameters. No reason, other than the invisible shackles that, even now, kept me chained to the pain of the past.

Staring at my hands, white-knuckled on the steering wheel, I realized that the shackles weren't invisible. They were imaginary. All of the things that had prevented me from taking a chance on love, on life, on Zach, were in my mind. I had created the barriers when I let fear control me, when I let my past with Geoff obscure the possibility of a future with Zach. I had been locked in a prison of my own making for eight years, and I was the one who held the key. If I was going to take a leap of faith, I had to cast off the chains, once and for all.

A sense of peace, of power and certainty, washed over me, sweeping away the fear on an awesome riptide of determination. I tromped on the gas, and the SUV popped over a hill like a Baja dune buggy. For once in my life, I was going to have one bold day.

"Whoa, careful!" Becky braced her hands on the dash to keep from being buffeted around in the car. "You're in a hurry."

"Maa-a—om!" Sydney complained as the SUV fishtailed around a corner and popped over the rim of a canyon. "Oh, my gosh! Look out!"

I hit the brakes and the Jeep skidded sideways, then squealed to a halt. Ahead in the valley, the road disappeared into a slew of mud surrounding a narrow creek that must have flooded with the recent rain.

Becky stuck her head out the window. "Oh, shoot. The creek's up." Pounding both hands against the window frame, she flounced back into the seat. "Shoot. We'll never make it back around the long way. I won't be there to serve at the cake table, and Mama Hawthorne will kill me."

I surveyed the bog ahead. There it was, the only thing standing between me and the possibility of a second chance with Zach—a messed-up mass of mire, and muck, and water under the bridge. An appropriate metaphor for my current life situation.

This time I wasn't going to be stopped. My heart beat faster, and I clenched my jaw, revving the engine and tightening my grip on the steering wheel. "Roll up the windows and check your seat belts, girls. We're bustin' through."

"All right!" Becky cheered.

"Go, Mom!" Sydney yelled.

"Hang on!" Holding my breath, I let off the brake and hit the gas. We rocketed down the hill and into the creek in a hail of wet gravel and dirty water. The tires spun in the mud, found traction, lurching the Jeep forward, then bogged down and spun again. "Come on, come on . . ." I muttered, pushing the gas pedal to the floor. In the backseat, Sydney echoed my plea, and beside me it looked like Becky was praying.

The tires caught solid ground, and the Jeep jerked, vibrated, then blasted out of the mud hole. I didn't start breathing again until we were on the other side and there was nothing left to hold us back. Two more hills, three curves, one small mud hole, and we reached the cattle guard that marked the end of the shortcut. When we turned onto the county road, I recognized it immediately. Becky's shortcut had taken me right back where I'd started from. The Lover's Oak loomed large ahead.

"The wedding lunch is out behind the Big Lizard." Becky pointed. "In the trees by the river." She checked her watch as we sped past the Lover's Oak and through town. "Oh, thank God. I'm gonna make it in time to serve Mama Hawthorne's cake."

I pulled into the ditch near the Over the Moon, because the

diner parking lot was filled with an odd conglomeration of cars, pickups, two tractors, three delivery trucks, a UPS van, a propane tanker, and two sheriff's department vehicles parked haphazardly in the ditch. Everyone in three counties must have come for the wedding festivities.

Becky opened the door before the Jeep stopped. "Thanks, Lindsey. Really. I don't know what I would have done if you hadn't shown up. Come on and eat lunch and stay for the wedding, OK? Everyone's welcome. You haven't seen a wedding until you've seen one under the Lover's Oak. Even when it's just old folks doing a repeat, it's really special." Widening her eyes insistently, she gave me a pointed look. "Zach's here."

"I know," I said, gazing speculatively toward the Big Lizard. Now that we'd arrived, my courage was waning. What if he didn't want to see me? Could I handle getting rejected in front of a crowd? And what about Sydney? Whatever was said, she would be right there listening. She'd already been privy to too much adult romantic drama this summer. Maybe it would be better if I took her to Dad's place. "It might be better if I came back later." The drive to Killeen would give me time to think about what to say to Zach.

Or time to chicken out . . .

"Come on, it'll be fun," Becky prodded, as if she knew that I was waffling. She turned to Sydney in the backseat. "There's lots of kids. The girls are serving at the buffet tables. You can help me with cake."

"Cool!" Sydney said, tossing her earphones down and scrambling into the front seat. "Mom, can I go?"

Becky and Sydney looked at me with equal amounts of expectation.

"All right," I said. *No more delay tactics, Lindsey. Time to stop taking the coward's way out. For once, face life head-on and see what you can make of it.* "I'll pull up into the shade for the dog, and be there in a minute."

Sydney scrambled out of the seat and stood looking adoringly at her new best friend. Becky patted her on the head. "Don't worry about her. I'll keep her with me." I knew she was trying to give me time to talk to Zach.

"Thanks."

Becky shrugged. "No problem. You did save my life, after all." Just before closing the door, she leaned in, her eyes earnest. "You know, the other day when we saw you and Zach at the horse camp, he looked happier than he has in a long time." She closed the door without saying anything else. She and Sydney hurried off across the parking lot, Sydney jumping like an excited puppy and Becky doing her best to run in high heels.

Pulling into the shade, I cracked the windows and headed for the Big Lizard. The closer I got, the harder my heart pounded. An invisible fist clenched my stomach tighter and tighter, pressing it upward into my lungs until I couldn't breathe. I stopped, my head whirling. I could hear a crowd behind the building. Tiny rivers of perspiration beaded under my T-shirt and dripped down my back, and a dozen what-ifs ran through my mind.

What if Zach doesn't want to talk to me? What if he doesn't feel what I feel? What if he rejects me in front of everyone? What if he doesn't? What if I end up falling for a guy who lives a thousand miles from my home? What if Sydney gets her hopes up and things don't work out? What if Zach isn't looking for something serious? What if he walked away because this was just a casual thing to him? What if I'm making more of it than it is?

What if this is my one chance, and I fail to take it?

I gazed down at my feet, frozen in place, just like in the horse corral.

TWENTY-THREE

THE SOUND OF VOICES AND SHOES SLIDING ON THE GRAVEL YANKED me from my thoughts, and I looked up just as Gracie, in her deputy's uniform, rushed around the corner of the diner. Zach was behind her, followed by Robert, the deputy from horse psychology class, who was fumbling with his radio while cramming a hot dog into his mouth. Becky was trailing them in her high heels, panting with her eyes wide.

Gracie slid to a halt when she saw me, and Zach sidestepped to keep from colliding with her.

Panic whipped through me. Sydney wasn't with Becky. Had something happened to her? I had a fleeting vision of my daughter falling into the river and being swept away, like in my dream. "Where's Sydney?" I glanced toward the corner of the building, hoping Sydney would come trotting up the hill after Becky.

Becky stumbled to an unsteady halt at the edge of the gravel, giving me a bemused frown. "She's down helping Pop make ice cream. She's fine." She glanced from Zach to me, as if waiting for some exchange to begin, then finally gave him a peeved look and added, "Gracie thinks they found the Jubilee tracks."

Zach stared past me toward the sheriff's car, his expression hard and narrow, preoccupied. He looked closed and impassive, yet I felt the pull of his nearness. I wanted him to meet my eyes, just for a moment, so I could look through that wall and see what he was thinking.

"The Internet tip from Geoff Attwood paid off," Gracie explained, seeming oblivious to the tension between Zach and me. Nor did she notice that both of us stiffened at Geoff's name. "Yesterday a dealer in Dallas forwarded an e-mail about theropod tracks someone was trying to sell anonymously. The sender wasn't very Internet savvy, because the script on the e-mail led right back to the computers at the San Saline library. So we had the Dallas dealer send a reply asking for photographs of the fossils, and we staked out the computers to see if the seller would come back. Yesterday—nothing. This morning—nothing. But just a little while ago, up drives the B and B Windmills truck. It parks right in front of the library, and one of the Bales brothers goes in. When the sheriff went inside, there was Bo Bales, plain as day, answering the dealer's e-mail on the library computer. How stupid is that? I guess he thought it was like using a pay phone—nobody would be able to trace it. When the sheriff confronted him, he claimed he didn't have anything to do with stealing the Jubilee tracks—said he saw the newspaper article and was trying to help track down the thieves. Anyway, we just got the call that the sheriff is picking up a search warrant and heading out to the Bales's place. He has a feeling we might find the tracks out there, or at least some of the equipment that was used to remove them. Bo and Benny would be the type to try to make a quick buck like that. The sheriff's been wondering for a while how they were making a living, given that they haven't installed any windmills since they took over the business from their father. The sheriff thought maybe they had a meth lab out here, but we never could find anything. Bo was a park ranger over at Fossil Ridge years ago, so it makes sense that he would know a little bit about fossils."

The pieces fell together in my mind. A truck used to install windmill towers could have a hydraulic lift, generator, and pneumatic tools—all the things needed to extract a large slab of rock. "Jocelyn said something about a windmill salesman the day I came to the Jubilee." I glanced at Zach, feeling all the significance of windmills. He was waiting for the Bales brothers' windmill service the day we met. We'd had one of our first kisses atop a windmill. . . .

He didn't look at me, just scanned the parking lot, his eyes a frosty green. If he was thinking of windmills, or me, it didn't show. "My truck's blocked in." He addressed Gracie instead of me. "I'll ride with Robert." Without another word he strode off across the parking lot, with Robert hiking his pants and downing the last of a Dr Pepper.

Gracie slanted a glance after him, then back at me, her tongue tracing the outline of her straight white teeth. "What in the world did you do to him? I've never seen him like that."

"You weren't livin' here when Shawna took Macey away," Becky muttered, shoveling a load of guilt on my shoulders.

Gracie clearly didn't want to step into the muck of that conversation. "I'd better go," she said as Robert's car started and pulled onto the road. "I'll let you know what we find." She headed off across the parking lot, jogging like a basketball player headed for a free throw.

I vacillated, my mind moving at light-speed into the universe of what-if. What if they found the Jubilee tracks, and I wasn't there to see it? What if the other Bales brother had a gun? What if things got dangerous? What if something happened to me, and Sydney was left alone? What if something happened to Zach? What if he got angry and reckless and did something rash?

The idea clenched my stomach with surprising power. "Becky, will you ask Collie or Laura to watch Sydney?"

"They're not here yet, but Pop and I will watch her. Don't worry. It'll be fine. There's lots of kids here."

I vacillated again. On the roadside, Gracie was getting into her car. Ramming her hands onto her hips, Becky huffed impatiently. "Gosh, go already, will you? You know you want to."

"The dog's in the car."

"I'll check on the stupid dog, OK?" Smacking her lips, she rolled her eyes. "Geez. It's no wonder Zach likes you. You're as much of a pain in the butt as he is. When you want somethin', you gotta just say so. If people don't like it, tough."

"You're right," I said, then turned and dashed after Gracie, hollering, "Gracie, wait. I'm coming with you!"

To her credit, Gracie had the decorum not to ask about Zach and me as we sped down mile after mile of gravel road, skidding around curves and kicking up loose gravel. Gracie piloted the vehicle like a NASCAR driver, and by the time we reached the fence of corrugated metal that surrounded B & B Windmills, we were right behind the other sheriff's department car. Gracie whipped past him at the driveway in a maneuver that knocked me sideways.

"Sorry about that." She glanced in the rearview with a triumphant smirk. "There's a little competition between the girl and the good-ol'-boy network around here."

When I uprighted myself, we were moving through a boneyard of sideways windmill towers and decaying skeletons of fans and fins that must have been building up for years. The kind of place where anyone or anything could be hiding.

The thought sent a heebie-jeebie through me. I sank lower in my seat. Gracie surveyed the junkyard as we moved through, then pulled up in front of a two-story metal shop building with faded yellow paint and rust in an oozing pattern like dried blood. "Must be the sheriff's not here yet," she said, peering down the lane toward a rotting house that appeared to be abandoned. Opening the car door, she climbed out in one lithe movement, adjusting her gun holster like she expected to use it. I exited the car and stood near my door, listening for human sounds. There was nothing but the rhythmic clang of loose tin slapping against iron pipes, which was quickly drowned out by Robert's approaching cruiser. They parked beside us and Zach got out, staring at the barn with his hand still on the car door as Robert unfolded himself from the seat with a groan, stretched, and tucked in his shirttails as if he were headed into the diner for coffee.

Gracie leaned casually against our car. "Guess I'm first on the scene again."

Robert sneered. "Yeah, yeah. We gotta wait for the search warrant, anyway. All that college education, you oughta know that. Didn't they teach—" He glanced up as Zach slammed the car door and started toward the barn. "Hey, Zach, wait. We gotta get the ..." Zach was already slipping through the door into the barn. Robert lifted his hands helplessly, turning back to Gracie. "Well, now what?"

"Leave him be." Gracie drummed her fingers against the cruiser's hood. "There's no one here. If *he* goes poking around in there, it's just trespassing. If *we* go in, it's illegal search and seizure." Inside there was the sound of metal against metal, and then the hollow slap of something hitting the cement floor. Gracie exhaled irritably, checked the driveway, then motioned to me. "Go tell him not to touch anything in there. The sheriff will be here any minute."

"All right." Closing my door, I walked to the barn and slipped through the gap between the doors, where Zach had disappeared. The interior was dim and the air smelled of musty hay and old grease. I stood for a moment, waiting for my eyes to adjust.

"Zach?" I called.

No answer.

"Zach?" I took a few steps farther into the barn, the interior coming into focus until I could see that it was cluttered with stacks of hay on one side, parts of windmills and towers lying in the center of the aisle, and a variety of tractor implements parked in the far corner. Near the farm equipment there was a small office door with a poster of a buxom Valvoline girl.

I heard someone shuffling in the loose hay behind the tractor implements. Crossing the room silently, I had a fleeting vision of old Western movies, where the good guy gets ambushed in a cluttered barn and lies helpless while the heroine walks blindly into a trap.

"Zach?" I whispered again, moving closer to the farm equipment. No answer, and the sound stopped. I inched forward, trying to peer around a wagon. If it was Zach back there, I was going to kill him for scaring me to death. If it wasn't ... If it wasn't, I didn't know what I was going to do. Crouching down, I tried to see under the wagon wheels. Against the wall I could make out a shadow, moving just slightly, and I heard a low sound, between a growl and a groan.

A new possibility rocketed through my mind. Maybe whatever we'd heard falling had landed on Zach and he was hurt. "Zach!" I called.

"What?" The door with the Valvoline girl swung open, and I jumped like a clumsy cat, landing on my rear end in the dirt. Zach stood in the doorway with his head cocked sideways, like he couldn't imagine what I was doing there.

"Geez, you scared me to death," I complained, standing up and dusting myself off, forgetting for a moment that we weren't on speaking terms. "I thought you were hurt or something."

Stepping out, he closed the door as casually as if he weren't trespassing and potentially messing up a police investigation. "Why would you think that?"

"I heard a noise, and then you didn't answer. I was worried about you." Was it my imagination, or did he, just for an instant, look pleased when I said that? "Anyway . . . well . . . Gracie says not to touch anything."

He shrugged, looking past me toward the door as if he wanted to be out of there, away from me. "There's nothing here, anyway. A three-foot slab of limestone would be pretty hard to hide."

"I heard something over in the corner."

"Coons, probably. The barn's full of them." He kicked a tuft of old hay, which was crowned with what I assumed was raccoon poop. "Which also means there hasn't been much work going on here. This place has been left to the coons for a while." Turning his shoulder toward me, he started for the front door.

I sidestepped to stop him. "Isn't that strange, though? If they were really doing business in windmills, wouldn't this workshop be in use? There wouldn't be coon scat everywhere." What I really wanted to say was, *Zach, I'm sorry. Don't walk away. Talk to me.* Instead, I was talking about raccoon poop. Looking up at the ceiling, I took a long breath, then let it out. "Zach, listen—"

"I can't, Lindsey." He cut me off, reaching out and grabbing my arms, setting me out of his path like a tin soldier. "I'm doing the best I can to give you what you wanted. You said no more, you had to leave, you couldn't do *this*." He motioned to the space between us, throwing my own words, my actions, back at me in a sharp ricochet. "I can't be your *friend*, Lindsey. I can't chitchat long distance about the custody battle and the ex-husband, or exchange cards at Christmas, or play Watson to your Sherlock until you decide it's time to pull out and head home. It's too hard. I'm sorry. I'm past the point of playing games." He strode toward the door, and I could feel the space growing inch by inch.

My heart clenched, wringing tears into my eyes. This was it. All or nothing. My one chance. "Why didn't you tell me about Macey?"

He stopped, stood statuelike in the stream of light from the door. The moment seemed to stretch on and on, the air silent with the scents of dust and old hay, waiting for movement.

Outside, a car door slammed. Gracie hollered something as a second door closed; then engines roared and tires squealed, flinging gravel against the barn. Zach and I jerked to life, running through the maze of junk to the door just as both police cruisers sped toward the old house, in hot pursuit of a black truck bolting cross-country over the pasture. The truck blasted through a barbed-wire fence, then hit the county road and disappeared in a cloud of dust with the police cars following.

We watched the road until the dust settled and the sirens faded into the distance.

"Guess we're stuck here," I said finally, sitting on an overturned barrel and looking at my hands. I wasn't sorry we were stuck. I wanted him to answer my question. "Zach, why didn't you tell me about Macey?"

He shrugged like it didn't matter. "Why would I have brought that up?"

I felt a pinprick near my heart, the adrenaline of the last few hours slowly draining away, leaving me confused and raw. "Why wouldn't you have?" I countered. "There I was, pouring my heart out to you about Sydney and everything we've been through this past year. How much I've missed her this summer. How hard it's been to be separated from her, and you don't say a word about having a daughter of your own?"

"Macey isn't mine, Lindsey." He leaned over a rusty metal barrel, gripping it with both hands like he might pick it up and throw it somewhere. "She isn't coming back at the end of the summer. Her mother took her away and gave her to some guy who happened to have the right DNA. I don't see her. I don't hear from her. All I can do is hope she's safe." Closing his eyes, he let his head fall forward. Every muscle in my body ached to comfort him.

"I know that, but I could have—"

"Could have what?" Throwing himself away from the oil drum, he paced a few steps, then turned back. "Commiserated? Joined me in raging against the machine? What good does that do?"

"Listened," I corrected. "I could have listened. I know I can't make it go away, Zach. Reality is what it is, but Macey is part of you. She's part of who you are."

Sighing, he shook his head, then stared out at the horizon with the faraway look I'd first noticed in the newspaper. His eyes moved to a pattern of invisible thoughts, then finally refocused on me with an intensity that held me motionless. "Lindsey, I didn't tell you about Macey because . . . " He drew a breath, let it out, closed his eyes for a moment, then opened them again. "Because I didn't want you to think I was looking for an instant replacement."

Rising to my feet, I moved closer, my hands outstretched in the space between us. "I never thought that."

"I knew when you found out, you'd think I was after a quick fix, a stand-in mother-daughter package to take the place of Shawna and Macey. It wasn't like that, Lindsey. You and I were a totally different thing."

I winced at the word *were*, dropped my hands. Maybe the damage I'd done was beyond repair. Maybe I'd destroyed whatever was between us. "I know that, Zach. I knew it even after Pop told me about Macey. I just . . . I wasn't strong enough to go with my heart. I used the news as an excuse to run home, where things are safe, and predictable, and there isn't any risk. It's what I do. It's how I . . . get by."

His eyes met mine, and for a long moment we looked deep into each other. I felt my heart pull from my chest and fall in again, just as it had beneath the Lover's Oak. I wanted him to say something, to make the leap with me. I ached for it, but the answer didn't come. Instead the wail of a siren broke the silence, growing steadily closer until he turned to look. I watched the strong profile of his face, my soul filled with a yearning like I'd never known. Unable to bear watching him any longer, I looked down at my feet. Gracie's cruiser was coming up the driveway. The moment was gone.

Something caught my attention near my foot, a piece of rock, freshly chipped, not the right color or composition for the gravel driveway. Squatting down, I picked it up, spotted a smaller chip, and grabbed it, too.

When Gracie pulled up, I held out the chips to her. Looking around, I could see several more. "Evidence," I said, as she took them from my hands. "These are all over the place. I'd bet almost anything they came from the riverbank at the Jubilee—all the components are right. If we take these to the track site, I can say for sure." Zach flicked a glance my way. Was he wondering if I was going to stay? Was he hoping I would?

Gracie nodded, setting the rock chips in the seat beside her. "The sheriff cut Benny Bales off down at the crossroad. They're taking him back to the department for questioning. We'll show him these rocks and tell him we've got an expert who's pretty sure they came from the Jubilee track site. I doubt if it'll be long before he comes clean after that. Benny's not the smartest egg in the basket." Fingering the rock chips triumphantly, she unlocked the back doors. "Hop in. I'll take you two back to the wedding. I have to lead the processional out before I head to the office."

Zach and I climbed into the car, silent, not looking at each other. I turned toward the window, feeling the sting of tears. I wanted this to work out. Somehow this had to work out. It couldn't be over.

I laid my hand on the seat, wishing he would slip his fingers over mine. Nothing. No movement toward my side of the car. He only stared ahead thoughtfully.

We arrived back at the Lover's Oak just in time. Beneath the yawning tree there was a wedding about to take place. Gracie dropped us with the onlookers, then parked the cruiser in the road with the lights on to stop traffic, in case there was any, which seemed unlikely, since everyone in three counties was at the wedding. Gathered around the tree in bright dresses and starched Western shirts and jeans stood all the inhabitants of Loveland and most of San Saline. They'd come to watch something special, to celebrate the renewal of vows of two people who knew forty years ago that they were in love, and nothing else mattered.

An usher hustled Zach to the front, where Jocelyn and Pop stood with Sydney. I waited silently in the back, feeling uncertain. Nearby a guitarist began playing the wedding march, and I realized the musician was Laura's husband, Graham. He missed a note and winced, and my sister smiled at him as the wedding procession began weaving through the crowd toward the base of the tree. At the head of the column, Collie's tiny daughter, Bailey, toddled bravely along in a diaphanous white dress, her chubby hands spewing flower petals along the path, her curly red hair adorned with a ring of yucca blossoms. Behind her Collie and True smiled at each other, holding hands as they ushered Bailey through the crowd.

Near the base of the wedding oak, Dandy Roads looked like an old-fashioned circuit preacher, dressed in high black boots, black jeans, a black brocade vest, a white shirt, and a tall black hat. Holding a worn Bible, he read from Paul's letter to the Corinthians about the true nature of love—what it is, and what it is not. It is not boastful, not proud, not self-seeking, not easily angered. It does not hold a grudge. It is patient and kind. It protects, trusts, hopes, perseveres, and never fails, even when we turn away from it.

Love believes, and believes, and believes, even when it has been disappointed, and wounded, and thwarted by the weaknesses of the human soul. Standing once again beneath the ancient oak tree, I knew I wanted that kind of love. The bold, brave, never-ending kind. I knew I had it to give, and when I looked at Zach, I knew he was the one I wanted to give it to.

As the crowd shifted to let the procession depart, he fell in with the line, following Becky and the Hawthornes until he reached me. Slipping out, he stood by my side as Graham and Laura passed by. Graham was playing "Happy Trails" on the guitar. Laura grinned and gave me the OK sign. On the road, Gracie blasted the cruiser sirens, leading the wedding party toward two white horses in shiny black and silver saddles waiting to carry the bride and groom off into the sunset.

I looked at Zach, and he smiled just slightly, and my heart floated up and up and up. In his face I saw the mirror of everything I felt, and I knew that the passage from Paul's letter had made him see the truth, just as it had me. What we felt for each other was a gift, a miracle beyond the comprehension of human logic.

"Hey, Doc," I said to Zach as the crowd moved on. "Done surgery on any windmills lately?"

"Nah." His eyes twinkled, the deep, dusty green of wild sage. "My nurse quit on me."

I dropped my gaze to the spray of flower petals blowing through the grass. "She shouldn't have. She's an idiot for running away."

Nearby, Gracie's siren blew, and Zach and I turned to watch as the bride and groom rode their white horses off the pavement and turned onto the shortcut road. Waving to the onlookers, they kicked their mounts into a run and disappeared over the hill.

I stood with Zach as the procession came back, with Sydney, Bailey, and some other children now riding in the police car, which came down the road with sirens blaring and excited children making airplane hands in the window draft. Beneath the Lover's Oak, Gracie stopped and Sydney leaned out the window. "Hey, Mom, isn't this *boss?*" Another one of Whitney's words.

"It's boss," I agreed.

"We're gonna go down to the diner and have leftover cake, 'K?" Sydney asked, and Bailey echoed, "Edober tate, 'K?"

" 'K," I said, then waved as the cruiser drove away. When it passed my jeep, Mr. Grits poked his head up, let out a long, mournful howl, then squeezed himself through the window, which Becky had left open way too far.

"Looks like we might have another dog chase on our hands," I said, watching Mr. Grits greet the passing crowd as he trotted toward us.

"I think I know where he's headed." Zach nodded toward the tree. Turning to me, he took on an earnest look. "I never should have let you go." He stroked my hair and I leaned into his hand. "You had something of mine."

"You had something of mine, too." Whether it made any sense or not, Zach Truitt, cowboy veterinarian, occasional Tonto, and tilter at windmills, had my heart. I slipped into his arms, and all felt right with the world.

His lips parted into a wide smile. "You realize, of course, that Becky is taking credit for bringing you back here." He shrugged over my head, and I swiveled around to see Becky giving the Blum sisters an earful as they walked toward the diner. I could tell by the hand motions that right now she was illustrating our harrowing trip through the mud pit. "She's pretty proud of herself, because usually she's the one tanking other people's relationships."

"Guess there's hope for all of us." I laughed, turning back to Zach.

"Guess so," he agreed. "Of course, the Blum sisters will tell her it's the Lover's Oak that did it."

Leaning back, I considered the ancient canopy of branches overhead. White rose petals hung tangled in the leaves for just a moment before they pulled loose and floated upward. I watched them swirl on the breeze, in no particular hurry, until a whiff of Texas wind grabbed them and whisked them off into the unknown.

Turning back to Zach, I looped my arms around his neck, and he pulled me close and twirled me in the air. From somewhere nearby, Mr. Grits let out an excited yip as Zach stopped at the base of the old Lover's Oak, pressed me up against the tree, and kissed me. A kiss of pure magic, of true love, of trust and hope, and all the things they write about in fairy tales.

The Blum sisters saw it all, of course. When I opened my eyes they were standing there staring as the procession passed by. I smiled and waved, and offered a giddy, "Isn't it a beautiful day?"

The sisters flushed and pretended to have been checking the condition of the old tree. "Oh, my goodness, Zach," the taller one said. "We didn't even see you there. We were just noticing that the Lover's Oak looks in fine form today." Linking arms, they toddled off down the street, whispering something about secret bones and the FBI.

Zach chuckled under his breath. "Guess we should go have some cake before people start to talk."

"I think they already are," I said, looking around for Mr. Grits, who had settled into a cool spot beside the old stone sign. For the first time I noticed the words etched into the base, *Ende Gut, Alles Gut.* The same phrase that adorned the door frame of the pioneer house that Caroline and Jeremiah built.

"What does that mean?" I pointed as Zach and I turned to leave.

He smiled at some private irony. "Ending good, everything good," he translated, slipping his hand over mine. "All's well that ends well."

Laughing together, we headed off toward the Big Lizard Diner, hand in hand, already over the moon.

And all the Lindseys lived happily ever after.

Ende gut.

Wandering Shepherd

by Colleen Collins

There are times when a story transcends the ordinary and ignites the imagination. When it happens, a writer can either stick to the facts, or suspend disbelief and report what might have taken place. As always, I report the facts, and leave you to decide on which side of the coin you'd like to fall. This is the tale of a wandering shepherd.

The part Great Pyrenees sheepdog in question, nicknamed Mr. Grits (among other things unfit to print), was first sighted in late May by Elva Bradshaw of Turkey Creek Ranch. According to Mrs. Bradshaw, she discovered the dog in her vegetable garden, when she headed out to check her wax beans.

"It was the biggest thing I ever saw," said Mrs. Bradshaw. "I thought it was an albino deer or a hairy calf or some such."

Upon closer inspection, Mrs. Bradshaw realized the invader was a very large canine, apparently digging up her bean plants.

"I got my grandson's BB gun and run him off," said Mrs. Bradshaw. "I was hoppin' mad, I'll tell you. It wasn't until two weeks later when I was cleaning out the bean row that I found a huge rattlesnake

half-buried in the dirt right there where the dog was digging. The head was chewed clean off. I'd of got bit by that thing for sure if the dog hadn't killed it, and I live here all alone. I sure felt bad about shooting that dog in the butt after that."

Two days after the Bradshaw sighting, Mr. Grits was discovered in the bathtub of Esperanza Alvarez, three miles outside of San Saline.

"I am awakened by a noise in the bathroom very early in the morning," said Mrs. Alvarez, who is the mother of three-year-old triplets. "My husband is gone to work, and the babies still in their bed. When I go into the bathroom, there is this white, hairy animal in my tub, trying to open a container of cottage cheese. I am scared out of my mind. I think, I am having heart attack!"

Mrs. Alvarez closed the bathroom door and called the volunteer fire department, which removed the dog from the bathroom, and chased it out the back door.

"We wasn't about to try to catch it," said volunteer fireman Dub Monroe. "But while we was in the bathroom, we sure enough smelled propane gas. Sometime during the night, the pilot on the hot-water heater went out, and it was leaking gas. No telling what could have happened."

Mr. Monroe theorized that the failure on the pilot light and the dog's presence in the bathroom might have had something to do with thunderstorms the previous night.

"Dogs are smart about bad weather," said Mr. Monroe. "They look for a safe place to take refuge."

Shortly thereafter, Mr. Grits was spotted in the fellowship hall of the San Saline Baptist Church.

"We'd just set everything up for potluck supper after Sunday service," said June Hawthorne, coordinator of the church hospitality committee. "We went into the sanctuary to gather everyone up for the blessing, and when we came back, we found this huge dog halfway up on the table, helping himself to the coleslaw. I didn't think dogs ate coleslaw, but there he was, bigger than daylight."

Church elders attempted to capture the dog, but were unsuccessful.

"We had to throw the coleslaw away," said Mrs. Hawthorne. "The Blum sisters were hopping mad, but turns out it was a good thing. Two weeks later they made potato salad with that same jar of mayonnaise for the Ladies' Bridge Club, and everyone came down with salmonella poisoning."

According to the Blum sisters, the questionable jar of mayonnaise had been newly purchased at a surplus store in Killeen. "We'll never buy discount groceries again," said Alva Blum. "Of course, we may never eat potato salad again, either."

Over the next two weeks, the escapades of the bandit dog continued around town, including a late-night raid of the San Saline locker plant, during which the animal made off with a partial leg quarter of beef.

"We figured out later that the dog was able to get in because we had an ex-employee entering the building late at night and stealing hamburger," said plant supervisor Wendel Wright. "After the dog incident, we put in a new back door, and suddenly our inventory stopped disappearing."

The ex-employee was discovered several days later during a stakeout by the county sheriff's department.

"He was pretty shocked when his key didn't work anymore," said sheriff's deputy Gracie Benton. "We found him there, trying to get his key back out of the lock."

After raiding the locker plant, the dog turned up in the nearby town of Loveland, where he caused a stir at the Jubilee Ranch.

"We thought he'd chased a bunch of cows through the fence," said ranch foreman Dan Daily. "But later on we found out we had a pack of feral dogs on the loose that had been killing calves and baby goats. The sheepdog was probably trying to run them off."

While staying in Loveland, the dog made his presence known by helping to ward off a gang of fossil thieves, who were later apprehended near the B & B Windmill company, where numerous stolen fossils were discovered hidden beneath a haystack. Among the specimens that had been illegally offered for sale on the Internet were the heisted theropod tracks from Jubilee Ranch.

"I was staying in the cabin just above the track site," said visitor Lindsey Attwood. "In the middle of the night the dog started barking. When I ran outside there was a truck heading down to the river. The dog chased them away, and the next day I reported it to the sheriff."

That clue, and an Internet tip sent in by paleontologist Geoff Attwood, helped lead authorities to a ring of individuals allegedly dealing in the illegal sale of stolen antiquities.

While in Loveland, the sheepdog was also reported to have aided in a matchmaking scheme involving Jubilee Ranch native Zach Truitt and out-of-towner Lindsey Attwood, who are engaged to be married in September.

"We saw it all," said Loveland resident Alva Blum. "That dog led them on a chase all through the pasture, and when he stopped, he stopped right under the Lover's Oak. When we drove down to check on things, there was Zach Truitt and this lady from the FBI together under the oak, wrapped around each other like lizards on a beanpole."

According to Mrs. Blum, local residents knew immediately that true love was in the works.

None of this surprises the dog's owner, who, it turns out, is Mrs. Jada Bell of Lometa. According to Mrs. Bell, the dog, whose name is actually Noel, takes a notion every once in a while to leave the sheep and the other sheepdogs and go on a mission.

"It's my fault, I suppose," said Mrs. Bell. "Those dogs aren't supposed to be pets, but that one was born Christmas day out in the field the week after my husband, Floyd, died. Noel was the only one in his litter that survived, and I was so lonesome, I brought him inside to raise. He comforted me through a hard time, and I just figure that every once in a while, he gets a hankering to do that same thing for someone else. He comes and goes as he needs to, and that's fine with me."

According to Mrs. Bell, over the years the dog has stayed with a child who'd been injured in a car accident, a widower whose wife just passed away (whom Mrs. Bell eventually married), a man who'd recently lost his eyesight due to glaucoma, and several others. A family in Lampasas credited the dog with alerting them to a house fire, and a college student from Brownwood was reportedly accompanied to safety late at night by the animal, after being forced off the road by a suspicious man posing as a police officer.

"Most of my information is secondhand, after the fact, so all of those things may or may not be so," admits Mrs. Bell, who smiles knowingly as she leafs through the scrapbook she has compiled of the dog's reported travels. "But sometimes it's the things that require a leap of faith that we need to believe in most of all."